Morgan, Michael
Hamilton.

The twilight war.

DATE			

The Twilight War

The Twilight War

by

MICHAEL HAMILTON MORGAN

A DUTTON BOOK

DUTTON
Published by the Penguin Group
Penguin Books USA Inc., 375 Hudson Street,
New York, New York 10014, U.S.A.
Penguin Books Ltd, 27 Wrights Lane,
London W8 5TZ, England
Penguin Books Australia Ltd, Ringwood,
Victoria, Australia
Penguin Books Canada Ltd, 2801 John Street,
Markham, Ontario, Canada L3R 1B4
Penguin Books (N.Z.) Ltd, 182–190 Wairau Road,
Auckland 10, New Zealand

Penguin Books Ltd, Registered Offices:
Harmondsworth, Middlesex, England

First published by Dutton, an imprint of New American Library, a
division of Penguin Books USA Inc.
Distributed in Canada by McClelland & Stewart Inc.

First Printing, May, 1991
10 9 8 7 6 5 4 3 2 1

Acknowledgments
Excerpt from *Terra Nostra* by Carlos Fuentes. Translation
copyright © 1976 by Farrar, Straus and Giroux, Inc.
Reprinted by permission of Farrar, Straus and Giroux, Inc.

REGISTERED TRADEMARK—MARCA REGISTRADA

LIBRARY OF CONGRESS CATALOGING IN PUBLICATION DATA:
Morgan, Michael Hamilton.
The twilight war / Michael Hamilton Morgan.
p. cm.
ISBN 0-525-93315-8
I. Title.
PS3563.08713T9 1991
813′.54—dc20 90-22048
CIP

Printed in the United States of America
Set in Janson
Designed by Eve L. Kirch

To my father, who fought in a real war;
and my mother, who fought for women.

ACKNOWLEDGMENTS

My thanks to Geri Thoma, for keeping the faith; to Kevin Mulroy, for editorial guidance; to Dr. George Krizek, for his help with the Czech language and landscape; to Juan López Díaz, for showing me his Guatemala; and to Pat Gabriel, for a glimpse of the future.

I make peace, and create evil; I the Lord
do all these things.

ISAIAH

San Carlos de Chixoy, Guatemala
September 23

Miroslav Lhota, that voice shouted out of the storm.

Half drunk, the man called Lhota was attempting to run up a path that curved through a mountain jungle shrouded in night, just as a storm was coming on full force. The cracks of lightning felt so close he expected one on the back of his neck any second.

He tripped over a squealing pig in the dark.

One of his shoes came off.

He sensed he was about to be shot.

I am the stupidest *osel* on earth, he cursed to himself.

He'd departed the town—if you could call the cluster of a dozen rotting wood-and-adobe structures a town—rather hastily, and he was stumbling uphill and through the jungle to an even lesser place, a place that in any other land would not have been a place at all, so small and forgettable was it. But here in this country of human sparseness it even had a name and an identity; it was his destination and a possible refuge at this precise moment. He couldn't yet make out its lights, the two or three cooking fires and lanterns hidden by forest or taken inside to escape the blast of the storm. In fact, he could see nothing at all except the path and panorama lit up by intermittent flashes of lightning. It was so dark an airborne chicken hit him in the face. He was stumbling. He was drunk. He was now about to be killed by someone he had so cleverly arranged to kill himself.

So he cursed.

He guessed his pursuers were still downhill and behind him, one of them calling him by his old name, a name from his other life, a name no one had used publicly in years. The shouts ringing on the edge of the storm made the whole thing seem like *the dream*, the nightmare of exposure and death he'd had for many years but that had never been staged quite this way, in tropic jungle on night of fevered storm. No, they'd always hunted him down in a granite forest of Gothic parapets and cobblestoned streets, the chill fairy-tale townscapes he had been born into, which had shaped his life and the way he thought. In his dreams they always caught him *over there*, not here.

Zatraceně! he cried into the squall, coughing and gasping, now falling more than running uphill, hearing his name and a command being called toward him out of the storm and the night, his memories and heightened senses ballooning those precious seconds out into another lifetime, a vista of a mythic army of liberation and a revolution, huzzahs and cheers, and a red flag flying from a medieval clock tower. He'd been there with them shouting as a young man, cheering about the possibilities of the future, and now he was an old man, running uphill into a jungle away from his own name: this was the future he had created for himself.

Miroslav Lhota, the pursuer called, *stop and face me*.

He'd been sitting on a log drinking his *cerveza* outside the miserable little *bodega* watching the storm blow up when he heard that voice before he even saw any faces, he heard that voice coming out of the newly arrived pickup truck before they even opened the door, the sound of its diseased tubercular wheeze striking fear and astonishment into him as sure as any blow. He'd been trembling as he pulled himself up as discreetly as he could and began making his way out of the village and up the path, up the path and away, all thought swept from him for a moment, hoping against hope that he had not been seen, praying with every cell of his body that he would be delivered into the refuge uphill, into the company of his newfound associate uphill, who would somehow help him reformulate the plan now that things had changed: he could think of nothing but getting uphill and getting delivered.

But he had not been delivered; he'd been seen. And what else could he have expected in this town made up of only a dozen squat edifices that were little more than humps in the dirt, animal mounds like anthills or foxholes, where he was as conspicuous as Santa Claus at a Japanese tea ceremony, he an old Carpathian in new American polyester safari suit sitting half drunk on a log in a pathetic Maya village with a total population of fifteen people?

You stupid *osel*, he cursed to himself.

Miroslav Lhota, that voice called again, and Lhota nearly turned around this time, the repetition of the name echoing in his head; he had not heard it in so long, not shouted publicly like this. He was astonished at how it made him feel, as if this pursuer were an old friend, someone from back there, maybe someone from his boyhood, the sound of it so warming him in his drunkenness that he very nearly did turn around.

Two men were after him; the old one he knew by voice from long ago, the younger one he knew only by instinct. Lhota had simply known *what* he was and why he was there. No, the younger man was recognizable only by an aspect, an aspect entirely independent of his almost concave Iberian face, a square cleft chin darkened by stubble, the top of the high forehead capped by a widow's peak, a head that belonged on a larger body and not on this wiry, fatless, almost bandy-legged form, the thinness of a shipping clerk or a door-to-door vendor, a combination of face and build that was common to the streets and alleyways of the Latin world.

Turn around and face me, the older man called, that horrid voice sounding somehow closer this time, which was impossible: the old one was even older than he; how could he be catching up? This would have demoralized Lhota even more had he not now seen a distant light that had to be the light of the refuge, giving him a last bit of hope, even quickening his step. For he was now mostly up the incline and onto a patch of cleared level pasture where a lone cow grazed by day, rimmed by palms and mahogany and mango now turned into dark flailing giants by the night and the storm.

Gabriel! Lhota dared to call up ahead in his own choked voice, hoping to alert his colleague, get him into action, *Gabriel!*, but he could have no assurance that his voice would go that far yet over the roar of the storm. Now he was running again, some final bit of adrenaline giving him the strength and the clarity of mind to roll up his shirtsleeves as a signal to a friend far away, and to pull out his own pistol and cock it in preparation for use, envisioning some kind of last stand. He was even to the point of estimating distances, available cover, lines of fire, when a third man sprang out of the darkness at his left and either kicked or knocked the pistol from Lhota's hand, leaving him standing there defenseless facing this third unexpected pursuer. Visible in the flashes of lightning, the third man was as alien to this place as Lhota and the old one were, this one a slim, goateed Arab with a pistol and silencer aimed at him, grinning that unpleasant grin of crude desert victory untempered by the slightest bit of humanity or mercy, a purely animal grin that meant this was the end of the line.

Now the other two, first the widow's peak and then the old one, came closer, the old one's breathing growing louder and uninhibited with the relaxation of a race won.

Miroslav Lhota, this old man grunted from behind, *turn around and face me.*

Having no reason now to refuse, Lhota did so.

Why? he thought to ask the man whom he had tracked for twenty years and whom he'd intended to trap here several days later, but who had in fact trapped him.

So I can shoot you properly, the old pursuer replied, and he did, somewhere in the upper half of the head.

Miroslav Lhota was amazed that he lived as long as he did afterward, remaining fully aware of his identity and situation for some moments after the flash and the impact, having lost his eyesight, speech, and motility in the explosion but still conscious of the raindrops that fell down out of the sky and burst in thrilling little impacts on his face, on his neck, on the bare skin of his forearms. And he heard with clarity the chorus of overjoyed tree frogs as they sang their joy at the rain: saved again, they sang; they would not die of drought this time. How deeply he appreciated the song of these creatures tonight, a realization that at first made him sad, for he knew in all honesty he could not sing the same song with them; but in the remaining seconds their sound soothed him, filled him too with a joy, joy at the welcoming song of a refuge he had sought, sought for a lifetime and never found, until now.

Pettyville, North Carolina
July 19

Something particularly miserable about insomnia in the summertime, Robinson thought. He hadn't slept more than an hour or two, the remnant of the Equanil giving him a headache to complement his burning eyes. Finally he gave up the effort to sleep and went outside, but rather than slipping into the merciful shroud of a dark winter morning, he was swallowed by the hot breath of a southern July, sun, air, and sky already merged in a seamless white-hot gas: it was only nine in the morning, so what would two in the afternoon be like?

Where the hell was he?

Pettyville, North Carolina, was a small town dead center of the vast eastern part of the state, a flat alluvial plain stretching from the capital at Raleigh down into black-water swamp, a zone of tobacco and cotton fields, lone brick ranch ramblers sitting treeless on vast acreage, gaudy pecan-candy comfort stations, and bleached frame Baptist churches sitting back in little stands of uncut pine. An occasional tar-paper shack stood with rusted washing machine on collapsing porch, each ruin magnetically drawing a half-dozen old car bodies to worship where they had fallen, all run through with jungles of kudzu and honeysuckle. Signs advertised Kiwanis, Lion, 4-H, and products to combat tobacco suckers.

The familiar goggle-eyed visage of Senator W. A. (Buddy) Blisterson glowered down from its own billboard, face haloed by a bunting wreath of American flags and screaming eagles, the block letters below confirming: NORTH CAROLINA IS BLISTERSON COUNTRY!

Dany, Lhota said, *I know this a complete violation, but I simply must talk with you, face-to-face, please, make every attempt to come down, and tell no one, I will explain. . . .*

Daniel Robinson was walking from his room in the Wisteria Motor Court to the motel coffee shop on a Saturday morning to meet with Miroslav Lhota, who did not go by the name Lhota anymore and had not for some years, but rather answered to the new legal name Morris Krámský. He was owner of Kramsky's Sportworld, its colossal plastic signage clearly visible in the shopping plaza across the highway from the motel. Robinson had driven down from Washington the night before to see him, in response to a badgering, then desperate, phone call.

Of course it's a violation of the rules, Robinson said, *I don't even exist for you anymore, and you don't for me, at least let me clear it with somebody*. . . .

But Lhota had begged him to come. He had pleaded, saying lives depended on it. He had made Robinson remember the good old days, when they were friends and colleagues, the Czech informer and his American spymaster, both on the way up. And so Robinson had consented to come. Robinson and the United States owed this man a debt, having used him liberally, a debt that had never been fully repaid and perhaps never would be.

Lhota had come to this improbable place to take part in the boom that was occurring there, because out in the tobacco fields there also now stood vast, silent, windowless industrial enterprises in the flatlands, making telephones, microchips, aircraft propellers, chemical solvents. For no discernible reason, dozens of multinationals and thousands of outsiders had come in.

"That's why I bland in so easily," said Lhota in his dripping Slovak accent as they sat down for breakfast, Lhota showing off he could speak English. "To locals, I'm just one of many."

"And a devout Catholic, no less," said Robinson.

"I'm only non-American Catholic here," he said. "Nobody from old country. Just young transplants from New Jersey. Church meeting in corrugated-metal warehouse until we build own building. I'm on building committee. Nobody wonder about national origin."

Lhota a Catholic refugee? Who in the Agency had devised that? The man opposite him was sixtyish, heavy-jowled, those watery sentimental eyes of Slovakia and the breath forever strengthened by a recent consumption of sausage, a reserve link of which was carried in a coat pocket: Miroslav Lhota had to have been the only diplomat in Vienna who carried *klobása* around in a coat pocket, and mercifully so. His name at birth had been Lehota, but as a young Communist in Prague he had taken the Czech spelling; he had gone back to his Slovak homeland to help infiltrate the Catholic Church as a young party *úředník*. He was mostly bald; the remaining fringe of hair hovered between brown and gray. He was wearing a McGregor golf shirt, pyrethrum-yellow Sansabelt pants, and white shoes, all things he must have liberated from his own store racks.

The Wisteria Motor Court was a large new facility with a singularly active cocktail lounge, which had boomed until the wee hours the night before.

"Lhota, how do you like it?" Robinson asked. He was still astonished to be sitting in North Carolina with his old colleague.

"Oh, isn't perfect." Lhota took a puff from his cigar. "Strictly small-town. Hardly any of locals ever been out of state, much less country. Big thrill is to go shopping in Raleigh on weekend. And I can't get native favorites, like fried cheese or real Plzeň beer."

"Anybody onto you?"

Lhota laughed. "Not even fiancée knows."

"Fiancée?" asked Robinson. "Congratulations. Who is she?"

"Local girl. Blonde. Twenty years younger. Divorced, with two kids. Sings country and western part time. Southern Baptist."

"Already marrying outside the faith?"

"Totally in love," swore Lhota. "She convert anytime I say."

Out on the highway that ran by the hotel, which was the main highway connecting Raleigh in the west to the swamps in the east, leviathan trucks roared by, sending slight tremors through the plateglass windows as they passed. Inside, some of the locals Robinson recognized from the night before in the lounge were sliding in for breakfast. The waitress was classic Southern, in canary polyester pantsuit and a strontium-white bouffant hairdo.

"Dany," said Lhota. "Pardon me, but you are well? Maybe due to beard, but you look terrible. You lose weight?"

Robinson wanted to change the conversation.

"The divorce," he said. "Harder than I thought."

Lhota nodded, watching him closely.

A black woman moved past, mopping the tile floor and carrying with her a cloud of cleanser odor, a wash of citrus pheromones.

"How's the sporting goods business?"

"Great," whispered Lhota. "Actually making real money now.

Probably first CIA investment to ever make profit. When ex-Communist is hungry enough, he can hustle. People here sports crazy. I sell top-of-line football uniforms to every kid over age of eight, baskbetballs by hundreds, weights and gym equipment. And guns."

"Ah ha," said Robinson. "Now I see the connection."

"Don't make fun," Lhota said. "More guns fly around here than Czech State Security ever dream of. Everybody packs gun. Truck-drivers, preachers, little old ladies. Ready to open fire."

"Be careful," said Robinson. "Who are your wholesalers? You might bump up against one of your old cohorts."

"Americans or Czechs? By God, Dany, of course I'm careful. I don't cut deals with anybody in Geneva or Monte Carlo; nobody overseas as matter of fact. So I think I'm okay."

The waitress brought Robinson a pair of waffles and coffee. She brought Lhota two scrambled eggs, five brilliantly pink slices of ham, a steaming pile of hash brown potatoes, a bowl of cornflakes, orange juice, a half grapefruit, and coffee.

"I'm glad to see you're eating well," said Robinson.

Lhota's comment was lost as he inhaled the hot hash browns.

"I hope you live to your wedding day," Robinson said. Lhota only grunted. A slight perspiration had formed on his face.

"Lhota, I'm impressed with your English."

"I spend years talking to you guys," Lhota grunted. "I spill enough to fill fifty file cabinet."

"You were considered productive," said Robinson. "A good investment."

"Humph," said Lhota. Now he was working on the toast, first thickly buttering it, then smearing on livid grape jelly. Robinson finished off his waffles and watched Lhota eat.

"*So whom did you tell about my call, Dany?*" the older man finally asked, switching into Czech, mopping his lips and face with a paper napkin.

"Nobody," Robinson said. "I'm taking a risk even coming down here. I'm sure not going to advertise it."

Lhota looked at him for an interval, studying him. It unsettled, even angered, Robinson to have this old friend scrutinize him for signs of lying.

Lhota was apparently placated.

"So who hates me up there?" Lhota asked. *"Garibaldi? Tabor? Who's my persecutor?"*

"Ha," Robinson laughed. "Don't be so dramatic. Nobody hates you."

Now he *was* concealing, and both of them knew it.

"Are you one of them, Dany?"

Lhota was looking at him through those watery sentimental eyes, that look, that look of irreconcilable truths battling in his head, the same look he'd given Robinson from the Air Force stretcher as he was being flown out of Vienna in 1977 to freedom, a look too close to that of a dying man because he'd been shot through the gut by the KGB, the look that said: It is not possible you or the great United States of America would have kept me waiting so long to cross over. It is not possible you or the United States would have left me exposed for those two months as they asked me to perform one last operation for them, even though I was afraid, even though the KGB knew of my plans. You and the great United States would not do such a thing.

Tell him he's protected, the station chief had said. Lie, stroke him, tell him anything, say our asset in the KGB station'll cover him, but no way in hell is he coming out now.

Lhota never said it outright, and he certainly would never have been so direct as to accuse Robinson or the United States of participation in his betrayal; it was always somebody else, some detractor, some isolated individual who perverted the essential goodness of the United States of America.

The look, the memory, made it difficult for Robinson to keep a distance.

"Why do you think you've got enemies?"

"For one thing," said Lhota, *"sending me here. I mean, not to run down the good people of Pettyville. But, Dany. This is nowhere. They might as well have sent me to Olomouc. Is this any kind of payoff for helping them break the Czechs in Vienna?"*

"Maybe they were thinking of safety."

Lhota snorted, then looked around the room.

Robinson did the same, involuntarily. The sweep of his glance revealed only truckdrivers and busty women from the lounge last night. No one even remotely suspicious.

"You aren't worried about your safety, are you?" Robinson asked. The question sounded ludicrous to him. Lhota'd been written off, forgotten long ago by Prague, Moscow . . . even Washington. The stories he could tell were all ancient history, irrelevant to the new order. No one was out to get him. Much bigger defectors than he had been totally forgotten in the rush of the Wall falling, turned into embarrassments now, anachronisms. Emissaries of *perestroika* now dazzled New York and Washington cocktail parties, gave talk show interviews, wrote books. Retired KGB directors now had grants at the Carnegie Endowment and Brookings. This was the new age.

Yet Lhota sat there, smirking, shrugging slightly. It was his look that said, Who knows?

The Agency rumors and gossip ran through Robinson's head again. Theatrical Lhota, delusions of his own grandeur. Post-defection depression. Will say or do anything to get back in the limelight. And the ugly stuff, whispered: Lhota still a Soviet double. Planting disinformation.

"It wasn't terribly smart inviting me to come see you, if you're worried about being found out. Somebody could have followed me down," said Robinson.

Lhota smirked again. The implication was: It's too late. "They" already know about me.

Robinson found the whole thing absurd, and he didn't want to pursue it. He stirred the melted butter in his plate with the prongs of his fork. The waitress brought them a copy of the *Pettyville Daily Reflector*.

"*So what is going on in the bureau?*" Lhota finally asked, seeing Robinson wouldn't rise to the other bait. "*You can tell me. Is it Garibaldi? Is he going senile?*"

Robinson didn't say anything.

"*I know what he thinks about our new painter-President,*" said Lhota. "*Garibaldi's blown the President's German grandmother into a plot to give the Sudetenland back.*"

"What do you think about the *President?*" Robinson asked, astonished Lhota knew what had been discussed in the bureau, but not willing to confirm it.

Lhota rolled his eyes and shook his jowly head in exasperation. It was as if he was saying, You stupid Americans. Do we have to lead you by the hand? Robinson knew. He had heard these comments countless times over the years.

"Didn't you keep a close eye on him when he was a dissident?" asked Robinson.

"Of course we did. Although he was one of many, just barely out of school in those days. His uncle and family were of more concern."

"And?"

"And he's what he seems. He's a good man, a great man. My old colleagues made him a greater man than he would have been, they gave him such sweet suffering to inspire his art. Only my people could elect a painter as President."

"Is he apolitical?"

"Who cares?" snapped Lhota. *"He's a saint, a wonderful man sitting on top of the forty-year garbage heap of our Communist revolution. While little Communist toads hide deep in the mud, waiting for all this to blow over."*

"But they can't survive in the mud for long, Lhota," Robinson said. "All those people will be swept away in time."

Lhota coughed. He ground out his cigar in the plate where eggs had been. He scratched the back of his neck. Outside, the morning was dissolving into a full late-summer day in the backwater South: Amazonian humidity, vegetation just aching for a chain saw, glinting explosions of sunlight jetting off the windshields of cars and trucks on the highway.

"You're trying to make me think I'm a foolish old man," said Lhota, *"that I don't know my own people, my own country. That the world has changed so much."*

"But it has changed," Robinson finally said. "It's changed so much I wonder if I can even do my job anymore. All the old players, the configurations, swept away. Lhota, we're just pretending to work up there. The *New York Times* knows more than we do."

"Have you forgotten every lesson I ever taught you about them?" he finally said. *"This is their game. Never, never take something as it appears. Look for its inverse. Every surface is false."*

Lhota lit another cigar. His face was enveloped in smoke, like some kind of rocket at liftoff.

"Lhota," said Robinson after a moment. "Why did you call? It wasn't just to go over all this again, was it?"

Lhota sat scowling, a mixture of old man and infant, petulant that the world wasn't going his way. He looked disoriented in that instant, making all the rumors and gossip back in Langley seem true.

Post-defection depression. Loss of limelight. Conspiracy everywhere.

In the silence, Robinson looked down at the *Daily Reflector*. Stories about football practice at Central Carolina State College. County Manager Urges New Reservoir Plans. A tiny buried corner story about the reunification of Germany.

"Because I still trust you," said Lhota. *"Dany, try and get them to end this love affair with the new faces. They're being suckered."*

Robinson must have rolled his eyes or sighed, because Lhota suddenly gripped him on the forearm.

"Dany, this is serious business. Don't be seduced by the party in the streets. There's another show."

"And what is that?" asked Robinson tiredly. A three-hundred-mile trip for more far-out scenarios. Now he was genuinely pissed.

"The story is this. While you drool over our painter, the old conspiracies go on. The STB international section hasn't been touched. The KGB hasn't been dismantled. An old enemy of mine, a dead man, has come back to life."

"Who?" asked Robinson, knowing he would be told whether he asked or not.

"I knew him only as Emil," said Lhota. *"He's alive, in Central America."*

Robinson was tapping a series of indentations into a soft pat of margarine with the tip of his knife.

"He was supposed to have died in Ethiopia, in 1978," said Lhota. *"A plane crash, they said. He was on Warsaw Pact detail to Mengistu's forces in Eritrea."*

This didn't merit a response, simply a respectful hearing for old time's sake, and then goodbye. Robinson shifted in his seat. He still felt a buzz from the tranquilizers of the night before. But he had to take them. Otherwise the dreams came without warning.

"Miro," he finally said, "put it in a letter, with names, dates. Write it to your resettlement officer. He'll get it in the proper channels."

Lhota was livid. *"I wrote the letter four months ago. Nobody will pay attention to me."*

Robinson exhaled. "So what are you telling me?" he asked. "That this man is really alive and running the revolution in Central America?"

"*I don't know what he's running*," said Lhota with uncustomary modesty. "*I want you to tell your people to dig on him. Don't say I tipped you. Use whatever pathetic network you have left in Prague to find out where he came from. All sorts of people are singing now, all kinds of former secret police who say they always sympathized with democracy. Marvelous opportunity to clear up old questions.*"

Robinson coughed. All this buildup for nothing. Central America had fallen far down the priority list. The grand conspiracy was grand only to Lhota.

"*You don't believe me*," said Lhota. "*You think this is my fantasy, my delusion. Just like the others back in Washington.*"

Robinson said nothing.

"*They've gotten to you*," Lhota said, looking out the window. "*I've been written off. Out of vogue. They think I'm a puffed-up former cop who got carried away with the thrill of being a defector.*"

Robinson found all this depressing. It was like seeing the death of a loved one.

"*I could say worse*," said Lhota quietly. "*I could say mole, Dany. There's a mole up there, turning you all against me.*"

"Don't," said Robinson, shaking his head. "Moles are very unfashionable right now."

Lhota was quiet, and sad, for a minute. How had things gotten so bad?

"*Dany, we did have some good times in Vienna, didn't we? Remember those weekends up in the Tyrol . . . who were those girls anyway? What happened to them? And the running around and playing cops and robbers. God, I miss all that. I knew it couldn't last, but I miss it. Remember our agreement, Dany? If ever in trouble, meet at the Salzburgerhaus?*"

How could he forget?

Lhota smoked and scratched his head.

"*Remember our summertime signal, Dany? If I'm being followed to a rendezvous, I'll have my sleeves rolled up?*"

Of course, of course. Why was he doing this?

"*Dany, I made you. I taught you everything you know. Finish up what I couldn't finish.*"

Robinson couldn't respond.

"*Dany, we dug on Emil years ago. We dug and tailed him and tried to entrap him. I mean, the boss was really worried. This was a year or two after the Soviet invasion.*"

"Why were you even wasting your time on him?" Robinson asked.

"*Because the boss was scared. We knew Emil landed at Ruzyne with the Soviet troops in 1968. Others swore they saw him in the Kremlin that next day, when the Russians flew Dubček and Svoboda to Moscow as captives, to be badgered by Brezhnev. The boss wanted to know, who the hell was this Emil Užhok? The boss was upset. Husák thought he had the ultimate channel to Brezhnev. Užhok was evidence he didn't.*"

"Why didn't Husák just ask who he was? Couldn't he have called up his protector in Moscow?"

Lhota smiled, winking.

"*Dany, he wanted to keep his job. He didn't want to stir up the crocodile any more than he had to. That's why he put me on the case. I was to sniff and dig, but not to alarm the KGB. Very discreet. Very quiet.*"

"What did you find out?" Robinson asked, out of courtesy.

"*Certain strange facts, and big gaps. We believe he was a Ruthenian, from way out east, before Ruthenia was taken from us and given to the Ukraine. He used a Ruthenian last name—Užhok—but it was almost certainly false, the name of a village on the border. He was supposedly interned at Terezín concentration camp by the Nazis during the war; when the Red Army liberated, Beria gave him a Star of Lenin for his service to humanity. He was called one of the 'Angels of Terezín'—an* anděl*—for saving children's lives. Then he was invisible until the 1960s. We presumed he was in Moscow. Then he came back to Czechoslovakia for some kind of staff job with the Defense Ministry in the mid-1960s.*"

"Sounds like you managed to find a few things."

"*But, Dany, there was a KGB wall around Emil. Every time I got onto something specific—a date, or a place, or a job—I hit the foggy wall. Oh, we could find backdated records, erasures, omissions. Originals destroyed, the duplicates would say. Or there were blanks. Things just stopped.*"

"You did this alone?" Robinson asked.

Lhota didn't answer. He was holding something back. Robinson made a mental note of that.

"But what about his official biography?" asked Robinson. "It can't all be fake."

"*Come on. Half the people working for the Party were the same way in those days. Thugs like me. My former bosses and colleagues.*"

"Why is it so suspicious in this case, then?" pressed Robinson.

"Because of the stone wall," said Lhota. *"In all other cases the fabrications were by the Czechs. But this, this was different. KGB written all over it. This man, this Czech, was being kept secret from us loyal Communist Czechs."*

"It's too thin," said Robinson. "Central America isn't hot anymore. We've always known there were some Pact people in Nicaragua."

"But he was sighted in Guatemala," interrupted Lhota.

"So maybe he was helping the guerrillas. Or whatever. Central America isn't my area. God, Lhota, if you Czechs couldn't find out about Emil, how could we? It just isn't worth it."

"Dany," said Lhota, *"our own secret police weren't even allowed to investigate this man, this Czech citizen. He supposedly died in Ethiopia. And now he's been seen in Guatemala. He's deep cover for something. This is what you should be doing, not writing reports about the new* President."

Robinson digested that for a second. Perhaps something was buried there. But it was more likely a case of mistaken identity, the sighting in Guatemala, combined with Lhota's refusal to let go, his fantasies of conspiracy. More practically, the Agency would immediately suspect Robinson if he even tried to raise it; they would smell Lhota three hundred miles away. It could cost him his job.

Or a more sinister explanation—a thousand things were running through Robinson's head. Like: Who was Lhota working for? Was it some faction in the Czech secret police? Were Husák and his gang still running Lhota, from retirement?

Was it some ancient ethnic, tribal thing?

"How did it all end?" Robinson finally asked. "The investigation?"

"I traced Emil's 1966 Defense Ministry stint to a job at Hostivař, outside Prague. Pure KGB, locked up tight. My friends said, Don't touch it. Certain death. I kept pushing. And then somebody fired through my Prague kitchen window, Dany. This was taken as a warning shot. So Husák said, Investigation ended. Never existed. I guess it just embarrassed him to learn how powerless he was. Instead, they assigned me to watch Dubček for a while."

"Dubček?"

"After he was expelled from the Party. And it wasn't even so much an anti-Dubček thing. It was more protection, actually. Dubček had been fairly close to Husák. Nobody remembers that. It's all on paper, Husák praising

Dubček, even after the invasion. Husák said he was honored to serve with this man. Even after the Russians were in there."

Lhota could be seductive, even with his most outrageous tales.

"*And then the second shot came. They hit me this time, on a Sunday afternoon, a stroll on the river. That's where my shoulder scar came from. So Husák said, Get Lhota out of the country. That's how I became a diplomat, Dany. They wanted to hide me away, put me out of harm's way. No aptitude or language tests for Miroslav Lhota to see if I could actually do the job. No, get me out of Prague.*"

And yet the ground was soft; Robinson felt lost in a fog. This happened more and more. It was making him sick.

"*Dany, Emil was behind those shots. If it hadn't been for Emil, I'd never have been in Vienna to begin with, I'd never have met you, I'd never be sitting here. And it was Emil or his people who found me in Vienna and who tried to kill me there. These people hounded me right into your arms.*"

Robinson drank some leftover dregs of orange juice.

"*But now at long last, things are breaking. They've found a journal in Prague, from Terezín camp. It supposedly tells all about Emil, what he did there, clues to what he was doing later for the Russians, what he's doing now in Central America. It's just waiting over there to be picked up.*"

Who's he working for? thought Robinson.

"*It's my own fault,*" said Lhota. "*It's why you and your Agency loved me, and now hate me. I went from being brilliant, to a tease, to a liar. That's why they concocted this ridiculous new identity and exiled me to Kramsky's Sportworld in Pettyville, North Carolina. I was a virus. They wanted me out of town.*"

"We all fall prey to our imaginations from time to time," Robinson said. "This business encourages it."

The sun was midway up into the sky. The breakfast crowd had gone. The waitress had cleared away most all the other dishes. She sat on a stool behind the grill and polished her nails. Robinson imagined she was ready for them to leave, although she was too polite to do anything about it. That was the nice thing about the South.

"*I can see you won't do it,*" said Lhota after a time. "Můj adoptívní syn, *there's such a gap between us now.*"

Lhota sat looking at him intently for a moment. Nothing was said. Lhota had on a Rolex watch that must have cost two thousand dollars.

"*Forget I ever said it*," said Lhota. "*I'm your old* kmotr, *going dotty*."

It was Lhota's sentimental old paternal tone that on one level—the emotional—spoke to the fatherless Robinson. But it also made him wary; he sensed manipulation.

The waitress had turned on a radio, and the loud Wayne Cochran song further signaled that breakfast hours were at a close.

"*Dany*," said Lhota after a minute. "*Pardon me for saying so, but you don't look good. You aren't like the Dany I knew in Vienna.*"

"How do I look?" Robinson asked, not wanting to hear.

"*Scared*," said Lhota. "*Older, like your colleagues. Going by the book now, when you used to make your own rules. Garibaldi must be bad news.*"

Robinson resented this. He watched a huge sixteen-wheeler hauling refrigerated chicken breasts for Southern Poultry Outlets turn into the parking lot. The driver jumped down to the pavement.

"*Dany, I have one last favor to ask. A small thing.*"

His Slovak village code of behavior meant that a major humiliating turndown, such as Lhota just suffered, could be canceled by a personal favor. Robinson was obliged to meet it.

"Yes?" he asked.

"*Dany, my* tetka *Věra died this spring.*"

"I'm sorry to hear that. She was close, wasn't she?"

"*Like a mother. Poor old thing. Anyway, she was the last relative.*"

Robinson nodded, waiting.

"*Dany, she left some things behind. Not much: a few sticks of furniture, clothes. But her personal effects were rescued by a friend. He's holding them for me.*"

Robinson didn't like it.

"*Your people go in and out of there all the time. Could I ask one of you to pick it up for me? It's nothing of value. Just the Lhota family Bible, some old photographs of my mother and father. Nothing.*"

Robinson was torn. Maybe Lhota was telling the truth. But to risk one of his people on a pickup like that was dangerous. Maybe it was a setup.

"Who's got it?" Robinson asked.

"*A friend*," said Lhota, shrugging.

"You know you've broken the rules, maintaining contacts with home. Lhota, they could nail you on that alone."

"*Dany, I'm a human being. And I've been careful. You know how careful I am. I've run it through some exile circles in New York; they can't trace me. They don't know my name or address, not even my state.*"

"Who's the friend?" Robinson asked. There was no way he was going to be able to do this one either.

Lhota wrote out an address, handing it casually to Robinson.

Kampě 38, Praha.

"*You don't know how homesick I get*," said Lhota.

The driver of the poultry truck waved to the waitress through the window. She turned off the restaurant radio and ran to the door. She stood half inside and half out, conversing. He was wearing black boots and blue jeans.

Back in his memory, Robinson thought he knew this address.

"*The world is going to hell*," said Lhota. "*For a while I thought you Americans could hold the line. Now you let Iraqis and Germans and Japs kick you in the face.*"

Kampě. The little island under the Charles Bridge, along the shore of the Vltava. Cobblestones, damp river breath in spring, steam in summer.

"*Europe's going off in its own direction now*," Lhota said. "*America saved Europe, and what thanks do you get?*"

"Jesus," said Robinson, remembering. "This is Dvořáček's address."

Lhota was reddening.

"This is absolutely impossible," Robinson said.

"*Zatracene!*" sputtered Lhota. "*Why not? He's safe, secure.*"

"Is he your man?" gasped Robinson. "Lhota, we can't touch him. He's a Soviet double. Pure poison. On our shit list for three years."

"*Bastards*," swore Lhota. "*You cut him off, after all he did for you. Based on rumor. Pure American rumor. Created by a bunch of idiots sitting around playing with each other in Langley, most who've never even been to Czechoslovakia.*"

"I've never been there," said Robinson.

"*You abandoned him*," said Lhota. The sound in his throat was the curious warning of a normally pacific animal such as a badger, cornered, ready to pull out all stops in defense.

"*You left him to hang over there*," said Lhota. "*One of the cruelest betrayals of all time.*"

"He was judged a double," said Robinson. "Probably pulled you into some operation right now. That's what this is all about, Lhota. Being used, maybe to set me up."

Lhota sprang up from the booth; Robinson thought he was about to be slapped. Lhota trembled; and then he seemed to contain himself.

"*Little boy*," he whispered, "*I know my country and my countrymen a thousand times better than you. I know Václav Dvořáček. He survived my defection because he was clever. The fools in Langley thought there was a clear line to be drawn. But their opinion is mush. They never saw the gray, gray that everyone had to live by. Maybe Václav kept on pretending to work for the STB; maybe he told them a few little facts, and great big lies that kept them happy, that protected him from vengeance over me. And, Dany, don't forget, he had Husák for a patron all those years. I know Václav's heart. I know his mind. He was one of us, and he was a silent hero left to die a slow death in a prison land more hostile than you can even imagine. Every day, every waking minute, for him was five times worse than death. You cannot imagine.*"

Robinson was sorry this old sore had been reopened.

The waitress pushed the driver away, laughing. Rocked back on his heels, arms at his sides, he was like a cowboy straddling an invisible bronco.

"Hell far," Robinson heard the driver say through the glass and the half-opened door.

Who was Lhota working for?

Lhota was only looking at him, looking through him. It was as though he were looking back fifty years. There was no sign of friendship in his eyes.

"There's no way in hell I can go in and pick up photos for you," said Robinson.

That was all he said.

The truckdriver had given the waitress a cigarette, and they had both lit up. The man had the knack of letting a cigarette hang stuck from his lower lip, and he slouched in a tribal redneck stance somebody needed to record, for posterity.

"*There's someone inside Langley*," Lhota said, quietly. Then he withdrew down inside himself. He was still watching Robinson closely.

Robinson instinctively laughed at the mention of moles, it sounded so ludicrous. But his own body was trembling slightly. The waitress laughed also, and came back inside. The driver went around toward the motel registration office. Robinson took a slow breath.

"Lhota," Robinson said, regretting it even as he spoke, "who are you working for?"

Lhota did not move his body, but his mouth moved.

A piece of paper spiraled by the window, in slow motion.

"*I am working for me, and for you,*" he said.

Robinson took that.

"*If you have to ask,*" Lhota said, "*we aren't father and son anymore.*"

Robinson couldn't respond. That was the worst thing he could have been told. Something was being killed right here. His faithful friend Lhota, the champion defector. His mentor, his longtime friend. Now the two of them were using the careful probing you used with the enemy.

The whole encounter had gone foul.

Robinson looked at the *Pettyville Daily Reflector.* How blissfully unaware it was of things happening elsewhere. Lhota was lucky to be here.

Looking at his watch, Lhota shifted in preparation to stand and go. Robinson noticed the great sweat stains further darkening the electric-blue golf shirt. A paunch hung over the yellow Sansabelts.

"Are you a golfer now?" asked Robinson, the words sounding false rather than collegial.

Lhota didn't answer.

"When's the wedding?"

Lhota said nothing.

"Am I invited?"

Lhota looked at him, a slight tremor jolting his head. He was so far away.

"*Dany,*" said Lhota, shaking his head. "*I should never have called you.*"

Lhota put a five-dollar bill down on the table and started to walk away. Robinson had never seen him this abrupt, angry. Impulsively he stood, to try and calm him.

"Lhota, cool off," he managed to say. "You've thrown some heavy stuff at me."

Lhota made a grunting noise and continued on toward the door. The cleaning woman was watching them, aware of their dispute.

"Miroslav. Don't do this. Don't mix business and friendship this way, eh? We live differently. . . . It's not Vienna anymore; our lives have turned over, our world. Our spy thing is over with. But we're still friends, as much as ever. . . ."

Robinson laid his hand on the older man's arm, but Lhota pulled away, walking through the door and drawing them both out into the wall of humidity.

"You're acting childish," Robinson repeated. "You're asking me to break rules, laws. I could be fired for even being here. Don't do this to me."

Lhota turned to glare at him, blue eyes wet with fury, mouth pursed.

"We have always mixed business and pleasure, you and I," Lhota said, voice quavering. *"They were one and the same, built on trust. Now you do not trust me. Therefore the friendship is dead."*

"But it's not—"

Robinson reached out to detain him again, but Lhota pushed Robinson away and plowed ahead across the parking lot. A convoy of rusted troop carriers was rolling past on the highway, bound from an army base that had been shut down farther east. These would probably be sent to Texas and cut into scrap, or sold.

"Don't do this," Robinson said.

Lhota climbed into a huge new Oldsmobile and shut and locked the door.

"Miroslav," Robinson said, knocking on the glass.

The engine had started.

"Miroslav."

With a roar of tires on gravel, Lhota drove off into the haze. Robinson stood out there a moment, watching the car move away down the highway. He stood there genuinely devastated. He had not felt the impact of a loss like this since the divorce, and was astonished.

Back inside, the waitress was nowhere to be found, and Robinson had to go back into the kitchen to find her and pay his bill.

The mephitic haze of Pettyville followed him back up to Washington, and by the time he reached northern Virginia in late afternoon the heat and humidity had built up into one of those supercharged black-ceilinged storms that preview world's end, enormous discharges of thermal and electric and sonic force occurring overhead and rain cascading out of the black heavens as if entire oceans had been sucked up into the sky, the capital gone, the capital lost, you could see nothing but a low charcoal void hugging the earth.

Robinson fell into a chair in his apartment, which overlooked the river. He knew the city was beyond, but the rain was so heavy that visibility ended out over the water: he was looking at a new sea where land and people once lay.

There was a message from his girlfriend, Leah, on the machine, she'd called on impulse while out shopping, voice full of music, wanting to get together that night, to go camping in the Blue Ridge with a bottle of Scotch, a last-minute thing. So much fun it would be, even in the rain, so far from all this.

But he didn't return her message, sitting there instead to brood in the squall's darkness, never more unsettled and anxious in his life than now, unsettled in part because nothing was solid anymore. He had hurt a friend, he had denied an appeal from the person who more than anyone else had launched his own now-failed career. Without Miroslav Lhota, Robinson would probably have been dismissed within the first three years of his traineeship.

All Robinson's initial concern that Miroslav Lhota was lying to him, or working for someone else, was subordinated now to this feeling of having betrayed a friend, of having failed a mentor. Miroslav Lhota had risked his own life for Daniel Robinson; Daniel Robinson was unwilling to risk a little more career damage for Miroslav Lhota. That paradox sickened him, made him ashamed of himself.

Although he should have either called Lhota and made amends and done as he asked, or followed through on his original cold assessment and told the Agency the next Monday morning about the Pettyville meeting and all the wild talk, Robinson did nothing. He sat on it, sorting it out in his mind. He sat and sorted, turning the whole process in on himself, one more symptom of the mess his life had become. What, what was the answer?

Before he ever figured that one out, other news had come with the end of summer and descent of autumn, changing the whole game.

Miroslav Lhota was dead.

Langley, Virginia
The following January

And now it was winter, and Daniel Robinson sat with a group of men and women in a building hidden far out in a Virginia forest. Projected on the wall before them was a face, enlarged enough to reveal the grain and imperfections of the original photo. For the audience, this man was a comet soaring inexplicably into the heavens of another universe, parallel to but remote from their own.

The face was of the new painter-President of Czechoslovakia, and his features were best described as soulful. His was a particular kind of Central European face, a face more often found in the coffeehouses or the universities than at the head of a new government born in the streets. The mouth was unusually full and sensitive for a man holding a job once held by a commissar; the eyes surpassed the mouth, carrying both the shadows of sadness and the sparkle of humor that only a great soul could have.

This man was now the head of state in what had once been a dictatorship of the most rigid cut. And, thought Daniel Robinson, not only was he a total break from those who had come before; he is something totally alien to these people sitting around me today. Not many of us in this room could be described as soulful, he thought. Nor could many, if any, of the leaders of my own country in this century.

As the task force sat, looking, Daniel Robinson thought: This man threatens us as much as he does those he overthrew. He threatens our own dark profession.

The others in the group were struggling to find something false, something sinister, something devious about this man, so as to justify their own employment. Robinson was sickened by it. He could not help but let his mind wander back to Lhota, and what Lhota would have said about it all.

The new leader—the painter-President—is a wonderful man, Lhota would have said. He is what he is. But don't be distracted by him. You Americans are so deceived by appearance. A result of your glittering television imbecility. You must learn to think like Eastern Europeans. Expecting conspiracy in all things.

But Miroslav Lhota would never say those things, Robinson reminded himself; Miroslav Lhota was dead.

"Sings a song of innocence, but I smell something else," said a florid, garrulous man who had no neck but rather a curious shaved doughnut of fat between his chin and shoulders, like a life preserver.

The speaker was offering his opinion of the new President. The speaker's name was Garibaldi, he was the Area Director, and he had convened them to write something called the six-month pol/mil sitrep.

"What do we know about his possible KGB contacts?" asked a man in the rear of the room, an interagency liaison, who was taking notes.

"Too obvious," said Garibaldi. "Give me something sexier."

"Now let's not be hasty," whined another man. This one was very bald, an avian thinness to his limbs and frame, a deep air of exhaustion about him, resembling nothing so much as a piece of worn-out human carpet. Defensiveness rang in his voice, because his office was responsible for such knowledge, or lack of it. He was Tabor, and he was the Country Officer. He was Robinson's nominal superior.

"We do know," said Tabor, his slight vocal quaver learned from years of deference to authority, "that he did go to Moscow on a youth exchange when he was twelve—"

"Tabor," interrupted Garibaldi. "It won't fly."

"Intelligence Committee wants more," said an alcoholic Virginian named Buford Doswell, whose job it was to drink liquor with congressmen and their staffs and try to win more money for the Agency's budget in these difficult times of peace and a fading enemy threat.

This is pathetic, thought Robinson. We're looking in the wrong place. We should be figuring out why Lhota, a man who worked very hard for us, was killed; not manufacturing scenarios about the painter-President.

The single window, which ran the entire length of the room, had half-closed blinds dividing the outside world into a series of half-inch strips of a vast forest panorama, motionless, denuded, like some partly reconstructed satellite photo from deep space. Looking outside, Robinson noted how even the evergreens had drawn down to a minimum flow of grayish verdure, life force barely moving through frigid needles. Straight trunks of bare oak and maple descended to the banks of a frozen brook.

The sky was broken into bars of smoky winter light.

Facing Robinson, the painter-President stared down like a billboard.

He seemed to be addressing Robinson personally.

Is this, Robinson thought, how it went with Lhota? He just got pulled in and couldn't let go?

Daniel Robinson wondered if he too was going crazy. It was worse today than it had been in weeks.

"We've talked about the family angle," Garibaldi stated, for the record. "We've talked about aristocratic roots, German ancestry."

Tabor nodded. Robinson thought: This is theater, for the benefit of a tape recorder or the rapporteur.

"Colleagues," said Garibaldi. "We have a three P.M. deadline for the Director. I think it time we define ourselves."

This means Garibaldi will impose his view, thought Robinson.

"We will report that our new head of state will continue to pursue the rapprochement with greater Germany, in pursuit of investment and capital. We see a tilting away from the Czech-Slovak equipoise, into a new Czech-German financial partnership, with the Slovaks on the outside. He's had no need to offend the Russians by withdrawing from the Warsaw Pact, because the Pact's evaporated."

Evaporated, Robinson thought.

Robinson thought: Why do we pretend a man wasn't killed?

Seen through the window, the sky grew cinereous. The clouds were imperceptibly thickening, an increasingly solid layer overstretching the earth. They would thicken all afternoon, and that night, when some critical mass was reached, snow would fall. Flakes of crystalline perfection would settle from the sky and accumulate on metallic ground. Beyond this empty forest, children would play.

Cars would make their way slowly along frosty windswept lanes.

A landscape more suited to Grieg than to us, thought Robinson.

"Anything else?" Garibaldi intoned rather than asked. Someone coughed, and Tabor sat like a shriveled mummy, sipping coffee from a Styrofoam cup.

Lhota knew more, Robinson wanted to say. Lhota died because of what he knew.

The clarity of that thought took him by surprise, made his pulse jump. He wanted to say it aloud, to Garibaldi, to the painter-President looming down at them.

God, am I sick, he thought. The room spun again; he could feel the craziness fighting its way up through the Equanil he'd taken at breakfast.

"Draw up the paper," said Garibaldi. "Move along, ladies and gentlemen, so we can have it to the front office before deadline."

People coughed, cups were retrieved, newspapers rustled. Voices and bodies were extruded through the single door out into the hallway. Robinson was the last one out. Someone forgot to turn off the slide projector, so that the wall-sized illuminated painter continued to beam down at the empty chairs in disarray, the dust-filled tube of the projector's light twisting and writhing like a new galaxy in formation.

As Robinson walked out, he took one last look, as if in farewell to a friend. It was the farewell he had never been able to give his friend Miroslav Lhota.

You must know when to let go, Lhota had told him years before. Controlled paranoia is the spy's fuel—but too much, and you are destroyed.

Is that me? he thought. Has that happened to me?

Tabor was somewhat ahead of him and to the right as they walked down the corridor together, away from the conference room. Never an ebullient man, Tabor seemed to sag a bit more than usual.

The others, including Garibaldi, were moving quickly out of earshot. Tabor was attempting to do so too.

"The gospel according to Garibaldi," said Robinson, not willing to let Tabor escape.

Tabor avoided talking to Robinson these days. How he hated things that were uncomfortable.

"Well," Tabor said after a minute. "There's major editing and rewriting to do. I guess the deadline can be met."

"I'm more than willing to help," Robinson said, knowing there was nothing Tabor wanted less than his help.

And he was thinking: You are even more of a coward than I. You read my memo on Lhota's death, which went into Garibaldi's safe and for all we know no longer exists.

"Don't worry," Robinson finally ventured. "This morning I have my semiannual date with Ruthie. I don't have time to help."

Mercifully for Tabor, their paths at last diverged. Tabor continued on down to the Country Affairs Office, while Robinson paused at the elevator that would take him to the fourth floor, and Security, where he had his date with Ruthie, the chief security officer for the Eastern Europe section. Everyone was fluttered, without fail, semiannually. One used it to mark the passage of the seasons, the passage of life. The flutter was a rite, a ritual cleansing, one people hardly ever thought of after it was done. It was part of the job. Why was he worried today?

A slight rush of heartbeat moved his chest as the adrenaline flowed. He was due there in five minutes.

This would not do at all.

Security always had a special feel to it. Although you could hardly say any office in the building was a place of wild abandon, Security had its own atmosphere. The women were hard. The air smelled of smoke. The men had coplike looks to them. Were they of a different personality type? Did the work make them squint?

And now, with the budget cuts, the air was even harsher. There were many empty desks and darkened offices piled with cardboard cartons, presumably stuffed with files that nobody had time to look through anymore. The incoming work never decreased, the folders wrapped and sealed with "Top Secret," the in baskets piling up, while the people to do it were fewer, newer, lower paid, inexperienced. There was hardly any institutional memory anymore. The wheel was reinvented every day. Somebody had decided that the bulk of the horrendous budget cut of the year before would fall mostly here, and the wound was open and gaping.

Robinson looked at the side offices, searching for familiar names, faces. But Creelman, Masselink, Rinaldo, Tsao . . . none of them were to be seen, no nameplates on the doors at all. Had they all been retired?

But Ruthie was still here. Ruthie Lowenson was the best, destined to be where she was. She'd fluttered Robinson for a decade.

The receptionist looked up without greeting.

"I have a nine-fifteen with Ruthie."

The receptionist called, but Ruthie was already beckoning to him from her office door across the room. He went ahead.

"Danny boy," she said. "Getting a little gray hair, eh?"

He smiled.

"I told you to shave that awful beard off, didn't I? It ruins your profile."

This blond beard he had grown at the time of his divorce two years back. Why did people react to it so strongly?

"How's my favorite inquisitor?" he asked bravely. She squeezed his arm in comradely fashion.

"Can you believe what they've done to us?" she said, the statement sounding more like a litany than a question. She'd obviously said it before.

"I was almost wondering if you'd still be here," he said.

"Danny, Danny," she said. "I'll be the last one here. But I'm only as good as my people, and my people have been decimated. How can they expect us to do a job? Look out there, look what they're giving me to replace ten senior officers who were RIFed. Three juniors. We're talking ex–security guards. Some can barely read. This is not even second-rate."

Ruthie's desk was piled with the files, the Top Secret binders. Two had burst open and spilled onto the floor. Her window was darkened by boxes. She had triple in baskets, each a foot thick.

"Oh, it's not just us," she said, off into the air. "It's the same for the feds everywhere; the Congress too. This whole thing, the capital, is dying. I feel like we're all in some great diseased Third World bureaucracy, the Egyptian Ministry of Fertilizer, just coming in here to sit amongst the boxes and drink coffee and do our nails. I was over at the Pentagon yesterday. They're spending something like ten million dollars a week in penalty fees alone, because there aren't enough budget clerks to process their bills, write the checks. They've got the funds; they just can't process."

"Go private sector," he said.

"That's treason," she said, shocking herself, then laughing. "I'm career. I'll do my duty until retirement."

She lit a cigarette, waved her hand at the heaped in baskets.

"They cut us, then they expect us to track all sorts of new enemies. Iraq. Germany. Japan. Can you imagine? Tracking every contact you guys have with Germans, Japs? We're spread so thin."

She billowed smoke, coughed.

"I don't want to know how many things are slipping through right now. Right this minute." She looked squarely at him as she said it, striking him as rude, invasive. How dare she. But it broke the moment of intimate confessions. They talked briefly about whether it was going to snow that night, whether they would get the day off tomorrow. But Ruthie already had the arm-wrap in her hand and was ready to get down to business.

He let her put the wrap and the sensor needles on. It was 9:20 A.M.

"You know this by heart, don't you?" she said more than laughed.

"My catechism," he said. But the change was coming over her. Good friend Ruthie's voice was changing; she was going by the book. She even went through the formalities of showing him the presidential order that allowed her to violate his constitutional rights so liberally. He had read and submitted to it thirty times in the fifteen years of his employment.

"Let's start at the beginning," she said. "Daniel, any unreported contacts with Warsaw Pact country nationals, or nationals of any country on the list?"

She showed him the list, and he looked at it with some interest, for these names did change periodically, reflecting the fall of potentates, the shifts in alignment.

He read North Korea, People's Republic of China, Socialist Republic of Vietnam, Democratic People's Republic of Kampuchea, Republic of Cuba, Libyan People's Jamahiriya, Albania, Nicaragua, Mongolia, Iran, Iraq.

No, he said.

She repeated the question, with slightly different words. And he said no again.

Any unreported travel to bloc countries, or countries on the list?

No.

Any unreported approaches from bloc-country nationals, or countries on the list?

No.

Purchase or receipt of any literature or correspondence from bloc countries, other than those acquired in the work environment?

No. He thought: Does that cover my purchase of Gorbachev's *New World?*

You smile, she said. Why?

Nothing, he said.

What? she said.

Nothing, he said.

Any sign of surveillance on you by a foreign power?

No.

Do you have any family or romantic ties to anyone from a bloc country, or countries on the list?

No.

Please give me the dates of your travel to all bloc countries, and countries on the list, including month, year, purpose of travel.

He quietly sighed. She had heard this all before. It was in the files.

Ruthie, I haven't been anywhere in the last two years.

She paused a moment.

From the beginning, she said.

Ruthie, he protested, this stuff is old. It's in the files.

Danny, she said, you know the rules. Every two years I have to go back through the whole thing.

He sighed, seeking to reconstruct. This they watched closely. They would compare dates, and go back to the files, and call you about any discrepancies.

Beginning with Budapest, Hungary, in August of 1969, he recited to the best of his memory every date and time and purpose of travel. It took him, including her follow-up questions, in which she exercised her skill at trying to trip him up and poke any holes in his story, a full thirty minutes.

It was ten o'clock.

He poured a glass of water.

Let's talk love life, she said. Still unmarried?

Yes.

Cohabiting now or at any time in the last six months?

No, he said, because he and Leah still had two places, although she stayed mostly at his, since hers was just a rented room.

Any roommates?

No.

Ruthie had a slight twinkle in her eye. Any sexual intercourse during the period?

He sighed. Yes.

Where and when and with whom? she asked.

He tried to run back in his head. When had six months begun?

It was the epoch of Leah. What would he say about Leah?

It was the first time he had been asked by anyone in this building about his relationship to her. How revolting that it be here, in this setting. He resolved to minimize it.

I have a sort of girlfriend, he said.

Congratulations, she said. Name?

He gave her Leah's name.

Normal heterosexual acts? she asked.

Yes.

Any homosexual contacts?

No.

Any feeling of attraction to men?

No.

Any approaches from men?

How could he remember every pair of rolled eyes on Connecticut Avenue?

Any purchase of pornographic literature or materials?

No.

Any contact with prostitutes or escort services?

No.

She paused a moment to take some notes, then lit up a cigarette. She was enveloped by clouds of smoke that made her squint like her colleagues.

She was blondish, a Philadelphian, fortyish now, with a cleft chin and a face slightly pockmarked from a distant adolescence. As far as he knew, she was still a spinster.

She was good at her job.

What does Leah do?

Secretary, he said.

Government? she asked.

No, he said. Lobbyist.

Washingtonian? she asked.

No, he said.

Politics? she asked.

None, he said.

Last name? she asked.

Murphy, he said.

Any bloc or list country ties or travel? she asked.

I don't think so, he said.

But you don't know so, she said.

No, he answered.

Shall we do a check on her? she asked.

Don't, he said.

You know the rulebook, she said.

We aren't married, he said.

Cohabiting?

Not really, he said.

Age?

She's twenty-seven, he said.

A lot younger.

Fifteen years, he said.

I'd feel better with a check on her, she said, watching her needle.

Ruthie, she could care less about government or foreign policy. She's a free spirit. I don't think she even knows who the Secretary of State is.

You were in the White House, Danny, she said.

But I'm not anymore.

But you know your way around.

Ha, he said.

Do you love her?

He didn't say anything.

Do you love her?

I don't know, he said.

Any likelihood of marriage soon?

To Leah? he asked.

To anybody, she said.

No, he said.

How are you adjusting to losing your daughter?

There was a fluttering down inside him, a pulling downward. The thought made him weary.

Fairly well, he said.

Do you love your daughter?

Yes, he said.

Do you still love your wife?

He didn't answer.

Are you using any controlled substances?

No, he said quietly.

She paused a minute.

Are you using any illegal drugs?

No, he said.

Are you using cocaine?

No.

Heroin?

No.

Alcohol?

Yes.

How much?

One or two drinks a day after work. Maybe three or four on Saturday night.

Have you used any controlled substances in the last six months?

No. He felt the fluttering again, made his breathing deliberate.

Any marijuana?

He hesitated.

Any marijuana? she repeated.

Uh, yes, he said. Now the door was open.

How much, when, with whom? she asked.

Oh, twice or three times, I think, he said.

How many—two or three?

Three.

When?

Back in the fall.

Give me the dates and places, please.

He looked over at her desk calendar. He guessed.

With Leah? she asked.

Yes, he said.

She paused a moment, made some notes.

None since? she asked.

No, he said quickly.

Any heroin?

No.

Any stimulants, speed, uppers?

No.

Any mescaline, LSD, psychedelics?

No, he said.

Any antidepressants, sleeping pills, tranquilizers?

No.

She looked at her needle, made notes.

Are you now or have you at any time in the last six months been under the care of a psychiatrist?

No, he said quickly, before she had quite finished the last word.

She looked at him briefly.

He thought: She sees.

She repeated her question, watching him.

He repeated his answer, breathing evenly.

He thought: She sees, even though her machine does not. There was the slightest hesitation in her face as she was pulled between her scientific training and the deep instincts that had made her such a success.

She'll pop back on that one, he thought. She'll go off into something else and circle back to that to surprise me.

Are your finances in good shape? she said.

Yes.

Any debts?

Car, condo.

Any outside income in excess of five hundred dollars?

No.

Any inheritances, gifts, gratuities, consultant's fees, director's fees?

No.

Any stock dividends?

About two thousand dollars this last year.

From what investments?

My Merrill Lynch account. Small potatoes.

Any foreign investments? Any foreign bank accounts? Any interests in foreign business concerns?

No.

Any use of stimulants, speed?

No.

She was watching her machine.

No Doz?

No. He was having a hard time getting his breath. She was watching him breathe.

She was good.

Were you promoted in the last cycle?

No.

Previous cycle?

No.

Two previous?

No.

Are you happy about that?

No.

Are you happy in this career?

Yes.

She watched her needle and wrote.

Have you stolen any money on your travel vouchers?

No.

Have you falsified any of your tax returns?

No.

Have you ever stolen anything from a place of business?

He paused.

When I was a kid.

What was it?

I stole a brand-new wrench once, when I was eight or so. I had no use for it. I buried it.

Anything else?

I stole a box of candy bars when I was six. Go read your files, Ruthie. You've heard it all before.

Are you taking tranquilizers?

No.

Do you love Leah?

I don't know.

Do you love your daughter?

Yes.

Would you betray your country for her?

He could not answer.

Would you?

I . . . might, if her life were in danger.

She wrote something in her notes.

Wouldn't *you?* he asked.

She looked straight at him, softened for an instant.

Never thought about it, she said.

Danny, she said, how often do you take tranquilizers?

He just shook his head.

Who's your psychiatrist? she asked.

He looked out the window. This was the worst.

Danny, she said, we're all human. You can tell me.

It was now ten-thirty. It felt like five in the afternoon. He was shot.

Danny, the law requires it.

He sipped some water.

How long, Danny? Psychotherapy? Is it tied to the drugs? Your lack of promotion? Divorce? Are you willing to take a urinalysis?

He was silent, looking out the window, far far away.

But he was thinking: Yes. Yes. Yes to any and all the above.

Now they knew.

The buried secret of his psychiatric care, and the tranquilizers he had been taking, was known to the Agency. At this very moment, phone calls were probably being made, a report was being written, and certainly that day a meeting would be convened to decide what to do about Daniel Robinson and his personal problems.

It was late morning. Although he had lots of projects to complete, he could get none of them under way.

Strangely, sitting alone in his office after the interrogation was over, he felt relieved, a warm sense of physical relaxation washing over him as when some terribly bad news has been received—the death of one close to you, or the departure of a lover—and in that lull, everything hangs suspended for an interval, clouded in a kind of protective warmth. At the same time, the important clearly stood out from the mundane. Surely it was something physical and genetic, something inherited from the animal kingdom that allowed the organism to function and deal with loss or defeat, to prepare its defense even though the odds of survival were impossible.

The therapist's office was not far from where he lived, on the Virginia bank of the river. He'd been going to her for several months, paying out of his own pocket and under an assumed name to protect his job. He would sit in her office at dusk and watch the lights of the evening exodus pour out across the city bridges, as they talked about the sudden slowdown in his career after an early meteoric rise, the unacknowledged loss of his wife and daughter, childhood feelings.

And in the end, what had it gotten him? It had cost him several thousand dollars. He felt more depressed than when he started. And it would surely damage his already-sinking career . . .

There was no point in trying to do any work. Robinson decided to take a walk outside, despite the weather. He put on his coat and walked down the corridor and out into the cold.

The day had continued its steady descent into snow, air well below freezing, ground frozen hard. He turned off into one of the jogging paths the Agency maintained for its employees, only a single jogger, a fiftyish man in a gray sweatsuit, lumbering past him, breaking off a few frozen twigs.

"Oh . . . you should know Lhota is dead," Tabor had told him one morning in late September. Robinson had heard nothing from Lhota since their painful summer conversation and therefore assumed the silence meant the friendship was finished.

The news had reminded Robinson that he'd never reported on the strange Pettyville meeting to his superiors, nor acted on Lhota's belief his life was in danger.

To complete the bluntness, Tabor presented a four-day-old copy of the Internal Bulletin, which was normally circulated only to department managers but came now to him because someone, probably Garibaldi, had finally decided Robinson should be informed, out of courtesy.

The management of information from above had always been irritating, but that day it was like a slap in the face: he found himself gritting his teeth and envisioning all sorts of violent physical acts in response. Robinson had been Lhota's case officer for four years, he knew Lhota better than anyone in the U.S., he should have been put on the death immediately.

The attached photocopied report from the Office of Security showed that a quick inquest had been undertaken upon the discovery of Miroslav Lhota's body in northern Guatemala, in highland jungle not far from the Mexican border.

"Acute case of post-defection depression," wrote the Agency field psychiatrist. "Subject was inherently unstable, with failed dreams and a sense of estrangement from his new homeland. All information indicates subject died a lonely, embittered, deluded man, on a solo Guatemalan hunting trip, although setting and circumstances could have lent themselves to foul play. Subject, frustrated by lack of usefulness after defection, had gradually slipped into depression. He hated the idea of old age, and of being put out to pasture. He was saddened that in his new home, America, he no longer had any influence. Suicide is not ruled out."

Robinson's first reaction was anger: Miroslav Lhota wouldn't have gone to Guatemala to kill himself. He could have done that at home.

Security investigator in charge was Pinky Restrepo, working out of Langley.

Robinson had stopped by unannounced to see Restrepo, a small, choleric, balding man with a wide face, who bruxed gum as he worked and pumped the air full of the odors of Juicy Fruit. The wall behind him, as well as the desk and the tops of adjacent file cabinets, had become a panoramic photo altar to the entire Restrepo clan: there were weddings upon weddings in eight-by-ten frames and christenings in polyurethane paperweights and proud servicemen in official shots, baby pictures in silver frames and summers at Ensenada in plexiglass holders and no doubt mothers-in-law and cousins, all wrapped in a shroud of ribbon and flower and commercial retouching, and Robinson wondered how a man sitting in this gush of family love could remain so humorless and nasty. He'd been a police detective in Los Angeles until he answered an ad promising adventure and exotic landscapes; now here he sat.

"What did it look like?" Robinson asked.

Restrepo kept at his task at hand for a minute to indicate his irritation at even having to answer such questions, then he took his right hand and made a pistol barrel and trigger with his fingers, pointing them into his own mouth.

"Think he killed himself?"

Restrepo shrugged. "Locals or *policía* stole his pistol; we don't know."

"Photos?" asked Robinson.

Restrepo narrowed his eyes, exhaled, and made an explosive popping sound with his chewing gum. He violently rifled a drawer for a minute, producing a pair of photos, which he slung at Robinson to further underline his message of hostility. The photos showed the corpse sprawled on the Guatemalan mud, roof of head blown away, hair standing on end, eyes open.

I grow old, I grow old . . .

Robinson asked who at FBI counterintelligence was running the investigation.

"Man, you don't quit," said Pinky. "FBI has faith in us; it's in our hands."

"Is that normal?"

Restrepo didn't even answer him but went back to his work at hand, signing papers.

"The FBI should be on it," Robinson said. "Corpse had its shirt-sleeves rolled, Lhota's signal to me he was being followed. We used it a dozen times in Vienna."

Restrepo just looked at him, chewing.

"The implication," Robinson continued, "is that he was murdered."

"Tell it to the Inspector General. I don't have time," said Restrepo.

Robinson had gone back to his own office, where an hour later he was called in by Tabor. They met in Tabor's windowless space, which was only marginally larger than Robinson's.

"Dan, let Security do its job," said Tabor, squirming with discomfort, the lining of his mouth white with the residue of the antacids he sucked to soothe his ulcerated duodenum, today so bad a slight rime of calcified residue rimmed his lips. He loathed administering discipline, especially to Robinson.

"He may have been murdered," answered Robinson.

"Lhota was a sick man," said Tabor. "You've got to submit to the Agency wisdom on this one."

"Do we look the other way when defectors get killed now?" asked Robinson, loudly. Robinson got up and walked out of the room.

Robinson's phone had rung five minutes later.

He was being summoned to Garibaldi's office.

Here we go, thought Robinson, up the chain. He wanted to do something primal and liberating, but he knew that day that he would not.

Garibaldi possessed a corner office befitting his rank, boasting not just windows but a vitreous riot and two exposures. He reposed amid blond Scandinavian furniture, a side cabinet displaying a silver samovar with matching service from a tour of duty in Leningrad, an enormous oxblood carpet from a Central Asian republic that might or might not still be a part of the Soviet Union. Garibaldi was talking on the phone, and for a moment he left Robinson free to look out on the hushed forest, maples already turning a flame crimson, other leaves falling in a hushed descent.

"Did I miss your transfer to Security?" said Garibaldi, just as he hung up.

A touch of humor? Robinson didn't know how to respond. The two men had barely exchanged words these two years since Garibaldi's appointment.

This entire meeting was a signal. The signal was: Cool it. Know your place. You have no need to know.

"I think Lhota was murdered," Robinson said slowly.

It had sounded so reasonable in his head. But now he sounded impertinent to his own ears.

"Lhota was sick," said Garibaldi, a creaminess to his voice, a condescension, his lips pulled back in a way both unctuous and hostile, the work of his verbalization sending little jolts of movement down into the tubular encirclement of neck fat. The neck itself showed signs of cut and irritation, the personal burden of having to shave on a daily basis this soft and mobile area. "He was paranoid. There's no telling what he may have gotten into. He may have actually believed he was being followed. So he left his signal to you."

Robinson took that. He thought it was possible. But in his gut he didn't believe it, just as he didn't think Miroslav Lhota was capable of suicide.

Robinson was searching for a way to cut to the heart of this, sensing it was the last such opportunity he would have.

"What if he was murdered?" Robinson asked.

"Security will find out," said Garibaldi. Garibaldi had lowered his head somewhat, so that his chin was fully lost in the neck. His lips, resembling in coloration and sheen nothing so much as those large earthworms known as night crawlers, were now pulled back over the small white teeth even more tightly, eyes saying this was serious business.

"What do we do if we find he was killed by the other side?"

"That's up to the President," said Garibaldi, as though that were a juvenile, unprofessional question.

And it had come suddenly clear to Robinson: this matter was closed, the organization had made its decision, and he was futilely trying to open the iron door. All he could do now would be to make a mess, or, better said, a stink, and ultimately a fool of himself, having seen it attempted before, one person trying to run against the institutional tide, an infrequent, dazzling, and ultimately tragic spectacle. All variations on the theme inevitably led to a single outcome, long foreordained.

Garibaldi was looking at his watch.

To preserve *perestroika* or the next summit, Robinson was thinking. To preserve the status quo with the other side, whatever it was, thought Robinson.

"Is it the defector resettlement program?" asked Robinson.

Garibaldi looked at him for a few seconds.

"Has come under criticism," Garibaldi said slowly. "One of our most attractive tools."

"We have someone big on the line?"

Garibaldi's face went into that no-need-to-know look of admonition, a look of such patronizing dismissal that it begged to be answered, but Robinson fought the impulse down, brought it under control, the play in Garibaldi's eyes suggesting he too had seen this inner struggle joined and resolved in a few seconds.

"Will you let me know what you find?" said Robinson, closing. "Whatever went wrong with Lhota these last years, I still think of him as a friend."

Garibaldi had lifted his head somewhat, and the distended lips resumed their full, vermiform shape. The eyes softened slightly. He smiled. But he did not say yes. He didn't even nod affirmatively.

"Could I be allowed to go to the funeral?" asked Robinson. "I really feel I should."

"The funeral was yesterday," said Garibaldi. "Resettlement represented us."

There is not a chink in this fortress, Robinson thought.

When it was over and Robinson was walking back down to his office, it was as though it had never happened at all. He looked at his watch. Time elapsed from call of invitation to end of meeting, four minutes.

Miroslav Lhota dead, maybe murdered, buried; case closed. So Robinson had quietly let the thing drop. The institution had in effect cordoned off the entire event. He had not even been able to see the funeral, the grief, the wailing.

Goodbye, Lhota.

In the following days, he had been prompted to think from time to time how much Miroslav Lhota had influenced him, his way of thinking, of working. Not especially smart for an American intelligence agent to shape his career on the teachings of a Soviet-bloc defector. It was a fact best buried after all.

It was beginning to snow now, beginning with a few isolated crystalline formations, tiny arid flakes that might have been bits of leaves or ashes from a distant fire but melted to his touch when he caught one on his sleeve.

The jogging trail was taking him back to the Agency, curving down through a dark forest loam formed of fallen and decayed oak and poplar leaves, a place of rotting bark and exposed roots and Piedmont clay, a gentle suburban forest long since rid of any danger or risk. He had no real sense of time, surprised when he looked down at his watch to see it was the lunch hour. He wasn't hungry at all; today he felt the absence of all desire.

The snow did something to him, triggering first memories of a Southern California boy high in the Sierra, wondrous, exotic, the antithesis of life in the desert. And then, in Vienna for his first assignment, workaday snow, and in the Alps, piled to the eaves of buildings. Snow for him was a release, obliterating the grayness and the grime, giving the world a reborn polar aspect—a different kind of world, life a little closer to the edge, a wrench thrown into human routine.

After Garibaldi's chat, Daniel Robinson hadn't thought of Lhota again until sometime in late October, when while skimming a stale three-week stack of the Morning Summary intended to be read on a daily basis and passed on, his eye paused on one entry from Mexico City.

> Ledesma Murder Suspect
>
> TopsecretNoforn 9/21 Mexpol air source claim sight Cuban DGI Camilo Ordóñez arrive Iberia Madrid flight 9/20 Interpol list Ledesma shooting Santiago 4/23/72 poss contract shootist PLO/Red Brigade.
>
> Seek confirm second source/passport/ID info.

It had caught Robinson's eye because that kind of person hardly ever showed up in Mexico, so close to home, then he realized the day of the sighting was three days before Miroslav Lhota died in Guatemala. He closely read the following summaries, finding no other mention of the matter.

On a thread at best, he looked through the Agency directory. LatAm Affairs, Mexico City desk: whom did he know there?

The only name he knew at all was Mary Faith Storch, the two of them having worked together briefly on a paper on Czech surrogate activities in Mexico City three years before, a very stale and tenuous connection indeed.

He pursued it anyway, stopping unannounced by Storch's office, vaguely fishing, hoping she would assume he knew more than he did and fill in the blanks for him.

Mary Faith Storch was a corpulent woman, barely past thirty but electing because of size and attitude to adopt the demeanor of someone much older, wearing heavy suits and scarves in dark institutional colors as if in mourning or in penance, her hair in a bun; she'd served some time in a convent as a younger girl but found her true calling in covert operations. She didn't like him; she never had: she thought he was flip and sexually fast, and sought in all her dealings to discipline and punish him.

"What more you hear about the Ordóñez sighting?" he asked, regretting he had even come into the room.

"There was none," she said, her body drawing some kind of strength out of her desk and neatly stacked papers. The desk was hers; the desk was Mexico; therefore Mexico was hers, and she would control every perception and analysis of it.

"I saw it in the Morning Summary for September 21," he said.

"It was wrong," she said.

"What?"

"The sighting," she said. "Nobody knows what Camilo Ordóñez looks like anymore, it's been twenty years since Ledesma, and what business is it of yours, sir?"

"Goodbye and thank you, Mary Faith," he said. Robinson couldn't sleep that night, seeing Lhota's opened head with hair standing on end, a dark stain congealed on the cracking Guatemalan mud. His eyes open. Growing old, old, wearing his shirtsleeves rolled.

Robinson had concluded that whatever the explanation, the matter of the sighting in Mexico City could not be discussed any further in the building, which prompted him to run through scenarios of explanation. Such as: If the sighting wasn't accurate, maybe the original report, or its inclusion in the Morning Summary, or both, had caused embarrassment. And the same if the sighting *had* been accurate. But why such embarrassment?

Yes, they could be protecting the defector resettlement program, might indeed have someone big on the line waiting to cross over, and no, it was not terribly enticing to one prospective defector to see another defector gunned down in Guatemala.

Nevertheless, Robinson still felt an obligation to Lhota even if the Agency didn't. The Agency had treated Lhota like cannon fodder over the years, and he wanted to make sure they hadn't done it again. And Lhota had been signaling him at the end.

Robinson called an ex-classmate, Beth Bodenhorn, now on the staff of the Senate Select Committee on Intelligence, an old friend outside and mostly free of the control of this building and thus more likely to actually tell him something.

"Heard any background on one of our defectors being shot in Guatemala?" he asked as casually as he could over dinner late one Friday night. The question touched off a look of incredulity on her Germanic face, teeth pushed into the American suburban ideal by long-ago braces or genetics; a protestation of: You're asking me? Why would I know something like that if you don't? Beth Bodenhorn like many Washingtonians was fueled by the chemistry of ambition, she was racing on pure Senate committee staff director's adrenaline, and she punctuated every silence with a quiet but audible staccato *teh teh teh teh*, the sound a steel brush would make on cymbal, her driving rhythm, fast.

That Lhota had died within a few dozen miles of the Mexican border, in a remote part of Guatemala, was suggestive of other possibilities. Knowing Lhota's politics, and his connection, albeit tenuous, to the gun trade through his sporting goods store, Robinson considered another road.

"Let's think Central America," Robinson said. "Know of any covert aid to groups that Lhota might have gotten mixed up in?"

"Hon," she said, "after Noriega and Ortega went, Central America was ours again; we have nothing going. That leaves Cuba; as far as I know, we're just sitting and waiting. But I can't speak to freelance operations."

"How about defector resettlement?" he asked. "Have you been briefed on somebody big coming over, or anything that might make Garibaldi more cautious and secretive?"

"Once again, you're asking me?" she answered. "I'm not aware of any. As for Garibaldi, you know my opinion: a leftover bit of the California trash that the Old Man swept into office. I was massively unimpressed during his confirmation hearings. The last thing the Agency needs is a political toady directing Eur/Sov, one more example of tired old thinking."

They had parted because Beth's beeper called her back to the Senate floor at eleven o'clock on a Friday night. It was the budget debate; the chairman needed her to overcome the threat of a filibuster led by Senator Blisterson. Robinson left disappointed he had not found definitive answers.

It was snowing hard now, the transformation from tiny ashlike specks to a silent avalanche of enormous flakes begun in seconds, triggered by critical changeover in the high atmosphere, the ripping of a barrier.

Dense windless air buried sounds of cars, machinery, aircraft he had heard clearly only minutes before.

Soil, curled brown leaves, frozen dead grass of last summer, were disappearing before his eyes. This would be a bad one.

He walked slowly back to the main building. The Director's limousine was there, engine on and tailpipe billowing a great djinn of exhaust, blackness of the hood and trunk being conquered by crystalline white, the limo particularly hearselike this day, a fitting symbol of the sense of loss and defeat he felt. Every defeat was a tiny death, a glimpse of what was to come, just as this day was a glimpse of the earth's end . . . cold descent into absolute zero, soft obliteration, a taste of stellar space, and a lonely spinning journey through darkness.

He thought of his own career coming to nothing, of the way he had been taught to look at things now rendered worthless and outdated, of his daughter rationed out to him by agreement, his ended marriage, the death of youth.

The phone had rung one Tuesday night in December, at about

seven-thirty. His daughter, Shannon, was spending the night with him and Leah, and he had prepared dinner.

The caller was Darlene Scoggins, the late Lhota's fiancée, visiting town, calling from a pay phone on the Beltway.

"I know this is a surprise," she said, "but Morrie gave me your number before he died. I have to see you."

"Eh . . . when?" Robinson had said.

"Tonight. Now," she said. "I know this sounds awful, but I'm afraid I'm being followed. I have some things for you from Morrie; he wanted them given only to you."

Robinson had never met this woman; he knew nothing about her, although he assumed Resettlement had checked her out in advance of Lhota's engagement.

She had to pass on the information in person, and he was to tell no one she'd called.

In the old days, this would have set off every alarm in his mind. It was called Setup. Weave the web tight. Compromise him. But the old days were gone.

"Meet me at the Potomac Yacht Basin parking lot," he found himself saying. Because she was from out of town, he had to repeat the directions twice, to the spot south of the city on the Virginia side of the river. The Basin was closed for the winter. He gave her a time to meet, knowing he would arrive earlier and make sure there was no setup, no hidden observers.

"What is it?" Leah asked. They had just sat down to dinner. It was to be just the three of them, the semblance of family.

"I've got to go out," Robinson said. He wanted to say more, he knew she hated the gulf caused by secrets, but he couldn't be honest. He didn't want Leah to go, or to know anything. She had no idea what Robinson did for a living, didn't really care other than to assume it was vaguely dangerous and exciting. She was still naive about Washington, which was why he liked her, and he wanted to keep it that way.

"What about dinner?" she said, astonished.

"It'll have to wait," he said.

As he began preparing to go, he was aware that Leah was watching him, incredulous. Robinson didn't even try to fabricate, because Leah would have seen through it immediately. Shannon ate wordlessly, her fork clinking on the plate as she speared green peas.

"Call me when you're free again," Leah said, getting up to go. This was her ritual of withdrawing to a separate place when tension arose.

"I'm sorry," he said, moving toward her. But his mind was already back on the subject of Lhota, and she knew he was elsewhere, and so she held him away when he tried to embrace her.

Leah went out the door.

Since Lupe, the baby-sitter, wasn't with them that night, Robinson would have to take Shannon with him. She brought a blanket—it was already unusually cold—and some dolls. She would play in the back seat while he and Ms. Scoggins talked in the front.

The yacht basin was deserted, as he had expected, its only activity being the distant surf of traffic on the Founding Fathers Freeway and the lights of a seafood restaurant about a half mile south, flickering as the windblown trees intervened in his line of sight. Five minutes late, her red Cutlass appeared. Darlene looked uncertain. Turning on his interior light so he could be seen, he motioned her ahead. She walked to his car with a cardboard box.

A voluptuous woman in her early forties, her huge head of wavy blond hair held rigid by hair spray and tied with a red bandanna, Darlene Scoggins wore a white pantsuit and a denim jacket and came in a cloud of perfumed air that quickly filled the car and distracted him from his thoughts. But Robinson could see from her face and manner she was incapable of guile. She was nervous and apologetic.

"I'm so sorry to do this," she said in a husky, almost cracking voice. "Hi, sweetie," she said to Shannon. Shannon said hello.

"Look at those pretty blue eyes," said Darlene Scoggins.

"What can I do for you?" Robinson asked.

"Lordy," she said. "All I know is that Morrie thought the world of you. He said if anything ever happened to him, I was to give his personal things to you and you alone. He made me swear to that, before he went to Guatymala."

"What did he want you to give me?" Robinson asked.

"Right here," she said, slapping the cardboard box. "These was things he kept in a safe-deposit box over in Wilson. Deposit box was his private things, which I've never laid eyes on before and don't wish to. He said they was to go to you, that you'd know what to do with them. And, honey, I done what he said. Even when the investigators come down from Washington. They asked me ever' whichaway what he did, who he knew, what he had. They went through his office, through the house, ever'thing."

Robinson took the box.

On top was the Lhota family Slovak Bible, at least 130 years old, its leather binding crumbling. Key verses had been underlined and scribbled on by generations of readers.

Below the Bible was a file folder containing an assemblage of Xerox documents and scribbled notes, all dealing with Dr. Emil Užhok. Most prominent was a report filed by Mrs. Alena Petchek Moskowitz, of Key Biscayne, Florida, with the Holocaust Survivors Council, describing her encounter with the "Angel of Theresienstadt" in a hotel elevator in Guatemala City in 1982.

Remembering Lhota's request to pick up family belongings from Dvořáček in Prague, Robinson asked Darlene if she knew of his receiving anything from Czechoslovakia, or Europe, before he died. Yes, she said, she thought he'd received microfilm of a journal or diary or something but was still waiting on some photos.

"Did Morrie have any mysterious conversations or dealings with anybody before he died?"

"Lordy," she said, "funny business was a problem from day one." First she was worried it was another woman. Then she feared he was doing something illegal, like drug dealing.

"When I pitched a hissy fit about all the sneakin', he tole me he was a-lookin' for an old boyhood friend," she said.

His name was Emil.

Secrecy in his activities had been important, Lhota told her, because Emil might be in trouble with the authorities and living underground in Guatemala.

"When Morrie went to Guatymala to hunt jaguars," she said, "he was a-thinkin' he might actually find Emil." As she spoke, Robinson calculated that Lhota had died just before or after finding and meeting with this man.

If Lhota had been murdered, then by appearances Emil was the murderer, or at least the trigger for Lhota's end.

But who was Emil? Lhota's continuing contacts with Dvořáček and others back in Prague had planted doubts about his own loyalties, and Robinson still could not take Lhota's claims at face value.

When their conversation in December ended, Robinson had told Darlene Scoggins to write letters to the FBI in Raleigh and to the

Pettyville police, with copies to her lawyer, stating her belief that she was under surveillance. That way, at least her concern was on record. He told her to hire a bodyguard if she could afford it.

And then, a message from another world, the most bizarre development of all. Only a week after Robinson's meeting with Darlene, a postcard arrived at Robinson's home, written in Lhota's hand. Dated September 23—the day Lhota died—and postmarked Huehuetenango, Guatemala, it showed a Mayan pictogram from the Popol Vuh of two warriors locked in mortal combat. And there was the following entry in Lhota's handwriting:

Veil/
the face of God

The postcard itself was smudged and water-streaked, as though it had languished in the rain and in innumerable Central American dead-letter offices. It had taken nearly three months to arrive in Virginia.

And now it was January, and he was standing in a snowstorm, looking back at the building that had been his place of employment for fifteen years. He had never really taken the time to look at it until now; today it seemed small, nondescript.

Out of the shock of his confession and exposure, all the peripheral worries were falling away, and just a few central things remained.

Nature was ahead of him; she had come to a definite conclusion. The wind was picking up, and the torrents of snow billowed and blustered. The air swirled with it, and more seemed to be rising into the sky than falling from the clouds.

He was on the Agency steps, stamping the snow off his shoes, brushing it off his coat and hair. He could see his own reflection in the glass doors, his eyebrows dusted. He looked like some kind of specter, and the security guards visibly tightened as he came in.

They didn't recognize him. He, a fifteen-year veteran of the Agency, in and out of here thousands of times, and they were standing up to ask in their paramilitary way if they could "help" him?

He practically knew these guys by name. And yet he had always felt the tinge of discomfort, even of anger, at having to flash a badge at them to be admitted. The two or three times he had forgotten his badge, they had kept him waiting at the desk until his secretary had identified him for a temporary pass.

Now he fumbled for his pass, presented it, and walked by without speaking.

He hated these rituals, these reminders that but for a badge, he did not exist, would not be admitted. It was as though you were never really here, a warning of how fast you could be excluded and forgotten.

It was not a warning he needed today.

Outside through glass, a roiling panorama of soundless atmospheric conflict, snowflakes spiraling through a Virginia landscape of pines and oaks that looked untouched by humankind.

Tabor was waiting for Robinson when he got back from his outdoor walk, and he uncustomarily invited Robinson to lunch. They were virtually the last people eating.

Tabor was consuming something called Swedish meatballs, a dish he'd been eating every time Robinson saw him there in the two years they had worked in the same section. Tabor was fiftyish, and thin in an almost prepubescent way, a brilliant man drained by servitude and deference. The hair on top of his head had worn away to reveal pallid scalp. His height had diminished during his government service, shoulders sagging, bruised pits of fatigue forming under the eyes. His voice was modulated and low, the sound of survival in a bureaucracy. Even his colors had faded, his skin tallow-hued, his remaining hair a dull glaucous color, tooth and eye achromatic.

They ate in what was probably one of the best employee cafeterias operated by the government of the United States. It was a small glass cathedral, situated at the silent vortex of the larger structure of cubist metal and pellucid paneling.

The room was designed so that the sound of conversation would float up to the ceiling and away. It was as if sound were being sucked away from them like smoke, like an offensive odor into a ventilator. Two black women in gray uniforms and white caps were removing dirty dishes and trays from tables.

"Rough weather," said Tabor, cutting his meatball into two hemispheres. It was as though he had cut the planet into two halves . . . a brown outer crust, covering a pink molten interior.

Tabor cleared his throat artificially. It meant something momentous was now about to be said.

"Dan," he said, "this is very hard for me to say."

Tabor coughed. Sweat formed on his brow.

"Med and Security have told me about your tests."

Robinson knew the jig was up. He didn't even need to hear the rest.

"Dan, they've recommended you be put on medical leave for a month."

Robinson sat there, hearing it from a distance.

"And the Area Director and I will have to go along."

Tabor's chest sank with the completion of his task. He took half a meatball thoughtfully into his mouth, then compressed it as though he were drawing out its vital juices.

"Dan, we all know how this job takes its toll. This pressure wears everyone down. We all need a rest from time to time.

"I've certainly not been immune," Tabor added.

In escape, Robinson's eyes wandered back to the snowstorm.

"Effective when?" Robinson asked. He didn't recognize his own voice.

Tabor was almost whispering.

"Today, Dan. Take the rest of the afternoon off. Spend some time with your daughter."

Robinson considered what this meant. Medical leave for psychiatric reasons was probably the end. Certainly for Operations, and overseas. Possibly even for Intelligence, where he had been stuck for two years now.

Oh, they might detail him over to I&R at the State Department. Let him clip Czech newspapers and write unread reports for the rest of his life, until retirement.

An overpaid clerk.

"Dan," said Tabor, "I know this hurts. But don't make more of it than it is. I don't see any reason why you can't bounce back, after a nice rest."

Tabor was forcing a grin, the first Robinson had seen in two years.

Bullshit, thought Robinson.

Tabor was now unbearably uncomfortable, acting as if he expected some explosion from Robinson. He seemed to be having trouble breathing.

Tabor consumed the other meatball half in silence, then wiped his mouth. He could not look at Robinson. He was cutting into a portion of lemon chiffon pie when one of the waitresses walked over to him.

"Phone for you, Mr. Tabor," she said.

"Excuse me," said Tabor, thankful for the excuse to get away.

Tabor had once said to him, in bureaucratic lesson number fifteen: Watch how fast your friends scurry away when you make a mistake. You will find out who your real friends are.

And you will be sorely disappointed.

Tabor was called away upstairs. Robinson finished his salad, then walked back down the corridor to his section. As he passed the front foyer he saw the Director, with Garibaldi and the other area directors, stepping through the snow into his limousine. The new Director was a longtime Washington attorney and close friend of the President, who himself had once been Director here in his long apprenticeship to power. In fact, he was the only President of the United States to have held this job.

The snow was furious. What would happen if the Director of Central Intelligence got stuck in the snow?

When Robinson returned to his office, he went through the motions of cleaning out his desk. A picture of the Czech painter glared down, mocking him.

Then Robinson spent the remainder of the afternoon in the language lab, listening to Czech tapes, studying his map of Prague.

The lab was filled with the young faces of the latest Agency class, cramming for their upcoming overseas assignments. They were madly muttering in Ukrainian, Polish, Mandarin, knowing their whole careers rode on this first shot.

An hour later, he left. Driving through billowing arctic clouds of snow that would become slush, he saw Lhota buried in the cold cold ground, imagining him in Sunday best, hair combed, hands folded. He imagined Lhota with snow, with rain, with summer heat and winter frost baking him, curing him, transmuting him.

Lhota was speaking to him, from the grave, his hands outstretched, asking a last favor. But Robinson could not make sense of the words.

A journal and photos, Lhota said. Veil.

The face of God, he said, holding his finger to his lips.

What on earth had killed Lhota? Robinson thought, driving through a landscape transformed. And why on earth was he still trying to draw Daniel Robinson into it?

Two days into his medical leave, Daniel Robinson drove down the griseous Patriots Parkway in the nearer Virginia suburbs. The road passed through a landscape that at one time might have been pleasing to the eye, but forty years had intervened, and too many people and automobiles had been forced into this territory. The little ocher-brick-and-shingle houses with their chain-link fences seemed overlaid with a rain of settled exhaust, particles from the passage of millions of tires, thousands of grinding engines.

A lingering bedrock of Virginia redneck lived here, overlaid by a sediment of new arrivals. The land was now home to immigrant owners of Iranian carpet stores and Vietnamese grocery stores and Thai restaurants and Afghan coffeehouses, to parishioners of small evangelical churches that catered to Salvadoran and Nicaraguan refugees.

Most of the taxi drivers in that part of town seemed to be from Ethiopia or Somalia. The Somalis in particular had high chiseled cheekbones and small fine mouths from which shone teeth impossibly white, an alabaster perfection that stood in such contrast to the umber brown of their skin that Robinson believed they had to be beings of more dramatic emotion, memory, vision. It was a wonder to him that their visual fierceness did not somehow leach out into this desiccated North American ground, this winter land of dim light and faded hue.

Yet the versicolor blend of people had not produced a rich cityscape of immigrants, like New York. Either they had arrived too recently or this drab suburban spread was just not conducive to the exotic ethnic expression you could find farther north.

He turned into the parking lot at Three Bears Childworld. The snow had been reduced by a drenching rain and the unending traffic to charcoal wastewater. Along the highway, people in ashen spattered coats stumbled through puddles and piles of muck. Robinson could see the children still at play inside, because few of the parents had gotten off work yet.

Washington, he said to himself, is a city of work. The city energy was given over to the great morning-evening movements of people to and from work. Work devoured most of their waking hours, and the remaining few were spent racing about doing the minimum to sustain life. Repairing old things, buying new things, seeking cars, furniture, food.

On weekends, people walked about as if in a daze, disoriented by the temporary lack of work. Many filled the time by working hard, on their tiny yards and small homes, on their cars with hoods up.

This is what he had told the therapist: You cannot expect me to have feelings in a place like this. It is a place of work, of cold achievement.

The children in Three Bears Childworld were hitting a large air-filled ball with paddles, and this large ball bounced up and down between ceiling and flailing paddles.

Adult women moved tall through the group.

Robinson could see his daughter, a bit out of the swirling center of the group but flailing nonetheless.

His ex-wife had named Shannon at a time when many Americans were doing that; there had been a popular television character with that name. It certainly was not in either family.

His ex-wife was now a research analyst at a large private consultancy not far from this center. She had been an analyst with the Agency when he met her, they had fallen in love and remained married four years, produced a child, then split apart. Her name was Jackie Frankowski, she had a doctorate in International Affairs from Georgetown, and she was an analyst of Soviet Strategic Forces.

Had he loved her? Yes, he had, perhaps still did. Or maybe it had been something else, the bond, and it was not now strong enough to keep them together. This was a question he had agonized over many times, for he had never envisioned himself a divorced man.

It was now four-thirty. Robinson got out of the car, went inside, and picked up Shannon.

Jackie was working late that night, on a special study of the impact of *perestroika* on the command structure of Soviet nuclear forces.

After ringing his office and finding he was on sick leave, she had reached him at his apartment and asked him to pick up Shannon and baby-sit until she got home. She was surprised to hear he was on sick leave; Daniel Robinson hardly ever took leave for anything, even when he was staggering with influenza.

Shannon was now five. Robinson let her sit next to him, with his right arm around her, as he drove. The way she nestled and clung to him tore his insides up again.

"When are you going to take me on a trip?" she asked. This was the perennial question.

"This summer," he said. "You and I will go somewhere special."

"Are you going on a trip soon?" Shannon asked.

"Yes. I'm making a business trip."

"Can I come?" Shannon asked.

"No, honey."

She was disappointed.

"Where would you like to go next summer?" he asked. "Anywhere in particular? The beach?"

"Yes," she said.

They drove down the shrieking Patriots Parkway for a time, then got off and orbited with a dozen other cars up a spiraling ramp and onto a vast nameless boulevard that was carrying people to drugstores, franchise restaurants, strip shopping malls.

This was new exurbia, the raw edge of the blastwave of American growth in the late twentieth century, rolling out across the land. The cars were newer, and hundreds of Anglo-Saxon teenagers shot by in down-filled parkas. People looked quickened and without shadow, all drenched in an iridian flash, an energy transfer under way, the juice of fast money moving.

At the Great Escapes Travel Agency, Robinson sat in the car a minute to reassure himself no Agency people were in evidence. You could never be absolutely sure. A number of his colleagues used this office.

Then he went inside and picked up his tickets to Prague. Shannon sat in a chair and looked at travel brochures while he did his transaction.

"Any problem with the visa?" he asked the Persian, an old business contact for years.

"Hamza always delivers, right?" Hamza's teeth too were blinding white. His Baha'i relatives were right now being shot back home by the mullahs, while Hamza hunched over his monitor and coursed the electronic fare tables of the earth, searching out the discounts, the connections, the restrictions. Hamza gathered up the fabricated British passport and the ticket.

"When do I get your GTR?" Hamza asked, holding on to the ticket as if he expected payment first. "The first time this happened, I didn't get reimbursed for seven months."

"They just cut the orders this afternoon," Robinson lied. "In the mail to you tomorrow."

"I hope," said Hamza, shaking his head. "I could have gotten you a nice stopover in Paris instead of London if you'd given me more warning. No extra cost."

"No time," said Robinson.

"No time for Paris," Hamza repeated. "I would have made time."

Robinson thumbed through the passport. Derek Richardson, it read, British subject. A simple tourist visa. Naked, and yet so simple. Robinson would be Derek Richardson, a Yorkshire trade unionist, on a union sport committee. He was going to Prague to discuss British union participation in the reconstituted and not yet renamed Spartakiade Games now that the Communist government had fallen.

Robinson's itinerary took him to London under another alias; there he would be issued a new ticket under the assumed name. No one could trace him through the airline computers.

Robinson thanked Hamza and stood up. Shannon carried a handful of brochures, which she could not read, of the Ginza in Tokyo, Rio de Janeiro, Cozumel. He would probably take her to Virginia Beach.

They drove back out onto the Parkway, which led to a smaller road. As they drove, still following a line of cars, he was lost in thought for a time, remembering the good part of the domestic life he had once led as a father. He was aware she was singing as they drove. It was not until some minutes had passed that he listened to her lyrics:

I've got the everlasting love of Jesus
Down in my heart,
Down in my heart,
Down in my heart . . .

She had a beautiful little voice. But what made it so touching was that she was singing with great feeling. Her religiosity had come creeping in gradually over the last six months. At first he had attributed it to the Three Bears staff, which was heavily salted with fundamentalists. Whatever the source, it had obviously stirred something in her.

They had had many discussions about heaven, God, Jesus, and the like, which he tried to answer as impartially as possible.

They turned into a new subdivision called Dominion Hills, drove across a hillside that had been loblolly timberland six years before, now covered with simulated Cape Cod and Victorian gingerbread houses so new they cracked and snapped with every step you took inside and still exuded paint smells and the ester odors from the insulation and carpet materials.

The house that they had bought and that now belonged to Jackie was illuminated but deserted.

Robinson and Shannon went inside. The furniture from Himmelfarb's, bought only five years before, had not aged well. The chrome and glass looked terrible; the upholsteries showed every stain.

Robinson sat and read stories to Shannon. That had always been their favorite activity, reading and telling stories. Tonight they were reading *The Lubberton Leopards Get a Divorce*, a cleverly written series that had enriched the authors, Larry and Lana Lubberton. Abruptly Shannon turned to him.

"Daddy, are you stronger than Jesus?"

He thought about that one for a minute. He pondered trying to differentiate between physical and spiritual strength, etc., but decided not to.

"No," he said. "Jesus is stronger."

She digested that for a minute.

"Daddy," she said, "why don't you go to Sunday school?"

He exhaled. There had to be a right way to do this for the five-year-old mind. Lengthy theological explanations were out.

Fortunately the phone rang, and Shannon answered. Shannon

had blond hair, like his own absentee father, and like him. He could see a hint of his own Amerind cheekbones, but otherwise she looked at home in this suburb.

"She's working late," Shannon said into the phone. She furrowed her brow. Then she laughed.

"Goodbye," she said, hanging up.

Shannon came and sat down next to Robinson.

"Who was that?" he asked, as he resumed reading.

"Chris," she said.

"Who's Chris?" he asked.

"Mommy's friend."

"What's he like?" Robinson asked.

"Nice," she said.

"He builds cabinets and furniture with his bare hands," she added.

He began reading again, and turned the pages.

He builds cabinets and furniture with his bare hands, Robinson thought.

Although he should have been happy, excited, that he was taking things into his own hands by going renegade to Prague, he was filled with that sick, dread feeling of the entire last year.

It was not too late to call it off, start a new life with Leah. A quiet, peaceful life, building cabinets with his bare hands, going to Sunday school with his daughter.

When, an hour later, the beam of Jackie's headlights illuminated the living room with a flash, it was as if some kind of small nuclear explosion had occurred—brief, painless, and silent, like a neutron bomb—killing people but leaving property intact.

Their greetings, Jackie's thanks, and his farewell were all perfunctory.

"Gladdens the heart," Wilson Raver boomed, his arm sweeping out over the panorama of small arms, satcom, medevac kit displays. "Free enterprise triumphant."

It was later the same evening, and he and Robinson were standing in Raver's display booth amid the annual Armed Forces Association hardware extravaganza, "Meet the Threat 2000!"—nothing so much as the weaponmakers' trade show–convention, held this year in the show hall of the Capitol Huxley. Raver, former army ranger elevated to CIA Operations by virtue of his God-given linguistic ability to capture the nuances of anything from Dari to Kurdish in a few minutes of close listening, and now the vice president of a security consultancy known as PeriMeter in War City, Virginia, seemed fully in his element. No matter that this former Arizona football player was now free-falling into elephantine middle age. Thirty pounds of lard added since their last drinking session six months ago, coupled with disappearing black hair and January suntan and one of those small noses that couldn't tolerate much weight or its small nostrils spread up and out like a pig's, gave him added presence, so he looked like nothing so much as an animate desert boulder wearing an over-stretched pin-striped power suit.

Robinson snorted, but Raver pulled him closer. "See the two cursed murdering Chicoms over there? Some of my best customers. Please don't tell Buddy Blisterson. And I'm just waiting on the bloc business to soar. Borders are falling, baby. The flow of capital. A force of nature."

"So you think this climate is good for business?" Robinson asked. "Treaties, budget cuts, layoffs?"

"Name of game is export or die, Dan. These poor suckers are just now waking up to what I've known for fifteen years. I didn't sell my soul to one great big fat customer. No, I plied the Third World middle markets, the dusky regional powers. I knew what my asshole competitors just found out: with nukes in the freezer, we get back to real war. When men were men, and you had to fight for territory inch by inch. Shoot, no—some of us folks are doing real well."

"But the missile people are definitely hurting?" Robinson asked.

"The fat boys, yes," confirmed Raver with solemnity. "That's a little out of my field, of course. But I hear there's still room at the bottom end. Got money to invest? Check out a flyspeck company called Avian. Builds a beautiful little missile . . . subatmospheric. Glorified Roman candle, cluster bomblets, maybe a hybrid neutron spray. Comes in under any of the treaty restrictions."

"So the fat boys are dead?"

Raver shrugged. "Heck, I don't know how the big talks will go; depends on if we have a Soviet Union to talk to anymore. But technology is stalled. Hasn't gone anywhere since MIRV. Oh, SDI sounded great, but that was the Old Man's fantasy; it'll never happen.

And the missile corps is moribund: retention, morale problems. But hell, if you're smart you can still make money there. I heard a little bandit named Psychometrics over in Gaithersburg—he's former DoD, psyops—sold a three-million-dollar contract to SAC to do a study on silo despondency. Silo despondency, Dan. That's where the poor trigger boys down in the tubes think because of the talks and Gorbymania, nobody loves 'em anymore, so they might not have the guts or the reason to launch on command, they're unreliable. Next this guy's going to pitch the navy into studying the nuclear sub force. He milks despondency for another five million easy. And he don't have overhead. He's got an answering machine and a temp secretary. Writes the bullshit himself, so no graduate student to pay. All gravy."

Raver paused a minute to wolf down a handful of peanuts.

"There's still money to be made," he said. "SDI's deader than a doormat and the Congress still put up three billion this year alone, just to jerk off with. I know a lotta people who bought BMWs off SDI."

Raver was distracted as a young woman in a grass skirt registered him for the Armed Forces Raffle. The grand prize was a trip for two to the island of Yap. Robinson didn't register.

"Lot of us company graduates here," Raver said. "Bump into anybody else?"

Robinson shook his head.

"Hell, old Chic Golden's here, with Remington now, happier, much better paid, plays with guns all day. Remember Hollis O'Dwyer? Cyberdata Defense. Shit, Robinson, half the firms in here are Agency spawn, or DIA."

"Any contact with the Agency?"

Raver pretended to look over his shoulder.

"Who, me?" he said, laughing. "I'm sure for some of these guys, especially supercomputers, HDTV, you can't say where one stops and the other starts. Money comes buried without line item in the DoD budget, big gobs of it here and there."

"Still no oversight from the Hill? I thought defense was being slashed."

"They can't shut the mother down," said Raver with awe. "Maybe in five years. But they can't get a handle now. Constituents are shouting about jobs lost. Shit, figuring out procurement could keep 'em busy for fifty years. Dan, we got something like thirty-seven thousand people in our government authorized to spend big bucks on defense. I'm talking wormy little captains, even sergeants down in the Pentagon basement buying things, with signing authority. Can't shut 'em down, can't even find 'em."

They were momentarily drowned out by the simulated firing of a terribly precise laser-aimed howitzer that had proved itself in the invasion of Panama.

"You want a drink?" Raver asked. "Let's go up to our suite a minute." They threaded their way through the crowd to the nearest elevator, then rode up with two girls in bikinis and army caps, labeled "hospitality escorts."

"Hospitality is off this year," acknowledged Raver. "Hospitality's been going down ever since the Old Man. Draws too much attention these days. Sharp knives are out."

He walked his way past the sentry into the PerîMeter suite. Inside, a lovely young girl in a frilly blouse served drinks, while small clusters of customers and PerîMeter staff held quiet conversations.

Raver brought over two beers and took Robinson into one of the bedrooms and closed the door.

"So what's up? You aren't going to try and suck me back in, are you?" Raver's smirk and intonation let it be known that he would favorably consider such an offer.

"Miss the action?" Robinson asked.

Raver laughed. "Dan, I got all the action I need. The private sector ain't as boring as it used to be. Like I said, it's hard to tell who's running who these days."

"Since the Old Man?"

"Shit, it was happening even back in the Peanut days. Subcontracting things, spin-offs. As much to save money as to push it under the rug. No, I've got everything I had before, and more. Travel, big bucks, freedom. Only one thing I don't got."

"What's that?"

Raver shrugged, looked down a millisecond, as if he were really confessing a secret, or just thinking something through.

"The imprimatur. The credential. It still do open doors."

Robinson nodded.

"Mostly with foreigners, Third World types. They could care

less about free enterprise. Don't understand, don't even comprehend this spin-off, subcontracting stuff. When it comes to serious things, they want Big Mama herself, big C-I-A. Those letters still reverberate."

Robinson knew.

"And it's good for business to stay in touch. To keep the lines open, etc., etc."

Someone opened the door, saw them talking, closed it again.

"So what is it, Dan? If it's former-bloc stuff, I'm real interested. A good, virgin market."

"Nothing earthshaking." Robinson exhaled. "Wilson, do you remember Miroslav Lhota?"

Raver thought a second. "We bugged his apartment in Vienna, right?"

Robinson nodded.

"When was that—'77?"

Robinson nodded.

"Came over, didn't he?"

Robinson nodded.

"End of story," Raver said.

"He's dead," Robinson said.

"I'm sorry," Raver said. "He was a friend, right?"

"Yes."

Raver swilled his beer, thought a moment.

"Something ominous here?" he said more than asked, winking.

"Hole was blown in his head in Guatemala," said Robinson. "Official story is hunting accident, possible suicide. It stinks."

"Whoa, whoa, whoa," sang Raver. "A thousand questions. Whose official story, Dan? I thought *you* were official. And how did he come to be in Guatemala? And most perplexing of all"—Raver took another gulp of beer—"since when do you work for counter-intelligence?"

There was no good way to answer the last one, so Robinson didn't. About the rest he told the truth.

"Someone blew him away. A certain layer in the company is holding to the suicide thing. I gather they fear news about a murder would hurt their defector settlement program, maybe with the Hill. Or maybe they have somebody big on the other side, ready to come over, who would be scared off. Or maybe other things."

"What other things?"

"A back-channel thing."

"For us?"

"For whoever."

"Why Guatemala?"

"Lhota told me he was tracking somebody, somebody who was supposed to be dead. He tried to pull me in last fall; I told him to fuck off."

"Who was he looking for?"

"A Czech. Emil Užhok. Know the name?"

"Why should I?"

"He died in your territory in 1978."

"Where?"

"Ethiopia."

"I was in Kurdistan in '78."

"He was in a plane crash in Eritrea. Warsaw Pact detail. The civil war."

Raver was thinking a moment. You could tell he was thinking because he would lower his head and rub his great hammy fingers across his orange-tanned forehead, trying to squeeze the ideas out. This and his general physical appearance and speech patterns sometimes led one to think he was not mentally endowed. Such an assessment was incorrect and could result in subsequent embarrassment.

"I think I remember the crash, actually," Raver said.

Robinson nodded.

"Dan, is this a personal thing?"

Robinson didn't answer.

Raver screwed up his mouth and looked at the carpet. He seemed to deflate a bit. He had thought there was an instant contract coming; now he sensed the trail was a little longer.

"So what can I do for you?"

Robinson thought of Lhota's handwritten card, the bits and scraps of fact he was assembling.

"Can you check around about the crash? Know anybody who tracked Ethiopia back then?"

Raver shrugged.

"Could you ask around about it? Don't make a splash. Just run it down: any atmospherics, speculation, whatever."

Raver nodded.

"Why was he looking for dead Emil in Guatemala?" Raver asked.

"There was a live sighting."

"Live when?"

"Nineteen eighty-two," said Robinson.

"Fresh."

"Fresh enough to get Lhota killed."

"It or whatever."

"Yes."

Raver was audibly swishing his beer around in his inflated cheeks like mouthwash, and Robinson fully expected it to come spraying out. But it did not.

"Any help you can give me, Dan? Any quote atmospherics, speculation, whatever?"

Robinson thought about what Lhota's fiancée had given him.

"Emil was apparently interned in Terezín camp by the Nazis. Some kind of hero. Has a tubercular, gargling voice. That's how the lady recognized him in Guatemala."

"Gargling hero, working for the Pact, dead in Eritrea, alive in Guatemala?"

"Yes," Robinson said.

Raver smiled sweetly, pursing his lips and nodding like an old lady at a tea party.

"Anything else?"

"Nothing, really. Lhota was trying to get his hands on a journal from Terezín camp that would clear it all up, tried to suck me into getting it out of Prague, but I never saw the thing."

"Anything else?"

"Oh, some words from Lhota, written on a Mayan postcard just before he died. Inscrutable."

"Words?"

"Yes. Veil / the face of God."

"Veil the face of God?"

"Veil slash the face of God."

Raver made a tonsillic exhalation through his nostrils and pushed his Arizona lips out in a pout.

"Piece of cake," he said. They sat there in silence a moment.

"Want me to check out anything else while I'm at it?" Raver said.

"Protocols of the Elders of Zion, Dead Sea Scrolls, why do the heathen rage?"

"Whatever you can do," Robinson said.

"I've got paying customers to serve first," Raver continued. "Ethiopia I can pursue, makes some sense. Guatemala, no thank you. I try to stay away from the cucaracha circuit. Don't get me wrong: the Latinos are good people, but they don't pay."

Robinson finished his beer.

"Look, Wilson, I've taken enough of your time. Call me when you've got something."

"I go broke doing favors," said Raver.

Robinson nodded and got up. When they went back out into the outer suite, the two Chinese were there, flirting in drunken martial fashion with the barmaid, punctuating their assault with syncopated brutal laughter probably honed in a school for interrogation and reeducation. One of them spun and, too loudly, greeted Raver, who was obliged to stand and bend elbows with them. Robinson excused himself, passed several other suites where laughter and music occasionally escaped from barely opened doors, then walked out into the misting January evening.

He awakened to the feel of Leah as she bent over the bed to kiss him.

It was sometime past midnight, and he had to be up early the next day for the trip to London and beyond. His first reaction was a grunt.

But something in him thrilled at this woman who stayed with him, despite his distance. She had let herself in with her own key. Out of the corner of his eye he watched her undress, lit by the winter moon coming through the sliding glass doors. The light swept down the form he knew so well, the lowering jeans, the turtleneck sweater being shed, the hair and breasts flying, and he thought he heard a low laugh from her. He could smell something. . . . She had been drinking, maybe with her friends over near Dupont Circle.

She was tall and leggy, a onetime equestrian who had then bounced around the country, around the world, without any plan, following impulse, ever since finishing college.

She was up against him now.

She had landed penniless in Washington nine months before, fresh from a backpacking adventure in Africa, and had taken a temporary job as a secretary in a lobbyist's office, planning to work for three months and save up enough money to head west, to the Rockies.

"Let's go west together," she had said many times, and he never responded. In his head he was thinking about career, child support payments, the entwining chains of age and obligation that made something like that seem impossible. Now she was kissing him, her tongue, her breasts, her legs up against him, breathing, laughing.

"I could fall in love with you," she said.

She didn't care what he did for a living. She had seen the picture of the President presenting the award to him in the Oval Office a few years back, and that was enough.

She had no understanding of the arctic lore of power, of Washington, she was young, naive, a drifter, and that was why he was drawn to her.

They had met at a party in the late summer, a random encounter; he knew she liked him from the beginning. He couldn't figure her out. She laughed a lot, she drank too much, she smoked and hung out with a crowd of Australians and waiters whom he couldn't stand.

Why did she like him?

"Oh, Dan," she said, and he was on top, his arms around her in spite of himself, that feel, that richness of embrace he couldn't remember ever having with anyone else. He was squeezing her rhythmically, which she liked, and he couldn't let go of her: he squeezed the breath out of them both.

They would go camping on the spur of the moment, two sleeping bags and a cooler of food and beer, and they would lie together in the summer and fall woods and he would think but never say: This is what life was meant to be. He would listen to her breathing and the sounds of their lovemaking mixing with the night sounds of the forest, and in spite of himself a happiness would come up that lifted him out of the world he had been in for too long, a world of divorce and loss of child and stagnation of career.

People said the two of them looked alike, wide-shouldered, olive blonds.

She was half Wasp and half Spanish, he was half redneck and half Seminole Indian. She came from Rhode Island, the family had money and she would take none of it, she wanted nothing to do with them. He grew up in a Bakersfield trailer park with an alcoholic mother and no father.

"Open up, Dan," she said. "Talk. Where's your head been the last two months? What's wrong?"

She was caressing his back, his buttocks, one leg over him as the sweat slowly dried.

"Talk to me," she said.

"I have to take a trip," he said.

The moon was out over the river and reflecting off the argent of the monuments and the temples and the braids of the highways going in and out, bouncing lactescent off the ice on the river and the snow on its banks, Lhota was dead and buried and there were mysteries to be uncovered and in retrospect he would wish he had had enough sense to pay attention to what she had been saying all those six short months together.

"I'm going with you," she said, suddenly animated. "I'm looking for an excuse to quit; this is it."

He said nothing. He was in his head, he saw Lhota in his grave and his daughter miles away, he saw snow piled high in Vienna and the Sierra, and Leah was like a child pushing at his darkened windows.

"Where are you going?" she asked.

He didn't answer for a minute, but kissed her instead, let his hand play down her skin, which was adhering slightly to his fingertips as if in invitation.

"You can't go," he said.

She put her foot on his calf and stroked it slightly.

"Then let's go west," she said.

"Not yet," he said. "It's not time yet."

She took that, considered it, then stroked his hair. In another moment she was down beside him, and again they were embracing. They slept, arms and legs intertwined, until the alarm clock blared out and tore them from the place they were in. The morning came burning, harsh, much too early.

They shared some tea and toast. She was with him when the taxi came to take him to the airport.

"Have a good trip," she said, and they kissed. He should have known from the length of the kiss, from the look in her eye, what it all meant. He should have known what she was going to do. But in his mind he was already out across the ocean, obsessed with Lhota, fighting ancient battles.

As the cab pulled out of his parking lot and toward the Founding Fathers Freeway, he saw her climbing into her rusted jalopy, not looking after him. He remembered later, thinking it a bit odd, after the warmth of the goodbye, not to find her watching him go.

Every decision, and even indecision, forever shapes the course of the future. He believed that she would be there, kissing him in the moonlight, when he came back. Once he got this Lhota thing out of the way, he would give her what she wanted. She had done him more good than all the months of the therapist.

The swarm of planes on the early-morning tarmac, the gushing traffic headed every way, the shrieking transfer of energy and matter, should have told him of a universe forever in movement, never resting, nothing ever fixed or the same. The airport itself gave him that empty dread he always felt when first setting out, the severance from familiar landscapes.

He was under way.

To the fraternal liaison,
Czech Communist Party

September 8, 1945
Terezín, Bohemia

Comrade, greetings:

I write this to you under cover of darkness and secrecy, so should it be difficult for you to read, please accept my apology.

I write to tell you of a unique case which came under the jurisdiction of the Red Army's Political Commissar for this sector. It is the case of Comrade *Emil Užhok*, a Czech Communist Party member, imprisoned at Terezín since 1942 by the Fascist forces.

It was the Soviet intention to free this man as all such prisoners were freed, in an expeditious way. Yet accusations came from other prisoners that Užhok was a Fascist collaborator. Such accusations are not dismissed lightly, and the Political Commissar takes them all into account. He had begun proceedings to determine whether Užhok in fact could have been charged with war crimes.

The only documentary evidence to be found was the so-called journal of the late Comrade *Dr. Radan Michalský*, a founding Czech Communist Party member, who had been captive of the Fascist SS since 1939 and who was *executed* by same in 1943. The Commissar judged this journal to be accurate.

Just before the hearings were to begin, the Commissar received a cable from the State Committee for Security (NKVD) in Moscow. The cable, signed by Comrade Chairman L. Beria himself, said:

"E. Užhok had direct and intimate knowledge of certain secret activities carried out by the SS and Fascist forces in the Terezín Prison Camp. The possessors of any and all knowledge about these activities are judged to be of particular value to the Soviet Fatherland and the cause of the Revolution."

Comrade Beria ordered that Užhok be immediately remanded into the care of the NKVD for transportation to Moscow. He also ordered that all penal actions against Užhok, whether Party, military, or civil, be suspended and that all documentary records be destroyed.

This has been done, and the case of Užhok has been closed from the Soviet standpoint. However, begging to differ with the esteemed Comrade Chairman, I have sent the Michalský journal to you in a spirit of fraternal solidarity. As you struggle to renew your Party in times of peace, I think it wise you know the full story about Emil Užhok, should he one day seek to reenter the good graces of your esteemed group.

I ask only that you forever conceal the existence of this letter and journal from the USSR, lest my renegade act be made known and the exposure of the secrets contained herein result in hardship for all concerned.

A Soviet friend of the Czech struggle
(Signed)

Being here consigned to an almost certain death, I hereby commit the following inventory of my sins to paper.

If it is only God who reads my words, then that will be enough. My life has been the dark journey of a lost soul and a sinner.

May the ages forgive me.

Yours in God,
Radan Anton Michalský

Vienna, 1909

Ah, you fickle temptress on the Danube!
You who bewitched me as a young man, and then discarded me!

I shall begin my story in Vienna, not because I was born and raised there, which I was not, nor because I had any roots there, which I did not have, nor because I harbored any great love for that grandiose city, which I did not love but quite frankly came to hate for the way it turned its magnificent cold shoulder to me the entire time I was a resident. I shall start with Vienna, I suppose, because in those days Vienna was the center of our universe, Vienna was the locus for those many millions of us Middle Europeans who found it our destiny to be born within its far-flung dominion, and because it was in Vienna that I grew to manhood. Not physical manhood; I was already in my mid-twenties when I arrived. No, rather I mean intellectual manhood. For while I was in Vienna, all the detached impressions, experiences, and germs of ideas that had floated inside me from childhood were crystallized, consolidating themselves long enough to become a *system* of beliefs, a framework for approaching life and approaching the world, that would truly define my life's struggle. And though this structure would later be changed by the buffeting winds of experience, indeed would even be totally rejected by me, it would nonetheless still have a kind of reverberative effect on everything I later achieved, or tried to achieve, or failed miserably to do.

Have you been to Vienna? Though I can have no assurance that when you read these words the place will even be standing, and not swept from the face of the earth by the conflagrations this century is so capable of creating, I shall have to assume it survives, and you have seen it. You have seen this curious island of oriental Germanic style floating far, far to the east, too far east, some Germans would say, its proud boulevards and parks and promenades and palaces rising up out of the windswept pasturelands of the Danubian plain, a city without roots in the land on which it stands, much more like a sovereign city-state of old than one of the modern nation-capitals of the new world. The city was to me in those days of my youth like a great gilded castle on a sea of grain, the scene going from onion-domed silos and haystacks and peasant farmers carrying pitchforks to Baroque imperial grandeur in just a few moments of the locomotive's puffing or the carriage's procession. And it was into that city I entered as though I were entering someone else's castle, a place to which I was drawn like so many others, and yet a place that hardly knew I existed.

Although I would spend two years of my life there, I never felt I had connected in any meaningful way with it. Perhaps it was the fact that I spent my time there in poverty, at the fringes of professional success, in the shadow of others who were better attuned to the ways of the Viennese and to their curious, insular, and seductive way of life. I was nothing more than one of the thousands of imperial subjects who had been drawn in by the mother city, to exist at its margins, be absorbed for a time and then be dispatched back to whence we had come. Perhaps it was because I was of mixed Jewish-Catholic parentage, and from Slovakia, which to the Viennese made me both a Jew and a provincial and so a lesser order of being on two counts; or perhaps it was because of my dark coloring. Whatever the explanation, I imagined I could see unspoken barriers to me in their gaze from my arrival in 1909 up until the day I returned to my native land in 1911, their dismissal of me as someone who was there only temporarily, someone who did not really belong.

A native son of Bratislava and a graduate of the University Medical School there, I was in Vienna to serve my obligatory internship as a neurologist at the Allgemein Krankenhaus, under the tutelage of Dr. Sigmund Freud. My assignment there seemed at first to have been sheer chance, for I might as well have ended up in Prague or Salzburg or Plzeň or any of the cities of the empire. But the vacancy at the Krankenhaus had drawn the special interest of my mentor, the great Jaroslav Stuchlík, who had introduced the psycho-analytic method to Slovakia and by extension to the Czech lands as well. And a further element of common destiny lay in the fact that the brilliant Dr. Freud had been born in the Czech town of Příbor and hoped, by bringing a promising young non-Austrian provincial like me under his wing, to promote the spread of his method to more Czech and Slovak practitioners.

How fortuitious my selection was! For within a few weeks after having been notified of my assignment, I read and was electrified by the strange new applications of hypnotism in the treatment of hysteria by the very same Dr. Freud, based on techniques developed a decade earlier by Dr. Jean Martin Charcot in Paris!

Also through my good fortune (and some merit on my part, for I do not want to make you think that I as Stuchlík's star pupil was totally undeserving of these opportunities that had befallen me), I was invited to become a regular attendee at the Wednesday gatherings under the direction of Dr. Freud. Although it was still called the "Wednesday Group," it had in fact evolved into the Vienna Chapter of the International Psycho-Analytical Association, which had already split into two rival factions, one headed by the mystic Carl Jung in Zurich, and the other by that clerk of knowledge, Alfred Adler in Vienna.

At the time of my arrival in Vienna in 1909 I was twenty-five years old, a taller-than-average man, quite lean from years of student starvation, with a profuse black beard that fought off the victory of any razor after a few hours. I was marked by the wiry hirsute muscularity inherited from my mother's family, the Levys of Bratislava, an attribute I had utilized during part of my student days as an accomplished, though part-time, gymnast. I had hollow cheeks, prominent nose broken at the bridge, deep-set black eyes, piercing gaze, and a cleft chin, features that in tandem must have startled people at first meeting. But I must say that although I would not have called myself handsome, I was often aware of a discomfort I produced in women, triggered by strong sexual attraction. Certainly not all women; but those who were drawn to me were sometimes induced to make indiscreet statements and invitations. It must have been provoked by my general dark aspect, which in this culture so enamored of the blond and the light transformed me into the forbidden, suppressed "dark" side of themselves and thus the lightning rod for all that repressed energy!

For reasons I will later detail, I declined all these invitations, save one.

When I attended the meetings of the Wednesday Group I usually sat at the back of the hospital auditorium where we met at lunchtime, or later, in the corner of the study of Dr. Freud's chambers at 19 Berggasse. In the beginning I rarely participated in the conversations and debates there, leaving that to the more eminent men who made up the group. Gathered in those days were Sandor Ferenczi, Wilhelm Stekel (until he was banished by Father Freud!), Otto Rank, Hanns Sachs, Isidor Sadger, and Oskar Rie, as well as students, interns, and others attracted to the brilliance of the elders. Although I found myself rarely liking any of the notables, I could not deny their expertise. But my general dislike was so strong that through auto-analysis, and even in session with Dr. Freud, I tried to understand it. Part of it was simple envy, me the provincial intimidated by these great minds. I was certainly among the youngest there, and so there was the natural enmity of brash youth toward age and experience. But more likely it was because I sensed that despite all their brilliance, they, like me, were outsiders. Indeed, the eminent Dr. Freud had to cower in the academic shadows, for he was accused of being a pervert, a sex fiend, and people even whispered of his Jewishness to further indict him. Others in the Group were Jews too, and seeing us all there together made me speculate about my own origins and my, our, attraction to this calling. Was there something in the cold introspection required for psycho-analysis that was innate to us, to truly brand it the "Jewish science," as it had already been nicknamed?

I do not know the answer to that. What I do know is that my initial concern on that point was soon overshadowed by my encounter with the psycho-analyst and artist Lou Andreas-Salomé. She was conspicuous in that she was one of the few women who ever attended the group, and more memorable because she was the only woman who ever dared to intervene in debate. Not only that, but she could talk circles round those graybeards!

And I cannot ignore that I found her ravishingly attractive.

Lou Salomé at that time was fifty years old, and yet she exuded a voluptuousness, a sexual energy, that would have been uncommon in a woman thirty years younger; in her, it seemed almost supernatural.

She had shining cinnamon hair with not a hint of gray, dark eyes like mine, crimson lips she unabashedly colored to the maximum, a tiny waist showing no sign of middle age nor of ever having borne children, and a well-sculptured posterior.

She would often let her blouse fall open, to reveal a partial glimpse of full, juvenescent breasts.

The second night I attended at Freud's home, she approached me.

"Have I had the pleasure?" she asked.

I could not speak. My throat filled up with mucus, and my nose began to run.

"My goodness," she said, laughing. "Both I and our leader's estranged friend, Wilhelm Fliess, should be flattered."

Fliess had for a time been Freud's dearest confidant and colleague, until a bitter falling-out five years before.

She looked around to make sure no one had overheard mention of Fliess's name, for it was now heresy to Freud.

"Fliess has staked his reputation on a connection between the nose and the libido," she said.

At that point I flushed totally red.

"Do not be embarrassed with me," she said softly. "The flows of the body, the rush of attraction and desire, are normal and natural, the life force at its most intense; they must be attended to forthwith, or neurosis, hysteria, will surely follow."

I felt dizzy with the implications of that!

After the end of that evening's meeting, she invited me back to her quarters on Schmidgasse for further conversation.

By midnight I found myself being ravenously devoured by surely one of the most passionate women who had ever lived. I, who by choice had up until that point enjoyed only the favors of prostitutes, was swept full speed into the flesh-hunger of a voracious woman, one who explored every sexual act, who was relentless and single-minded. I was repeatedly carried to the summit, drained, then comforted and fortified for the next round.

Once I sank into slumber, only to awaken and find Lou in my groin, whispering endearments to my phallus, which stood erect in the semidarkness.

"The penis is the source of the life force," she whispered, both to it and to me. "It rises, it falls, it is a primal god, and I am its servant.

"It is the living totem," she moaned in the dark.

"I am its high priestess. I urge it heavenward and draw it down into my dark nexus."

Her pubis was dark and rich, the most profuse hair I had ever seen on any woman's body, and beneath its black tangles her body was as smooth and damp as that of a Gypsy girl of eighteen.

"Fill me," she implored, and I obliged. Each time I entered, it was as if I was possessed, there only to serve another being, and only to do her bidding until I died.

"Death comes to you five times this night, and five rebirths," she said. "You cannot know the ecstasy I feel when a man ejaculates his seed into my womb."

Imagine my consternation when I heard this kind of talk. If it sounds absurd and fabricated to you now, be assured that I heard it with my own ears and then later saw the general theme confirmed in her clinical papers, theoretical texts, and memoirs. Suffice it to say that she, we, were all pioneers in what was yet a murky and undefined world, and no avenue was too strange for exploration.

I fell asleep again, only to find her atop me toward dawn, attempting to bring my phallus into her anus. It was excruciatingly tight for me and, that night after so much coupling, probably as painful for her. She gasped, she panted, and was covered with a thin film of sweat.

Afterward I felt as though I would faint. She rose and walked over to the window, through which came the greige light of a weeping dawn.

"Look at them going about their assigned tasks," she said, peering down at the street sweepers, the factory-bound laborers. "Look at their faces, a kind of death-in-life.

"We must set them free of this tyranny of misery," she said. Turning to me, standing nude at the gray window, she raised her arm as though she were exhorting a mob.

"We must remind mankind of the pleasures it knows but has imprisoned in the dungeon of repression."

Between our parting that morning and the next Wednesday meeting, I sent her three messages, but got no response. I stopped by her apartment once and rang, and although I thought I had seen a form flash by the window, she did not answer.

Nor did she appear at the next Wednesday meeting.

When I did see her, two weeks later, she was in deep conversation with Dr. Viktor Tauska, a promising disciple of Freud, not much older than I.

I sensed in that instant that I had already been discarded.

My fears were confirmed by a medical student named Lobl, who told me Lou was notorious. Although I did not ask, I inferred he too had been taken to her bed, and many others.

"She has been through at least five of our group since she began coming here six months ago," Lobl said. "She devours them, captures their 'life force,' then moves on.

"It is her fountain of youth."

Although I was supposed to be a sober and analytical man, I was secretly devastated by this discovery.

At that time I lived in a rooming house that stood near the Belvedere Palace on Prinz Eugenstrasse. To supplement the meager stipend the Krankenhaus paid, I was allowed to operate a small private practice on the side, which I did from a storefront office on Hutteldorferstrasse, conveniently near the tram line. I specialized in taking referrals of patients with limited means from the Krankenhaus.

In my own variation on Dr. Freud's techniques, I had my patients seated upright and facing a wall hung with an imitation Persian rug. I sat immediately behind and out of the view of the patient.

And it was there that I listened to the outpourings, the torments, of the lost souls of Vienna. Many, like me, were barely clinging to respectability, not knowing how to pay for the next visit to the vegetable market or the landlord. Amazing to me that this imperial city, regal and austere in its grandeur and power, could be home to so many of us.

There was so little difference between them and myself. My heart went out to the downtrodden, the grime-faced, who could barely scrape up enough to ride the electric trolley or buy a lurid red candy apple to serve as a lunch.

Although I was expected to charge a maximum of five schillings per visit, that figure might as well have been five hundred, so rarely did I collect it. I told my patients to pay as they were able. The fortunate would count out old groschen or lay down a loaf of bread; the truly needy would ask me to let them coast until next time.

How could I say no, when I too knew the pain of poverty?

How could I say no, when I too knew the pain of their torments?

You see, these patients of mine and I had much more in common than anyone of them could ever guess. It was my most painful secret, exposed only in my training therapy with Dr. Stuchlík. The fact was, while I was working as an apprentice analyst and healer of the mind, I myself was in the grip of a powerful psychological obsession. The encounter with Lou Salomé was in fact my most fulfilling relationship with a woman, certainly since childhood. But while Lou was my infatuation, she who knew my innermost self was a woman of the streets, a creature of shadow with whom I sought to act out an odd little drama that since adolescence had been first a recurring dream and then a daytime fantasy, until under the disorientation of my move to Vienna it came bursting out into the daytime world.

Her name was Lili. I saw her my first week in Vienna, in the shadows of the Rathausplatz, and knew I would have to make the attempt.

Lili, despite the harshness of her chosen profession, was quite young beneath the rouge and lipstick and jewelry, little more than a schoolgirl, slender, her breasts barely budding.

I was out one fall night, made both excited and melancholic by the smells of the Danube and the end of summer, still a total loner in this city. I saw her waiting, ready to accommodate the city politicians and civil servants who were working late.

I stared at her and watched her eyes glisten at me, her mouth widening in the leer she'd learned from her fellow prostitutes.

I approached. She twirled her purse.

"Come with me," I said with embarrassment, taking her by the arm and leading her back in the direction of my modest lodgings. I had waited until dark so that no one, particularly the landlady, would see me with her.

"Wait a minute," she protested in her accent of Hungary, whence she had come. "We didn't even settle on price."

"Whatever you want," I said. I had never thought it would go this far. In fact, I'd hoped naively that a move down the Danube would set me free.

"I won't stand for anything rough," she said, perplexed. "No punishments, any of that."

"None of that," I repeated. We turned onto my street. I recognized one of my fellow boarders, Tagacs, another Hungarian, this one a young engineer. Turning to the wall to try and obscure my face, I was relieved to hear his footsteps head down the other block.

I led Lili up the stairs to my room, brought her inside, and closed the door.

I pulled a schoolgirl's blue uniform from my bureau drawer, patent-leather shoes, a ribbon now somewhat timeworn, and handed them to her.

"Dress behind that screen," I said.

"Ha," Lili laughed, as she dressed. "I'm going to bust this skirt. And these shoes are pinching me."

When she came out, I made her wipe off her makeup and tie her hair in the ribbon. All was approaching readiness.

"Sit there," I said, pointing to my small, narrow bed.

As she sat, totally baffled, I knelt before her by the bed.

"Oh," she said, thinking she understood now. "Oh, teacher, do you want to take off my clothes?"

"No," I said.

She was already beginning to unfasten the buttons she had just buttoned, when I stopped her.

"Now," I was barely able to whisper, "put your hands on my shoulders and say, 'Dear Radan, I forgive you.' "

She was astonished.

"Say it," I repeated.

And so she forgave me, and I wept in her lap, the tears coming in a flood, as they always did in the dream and in the fantasy, into this schoolgirl's outfit that I had saved all these years, seemingly for this very purpose.

"Oh, Margret, Margret," I whispered, until the moment had passed and I was recovering myself.

"Here is your money," I said, paying her two schillings.

"Who's Margret?" she asked.

"Please go," I said. And she did so, shaking her head in puzzlement.

Another half-dozen times did I repeat that scene over the following two years with Lili, who learned to act out the little drama almost flawlessly and said it was the easiest money she made all day long. In my own way I grew quite dependent on her, and in time, as we talked, I came to consider her as a friend, even a family member, and finally revealed to her the cause and meaning of the theatrics—or rather therapy—in which she had become a regular performer. It was hard for me to reveal the origins of this problem to her, except over time, as I grew more relaxed with her. But I did tell her, as I did later tell my mentor Stuchlík, who in my post-residency analysis finally helped set me free of it.

And as I shall tell you, when I know you better. But now is not the time.

Late in 1909, my political and professional lives began to converge. During one of my first visits to the Wednesday Group, I had been impressed by an impassioned appeal to greater political involvement by psycho-analysts, given by Fräulein Adler, wife of Freud's loyal if obtuse lieutenant, Alfred Adler. Fräulein Adler was openly mocking of her husband's refusal to join her radical enterprises.

"Of what use is psycho-therapy if the world outside the therapy chamber creates and reinforces neuroses?" she challenged us. "We all know, but will not admit, that oppression by the oligarchs, the forces of militarism and nationalism, have wreaked havoc on the human soul. Doctors, rise up and make use of what you know."

Adler himself was clearly embarrassed by these outbursts from his wife.

"*Liebchen*," he would say, "what would you have us do? Take to the streets with red flags?"

Freud signaled by his glowering silence that he found all this distasteful.

"And why not?" she said unabashedly. "The revolutionary parties are open to your views. Your field is not reactionary but radical, revolutionary. You are delving into the human mind, breaking away the chains."

I must say that while the others sneered at her, she set me to thinking. I introduced myself to Fräulein Adler. Even in her did I detect a slight disdain for my provincial origins. But she invited me to a meeting of her party, which no longer even exists, long since splintered and subsumed in the many doctrinal battles of recent decades. I had gone to anarchist political meetings in Bratislava during my student days, but being in Vienna and feeling suspect and conspicuous in my foreignness, I had decided to abstain from this kind of activity until I was on home ground again.

"I'm glad at least one of these nervous sheep has some good sense,"

Fräulein Adler said. "They're so afraid they won't get their fat fees paid, they cater to the oligarchs." At first I wondered if her interest in me was more than political. But it was not; a plumpish, garrulous woman, she made clear in unspoken terms that she wanted no more than political comradeship.

Attending that first meeting with her, held in a cellar beneath a packing house off the Danube, I listened first to a tedious discussion of the group's finances and a labor march to be held in two weeks and who would take care of making the signs and banners. Then they showed a silent film feature about V. I. Ulyanov of the Russian Social Democratic Party. As the film ran, they played an accompanying record on the gramophone.

"He is a tireless fighter for the rights of the forgotten peasants and workers of his homeland," gargled the record. "Imprisonment, exile, assassination attempts—he has tasted them all, yet struggles on. His writings inspire the world. . . ."

The cinematic Russian who jerked before us was dressed in moleskin overcoat and Petersburg cap. Removing his cap to wave it, he exposed his pale baldness. The face looked as if it were about to break into a grin. But the grin never came.

We watched the Russian speak, unable to hear his voice but observing his eyes, burning with energy and power, a numinosity Jung would have immediately recognized.

The narrator predicted that the forces of reaction and capitalism would soon trigger armed uprisings by the masses against the monarchies of Europe.

"World revolution will sweep away all borders and unite the working classes in the common enterprise of human progress! It will be dedicated to the creation of a new man, one living according to communistic ideals in fraternity with his fellow workers. The new man will rise above petty self-interest into a shared class interest, culminating in a withering away of bourgeois government, armies, laws!"

While the group now argued the pros and cons of doctrine and strategy, agreeing with or disputing the path of Ulyanov, I was lost in thought. I began to wonder if the discoveries of psycho-analysis couldn't somehow be applied to the revolution.

In that damp cellar in Vienna, amidst those stragglers of the communist cell, was born an idea which, though it now stands revealed as hastily conceived and distorted by youthful passion, at the time seemed to have the real ring of truth to me.

Later that evening, alone in my apartment, I wrote:

> It is not enough to leave the development of the new world to external political structures alone. The new world must also be created from within the new man. The revolution must be a psychological event, a rebirth that sweeps away the outmoded patterns of behavior and personhood which delay, and even subvert, the outer revolution.

I began a long period (spring 1910–autumn 1911) of exploring how to accomplish my newfound goal. In my therapy with several patients, I found myself crossing the line from idle innovation to full-blown experimentation. I employed varying techniques. My experiments, which were duly recorded but not yet reported to the Krankenhaus, encompassed the use of several psycho-tropic drugs, including cocaine, which Dr. Freud himself had first begun to employ in psycho-therapy in the 1890s. On one patient I also began the use of a galvanic battery applied to the frontal lobes. On two others I tried varying types of hypnosis, attempting through speech and suggestion to alter or replace patterns of thought, phobias, and preferences.

These experiments covered nine months time.

In mid-1911 I approached Dr. Freud himself, in his office at the Krankenhaus, and asked that I be allowed to present my paper "On Psycho-Suggestion and Social Objectives." At that moment he was deeply immersed in a dispute with the hospital administration over how much emphasis and support the psycho-therapy program would be given, and he was hardly paying any attention to me as I spoke. He thumbed through his desk calendar and stroked his beard.

"Ferenczi was supposed to be leading discussion this week, but he's in Buda-Pest, certainly won't be back by Wednesday. There is an opening for a discussant."

My heart raced.

"Are you prepared to withstand hard questioning by a formidable group of psycho-analysts?" he asked, distracted as he looked over some correspondence from the hospital.

"I am," I replied, petrified. I left an outline of my paper with him to review. He was so engrossed in his other business he didn't even say goodbye.

The following Wednesday I began to read my paper, after a cursory introduction by Freud in which it became apparent he had not had time to look over my outline.

"In light of the current political and economic situation in the world," I began, "the psycho-therapist must be prepared to step beyond treating the patient alone and move toward treating the illnesses of the social mass."

Several men coughed; Dr. Freud was already scowling at me.

"The dream state is a window on the dark subconscious and on the subterranean workings of that shadow world Dr. Freud and his collaborators have so successfully described. The dream is a window on the phantoms of the past, which through their deep-rooted nature dominate the present, and the future.

"We therapists are the outside observers, standing in the garden of the present, watching the byplay of the phantoms of the past, in many cases mutated into full-blown monsters of trauma and hysteria.

"But just as the lighted window casts light and images from within onto us silent observers in the garden, equally can the window become a door, be opened, and allow us in to combat those demons and vermin that torture the patient and project his pain onto the world.

"Once inside, however, we must not be fearful of going the whole distance. Of what use is it simply to treat the personal trauma as though it exists independently of the world outside, and then send the patient back into the milieu which caused the original neurosis? For each of us is also a tiny mirror reflecting the world. The health of the patient cannot be obtained without obtaining the health of the world, for they are one and the same, the individual the cell of the social body.

"Why be passive and stand aside and allow primitive and antisocial behavior to perpetuate itself in our patients? Instead, colleagues, should we not forge ahead, across the threshold that now presents itself to us?

"Using the techniques of hypnotic suggestion, psycho-tropic drugs, galvanic shock, controlled transference, and Pavlovian reinforcement, whether as separate methods or in concert, according to the personality of the patient, we can erase the demons of old trauma and learned behavior and substitute new patterns of a socially desirable nature—indeed, promote behavior that is socially productive."

"I protest," said a young doctor named Klein, standing up.

"I also protest," said Alfred Adler, looking over at his wife as if to ask, Is this your doing?

"I request that I be allowed to continue," I said. All eyes were on Freud.

"He is building an entire structure on mistaken premises," said Adler. "The result will be political rubbish."

"I request that I be allowed to continue," I repeated. "It is the custom here for the primary presentation to be made and then debate to follow."

Dr. Freud was clearly not on my side. He was deeply regretting that he had not reviewed my paper before allowing me to present it. But I had quoted custom correctly.

"Continue," said Freud.

"Other methods, which I have not had the resources to examine but which bear further consideration, include use of direct photographic projection into the retina during sleep or hypnosis, extended listening during a hypnotic or narcotized state to phonographic recordings of music or any therapeutically relevant sounds, such as patterned voices like chanting, to duplicate methods of autogenic training as specified by Johannes Schultz.

"The key to the success of any of the methods is the skill with which the therapeutic opening of the darkened window of the subconscious is executed, and the dexterity of introduction of new material, events, ideas, and images after the excision of harmful and/or unproductive memory and experience.

"It is also my belief that the effectiveness of this therapy is inversely proportional to the age of the patient, beyond age five. Its effectiveness up until age five would seem to be unquestioned, although I have had no experience with infants.

"My observations are based on studies with five patients, conducted over five months time. The patients will be known as Klaus (adolescent), Gerhilde (child), Ulrike (child), Rainer (adult), and Otto (aged adult).

"It is not my pretense to claim that all questions or doubts about this thesis are resolved; but rather that the possibility and implications of success demand further investigation.

"The objective of my method, which I will call Psycho-Social Reconstruction, is the nurturing of individuals who will subordinate their petty self-interest to an egalitarian ethic; positive reinforcement of impulses such as communality and concern for the less fortunate—"

"I protest," said Alfred Adler loudly, rising to his feet.

The room, which had been like a drafty cavern for minutes, erupted, exploded, indeed resounded with protests, rebukes, disputations, discussions, jeers, boos, growls, laughter, fists being shaken in the air, and feet stomping on Dr. Freud's august parlor floor.

The room, the house, thundered.

Dr. Freud only shook his head and looked at me in an oddly parental way. He shook his head, and the jeers and tumult continued, a tumult louder than any ever heard before at that gathering.

"Out with him!" most people were crying. "Out!"

"No, hear him!" one or two dissident voices answered.

I stood facing the din, looking into those faces that had never been friends to me, feeling their hostility, trying to continue but being unable, being shouted down each time I started.

It was my one and only presentation to the Group. It was also the one and only time I seriously expounded my viewpoint, except in the obligatory publication of my paper in several Freudian journals (complete with many prefaces and disclaimers!), which in turn generated floods of letters, mostly hostile, before the whole affair was gradually forgotten. My only supporters were invariably of the left.

Embarrassed that I had been so rash as to formally expound something before these experts that might have been worthy only of an interesting dinner discussion, and moreover to have pursued it further with my own private experimentation, I early on made the decision to forever keep my politics out of my therapeutic methods. In a later day, my private experimentation might even have prompted withdrawal of my medical license. But I was lucky, because as I've noted, in that pioneering era many false starts were made and abandoned, becoming only embarrassing historical footnotes to many a distinguished career, Freud's own included.

I did stay true to my political ideals by becoming a founding member of the Czech Communist Party upon my move to Karlova Universita in Prague, where I joined the teaching faculty of the medical school. Sometimes I told myself I would get back to my theory of "Psycho-Social Reconstruction" and give it another look, to see if something of use could be salvaged from it. But that vow was ever more hollow in the passing years, as I myself matured intellectually, and as events in the outer world led first to the Great War in Europe and the Bolshevik Revolution in Moscow, and then to the utter collapse of the empire and the emergence of the little independent nation of Czecho-Slovakia out of the wreckage.

It was a time of rejoicing for many of my countrymen, and it was for me too. But I cannot forget my final vision of Vienna when I returned there for a brief visit in 1919, haughty Vienna, after all this tumult had concluded. For here was a city that had once reigned from on high, now brought low with the rest of us . . . armies of beggars and tattered war veterans searching through garbage piles for a bit of cabbage, fine motorcars reduced to hauling firewood and laundry, holders of imperial titles now forced to become dressmakers, and what was once a world center turned into a backwater. This made me feel tragedy where I had never expected to feel it, and perhaps more than anything served to restrain my earliest, most intolerant, inclinations.

Only hours later, Robinson was on the ground in the country he had studied so much from afar, whose destiny he had affected in his own small way. It was a damp winter morning in Czechoslovakia.

He walked across the drizzling cement taxiway, between the holdover Aeroflot and Cubana airliners but also the new flood from Lufthansa and KLM and Air France, Czech Army troops in their olive greatcoats gathered in gaggles, out of formation, laughing and playing cards, blank spaces in their caps where the red stars had been removed not too long before. On the terminal itself, only the Czech flag flew where all the Warsaw Pact flags had once flown. This building, which had formerly been the most forbidding in the country, as much a barrier as a gateway, seemed imbued now with a feeling somewhere between relaxation and disorder. Spectators had been allowed out on a long-closed observation deck, and they were shouting with glee to some of his fellow passengers, exiled family members, coming home at last.

He was overcome with emotion—accentuated by his feeling of disembodiment after a sleepless night and too many Equanils—finally to see the place he had studied and analyzed for so long, like a second homeland.

It had never been clear if Czech Intelligence had ever known his face or real name. Lhota had always sworn he'd run his game with Robinson absolutely alone. But the KGB had to have seen them together—and wondered—during those drinking sessions in the Tennessee Bar in Vienna. The cover for their Vienna relationship, working on a Czech-American shoe export project, was plausible enough to fool most everybody. But he could not assume he was unknown. He could not even assume that passing Soviet photographers hadn't photographed him entering and leaving the Agency every day, or the White House.

He was playing the odds that the fall of the old Czech order had disrupted things enough that he would be able to get in and out undetected. Or that if they were still watching, no one would immediately recognize him now, older, hair graying, bearded.

Yet standing here now, he couldn't get away from the old fears, which were like reflex. How many of the people in Czech Immigration, in Customs, from behind mirrors or through recessed cameras, were watching him? How many photographs were being taken, to be compared that night and tomorrow against the files in some deeply buried bureau of the STB not yet touched by reform?

But the scene inside the terminal was more disordered than he had expected. This entry routine, which he had practiced and heard described a hundred times, was going differently. It was loose, friendly, almost Third World. He scanned for the eyes that should be watching him, hidden on a balcony here, a coffee shop bench there. And he was getting nothing.

Was it just a false sense of well-being from the emotion of his arrival, or a result of the Equanil? At Immigration, a woman officer hardly looked at his passport.

"Hotel?" she asked.

Shock rushed through him. How could he have forgotten an advance hotel reservation? How could Hamza have let that happen? Would this be his undoing?

"Yes," he said, feigning confusion. "I can't seem to find . . ."

He fumbled for a minute, trying to fabricate alibis on the spot. But she stamped his passport and handed it over.

"I recommend Panorama," she said. "Hot pool. And new bosses."

She handed him the passport and actually smiled. The old advance reservation requirement had been removed. He moved on in a daze. A line from the inaugural speech of the painter-President was hung on a large banner above the airport exits.

May our time as prisoners teach us compassion, not rancor.

In Customs, they did not even open his bag.

The whole scene shone with a brightness and innocence, an effervescence, possible only in places that are still relishing those first days of release from what was thought to be a lifetime sentence to oppression. Certainly no American airport could duplicate it.

While a surprising number of businessmen were coming and going, most touching were the obvious homecomings for those who had been driven away years before, or the departures for those who had never thought they would see another world. The terminal was actually crowded.

For a minute he stood in that space just beyond Customs where he was inside Czechoslovakia but had not absorbed the reality. And then he was in a bus, making the gray approach to the city itself, across the windswept taupe plateau of Ruzyne, following the same route the arriving Soviet commandos made late that August night in 1968 when they first took the city.

As they wound down into the valley of the Vltava, it only then began to hit him, with a thrill that was almost euphoric, a kind of euphoria he hadn't felt in a long time. He was in.

To get his bearings after arriving in the city, Robinson paused for a few moments in a tiny cemetery in the heart of Old Prague.

It was the place where the Holy Roman Emperor told the Jews in the sixteenth century they could bury their dead, a somber and timeless place surrounded by a museum, an empty synagogue, and Baroque residences that had stood for centuries. Kafka lived briefly in one of them.

On that winter day, the damp trunks of the trees shading the place were black as coal, and their long-fallen leaves sheathed the hummocks of earth beneath which lay the remains of the dead. Because no additional space was ever allotted, bodies and graves had been piled atop one another for four hundred years.

The headstones of the graves stood canted and impossibly jammed together, stalagmites breaking up from the earth, one more geological formation. One could not easily make out the Hebrew inscriptions. He found it an overwhelmingly beautiful and sad place. He imagined he could hear a thousand voices rising up in a whisper, the whisper of moist winter winds, the whispers of a civilization gone forever.

Beyond the cemetery's mossy confines, above the noonday rattle of motorcycles and taxis, he could distinguish the dripping granitic forest of the Goths, the slate spires, the gilt-trimmed lightning rods and crucifixes, of old Prague. Nearby, a five-hundred-year-old cuckoo clock still performed its hourly mechanized drama of life and death. A toy skeleton emerged from a clock face adorned with mystic and astral symbols, to dance, pirouette, and disappear inside.

All these architectural treasures in this magic spot had been miraculously spared the destruction of the last war. The humans had not.

On that particular January morning, several people dressed in dappled gray colors moved among the graves. Two old women walked nearest, heavy-coated and almost inseparable from the wet tree trunks and headstones. Farther away, a young blond girl dramatically laid single flowers on certain graves of people who had been dead for four centuries. She looked like not a descendant of those buried here but rather a student from a university theater class.

Robinson stood before the elaborate crypt of Rabbi Low, the sixteenth-century sorcerer who legend says created the magical Golem. The Golem's duty was to protect the Jews of Prague. But he had failed, protecting only the belongings of the thousands who had been shipped away to death. The belongings, assembled by Hitler for his Museum of an Extinct Race, were now housed in the State Jewish Museum, next door to the cemetery. Thousands of Jewish-owned cooking pans, footstools, chamber pots, filled its chambers and display cases.

Robinson decided to go directly to Dvořáček as soon as he had checked into a hotel. He walked back out into the weekday bustle of the city. Carrying his overnight bag, he was conspicuous as a tourist. Money changers, taxi drivers, and hustlers for hotels and guesthouses pestered him across the square toward the river.

My, he thought, how the spirit of free enterprise has burst forth here.

When Robinson barked back at his pursuers in his best Czech, they were confused, then put off, taking him for a local and therefore penniless. And when he put on a cinder tweed driver's cap, such as many of them were wearing, they left him alone. By the time he was at the stone archway marking the approach to the Karel Most, they were gone and he felt he had blended in. In the falling mist, he crossed the bridge, passing between the mute basalt archbishops and kings who stood guard on the railing. Above him loomed Hradčany, largest castle on earth, built by the Holy Roman Emperors to rule over an empire long since fallen to dust. The fallen Communist kings had kept their offices here, and now the painter-President followed suit.

First he checked into the Inn of the Wandering Boar, a tiny medieval lodging that by a miracle was only half full. Then he walked down the steps at the bridge's foot to the curious little island of Kampě, which lay in the Vltava River.

Looking back, he was certain no one had followed him. The streets were randomly populated: a lone slender child with a dog on a leash, an old woman carrying a wicker-basket bundle, a couple of young lovers entwined on this Friday midday. He found his mind running back to old habits—to wondering what eyes watched him from the tall, narrow windows overhanging each winding street. He had once theorized that the STB domestic office could mobilize street watchers in every sixth house in the city. Awesome, to imagine such manpower devoted to surveillance. That, to him, was the essence of the evil he had dedicated his life to combat. This monstrous diversion of human potential.

Again he felt a disorientation to think that those days were coming to an end. The loss of a love was immediate and brutal, the loss of an enemy more hidden in impact. He found number 38 and knocked, could hear movement inside, but there was no sign he would be answered. He knocked again. A white-haired woman in a wheelchair finally cracked the door, looked at his shoulder bag.

"What do you want?" she asked.

"I must see Mr. Dvořáček," he said.

"Who are you?" she asked. The crack in the door narrowed.

"My *strýc* sent me," Robinson replied. My uncle . . .

The door closed and was latched from inside. He thought a curtain opened for a second upstairs, then closed. He thought he heard snatches of an argument. A door slammed inside; the woman rolled into the inner recesses of the house, down a hallway or into a back room.

There was only a chill cinder-water mist falling on his face. Robinson knocked, and knocked again.

Several uncomfortable minutes passed. He loathed being left out here on the doorstep for all to see. Then the door slowly cracked open again, revealing a void and the scent of scuffed floorboards and a garlic meal cooked hours ago, last of all a tall, unsmiling man in his sixties, dressed in tweeds, gray hair combed wetly back. The man wore glasses that gave him the aspect of an academic; his skin was sallow with age, the flesh of someone forever indoors.

"Who are you?" asked the man.

"My *strýc* Miroslav sent me," repeated Robinson.

Václav Dvořáček's head jerked slightly at the mention of the name. A flicker of movement crossed the face, the dimmest outward evidence of surprise, ideas, possibilities.

Robinson pushed his way inside. The door was closed.

"Miroslav emigrated far away," said the man, his eyes narrowing. "I hardly remember him."

He is totally off guard, thought Robinson. This is the last thing he expected.

"Uncle is dead," said Robinson.

Dvořáček was speechless. He was trembling slightly.

"Someone sent him to his death," said Robinson, gauging the damage he could do here. Strangulation. An old house on fire. Small confined explosions.

Dvořáček stood as still as an aging asthmatic could be. Yellow skin hung down from his cheekbones, and his breath carried the odor of slow, sweet decay, like a compost heap of coffee grounds and fruit rinds. His teeth were stained from smoking and coffee drinking. He looked consumptive.

"I think it was you," said Robinson.

He wondered whether the wife was in back, dialing State Security right now. This man had been judged to be a Soviet double; what kind of points could he win by turning in an American spy, even if a renegade?

They stood in a small entrance hall. The floor was bare ancient oak, and the plastered walls were sooted and fault-riven. Beyond, Robinson could make out a room heaped with atomizing books, stacks of magazines and newspapers. Windowpanes striated by the dust of a thousand rains were covered by shroudlike gauzy curtains. The resulting outdoor light filtered through in jaundiced hue.

It was a place of memories. Dvořáček's STB cover had been as a black-market rare book and periodical dealer.

"It is very foolish, coming to me after all these years," said Dvořáček, a surprising confidence in his voice. "After what the family did, abandoning me in my time of need."

Dvořáček stroked his throat, as if to ease his breathing. He was genuinely off balance. But he had made no move to take Robinson farther inside. They stood there, panting in indoor air so cold that slight clouds of moisture formed as they breathed.

"Why do you come to me in this way?" asked Dvořáček. "I was loyal to Uncle to the end. I count for nothing. I have passed the river Styx."

He is either bluffing, thought Robinson, or telling the truth.

"You had things for Uncle, from his *tetka* Věra. He received them. Now he is dead," added Robinson.

Dvořáček took that for a minute and then asked for more.

"Uncle was obsessed," said Robinson, "and you fed his obsession. You played with him. You poured water on a fire."

Dvořáček said nothing.

"Sending messages. Looking for things. Keeping secrets."

Dvořáček was very still. This will tell, thought Robinson. In the rear, the woman moved around on another bare floor. A television blared, and water pipes roared as a tap was turned on.

"I was loyal to Uncle," said Dvořáček quietly, but bargaining. "I owed him much."

Out through the arched windows and through the lutescent gauze, Robinson could see the Baroque facades of Kampě, of Malá Strana, and the Gothic towers and statuary of the Karel Most. The water in the little rivulet separating him from Malá Strana was slightly roiled by unseen currents, a moving sheet of the slate its sediment might become in a million years. The rain clouds were breaking up; the world outside lay wrapped in cool vapor.

"Who killed Uncle?" Robinson asked.

Dvořáček was motionless. He might have been carved of old ivory and placed there in the foyer.

"Who are you to ask these things?" Dvořáček responded. "Family secrets?"

Outside, a group of schoolboys walked by, their satchels swinging. Dressed in uniform, they sang a ribald limerick about a young maid who sat on a swine. They must have been twelve years old.

"Who killed him?" asked Robinson.

Dvořáček seemed to exhale, to deflate even as Robinson watched. His fixed gaze was now clouded over, and he was looking down inside himself.

"You are his *synovec* Jiří," whispered Dvořáček after a minute, almost to himself, his voice hoarse, jaw slack. "*Synovec* Jiří."

Yes, Robinson thought: I am nephew Jiří, I who ran Uncle Lhota, and through him you, and all those others Lhota drew with him. I who never saw you, nor you me; my name was never known to you except as the nephew. I have come to you now, after ten years.

And he also thought: You, Václav, were always the best, the kind of weapon we feared having in our own arsenal, should it ever be turned against us. We finally judged you more Soviet than American. But Lhota was right: Americans had a hard time evaluating the compromises men had to make on the other side.

Dvořáček was a "finder." He "found" people, traced them, tracked them down.

This was it. There was no more to say. They could have him in the dungeons of the Daliborka or on a plane to Moscow in ten minutes. Robinson would make wonderful headlines back at the Agency, causing incredible confusion. Was he a defector, or a mental case? Another enigmatic story buried on the back pages of the papers.

Dvořáček slowly turned and walked into the adjoining room. As he turned on a radio deliberately too loud, he beckoned for Robinson to come in. Here and there among the disintegrating books, the primordial newspapers and magazines, was tucked a chair, a worktable, a lamp. A disturbingly large cat sprang from one stack and disappeared across the room. Dvořáček pulled two chairs together, poured tea from a small electric pot that steamed in the cold air.

The radio was playing a medley of protest songs that had brought down the old government.

"What do you want to know?" Dvořáček asked, barely audible over the roaring music.

Robinson hesitated a minute. Stacks of the Communist Party paper *Rudé Právo* were on either side of him, and some of the new democratic dailies, a photo taken of the painter as he and Gorbachev signed the troop withdrawal agreement.

"What was Uncle searching for when he died?" Robinson asked.

Dvořáček put his cup loudly into the saucer. He shook his head, almost bemused, removing his wire-rimmed glasses to clean them. He was really quite a distinguished-looking man . . . a long, melancholic face, elongated body, birdlike sensibility and movements.

"A man called Emil," Dvořáček said.

Robinson said nothing. A pallid sun began to break through the wet acidic skies. Pouring past the yellow curtains, the light warmed the room for a few minutes.

An inexplicable smile had crept onto Dvořáček's face. In the filtered aureate sunlight, he seemed like a face out of Vermeer, Rembrandt. Dvořáček was now looking out the window, the music so loud Robinson was more reading his lips than hearing him.

"The old days are ending," Robinson said, motioning to the radio, to the pictures of the new leadership.

Dvořáček's body jolted in a suppressed laugh.

"So they are," he said. He had put his glasses back on.

"And yet someone killed Uncle," said Robinson. He lowered his voice so that the roaring music was triumphant.

"The dead wasp can still sting," said Dvořáček.

"Is it dead?" asked Robinson.

"An empire can take a long time to die," Dvořáček said. "The farthest outposts of Rome went on for years before they heard Rome had fallen."

"But things move much faster now."

"They do," agreed Dvořáček. The Czech poured more tea, added sugar, stirred slowly. The huge cat walked up to Robinson and began rubbing against his leg, purring. It was an atavistic cat, giant, like some kind of extinct breed of Central European lynx. Its purring was hoarse and unsettling.

"What killed Lhota?" Robinson asked.

Dvořáček winced slightly at the mention of the name Lhota. It was the first time it had been said in this conversation. Perhaps it was the first time since his defection thirteen years before that it had even been voiced in this house.

"Uncle and I carried out an investigation long ago," said Dvořáček. "In our search, we were frustrated to find many things beyond our grasp. Closed doors. Riddles. This is what killed him. We were fools to continue with it. It was his obsession, and he dragged me along. Better to live in ignorance."

"Who was Emil?" asked Robinson. Dvořáček looked weary, rubbing his deep-set eyes. He coughed a racking cough for a moment, then stopped to catch his breath. It was as if these questions, this visit, were wearing him down.

"I was responsible for Emil's ancient history, Miroslav the more recent events," said Dvořáček. "We were to dig quietly and report back. I found a few things, interesting only because they were so few. Otherwise great voids. Blanks. Questions."

The cat had caught a tiny mouse behind a bookshelf and carried it wiggling in its jaws.

"Emil Užhok." Dvořáček coughed. "A Czech citizen who arrived with the Soviet troops when they invaded in 1968, and was on the plane when Dubček was flown back to Moscow for his tongue-lashing by Brezhnev. A Czech who was kept a mystery to our own General Secretary by the KGB. Birthplace, age, ethnic origin unverifiable, but believed to be Ruthenian. Came to Prague at the time of the Hungarian annexation. Possibly enrolled in Karlova Universita in the late 1930s, member of student Communist cell. Possibly interned by the Nazis at Terezín, although no living witnesses to his being there could be found. And in the 1960s, actor in some Soviet research program at Hostivař we were allowed to know nothing about."

"What sort of actor?"

Dropping the stunned mouse, the huge cat jumped up into his master's lap, causing some tea to be spilled. Dvořáček stroked the cat's back.

"We have no idea," said Dvořáček. "We presume he had something to do with defense, for that is what was done at Hostivař. I couldn't venture a guess as to Emil Užhok's actual job. Perhaps placed there to supervise the loyalties of the handful of Czech workers at this most secret of installations. Perhaps a lowly informer. Or a specialist of some kind."

"But didn't you say he arrived with the Soviet troops in 1968?"

"We could never verify that. It might have been mistaken identity. At any rate, in this case, for years, all doors, all possibilities for an answer were closed to us. Until the collapse."

As he spoke, he had gone off into his stacks of newspapers. He rummaged for a minute, and the protest music soared to a crescendo.

"Until the collapse," repeated Dvořáček. "I was contacted by an acquaintance of mine on the Party Archives staff, someone infected with the desire to bare our souls, reveal our past sins. She remembered my interest in Emil from years ago. The collapse of the Party meant many long-sealed documents were being brought to light."

"Who in the Archives?"

Dvořáček made no move at all to answer.

"What did she tell you?"

Dvořáček came back to his chair and sat down. Coughing, he lit up a pipe.

"She said she had stumbled upon a certain parcel from the Terezín concentration camp, long sealed in the Higher Party Archives, inadvertently gathered up by the Soviet liberation forces. Among them was a journal that, in her words, would discredit Emil Užhok and his Russian sponsors. There were also some documents relating to the Red Army capture of the camp and Užhok's legal status at the time. The existence of this journal was something that Miroslav had believed in fervently. It seems that in his conversation with a Soviet contact many years ago, he had been told that such a document existed. But its whereabouts and precise contents were then unknown."

"What did the journal say? And the Soviet documents? Did the occupation forces arrest him?"

Dvořáček shrugged. "As for the Soviet material, it indicated Užhok was about to be investigated by the Red Army for Fascist collaboration, when he was rescued by Lavrenty Beria, due to some knowledge Užhok had of 'secret SS activities.' About the journal itself I don't know, because I was unable to read it, in microfilm form, with my bad eyes. Nor was I given even a summary of its contents. My associate was unable—even fearful—of doing so. Her energies were focused on getting this parcel well out of Czechoslovakia and into the hands of those who could make proper use of it."

I have one last favor to ask, Lhota said. My *tetka* Věra died. And she left some things.

Family Bible, photos, that kind of thing.

Please, Dany. Please.

"Why didn't she just release it to someone here? Why the need to get it out of the country?"

"Neither she, nor I, was yet confident that these materials would see the light of day if we tried to publicize them here. Our revolution has gone only so far, and people of dubious loyalty still exist. And besides, it was a rather esoteric matter from long ago, an affair that might not have interested a public or press more focused on today."

"How did you get it to Uncle?" Robinson asked.

"You must realize it was kept in the most restricted area of the Archives for forty-five years. Its removal and transport had to be done quickly, during the confusion of the Party's fall. Several people were seeking to possess it, thinking it might be negotiated for safe passage to Moscow in the event of a democratic crackdown on operatives of the old order. My friend, fearing its theft or destruction, saw an opportunity to export the papers, when Miroslav's own efforts to get a courier failed. It was shipped under diplomatic cover to Vienna, and from then into a network not even I would be able to reconstruct."

A journal, she said.

"Do you even know if it reached him?"

"My last message from him indicated that it did. Ironically, just as the journal went out, a packet of photos from Terezín also surfaced in the Archives. As far as I know, they are still there, awaiting some way of getting them to Miroslav."

"Who's your contact in the Archives?" Robinson asked.

Dvořáček was silent, dismissing the question.

"Was it Libuše?"

Dvořáček's eyes narrowed, and he lowered his head like an animal ready to strike.

It *was* Libuše, thought Robinson: Libuše, founder-goddess of Prague, sweeping down the valley walls with her peasant king, Přemysl, to found Praha, the Threshold City. Libuše, code name for Lhota's and Dvořáček's helper in the Archives, who had been part of Lhota's Prague network years before. And then abandoned, Lhota would say.

"Do not," whispered, or rather hissed, Dvořáček, "even think of approaching her. She is an innocent whom your family used without mercy and then tossed aside. Do not even think of it."

It was uncanny how this sick elderly man could marshal the impression of physical force. He looked as though he could unleash some kind of skeletal fury that would leave an enemy torn and blinded.

"Do you know anything at all about the journal?" Robinson asked.

Dvořáček paused a moment.

"I only know who wrote it," he said.

"Who was that?"

"Dr. Radan Michalský."

"Who was Michalský?"

Dvořáček relit his pipe and shooed the cat away. Now the sun was fading into clouds again, and the room went from saffron to smoke. It was as if Dvořáček had not heard. He was looking off into space.

"A prisoner. A doctor. A Jew."

The Czech reflected on that.

"And one of the founding fathers of the Czech Communist Party."

"So the journal and photo prove that Emil was in fact at Terezín?" said Robinson.

"I suppose," said Dvořáček after a time. Another group of schoolboys walked by the yellow-curtained windows. It was drizzling again outside.

"Why," asked Robinson, "were Michalský and Emil together?"

Dvořáček shrugged, then began coughing. His coughing fit lasted for a full two minutes. Afterward he could barely talk, and his eyes watered.

"Miroslav spent the last ten years of his life tracking Emil down, undeterred by the reported death in Ethiopia. How ironic that Miroslav would succeed in finding him, just as this journal emerged from nowhere, with its own secrets. How ironic that Miroslav would be dead when he was on the verge of finding the answers he had sought for so long."

"What does 'Veil / the face of God' mean?" asked Robinson.

The radio music abruptly stopped for a few seconds. In the interval, he could hear his own heart beating, and the rasping breaths of Václav Dvořáček.

"I have no idea," said Dvořáček, almost apologetic.

Strangely, Robinson almost believed him. He almost believed Lhota was right, that Dvořáček was loyal to the end, not a double but a victim.

"Will you kill me now?" Dvořáček asked, sincerely.

Robinson could not answer.

"Please, do so," said Dvořáček, placing his hand on Robinson's forearm. He gripped Robinson with that curious steely force uncommon for a man his age and health. This was morbid.

"You must," whispered Dvořáček, coughing between the two words. "Please do not leave me to them a second time."

"This is the new era," said Robinson, saying nonsense. "The peaceful revolution. They wouldn't dare."

Dvořáček's coughing was now thunderous rolling spasms that reached down into his abdomen. His sallow face was reddened with the impact of the coughs. He was coughing up flecks of blood.

"You see what they did to Miro and to my wife," said Dvořáček, almost apologetically. "At least they killed Miro. My wife they struck down on the street with a lorry. They broke her back and paralyzed her. Please, save them the trouble of trying again."

Robinson quite honestly had nothing to say. Dvořáček, despite his discomfort, rose from his chair. He was shaking his head, as if to say No. Robinson was being pushed toward the door by a sick, dying man. This is absurd, he thought. As Robinson was being backed into the foyer, the big cat sharpened its claws on the gauzy curtains, tearing great rips in the material.

"Aa," gasped Dvořáček, throwing a spoon at the cat and hitting it square in the back. It shot off into the stacks again.

"Who?" Robinson asked. "Who do you think it is? The KGB?"

Dvořáček tried to laugh, amid his coughing. But he could not. Robinson was up against the doorframe, Dvořáček's moldy breath hitting him square in the face.

"You and I," whispered Dvořáček. "You and I killed him."

It made no sense. Dvořáček was opening the front door, his crippled wife in the hall that led back into the living area, watching this melodramatic scene in horror.

"What do you mean?" Robinson asked, now out on the front steps. It looked as if it would rain again. Dvořáček glanced up and down the street as he pushed Robinson outside, and the door began to close between them. Dvořáček was in an ever-narrower frame, until he was just a thin strip of a man, eyes, portion of mouth. His steamy sick breath billowed out through the fissure.

"Leave us now," said the disappearing mouth.

"What do you mean?" Robinson asked the diminishing crack. "How did you and I kill him?"

"They will be here soon," said the darkness. "Be gone."

And then there was only an eye, and an iris, and the last escaping bit of steam, before the door closed. It closed solidly, finally, and was latched, and Robinson could hear Dvořáček receding deep into the bowels of the house. One of the neighbors, out to sweep her front steps, noticed Robinson, scrutinized him through eyes that had seen any manner of outrage. They were narrow, reptilian slits, revealing nothing but her hardness. Robinson shivered.

He made his way to the steps that took him off the island and back up onto the bridge. He was shaking, drenched in sweat. His body was limp.

Beneath his feet, the broad taupe flood of the Vltava broke over the exposed bones of this continent of ashen mist, this Gothic continent of fog and winter dreams.

Robinson walked the few hundred yards through the misting riverine dampness toward the Inn of the Wandering Boar. The heads and exposed shoulders of stone prelates and saints lining the medieval Karel Most bridge seemed burned black, scorched by a skyborne fire. Yet even in this weather and gloom he savored each step of the way, his first sightings of places he had long read of and studied, like a novice pilgrim in Mecca. It was his plan to remain at the inn the remainder of the day, sorting out impressions and possibilities raised by the talk with Dvořáček. The talk had given him nothing other than a vague confirmation of what Lhota had said: no supporting evidence and certainly no larger explanation as to why Emil, and Lhota, had been in Central America.

He saw a particular pedestrian behind him whom he had seen a few minutes before, maybe had even seen earlier that morning at the cemetery or the airport or somewhere in between. It might be a coincidence, but the possibility of being followed was enough to send him away from the inn and across the bridge toward the Old Town, hoping to lose this pursuer.

He crossed the bridge fast enough to make himself breathe raggedly. He slowed, wondering who else might be watching. With an occasional backward glance, he browsed for a minute in front of the Tuzex foreign currency store, where the post-Communist state still sold Bohemian crystal and fine linens. In the window's reflection he watched the spotty flow of people behind him and across the street.

Now a kind of physical paralysis was seeping into his bones. He walked away from the Old Town Square, perpendicular to the unseen riverbank, debating whether to fade into an alleyway or a doorway, carrying out a textbook evasive maneuver. The sooty Gothic facades of the houses reached up on either side of him, each fairy-tale structure begrimed by industry's fallout. Robinson stopped for a moment to read a playbill advertising a festival of dissident Eastern European drama, to be held at the Palace of Culture.

There was definitely a man following him. He was not a Czech but an Arab, a slender young man with a mustache and a wispy goatee. He wore no raincoat, but rather a shiny blue suit complete with vest that fit too tightly. He was hanging a bit in the shadows like Robinson, furtive. He moved, seen in the shopwindow's reflection, as if he would approach Robinson.

Robinson didn't need this now. What was it—a setup preceding an arrest?

But then the man brushed on by him, to an obviously well-to-do West German couple dressed in matching vulgar brown leather jackets and thonged leather leggings. They had orange suntans, as if they had just come from a week in the Canary Islands. In an instant, Robinson surmised that the man was in search of a drug deal or a currency transaction. Astonishing: freedom had brought with it the ability of foreign drug dealers to enter and do their business here. Robinson continued on, down a side street. He tried to remain outwardly unchanged, but a feeling of relief made his legs, limbs, rubbery.

One or two days, and then he had best be getting out.

Around him, trudging up and down the cobblestoned streets, were the worn denim knees and long tangled hair of the 1960s, of hippiedom suspended in time. No blow-dried hair or gymnasium-inflated bodies here, but the waxen faces, the prophetic beards and heavy boots, of a forgotten time in this gentle country of humanists. In his disorientation, Robinson felt the most unexpected nostalgia for his college days, for the revolutionary tide he had never joined—he was a GI bill student—but which he had watched in silent envy. Here of all places, in this former police state, was a museum of that time.

A roar of motorcycles preceded the speeding passage of two black Mercedes sedans, probably en route from the Civic Forum headquarters toward the seat of government in Hradčany Castle. He remembered how exposed he was on the street, and he slipped into the first available beer cellar to collect his thoughts. One geriatric drunk was asleep on a bench, where he had obviously spent the night draped with a newspaper to ward off a chill. A heavy woman wearing a hair net and sagging flesh-colored hose brought Robinson his beer. He drank alone, watching the feet of pedestrians through the sidewalk-level cellar window.

He knew what he had to do, whom he had to seek out, but he let Dvořáček's warning keep him there, immobilized, for the rest of the morning. He sat there as the tavern filled with the luncheon crowd, dozens of well-dressed office workers flooding in, people in their twenties and thirties, people who a year ago had been Communist Party technocrats but were now learning the ways of capitalist finance and unemployment insurance.

Still, Robinson was uneasy, expecting to bump into somebody who knew him from Vienna, even a familiar face from the American Embassy who would wonder why he was there. So many things could go wrong.

The din increased, the lights were turned up. A once-empty room now rocked with competing choruses of laughter. He had to give up his corner seat to an expanding group; then he had to choose between joining another group of young Czechs or leaving. They looked at him uncertainly as he decided. He was getting too conspicuous. He bowed and departed, walking into the drizzling afternoon.

For a time he played tourist, crossing paths with a huge group of former East Germans wedded to a tour bus. They were loud and unruly, angry that the agreement to come on this vacation had been signed two years earlier, before the peaceful revolution, angry that the union fund didn't have enough to send them to Paris or Rome. Several of them were drinking from pocket flasks, and the Czech pedestrians were staying out of their way.

Finally, after lingering for a time at the Church of the Crusader, he entered the Klementinum, asking at a small courtyard for directions to the Archives. A street sweeper directed him farther on.

The Archives looked as they must have in the Hapsburg days, the Czech state not having spent one cent on furnishings since. Imperial mahogany had seen its original scarred finish replaced by the burnished grime of a million hands. Dust-covered Bohemian crystal chandeliers hung overhead. The main reading area contained a dozen long tables with hard-backed chairs, a forbidding central desk, and behind the desk, cavernous stacks where shadow figures moved, retrieving documents, newspapers, records. The Archives, long a comatose place, now held dozens of researchers trying to find the truths that had been buried for so long. The desk was controlled by a fiftyish man in spectacles, bald, with a hairless yellow complexion. He refused to make eye contact with anyone, lifting his eyes from his tasks only when he could not avoid the whined appeals any longer. Requests for documents were filled out, presented to the deskman, approved, dispatched to the stacks. Robinson searched each face, each shadow, in the stacks, for the person he had never met but whom he had controlled from afar.

Of course he had seen her photo. But that was so long ago. He was looking for the woman placed in this job by Lhota a full sixteen years before, when Miroslav Lhota had never dreamed he would someday defect. A person who had become part of uncle Lhota's and then nephew "Jiří" 's network.

To justify his presence a few minutes longer, Robinson pretended to read a lengthy instruction document about the Archives, which hung from a chain attached to the wall. Closing time was only fifteen minutes away. He intently studied a fortyish woman who came from the ladies' room and took up her position at the desk. She was squat, short, with strings of reddish hair hanging down on either side of rouged cheeks.

Could it be she? Could she have changed so much? He halfheartedly wondered if he should approach the woman.

And then he saw "Libuše," his salvation, appear out of the darkness. She was a woman close to his own age, dressed in faded denim jeans and matching jacket. She was still slim, perhaps too much so, with dark-blond hair brushed back behind her ears. As she stepped out from behind the desk to deliver a requested book to a seated matron, he saw that she was wearing high-heeled black boots out of style in the West ten years ago but now revived by the kitsch dressers of New York and London.

Although she was leaner than his ideal, she moved gracefully. The old jeans had become molded to her form, and he could see a swell to her calves. She had been a dancer, he recalled, and perhaps still was.

Again he was reminded of his youth, and a flood of nostalgia came up, a memory of this network that had been his unseen family for two very intense years, carrying out his orders and risking exposure every day of their lives. With it came a memory of how he had been then . . . young, and without fear.

You aren't like the Dany I knew, Lhota said. *You're like the others now. Scared. Going by the book.*

He watched her but did not yet catch her eye, because it was too soon. He had no need of worrying she would recognize him, for she had never seen him, knowing only a disembodied entity named Jiri who communicated with her, fourth hand.

The Archives would close in ten minutes. Already searches in the stacks were coming to a halt, and many of the readers rose to leave. The bespectacled deskman initiated a clockwork routine of squaring up piles of the day's request cards, banging their edges on the desktop, binding them with rubber bands. Drawers opened and closed loudly. Books were summoned back to the all-powerful desk, for reshelving tomorrow.

"Five minutes," intoned the deskmaster.

Robinson went back outside, loitering in the empty courtyard. He busied himself reading a guidebook, while the last readers left. A final interval of five more minutes passed before the library employees also departed.

Libuše in denim broke his heart. She was walking with one of the stack workers, a chubby man, much younger than she. Robinson followed them discreetly, not toward the square from which he had entered but in the opposite direction.

A mismatch, he thought to himself. But book people are strange, like musicians. Then at the Staroměstská subway station entrance, dawn broke. With not so much as a kiss or a handclasp, the two librarians parted, and the woman entered the station while her friend headed on toward the Mánesův Most.

Robinson was madly trying to remember if she had had a husband when he was running her. Yes, he thought she had; in fact, he'd been a Party member, an opportunist rather than an ideologue, but a risk nonetheless. Libuše had been forced to run her whole game without her husband's knowledge.

Tickets, fares, coins Robinson had to deal with, and he didn't know the drill. The farewoman was dead asleep in her booth, while the people of Prague blew in and out of the concrete cave. It was modern and fairly classy, more modern than Vienna's. Daringly, he walked right through the entrance without putting in a fare ticket, following Libuše and two young Prague students who did the same thing. But of course, he thought: Ripping off the people's state was still commonplace.

Down the escalator he rode, with the salesgirls and destitute intellectuals of Prague. Faces from all the corners of the collapsing empire surrounded him too, on trade and exchange agreements that hadn't expired yet: Uzbek and Mongol technicians there for a training course; East Germans in their ersatz Adidas and down-filled parkas; Czech Army officers in olive-and-red dress uniforms, all oblivious of him.

Ten yards ahead of him, she was pushing onto an already engorged car. Impulsively he ran toward the filling car. He forced his way into the sardine mass just as the door closed.

"Pushy krauts," somebody muttered farther inside. He groped for access to a rail that would keep him from falling. A grandmother with a huge bag stood heavily and unmoving on his foot. And then the train pulled away. Dozens of other commuters pressed unsuccessfully at the closed doors. The wheels turned, and Robinson was being sucked away into the underground. The roar of the wheels on the track and the rush of air elated him, and he laughed out loud into the roar.

At Můstek, the first stop on the A Line, a few people struggled off, but another impossible boarding crush followed. Robinson continued with the woman to the next stop at Muzeum. There they tranferred to the B Line headed south out of the city toward the terminus at Cosmonautů. He passed two stops with names of historical resonance: I. P. Pavlova and Gottwaldova, named for the first Communist prime minister, and soon to be renamed. After Pražského Povstání, she exited at Mládežnická.

He trailed her by ten yards up the escalator. When they emerged, the misting sky was fading into achromatic dusk. Several boxy towers loomed over an expanse of concrete and dead lawn. The Hotel Panorama was in the distance about a quarter of a mile away, while the circular Tuzex building stood nearer. Dozens of people were pouring inside it, including the librarian. He stopped short, staying outside to gaze in through the shopwindows. People were queuing up to make payday purchases of tape players, transistor radios, cassettes, and cameras. The prosperity was something of a surprise, just like the dress of the crowd. The hippies of downtown were not visible here; instead, down-filled parkas and running shoes, corduroy pants and new sport shirts, shot by. Try as he could, Robinson could put no finger on a difference between the faces and clothes here and ones he might see on the other side of the line, save an indefinable sharpness, an Eastern edge.

Robinson took a moment in the shadows to gather his thoughts. Mongolians trooped by, headed for the Panorama, followed by Russian women carrying great shopping bags. A pair of Aeroflot liners were making their approach to the airport, flying down the valley of the Vltava. In the near distance, old Prague was already shimmering like a jeweled canyon. The lights of Hradčany had come up, and the ancient castle shone with a brightness that would have warmed the hearts of the first Libuše and her peasant king, Přemysl: A great city they decreed from their heights, Praha: the Threshold City it would be, renowned throughout the world.

She emerged from Tuzex carrying a plastic bag, heading back toward the subway station. Beyond it, towers of new apartment blocks and their illuminated windows were a thousand tiny stages. It was part of the Pankrác housing estate. Aside from a total absence of flair, it might have been any of the high-rises slapped up around the perimeter of Washington since the 1950s.

Abruptly she looked back at him; he almost spoke, but held back. They passed the first row of buildings and approached the second.

"Excuse me," he finally called, loudly. She stopped and faced him, hearing his accent come through.

"I'm trying to find my way back to the old city," he said. "I seem to have lost my way."

She seemed skeptical of that.

"Do you have a car?" she asked. Apparently she had not noticed him on the train.

"No. I came out on the subway."

"You just walked past the station," she said. "Back there, across the highway . . . did you not see it?"

"No," he said.

He was quickly sizing her up. She had no wedding band. Her blond face was structured by fragile pointed cheekbones. She was blue-eyed and wore bluer eye shadow, with a fine lacework of wrinkles at the corners of her eyes. She was more attractive than he had realized. Despite her age she had a gaminish look.

"Would you like for me to show you the way back?"

"You have to forgive me," he said. "I don't mean to make trouble for you."

"German?" she asked.

"No," he lied, gambling. "English."

She nodded, surprised. "You speak good Czech; for a minute I wondered if you were one of us."

He was dying to ask a few questions that would tell him for sure, but he was still uncertain. Not of who she was, but of what she might have become. They were now approaching the thoroughfare, beyond which was the subway station, totally conspicuous and impossible to miss.

"There is your stop," she said. "Where in town are you going?"

"To Malá Strana."

"It is quite simple," she said. "Take the train to Muzeum. Transfer there. Two stops to Malostranská."

"You have been so kind," he said, in a frenzy.

She began to walk back into the huge complex. Cars were roaring up and down the road with the energy of the gathering Friday night. In new Prague white light shone everywhere, giving all an icy look; none of the multicolored hues of capitalism yet. White street lights, window lights, utilitarian signs. Old Prague was a distant enclave of castles and cathedrals, with Hradčany standing above all.

"Wait!" he shouted, when she had gone halfway back. "Wait!" he shouted, to make himself heard over the traffic. She turned, alone on that concrete sidewalk, a damp night wind blowing around her. She stood there puzzled. He walked, half ran, to where she stood.

"You must forgive me," he said. "I was not entirely honest with you." She wasn't smiling, not knowing what to expect.

"I have another interest," he said hoarsely. "The Přemyslide dynasty. I've done some research."

Her face was changing, a combination of astonishment and something else; he guessed pain.

"The matriarch or the patriarch?" she managed to ask.

"The matriarch," he said. "Libuše."

The cars roared behind him. A string of airliners were strung out to the east, awaiting landing clearance.

"Could I ask you to join me for dinner this evening?" he said. The noise of the aircraft was harsh and metallic overhead.

She paused a second and looked down at the ground. He thought she was going to say no.

She wore a light-colored lipstick that dated back to the 1960s. The floodlights were making her too pale, her cheeks too hollow. But he could see why Lhota had been taken with her years before, when she was still a student and Lhota already middle-aged.

"Shall we go?" he asked.

She looked at him, then shook her head.

"It is best we go to my place," she said.

They walked together back down the canyon of gray ice cliffs to where she lived. They entered her building, passing an older woman wearing an apron, seated at a table by the elevator. Simona nodded to her, and the woman beamed back.

On the way up, in the scuffed tiny elevator, Simona was able to smile.

"She thought you were my long-lost husband," she said.

They rode up together in the elevator—a scarred metallic enclosure of crude construction with a door that did not open automatically, which stopped a good six inches above or below each floor. They got off at the fifteenth floor, walking out into a windowless, dank, and grubby hallway. Either a vent was open to the outside or the hall was unheated. As they passed each door, Robinson could hear the domestic scenes of night Prague being acted out: a television blaring the news, two young girls taunting each other about a bottle of grape juice, a woman carping at her husband about his failure to pick up cheese on the way home. Babies cried, dogs barked, the hallway stank with the captive odors of a hard life. A door opened and a blond man in a sleeveless undershirt started out, then saw them approaching and withdrew.

"Hope you don't find it cold," she said. "Heat doesn't come on until seven."

Her apartment consisted of one modest room with an alcove kitchen and a recess with a small bed. She had a closet and a bathroom equipped with toilet and metal shower. The sink and mirror were in the kitchen.

"Cold air is healthier," he said.

The wall was hung with one Jan Rusek's diplomas from Karlova Universita, and pictures of Simona and a man, presumably Jan, together in student days, when her face was fuller and her hair more lustrous. Frames held several playbills from 1968, as abstract as the ones he had seen on the street, but these advertised Czech productions of Miller, Handke, Čapek. Simona's degree in library science was also displayed.

Simona had a television, two lumpy old armchairs and a small couch, and a hooked rug only partly covering the linoleum floor.

"You're lucky to have your own place," he said.

"I am fortunate," she replied. She was looking into the half-sized refrigerator.

"I have two beers left," she said from inside the fridge.

"Beer is fine," he said.

Simona Rusková, read her diploma, Bachelor in Archival Sciences, 1974.

"Where's your husband?"

"My ex-husband is with the U.N. in New York now," she said. "Quite honestly I've been too busy to clean out his things."

Robinson saw from the photos that Jan had one of those cutter-sharp Czech faces—pointed nose and chin, piercing eyes. Maybe the face of an artist, or a zealot. A cabinet door closed, and Simona put a slab of cheese on a plate.

Robinson saw drama texts interspersed on the single bookshelf with *Systems of Distribution in a Socialist Economy* and *A Basic Revolutionary Economic Primer.* He saw García Lorca, Albee, Chekhov.

"Are you the secret dramatist?" he asked.

"Those were Jan's," Simona said. "He started at the Universita wanting to be an actor. Then came the invasion, and he saw what was happening. He changed his specialization to economics."

. . . Spring blossomed into summer, summer into fall, fall into a winter of frost and wind. Spring was ecstatic liberation, summer sprouted the first doubts like fungus and toadstools, fall brought disintegration, winter an imprisonment of the soul. People walked through the streets with clouds of frigid vapor billowing from their mouths, but they said little, as though they were blowing phantom ideas, words, heresies, into the air. It grew ever more

silent in that winter. With freedom and hope gone, the tanks stood in their place for a time, and then even they slipped away. Desperate acts of rebellion became fewer, and then they ceased altogether. . . .

"Here we go," she said. "Our best Plzeň beer and some cheese from Moravia. Even have some Moravian wine, if you would like."

"Excellent," he said.

She pulled open the curtains to reveal the Threshold City, the city decreed by Libuše and Přemysl. Hradčany shone above it all. Even seen through the single soiled pane, the place was otherworldly.

"Music?" she asked.

"Of course," he said. Out of the tiny portable tape player came some Scandinavian rock she'd just bought that night.

He knew the air was poisonous: he had read of the acid rain and the trees dying in Bohemia, the dying lakes; but above the city tonight the wet hazy sky was luminous, like the aurora borealis.

She was standing next to him as they looked out over the electric city. At the foot of the Petřín People's Observatory stood the illuminated Strahov Stadium, where the Spartakiade Communist sports festivals had been held since 1955, vast totalitarian displays of physical culture and regimentation, huge faces of Party leaders formed by thousands of red and white cards held by high school kids, titanic faces of forgotten Marx and Lenin and the now-fallen dictators.

"Prague the magnificent," he said.

"Yes. When I was a young girl and we would come to Praha, it was like going to . . . Paris, I guess. Although I have never been to Paris. It must be quite beautiful, isn't it?"

"Yes," he said evenly, never having been one of the millions who worship the City of Light.

The cassette ended prematurely, and for an interval there was no sound but the humming of the refrigerator, the dampened noises of the apartment building coming through the walls.

"Why have you come?" she asked.

She turned on the television, replaying the ceremony of departure of the Soviet troops months before, as helium balloons went up into the sky and a line of Soviet troop carriers rolled off toward the east.

"Because Uncle is dead," he said. "There were things he was searching for, things he wished to retrieve. I've come to see if you can help me find them."

That was all he said, all he could say. She had changed the

television channel, to an interlude of Slovak folk dancing, complete with apocalyptic mountain horns and flashing black boots, peasant girls and Carpathian athletes, the particular styles of this little forgotten bit of humanity. She took what he said and considered it, and he guessed that she found its power limited, small and lost in the sweep of greater events, distances, time. She looked out the window, out into the mist and rain, as if she were looking back, back on a day that was best not remembered, for that is often the experience in these lands, as with people everywhere who have suffered trauma—push it away, bury it; look forward, not back, for back is the way of pain.

They decided to make a meal from the wine, cheese, and bread she had in the apartment. And gradually his hope that she would shed light on this mystery faded, beneath the reality that the pieces of evidence—if they did indeed exist—were few and scattered across the globe.

"Yes, I was the source who provided Dvořáček with Dr. Michalský's journal," she confirmed. She had known Michalský's name from Dvořáček's search for the truth about Emil, done a decade and a half earlier.

"I stumbled upon the journal back in the spring last year. It was when the people were growing impatient with the interim government. They had a rally in Wenceslas Square all afternoon, charging the Communists with trying to cover up their crimes of forty years. They began chanting to open up the Party records to the public. We were tipped off, and the Chief Archivist put us all to work trying to get the most sensitive material to another storage area. It was the first time most of us had ever been into the inner sanctum.

"It was then," she said, "I came upon the material. Although I had immediately deduced that the documents, kept in a special Terezín section and long sealed to all but the Chief Archivist and emissaries of the Central Committee, were relevant to Dvořáček's search, I hadn't been able to interpret them. Dr. Michalský's journal was in Slovak, which I read at a basic level but did not have time to translate. And the photographs I found had been altered, casting doubt on their value.

"Although I guessed instantly this was the journal Dvořáček had wanted years ago, I had very little time to evaluate what I'd found," she said, "being most concerned with getting the Terezín discovery to a hiding place from which I could retrieve it later." Not only was she concerned the demonstrators might inadvertently find the material or destroy it; she did not trust the Chief Archivist, trained at Moscow University and a Russophile of the worst degree. She feared he too might destroy them.

"What do you remember about the journal?" Robinson asked.

"Oh, a moldy leather binding, as I recall. Water spots, cracking paper. It seemed to cover his life, from long before the war to the end—his death, I suppose—at the camp in 1943 or so. It was written in longhand and was several hundred pages long, in a difficult-to-read ink script. The pages themselves were brittle, not having been sealed properly."

"What about some Soviet Army documents, about Emil's legal status when the camp was liberated?"

"Documents?"

"Dvořáček said you had documents."

"What I had was a letter, presumably by an anonymous Russian. The letter said Emil was suspected of being a Fascist collaborator, but because he had been a Communist, there was to have been a political hearing. But the NKGB—Beria—intervened, saying Emil was of great value to the Revolution, because of some knowledge he had. Emil was turned over to the NKGB and sent to Moscow. All proceedings against him were dropped. The writer of this letter had smuggled the journal to the Czech Communist Party, saying they should know the truth about Emil Užhok, should he reappear someday."

"Do you think Emil went to work for the NKGB?"

"How should I know that?"

"Because he turned up working in some capacity for the Russians at Hostivař in the 1960s."

"Hostivař," she repeated, curious. "He must have been valuable to them."

She looked at Robinson.

"I thought Hostivař was some kind of defense research center," she said. "What could he have done there?"

"I was hoping you could tell me," he said.

She shrugged.

"How about the photos?" he asked.

"Taken at Terezín camp. Most were SS inventory photos, of camp buildings and the environs, but several included inmates. The one that most interested me had been taken by the SS Records Unit in 1942; this was stamped on the back of the print. It was of two men posed before a barracks, in prison uniform. One was old and bearded, the other quite young, of student age. They were identified on the back as Dr. Radan Michalský and Emil Užhok. A third name was obliterated. I thought a third man had been in the original photo, but it had long ago been torn, so that only the two prisoners showed.

"It was just by accident that I discovered, taped inside the journal, an envelope of photo negatives. Quickly rifling them," she added, "I saw they duplicated the old SS prints, including the torn one. You have to understand I was rushed, the light was terrible down there, everyone was in a panic. But I confirmed that the torn photo of the two inmates did originally contain a third man, who appeared to be a guard or officer of the camp. Then I saw that the remaining bulk of the negatives were not photos at all but a microfilm of Dr. Michalský's journal.

"I had to make a quick decision," she said, "knowing it might be months before I would be able to smuggle the actual journal and photos outside of the building without arousing the suspicions of the Chief Archivist and the guard staff. I resolved to take out the microfilm and negatives right then, inside my boot." This she did in the confusion of the afternoon before the mob assault. From her the material went to Václav Dvořáček, to be included in the Lhota family Bible and articles, which were then sent by a network she did not know to the West.

"Is it possible this journal was a manufacture . . . a forgery created by some individual or faction?" he asked.

"Possibly," she said, "considering it had been seen by so few and had been so mysteriously concealed for forty-five years. But based on my own observations, it seemed to be as old as it claimed."

"How long have you known Václav Dvořáček?"

"Since I was hired at the Archives."

"How did you meet him?"

"He was part of Miroslav's network."

"Do you trust him?"

She paused a minute, a quizzical look on her face.

"I took him on faith," she finally said, "as I took everybody. Miroslav was our patron. I've never had reason to doubt either him or Václav."

"Do you think this quest was anything more than Lhota's personal obsession with Emil Užhok?"

"Anything is possible," she said. "But I had no reason to think otherwise."

"Do you know the meaning of 'Veil / the face of God'?"

Her face was blank. "I have no idea."

In frustration he drank, and that was on top of the morning dose of Equanil, so by late in the evening he was close to drunkenness and a sinister euphoria. He was half hoping she would invite him to stay the night; but whatever possibilities had existed in that area were now long dead, killed by his identity and questions and the pall of gloom over the whole Lhota affair.

He bade her good night and took a cab into the old city, to his Inn of the Wandering Boar. It was a windless damp night, somewhere between winter and spring, a feeling not far from balminess. The sheen of mist lay on the cobblestones and further blackened the dark stone of the city, each winding street stretching away to its disappearance in the inevitable curve like a tributary in a river. Robinson took a minute to speculate on how architecture can affect the human mind, feeling magic and conspiracy emanate from those same stones. He was well into that thought when, as he came through the inn's door, he very nearly collided with the State Department desk officer for Czechoslovakia, Bob Yamamoto, who was departing from a drinking session with a group of Czech journalists.

"Hi, Dan," said Yamamoto reflexively, slightly drunk. Robinson charged ahead, acting as if he hadn't heard. Mercifully Yamamoto let him go, perhaps wondering if he'd blown a covert mission. He and his group went out onto the street.

The desk clerk had seen this strange encounter; Robinson was sure of it. Once in his room, he cursed and pounded his fist against the stucco wall. Then he called Lufthansa to get his flight changed to the first one out; he knew no State Department people would be on Lufthansa now that Pan Am was flying in. The weary ticket agent said she would put him on standby for an early-afternoon flight to Frankfurt.

Then he called the desk clerk to see if Mr. Yamamoto was registered there. Yes, he was, but he was out at the moment; would Mr. Richardson like to leave a message? No, he would not.

Then Robinson downed another Equanil, which together with the wine produced a slow nauseating spin in his head and gut. If he closed his eyes, the swirl would become a maelstrom and he'd be sick. So he sat in the dark, eyes open, for an interminable time, devastated over the realization that too soon he would be up and on a plane out of here, so many questions unanswered. He tried to formulate some kind of scenario for dealing with Yamamoto, some way to ensure that he wouldn't mention this bizarre sighting to anyone, but a sea of panic kept washing him away from any hope of a solution. Hours went by. He focused his eyes on the rain-streaked window, descending rivulets of shimmering beads lit by street lights and far windows, and on the shifting, melting outlines of the city itself. Midnight came and went, and still he was forced to stay awake. Sometime afterward, sleep descended, in a black wall, and he fell into a violent seething pit just below the surface of wakefulness.

He dreamed.

He dreamed that he and Simona were preparing to make love. He watched her as she unzipped those ancient tight denim jeans and pulled them down to the floor. But then it was not Simona but Leah, his Washington girlfriend, bathed in moonlight and ready to climb into bed with him, her dark-blond hair flowing in the moonlight, her arms and the marble curve of her thighs welcoming him in.

He kissed Leah as he had never kissed anyone, in that intensity of arousal possible only in the dreamworld, the latent ecstasy of his first adolescent kisses recaptured. The sheer touch of his lips against hers brought him to a state of pleasure in physical love he had not known in waking life for many years. It was euphoric and primal, and he felt it in his heart.

He and Leah had a baby right there during their lovemaking. The baby was Shannon, born talking and fully clothed. Leah slowly metamorphized into his wife, Jackie, spouting Czech obscenities. Their Virginia tract house had been transported to a windswept hillside in the Tatry, and it was not a fake Cape Cod but the worst redneck trailer imaginable, exuding an odor of evil heightened by the presence of his mother, who now stood on the edge of the forest and motioned him along.

Look here, his mother said, and although he did not want to, he followed her. Shannon was lost in the trees—he could hear her crying somewhere for help, and it tore at his heart that he couldn't find her—but he was transfixed by the open grave that his mother had led him to.

There, dried by summer heat and frozen by winter cold, was the body of Miroslav Lhota, reaching out to him.

Veil, Lhota called from out of the ground. *The face of God.*

Robinson awoke to find himself sitting upright in a tiny room in the Inn of the Wandering Boar in the old part of Prague that had grown up at the foot of Hradčany Castle, grandest in all the world. A feeling of dread permeated his very skin, and it took minutes before his eyes stopped their mad search of the room's shadows for the figures of his nightmare. It was getting on toward dawn before he slept again, the approach of day marked by the quickening of steps on the cobblestones outside and the nearby rumbling of showering and packing and departure audible in other rooms. His last thought before falling asleep was that he would never fall asleep as long as he lived.

It was nearly noon when he woke up, startled to find the maid shaking him, telling him he would miss his plane.

He bolted upright, incredulous. His battery travel alarm had apparently bleated itself into deadness, and the clock itself had stopped running hours ago. This was the latest he had slept in memory. As the maid stood in the hall twirling her feather duster and waiting for his departure, he stumbled about in a fog, dressing himself, calling down for an airport cab.

The inn checkout was slow and disorganized, with confusion about credit cards and traveler's checks, a different room rate than he had been promised, elaborate handwritten corrections on his bill. As an afterthought, the clerk turned over a parcel from a morning visitor who had asked that Mr. Robinson not be awakened on her account. All the while, Robinson was expecting Bob Yamamoto to appear out of nowhere and greet him again.

The taxi was ready to go.

Robinson quickly looked inside the parcel's wrapping; it was a Czech edition of bibliographical references on the Přemyslide dynastic succession, autographed on the overleaf with an *L* . . . presumably for Libuše. He stuffed it in a side pocket of his bag.

The sun was coming out now, burnishing this landscape with a glistening umber, but towering dark clouds stood stacked over the hills, promising more rain. The airport routine was frenzied, because he was close to missing his flight; before he knew it he was in the security line, being sped along, his camera here, his bag there, pairs of hands and eyes quickly scrutinizing. All quite friendly, searchers and questioners dressed in civilian rather than military garb, jokes and quick movement, we're so sorry but you know, wink wink, out of our control.

As he was headed for the door and freedom, one of the security men, teeth dark from tobacco, tapped him on the shoulder. Robinson very nearly lost his breath.

"Is this yours?" the man asked, and winked. In his hand he held a torn portion of a photo. Robinson was dumbstruck, ready to deny, to play dumb, to lie. He literally could not speak.

"Hurry," said the man, giving him a friendly push. "You will miss your plane."

Holding the photo in his hand, Robinson stumbled out across the wet black runway, the engines of the aircraft in high whine, the Lufthansa stewardess waiting expectantly at the bottom of the mobile stairway.

In those final yards, he was neither here nor there, on the verge, already feeling suspended above earth by a few feet. In his rather emotional leavetaking, as he went up the aircraft stairway, he turned to look back again at the airport he had so often studied in photographs, analyzing arrival ceremonies, pecking order, personages once prominent and now in obscurity. As an afterthought he glanced up at the railed rooftop deck, which had for so long been closed off to spectators and now had been reopened to allow families one last wave and goodbye to their departing members, or a first welcome back to the prison now being swung wide open. And it was there he saw another familiar face, from the day before; a dark goateed figure in a tight blue suit, a lithe Arab man who'd followed him through the streets of downtown and then faded away; now he was up there, watching Robinson depart.

After exchanging glances with Robinson, the Arab turned and slowly walked inside. When he was gone from view, it was as if he'd never been there. Robinson was so dazed by the whole departure that it was not until they were roaring down the runway, lifting off over the canyons and brown fir forests of Bohemia, that he realized the photographic fragment he held in his hand was the one Simona had spoken of, the photo taken in 1942 at Terezín, showing Dr. Michalský and Emil Užhok, duly identified on the back.

Only when he concluded from the open suitcase pocket that during the security search the photo had fallen out of the Přemyslide book left by Simona, and was not a gift from Czech airport security, did he begin to calm a bit. "I found this little something that Uncle's family once treasured," read Simona's note.

The winter-green hills of Bohemia spread beneath them.

The aged look of the tear suggested the photo had been ripped apart years, perhaps decades, ago. And yes, he could see why Simona would think another man had been present; a stranger's arm and hand stretched over into the photo, onto the shoulder of the biblical Dr. Michalský, Jew, Czech Communist founding father, and camp inmate.

As Robinson roared out over the expanse of the Oberpfalzer Wald, over the Franconian Jura, this family photo seemed almost disappointing, an insignificant little memory tumbling out of Europe's closet. But he had no choice but to face up to it, because not five decades—a wink of the eye, an *Augenblick*—separated him from that time.

And in the case of Lhota, he was learning, even this curious old memory could be reason to kill.

Prague, 1926

Ah, Praha . . . nestled in a river's curve. City of philosophers! Mother to wizards and theurgists!

While I never formally "renounced" my theories of radical political psychiatry, I did cease voicing them. And to protect my growing private practice in Prague, I was not open about my Communist affiliation either. So it was that much of the high society of Prague came to me, to pour out their inner torments. My previous years of treating indigents in Vienna, motivated both by the terms of my internship and by my own sympathies for the downtrodden, were followed by these years of compromise and accommodation, during which time I saw hardly any indigents at all.

As father confessor to the most rich and powerful of Prague, I was placed in a curious position. For the first time in my life I had an entrée into respectability and high society. Yet concurrently, because of the nature of my profession and the still-lingering reputation of hocus-pocus or, worse yet, forbidden sexuality which surrounded psycho-analysis, I was relegated to a special role. If anything, I was for the grand dames of Prague a pet, like a popular artist or actor invited to their gatherings to give flair and a hint of danger but never admitted to their inner circle by marriage or full social acceptance. I enjoyed the salacious intimacy of the trusted subordinate, like the hairdressers and seamstresses to whom the Hapsburg princesses turned with their gossip but who for reasons of class and profession were still a breed apart.

That time was curious, and exciting for me. The flowering of the infant republic of Czecho-Slovakia, that new nation born out of the friendship of Woodrow Wilson and Tomáš Masaryk, was at its height. To be sure, I was a native-born Slovak and wary of these new Czech partners who had replaced the Austrians; but nevertheless

I was infected by the Czech effervescence, their testing of the limits. It was a gay time, intensified by economic boom, when the foundries and machine shops of Moravia-Bohemia did what they knew best, turning out railroad wagons and iron ingots and motorcars; it was embellished by a creative awakening, when drama and debate were on a parallel with the most avant-garde in Berlin and Paris.

Among my acquaintances at that time I counted the more flamboyant and unconventional sectors of Prague high society, including the Jewish princes of commerce and industry, politicians of all stripes, including the left, and artists, writers, poets, and others of artistic bent. The Jews came to me because they considered me a brother, albeit lapsed, the others because my profession was suddenly in vogue and the thing to do. And so I heard the dark confessions of many, confessions that were testimony to the painful and mysterious journey of life and growth, each one highlighting the psychological pitfalls, dead ends, and detours that beckon to all of us as we make the migration from birth to that fragile state called adulthood.

I realized that my profession was giving me an ever more tragic view of humankind. How ironic to come to this realization at such a bubbling time of hope and discovery, of artistic and national rebirth. Consider: There was a certain Czech deputy of the Social Democratic Party, now long dead and forgotten but then of some interest, particularly to representatives of foreign powers who felt he had a future and could play a role in swinging little Czecho-Slovakia into one camp or another. This gentleman, though originally of the left, had like his colleagues of the Socialist International resolutely spurned the friendships of the Communists and the representatives of the reborn Soviet Union, which had opened a legation in Prague soon after the October Revolution.

This gentleman also had a scandalous secret, confided only to me and perhaps to one or two other persons in all the world. Though married and a father, he was a secret sexual invert. Such personalities I encountered periodically in my profession, and there was nothing sadder than seeing someone of status teeter on the verge of exposure. There was a Sophoclean dichotomy between the rise of these individuals in career and status and, at the same time, the ever-greater risk they ran of being ruined. This gentleman was headed down that road and so had come to me in the hope I could hypnotize him out of the longings he so strongly felt. This poor man had never actually committed a single perverse act, but his yearnings on several recent occasions, including a conversation with a servant youth that had nearly led to seduction, confirmed to him that his long-buried fantasy life would soon burst out into the light of day.

I had read various studies on attempts at sexual reorientation, and although a handful of people claimed success, most notably De la Rue (1908) and Pfluger (1915), I was skeptical. In my opinion, these sexual fixations were so deeply rooted in the earliest infantile experiences, possibly even in prenatal influence, that no subsequent manipulation such as hypnotism could have lasting effect.

"But, *Doktor*," this poor fellow implored, "I have no other recourse. Otherwise I feel myself being swept away on a tide of licentiousness and depravity."

So I went against my own instincts and subjected him to hypnotic suggestion over a three-month period, knowing in my heart it would not work. But he was desperate. In the process, I was forced to listen to his hypnotic recitations of all sorts of detailed fantasy. I did see how he was in the grip of this fixation, and though I was repelled, as a fellow human being my heart went out to him.

During that period, I found myself at a reception in honor of the new chief librarian at Karlova Universita. I was approached by an acquaintance of mine from the Soviet Legation, an attaché of vague portfolio named Rodion. He seemed to have some interest in cultural and educational affairs, for it was at such gatherings that we would cross paths. Obviously he knew of my Party affiliation, for he would talk to me in knowing tones, but he never said anything that would incriminate me with another listener. My surprise at his knowledge of my private affiliation quickly gave way to encouraging winks and nods on my part, so bored and uncomfortable was I in my role of dormant member; in fact, I was so far underground that I felt myself dead and buried to the Revolution.

You see, dear reader, my Czech party comrades, surprised at the ease with which psycho-analysis was winning converts at the highest level of society, had quickly consigned me to a role of serving the Revolution by becoming a successful psychiatrist. Though I resisted mightily, wanting a more active, open role, they gave me no choice. The Central Committee, a committee of equals, many newer to the struggle than I, voted against my appeals. As our theoretician said, Radan Michalský was not a laborer, not an organizer, not a trade unionist, and not a rabble-rouser. He was a psycho-analyst, a doctor, and a scholar.

That was the root of my dissatisfaction with the Czech Party in those days. I still burned with revolutionary zeal, and becoming a successful professional seemed the way of cowardice. But no matter; once the assignment was made, I had only infrequent contact with my comrades, so my dissatisfaction stewed within. At times, I thought they had forgotten me altogether. After one stretch of nearly two years without any message at all, I assumed the Party had disbanded. But no, it still existed. And to my continuing disappointment, it seemed they had nothing for me to do.

This weighed heavy on my mind when Rodion appeared before me at the reception.

"Happy New Year," he said to me in Czech, and I accepted his toast of raised slivovitz. We both commented on the singular wealth of attractive young women at this event, although each one seemed without exception to be paired with a paunchy older male escort.

"You know why young girls go with old men?" Rodion said to me in the guttural tone that told me a ribald answer was to follow. I did not know the answer.

"Because they have thicker . . ." He paused a minute to take a shot of slivovitz and to prolong the suspense.

". . . wallets," he concluded. "But young women inspire greatness, even in old men. Remember what Pushkin said: The greatest poetry is written with white ink."

Rodion's semi-inebriated joke had been overheard by one of the grand dames of Czech society, and she gasped as only persons of her status and demeanor could, walking away and fanning herself.

We stood a moment, watching her recede from view.

"I hear," Rodion said softly, "you are treating a certain Social Democrat."

I immediately turned to look at him. I wanted to know how he had found this out.

"I have my sources," he said, smiling. "This man can be of real use to the Revolution. If he would only let himself be."

I sipped my slivovitz, wondering whether my medical oaths required that I end the conversation. But I was torn. I was so overjoyed to be talking with a fellow Communist after all these years.

"He was a correct thinker a few years ago," mused Rodion. "Then he seemed to have turned his back on the workers, to curry favor with the oligarchs."

Though crudely put, this was essentially what had happened with the man in question. His youthful ire at the monarchy had been tempered by pragmatism.

"Of late, he has also turned his back on the motherland of socialism and is kowtowing to France."

The new Chief Librarian tottered by. I thought to myself he would not live another five years.

"I couldn't care less what he pursues with the Czech workers," said Rodion. "But why is he so unfriendly to his Soviet brothers?"

I could not answer. But everyone knew that the bourgeois democrats of Czecho-Slovakia, while publicly trying to balance themselves between France and Russia, secretly yearned for Paris and not Moscow.

"Dr. Michalský. We would simply like our old friend to give us an equal hearing."

I did not respond. The whole conversation was disturbing me. The Chief Librarian had spilled slivovitz down his aging chin and onto his academic robes, and three secretaries were clucking over him, dabbing with napkins.

"What is his secret? What has he confessed to you?"

Clearly the Chief Librarian was inebriated. A protective screen of people assembled around him, and he was being assisted to a chair.

"For the good of the Revolution, we must know."

And so at last it came clear: after languishing for years, I was at last being called to mission by my comrades. What cruel irony that it should be this kind of mission, one that would compel me to the betrayal of confidence and a violation of my Hippocratic oath.

I hesitated, saying the matter was a complicated one, involving the sanctity of certain professional oaths.

"What is more sacred than the call of the Party?" Rodion asked, now bemused and suspicious. I had no good answer for that one, for it would lead down the primrose path of renegadism or insubordination, and I would be a marked man. I mumbled, begging my leave, saying I would be back in contact shortly, and thinking I had won at least a reprieve. Instead, I would later learn, I had planted doubts in the worst quarter, which would come back to haunt me later.

Nodding in farewell to Rodion, I took myself back to my study, where I pondered this issue long and hard. What kind of revolutionary, what kind of Communist, was I to quiver and quail so when faced with my first real assignment of significance after ten years of bourgeois masquerade? For hours I cajoled myself, these two voices, the revolutionary and the medical doctor, shouting at each other in my skull. Only under the merciful dullness of alcohol did the revolutionary shout louder, and I decided to contact Rodion for a subsequent meeting.

But the next morning old Hippocrates beat in my skull with the righteous hammer of the hangover. I vowed to stand firm and not reveal the Social Democrat's secret. It was a stance that filled me with a noble pride. No matter that twenty-four hours earlier I had nearly gone the other way. This is what I had decided. And so I awaited the inevitable call of Rodion.

The strength of my moral stance was never tested, for the call never came. Instead came the astonishing news that the Social Democrat had ended his own life, mystifying all but me. From that news, read in the *Národni Politika*, I deduced that the poor gentleman, either on the verge of succumbing to his urge or immediately after having done so, had found the torment unendurable and ended it.

Looking back, I see that episode as a momentous development, a major turn in my life that determined all that followed. After that, there was no turning back. But at the time, it seemed only one of many competing distractions. Because in 1926 I was still a young man—I was forty-two years old—surrounded by the gaiety of Prague's second flowering. Each night it was either the theater, where we attended the latest works of the young Karel Čapek, or a symphony by Smetana or Dvořák, or a poetry reading or gallery opening. Or it might be a political or literary discussion until dawn in some starving thinker's garret, where I was welcomed as a curiosity. All these things were bubbling around me.

And most important, I was in love.

I, who thought I would be destined to spend my life a bachelor, was certain I had at last found my life mate. A fascinating woman, an ethereal soul placed only by some error of destiny within my humble sphere—this rare being had taken over my life and made all else seem secondary.

Her name was Loki Leventhal. Named by her globe-trotting father for the Norse trickster god, she was more than a decade my junior, but I knew upon meeting her that she must be mine.

Iconoclastic daughter of the fabled Leventhal family, the Jewish royalty of Czecho-Slovakia, she sprang from a lineage that controlled the destiny of thousands, through ownership of banks, coal mines, steel mills.

How I loved her; and all the more when I saw that the power of her family meant nothing to her.

She was attracted to me for being dangerous, a psycho-analyst, an older man with no social connections. It was her means of rebellion against the family that wished to absorb her, control her.

It was through her friendships with the avant-garde that I met Karel Čapek and his contemporaries. It was she who saw that I was invited to the salons and garrets of artistic Prague.

Loki—poet, painter, dancer, free spirit—had come to me for treatment. She was in the grips of a hysteria manifested in frigidity so intense it had ended her first and only attempt at marriage, bringing some scandal down upon the family. So bewitched was I by her flashing blue eyes, by her red hair pulled back in a dancer's bun or tumbling in wild ringlets around her face, I could hardly concentrate on her free associations as she lay on my couch.

She delighted in shocking her family, going out of her way to mock their aristocratic pretense. To her it was an embarrassment, backward thinking, an anachronism. She had mocked them by marrying a penniless Gentile, a young sculptor by the name of Čestmír Mikuláš.

"Čest'a would kiss me—oh, how he would labor over me," and she sighed, remembering. "He did love me, and I in my way loved him. But never did my flesh respond. It was like I was made of stone, and sometimes I even felt . . . a devilish satisfaction at watching him labor so, for nothing."

"That made you truly happy, to see him suffer?"

She pondered for a moment.

"In a way. It was like I derived some kind of . . . happiness by showing him how . . . how unreachable I was. I was in a prison, and I delighted when he could see how tightly shut it was."

Who could ever have imagined? I thought as I watched her wild curls tumble over the couch cushion. To the unknowing she seemed the true wanton, her hair and unconventional dress suggesting something of the Gypsy, her face the very epitome of bursting female sensuality.

"Tell me about your relationship with your father," I asked. Though the question for me was routine and mechanical, having been asked of hundreds of female clients over the years, the shift in subject for her was discomfiting. I could see her struggling to answer.

Her father was Egon Leventhal, an errant son, sportsman, and youthful widower, who had never gone into the family banking house but instead hunted and played tennis and chased women around Europe, assured of enough income to carry out his lifestyle.

"I really . . . have no feeling for him at all."

"No feeling? No love? No anger?"

She trembled slightly as she pondered.

"Once I left girlhood, I saw little of him. Also after Mama died and he was traveling so much. We grew distant."

"Your mother died when you were how old?"

"I was twelve."

"What caused her death?"

Loki shifted on the couch. I noticed a fine hint of perspiration on her brow and upper lip. Her hands were fidgeting.

"Her lungs filled with fluid and she died."

"She drowned?" I asked, perplexed.

"No. She had a condition . . . of the lungs. One night they filled so completely with fluid . . . that she suffocated."

Her beautiful features were contorted in a scowl, a grimace of remembering.

"And you loved her very much?"

Loki said nothing, placing her hands at her temples and rubbing.

"You loved your mother very much?" I repeated.

She was not answering; her hands were firmly at her temples, her eyes closed.

"Your father mourned your mother?" I asked.

She was breathing in evenly spaced pants. Her skin had gone ashen.

"*Slečna* Leventhal," I said. "Is something wrong?"

For a minute she was stone rigid. Then I noticed her lips moving, as if in recitation. It was late afternoon, the spring light slanting in through blooming ivy and laurel.

"*Slečna* Leventhal, can you hear me? Are you ill?"

As far as I could tell, she had plummeted into catatonic shock, triggered perhaps by some memory or some part of my question, or a word. My own adrenaline began to flow, as I wondered if I had injured this beautiful soul.

To my total amazement she rose from the chair and, despite my protests, ran quickly from the room and out of my office. I stood in the doorway calling to her to come back, until I thought I might arouse the neighbors; but she walked purposefully away.

Concerned about her whereabouts and well-being, I called for her at her home a half hour later. I was informed that she was ill and was receiving no visitors, but that she was under a doctor's care.

She had recovered enough by the following week to return to my office. I sensed that the crux of the problem lay with her father, but a frontal approach wouldn't work. So, with her consent, I utilized hypnosis to delve deeper.

I shall not bore you with a transcription of our hypnotic session, which stretched over a month. What I shall do is reproduce a poem that she wrote for me when the process was completed, in fact when she had left my care. I am no judge of its literary quality; however, it does capture her state of mind and the source of her withdrawal from men.

THE DREAM WINDOW

Vyslyš mne, ó můj Bože!
Yes, hear me, O my God!

High up in nightworld's castle,
Wrapped deep in feldspar nestle,
A sleeping mineral child reposed,
Her frozen crystal smile composed.
Beneath a slate-rock parapet,
Below a basalt battlement,
She slept with virgin angel's face,
Curled in geologic embrace.

She breathed her pure and sinless breath,
Her stony calm a mime of death.
But someone's roguish footstep sounded,
Echo of his touch rebounded,
Winding up the tower's way
To where the sleeping statue lay.
Uninvited from Hell's depths it came,
Climbing up, it called her name.

Serpent's sinuous night assault
Brought it up from buried vault.
Turning, twisting,
Beauty glistening,
Up it climbed,
Stopping, listening.
Soundlessly rising, seeking entry,
Ever wary of dormer sentry—
Only her door could stop its rise.
Intruder heard the sleeper's sighs.

What pulled her out of mindless sleep?
What broke the wall of castle keep?
A smell of breath,
A sense of heat,
She thrilled to feel him brush her feet,
Felt him kiss her forehead's cliff,
He spawned a life in blinding riff.
Sapphire eyes once locked in dream
Opened to see his own eyes' gleam.

She saw a hunter
Fresh from chase.
Outdoor life
had browned his face,
Drenched in quarry's dying spray,
Drunk with ending life that day.
Boar's thick gush,
Deer's thin rush—
All God's creatures falling prey,
This man had taken life away.

Now tonight he'd bring it back.
Through a girl's midnight attack.
So she swelled with heat of blood,
Tearing stone in heated flood.

His movements lit by pallid moon,
Necromantic bent in fiery swoon.
Two mouths exchanged air and mist
From clever lips to lips unkissed.

She knew the flesh's quickening race,
He rolled deep down in death's embrace.
She felt it rushing through her veins,
Passion's bloodhorse free of reins—
She lived the thrill a touch can bring,
The cresting wave of wakening.
Arrival of life's prime event
Shook her young world's fundament.

But no, the moment wasn't right.
This foul attack hid deep in night.
When she looked through her dream-window
No brilliant dawn world spread below.
Instead she saw how chill moonrise
Lit moths and bats, not butterflies.
She knew it was her true soul's-night,
A nightmare world wrapped in false light.

She wanted to fly oh, far away,
And so transform her night to day—
But held fast by necromance,
She had not a living chance.
His hand was there to hold her back,
His foul intent turned bed to rack.
She gave a captive's distant moan,
Now lost to touch and blood alone.

A dying rabbit in fox paws,
A newborn hind in panther jaws,
No more than girl on surgeon's table,
Victim of this nightmare fable.
Hunter's breath was smoking hot,
Icewhite teeth showed moonlight spot.
No, she breathed, sickly no,
Yet still he taught what she shouldn't know.

Dreamy eyes saw reptile flash,
She felt a wound by serpent's lash,
Touch of lover who kissed, caressed
But then became a beast possessed.
Drenched in hunter's garlic breath,

She lived her childhood's sudden death.
Final tremors took him away.
Hunter expiring like his prey.

But no journey onto death's black shore,
He fell instead to â heavy snore,
And she too drifted, afraid to stir,
Feeling breath sweep over her.
Only then that real dawn came,
Hurling light on midnight shame.
Sun could not lift her depression,
Showering light on death procession.

While captive to her dread emotion,
Sounds came up of servant's motion,
The clip of hooves on cobblestone,
Chip of chisel on gravestone,
Sobs of Věra, coughs of Bova,
Mourning wail of Hrabánková.
Below the rape that left her unsteady
Mama's cortege was making ready.

Still he slept, full spent from lust,
Nighthunt's blood now morning's rust.
She pushed at him to no avail:
Evil knight had found his grail.
Black, jet black his tangled hair
Ungrayed by age or workday care:
Still young this demon nightmare lover
Thief of what she'd never recover.

She gazed in pain upon his charms:
Mysterious chest and folded arms,
Hardened curves of hunter's rear,
Dark curls touching sculpted ear,
Black mustache, a face unlined,
Two hands heavy yet so refined,
Able to give the softest stroke
Or twining tight to make her choke.

She stroked her lover, stroked his mane,
Traced the course of arm's blue vein.
But out through window a shouting maid
Recalled her evil, made her afraid.
Even with sun now edging in—
It threw sharp glare on midnight sin:

Bright on rooftop, white on marsh,
Light burned her eyelids, raw and harsh.

Places that rest most times in dark,
Were hotly lit with dawn's rude mark.
Arrival of day made heart beat faster.
She had no choice but to rouse the master.
While Mama was lowered to her grave,
Another held child in sin's dark cave.
The loathsome truth no more ignored,
Her midnight raider was father and lord.

This poem provides a unique answer to my question about her relationship to her parents. My beautiful, my beloved Loki was in the grips of a curious psycho-sexual bond with her father, a direct effect of incest committed on her mother's burial day. And via this act Loki had in her own mind become an accomplice in her father's "murder" of her ailing mother. To my training, at least, nothing could have been more tailor-made to produce an aversion to men than this bizarre Oedipal alliance. The repressed memory, which was scuttling any possible relationship with a man, was a painful wound which through her art had been turned into the pearl within the oyster. I immediately began reading her published poems, finding now everywhere clues to her adolescent trauma. I found them much more useful than her own free association. Her poetic state seemed to serve as a numinous window on her roiling subconscious.

My fascinating reading and work with her, however, could not erase my growing realization that, first, there was little I would be able to do with this beautiful victim spread on my couch; and, second, that I was falling ever more powerfully in love with her.

After six months, I felt compelled to tell her.

It was an autumn afternoon, warmer than most, but you could tell the year was falling inexorably into winter. The leaves of Prague's parks and boulevards were ablaze, and many had begun to flutter earthward.

"Loki," I said at the end of our session, "I must give you some disturbing news. Regretfully, I must inform you that this is our last session together."

She looked shattered, totally stunned.

"Loki, there is a phenomenon in my profession that is essential to the process. It occurs when the intense psychological intimacy of the therapist and patient causes the patient to develop a deep emotion with roots in childhood, transferring that primordial emotion to the object at hand. And there is another phenomenon, which the therapist must forever guard against, for it can be most dangerous. . . ."

She looked at me, confused. She flushed, had difficulty breathing. It was clear I had hit another exposed nerve.

"Are you saying I am in love with you?" she blurted out, almost sobbing. Then, before I could say anything, she jumped up and ran from the room. I walked to the door to try and stop her, but she was gone again.

In the intervening week I had much time to ponder what had been said. Why had I even brought up the subject that way? I could have ended the sessions for some fabricated, obscure reason.

My God, I pondered; how unprofessional I had been. To be giving her what amounted to a confession of love and extorting her own oblique confession in return. I had probably traumatized the poor thing even further.

One evening the following month, when the breath of winter was really making itself felt, I was alone in my apartment, which at that time was in Malá Strana. Although spacious, it suffered a problem endemic to all such structures built in the Baroque era: lack of heat. The fire in my study fireplace seemed to create a narrow margin of warmth directly in front of the hearth, but the cold air it drew in from the outer reaches of the library and hallway made one even colder.

There was a knock at the outer door. It was nearly nine. Who could be calling? Someone from the Party?

I went downstairs in my dressing gown.

I opened the door to a blast of cold stormy air and to the sight of Loki, hair disheveled and flying in the wind, eyes wild, cheeks ashen.

"Loki," I breathed.

She pushed her way inside, then like a madwoman embraced me and drew me into what was surely the most urgent, imploring kiss of my lifetime, before or after.

It took my breath away.

We stood there in the cold foyer, kissing for an indeterminate time. Her kiss was frantic, frenzied, and for the moment the bold onslaught of her passion put me off slightly.

She smelled so young, so fresh to me, her skin the softest imaginable. She felt like a child in my arms.

Abruptly she began pulling me upstairs, so quickly that I stumbled repeatedly, laughing.

"My God," I said. "Slow down or you will kill me on the way up." As we passed the hallway mirror I saw the contrast in our appearances: me the bearded hairy shadow at the side of this glistening auburn vision.

"Where's the bedroom?" she muttered. I steered the right way. As we fell inside, she literally ripped my robe pulling it from me. Then she pushed me to the bed, madly stripping off her own clothes.

As she lay atop me, I took her in a kiss that matched her first one for length and fire. She jerked about on me madly, biting at me and muttering obscenities.

How will I keep up with this? I thought.

Then, to my amazement, when my need for her was truly awakened and that was made clear to her in the power of my kisses and caresses, she went stone cold.

I was suddenly a man alone, kissing a statue.

Whatever interest she had had was totally gone. I kissed her, and it was not returned. I caressed her in the most intimate places and got nowhere. She was dry, her skin cold. Coitus was out of the question. In her rigid state, it would have hurt me more than her.

"Is something wrong?" I asked, knowing of course what was wrong. Her frigidity was undiminished.

And so it went with our love. Time after time we would start down that road, only to find a thorn-covered gate barring the way. In a sense, I think it intensified my love for her, transmuting it into something ethereal and unattainable.

I was fully prepared to marry her and make it my life's work to help this beautiful creature out of her prison. She too seemed so inclined, for we discussed it often.

We were even to the point of setting a date by midwinter 1926–27.

It was on one of those frosty afternoons, just as I was leaving the office, that I received two telephone calls.

The first was from Party headquarters. An urgent matter had come up involving the Soviet Union, and they needed my immediate presence.

The second was from Loki. Although she could not speak at length, she frantically needed to see me.

I made a snap judgment, which I would forever regret, to do the Party's bidding first.

"Loki," I said, "I will come as soon as I take care of this business. I will be there in an hour or two."

Although she seemed disappointed, she said little.

Why did I not pay more attention to her?

The Party business was truly urgent, for they dispatched a car and driver to collect me. I was driven by Josef Blazek, who would one day become my personal valet and confidant, and with whom I would enjoy a comradely friendship until my incarceration.

I was sped to a small villa at the south of Prague that had briefly been the White Ukrainian legation but upon their defeat by the Red Army had, after brief legal skirmishing—and on rather specious grounds, I might add—been transferred to the Soviet government. The original Austrian builders had used it as a hunting lodge, but the Soviet comrades now combined its use, as a recreational facility for the new Soviet legation staff and a guesthouse for visiting high dignitaries from Moscow.

"Blazek, what has happened?"

My future friend could only shake his head.

The Soviet guard admitted us.

As we came up the driveway, I recognized several legation license plates, together with two belonging to the Czech government.

I even recognized a young staffer from the State Prosecutor's office, smoking a cigarette.

We nodded to each other. I was taken into the villa, where my Soviet diplomatic acquaintance Rodion greeted me. I lowered my eyes in memory of the last encounter, but Rodion seemed to have forgotten.

"What has happened?" I asked. "Has there been some accident?"

"A terrible accident, yes," said Rodion, arching his eyebrows strangely. He took me through the house, down the central corridor, and, passing through the kitchens, out into the back garden.

We walked down a frozen path into a wooded area. Through the trees shone lights of a small cabin. The tiny village of Prasky lay beyond.

"Well," I continued, "aren't you going to fill me in?"

"You will see for yourself."

So cryptic, I remember thinking to myself. This looks serious.

As we came down to the cabin, the state's coroner emerged from the back door.

The cabin was larger than it seemed from uphill. It was built in the Alpine style, with a great fireplace the height of a man, exposed beams, and wide pine floor. The fire had long since burned down. The smell of smoke, whiskey, sweat, and garlic drifted in the air.

The floor was littered with broken glass, which several of the Soviet staff were noisily sweeping up even as Czech police ordered them to stop. The Soviets, feigning no understanding of Czech, continued sweeping up what was presumably evidence.

More Czech police were arguing in a corner. Two staffers from the Foreign Ministry stood ashen by the front door, which faced down toward the village of Prasky. One of them was shouting at the police photographer; the other clutched a telephone.

It was apparent a Czech-Soviet confrontation was under way, as well as one between competing factions of my own government.

I was taken into a small side bedroom.

There on the small bed was a form shrouded in a sheet. The prosecutor and the deputy coroner pulled back the sheet to expose a girl of about seventeen, dead, her eyes wide open.

"She was strangled to death," intoned the prosecutor.

Rodion stiffened at this verdict.

"A terrible accident," said the Soviet vice minister of legation, a fat Central Asian whose shirt was soaked through with sweat.

In a corner chair snored a man in his late thirties, shirtless. He was barrel-chested, unconscious, wearing khaki pants and no shoes. Despite the fact that his head lolled back in stupor, a pair of pince-nez glasses remained firmly in place on the bridge of his nose. It gave him an odd air of both slovenliness and erudition. His hands were clasped.

"How did the police get in here?" I asked the prosecutor. "Isn't this Soviet property?"

The prosecutor smiled.

"You ought to be working at the Foreign Ministry," he said.

"No, my good doctor, it so happens this cabin is on Czech territory. The legation has been leasing it for five years, first as a gardeners' barracks, and through habit began to consider it part of the villa compound. But it is not. Apparently the suspect was having a private . . . party earlier this afternoon and, in the state of intoxication you see him in now, committed this assault. The crime was exposed when the shouts and shrieks of the young girl were heard down below and the villagers burst in. This poor thing is of a family down there, although they are at evening mass and don't know yet what has befallen their daughter. . . . She was lured up here with the promise of a job."

Rodion came over to me.

"Radan," he said, "this is a wretched situation. If unchecked, it could result in terrible complications between our two countries."

"Who is he?" I asked, glancing at the intoxicated man in the chair.

"Comrade . . . Luchenko. From the Ukraine."

The criminal's real identity was being concealed.

"Why have you brought me here?" I asked.

Rodion ushered me into the great room.

"Radan, this prosecutor is the worst. He is determined to push this thing to the limit and bring on a confrontation. He wants to arrest this man."

"So what do you expect me to do?" I said. "A murder has been committed on Czech territory. Claim diplomatic immunity."

The Foreign Ministry staffers hovered nearby.

"Your constitution is a little ambiguous on that point," said Rodion. "Your foreign minister was able to extract one concession from this very troublesome prosecutor, who I gather wants to run for president himself someday. He is willing to consider this an accident, if a Czech M.D. will so certify."

"An accident!" I erupted. "You want me to say this poor thing slipped and strangled herself? I'll have no part of it."

I was truly disgusted, moving toward the rear door, through which I had entered this grotesque scene.

One of the Foreign Ministry minions had the phone in hand.

"The foreign minister is on the line," he whispered to me. "He urges you to deeply consider how this might affect relations with such a . . . powerful neighbor and ally."

The young prosecutor, a crusader who had won my admiration over the last several years, stood smirking in the bedroom doorway.

His eyes seemed to say, Are you too a whore?

I was now outside. I felt as though I were going to vomit.

"Listen, Radan," said Rodion, more forcefully now. "You are in no position to be squeamish."

I shook my head.

"You can't intimidate me," I protested. "I'll have no part in murder."

Rodion tightened his grip on my arm.

"Listen," he growled at me. "This has the attention of powerful people in the Party in Moscow. This drunk gentleman has important friends."

"Who is he?" I sneered, pulling my arm free of his grasp. "I've never heard of any Luchenko. I'll certainly not pervert the law for that."

Rodion's eyes burned at me through the darkness.

"Very well, you fool," he said. "The man with the bloody hands in there has been deeply involved in the counterrevolutionary campaigns in Georgia and the Ukraine. He is a defender of the Revolution of the highest order. This little slipup matters not in the big picture."

"So tell me," I said. "How am I to call this an accident? The girl has bruises on her neck. Apparently there are witnesses."

"Forget the witnesses, the girl's family. They will be well compensated by the Soviet Union. What is required is a certification by a member of the Czecho-Slovak Medical Society that by accident Comrade Luchenko . . . ingested a contaminated quantity of wine, producing a violent reaction. That the resulting death was accidental and unpremeditated. And he will be released into Soviet custody."

I could not help but laugh.

"What are you talking about?" I asked. "Delirium tremens? I've never heard of such a brutal reaction. And the prosecutor will accept that?"

"Apparently he will. The Czech foreign minister has taken the initiative on this. Your President has been totally equivocal, unable to make a decision. Everyone knows he is intimidated by this young prosecutor and thinks he will be a rival someday.

"And of course," added Rodion, "the minister does not want to offend the great Soviet Union either."

"And why me?" I protested. "I'm sure you can find some member of the Medical Society who will do this for a sufficient fee. I am not for sale."

Rodion only glared. He lit up a cigarette.

"Let me say this," he said, exhaling. "We don't have time to go shopping. If you decide to fail us here, not only will your country suffer but so will you."

He held the hot tip of the cigarette about an inch from my face. For an instant I thought him truly capable of burning it into me, right there.

"I would not want to have to explain what all that means," he said.

I shook my head in disgust and went inside to make a phone call. I dialed our Czech Party secretary. He confirmed that an arrangement had been made with the President: to help the President out of this difficulty, in exchange for some "major future benefit to the Party" that he was not at liberty to discuss.

A deal had been made at the top: It must have meant a cabinet post for a Communist.

I hung up the phone. The Foreign Ministry aides looked at me rather expectantly.

"Where is the police report?" I asked.

The prosecutor only smiled. He was already imagining a future political campaign built around the "D.T. murder." A sergeant brought the report to me.

I duly wrote out the preposterous "certification" of the "unfortunate allergic reaction" of Comrade Luchenko that resulted in involuntary hallucinatory assault.

With loathing, I signed my name and the date.

I spoke briefly, and rashly, to Rodion on my way to the car.

"Never come to me again with your requests," I said. "The next time I shall refuse, no matter what the consequences to me or the Revolution or our fraternal association with the Soviet Union. If it comes to expulsion from my own Party, then I shall accept it gladly."

He smirked during my entire statement.

I was filled with self-loathing all the way back to the city, taking no comfort that my complicity had the support of the highest levels of the Republic, much less the Party, and was supposedly in the national interest, preserving our fiction of independence and sovereignty.

Nor was I especially gratified when a week later I received the following note via Soviet legation courier:

Moscow
January 17, 1927

Comrade Doctor Michalský,

I am forever indebted for your professional expertise and assistance during the recent misunderstanding in Prague. My staff tells me your work resolved what would have been an otherwise grave situation. I only regret I was unable to meet and thank you personally.

If I can ever repay you, do not hesitate to ask.

Sincerely, L. Beria

A ghastly new tidbit for my memory album, I thought. I did end up keeping the letter.

But by the time I received it, I was still in the grips of another, much more personal crisis. My return from the adventure at Prasky was delayed until after midnight by an extended stop at a tavern to try and obliterate the whole experience, which I partly succeeded in doing. But my immediate cure led to an emptiness that would last a lifetime. When I arrived home, my housekeeper handed me a note she had received two hours before.

I immediately recognized my beloved Loki's hand.

I had completely forgotten my promise to visit her that night.

I tore it open.

My dearest Radan,

It is now apparent I will not see you this evening. When I called, I was in the grips of a powerful depression and much needed to talk with you. But your absence, which was at first excruciating, forced me to confront my problems alone.

I have realized I will not rise above this situation until I make my own life, away from this city and family that bear down upon me like a curse. I have decided to take the overnight train to Paris. I have friends there and will contact you as soon as I am settled.

My love to you, for all your efforts on my behalf,

Loki

Hardly in the best of spirits before reading that, I sank to the floor in grief. I knew the train had already left, because on my way home I had seen it pull away from the station.

I had thought: See the beauty of that train moving west. It symbolizes freedom, movement. The magic of lands unknown.

I had watched its lighted coach windows glide off into the Bohemian darkness.

It had given me some momentary solace in my depression after the horrid encounter with the Russians.

What irony that the only love of my life would have been on that very train without my knowledge, headed west, leaving me, in my wretched loneliness, behind.

I do not think I ever fully recovered from the loss. For it soon became apparent Loki was determined to cut herself off from the past. My letters and attempts to find her went unanswered.

It was clear she did not ever want to see or hear from me again.

The airport limousine took the Victory Connector in, and then the driver picked up the Founding Fathers Freeway, passing the Agency entrance, which Robinson refused to acknowledge, choosing to gaze off instead into the dark, snow-patched forest on the opposite side of the road. Down he and the driver came, descending with the falls of the river below them, and Georgetown, the city, the sky, were lit with a frosty theatrical light, a gelid monumental light so chill that the panorama, though spectacular, conjured up in him only a grandiose emptiness, a feeling of a void. The ghost of the Old Man still hung over it, but the Old Man was gone now, together with the enemy who had created him, and so what this vista represented was a vacated theatrical set not yet claimed by anyone else.

The falls of the river were dying away in islands of rock and winter sheaths of rime ice, an overhead crisscrossing of bridges, and on the other bank the brick prison gloom of Georgetown, spires of its chapel and the National Cathedral beyond, all detail hidden in the fur of thick dead trees, the river cutting through the heart of it and descending right there from the end of Appalachia to the tidal coastal plain. The final walls of the river gorge soared on his right up into the lofty Virginia redoubts where household names dwelt, downriver of that into the instant urban gob of Rosslyn and the Iwo Jima monument, then on to the cemetery covering hill upon hill, the boys dead in declared wars and undeclared police actions, an eternal flame, a house where Robert E. Lee once lived, looking out in defeat over his vanquishers, looking out in defeat over the victory city, the new Rome.

This was the victory city, with all fatal passion, blood obsession, screaming vision, gone out of it. For what had defined this city for more than fifty years was the enemy, and now there was no enemy worthy of such a grandiose concentration of forces and egotism, such a nefarious aggrandizement of the state, rendering what now spread out on the land before him into the final marble blossoming, once-passionate ideas now rendered into memorial stone.

On the shady side of his apartment building, the snow was still fairly deep, while in exposed areas it was melted, evidence of a storm followed by sunny weather while he was gone. He saw his car, but he didn't see Leah's; maybe it was parked out of view, or she was with friends.

Claude the desk clerk handed him a small envelope, and inside, Robinson found a note from Wilson Raver.

Where the hell are you? Give me a call.

Just as Robinson left the elevator on his floor, he thought he saw a man turning away from his apartment door. But that was nonsense; the light was out at that end of the hall, and he was tired from two transatlantic trips in two days, and so it was probably a visual trick caused by fatigue and jet lag.

They passed in the hallway. The man was in uniform, carrying an exterminator's spray canister. Robinson noted only that he was dark, perhaps in his mid-forties. Since he wore a cap and kept his face down, he couldn't be clearly seen.

The man continued on down to the elevator, and Robinson to his door. When Robinson got there, he saw that the door had been jimmied open; there were scratches around the knob and lock. Stepping inside, he saw the den in disorder, his desk drawer files strewn on the floor. His computer was on, and he was certain he'd left it off.

Leah wasn't there at all. His first thought was that Leah had robbed him. The thought was ridiculous, sickening.

Just then he heard the elevator bell ring, signaling its arrival, the opening of the door for the exterminator.

The elevator door closed just as Robinson ran out into the hall. It was going down.

He ran for the service stairway and took the stairs two at a time, fast as he could. He fell once, but recovered. Down he spiraled, almost tempted to vault himself over the banister and down into the airspace. But it was too desperate, and he'd probably break a bone.

After twelve flights of stairs he hit the first floor and burst out into the corridor. The elevator door was open, no one to be seen. Robinson ran into the lobby just in time to see the man jump into a waiting mud-colored van and roar away. He couldn't identify the model, knew it only as an American panel truck, no markings, careening out of the parking lot.

"Mr. Robinson," Claude the desk clerk called. But Robinson was already out in the lot, key into the frozen lock of his Saab, which he hadn't driven in four days. He started it, watching the van shriek down Manifest Destiny Drive toward Patriots Parkway and presumably toward I-395. His own engine stalled once as he too raced out of the lot.

Fortunately, at this time of night—eight-thirty—traffic was easing off. Once on Patriots Parkway, he thought he could see the van about a quarter mile ahead, turning onto 395 South. He ran a light and was himself up the same ramp, perhaps a minute behind his quarry.

Now he was on 395, and he momentarily lost the van in a cluster of congealed cars and trucks headed south into Virginia. People were changing lanes, blocked by a pride of tractor-trailers accelerating into the slight downhill grade, while cars tried to get around them. The nearest trucks blocked his view of what was ahead. Then through a gap in the traffic he saw the van breaking free into open highway, pulling around the first tractor-trailer. He tried to push on through, but the gap closed.

By the time he got out of the cluster, he was passing through the assorted exit ramps and overpasses of Whirlington. He thought for a minute he saw the van spiraling up and above him on Quemoy Lane toward Alexandria, but by the time he too made the turn, it was gone.

Upon returning to his apartment building, he asked Claude if he had let any exterminators in.

"I let one in, to spray the basement."

"Since when do they spray at night?"

"Mr. Robinson," said Claude, lowering his head in earnestness, "he had a state permit. Commonwealth of Virginia. Emergency order. I don't mess with the state, no sir. If the state says Jump, I say How high. No sir."

Robinson couldn't help but curse. The clerk was nervous now, defensive, afraid.

"What did he look like?"

"Spic, I guess," said Claude, a fiftyish hollow-faced Southern white man who showed the ravages of a not-too-distant alcoholic period. The kind of white man one sees sitting in bus terminals or seeking day labor in mills and assembly plants across the South.

"Did he have an accent?"

"Yeah. Cubean or wetback."

"Cubean," Robinson repeated.

"Want me to call the police?" Claude asked after a minute.

"No, no," snapped Robinson.

"Did he bother you?"

Robinson didn't say anything but went back upstairs.

Other than the wrecked den, nothing had changed since he'd left. The breakfast dishes from five days before were still in the sink. The bed was unmade, the dirty clothes in the same spot where they'd fallen.

The closet where Leah kept some changes of clothes was empty.

I don't need this, he thought, sitting down on the bed. He was searching through his recollection of the departure for a clue. Had he hurt her? Of course she had wanted to come with him, but it was out of the question.

Four urgent messages from Raver had his message machine blinking madly. Leah hadn't called at all. He found her note on his desk, originally sealed but apparently opened and read by the "exterminator."

I've decided to go west. I'll be in touch soon.

Love, Leah

He looked up her friend Vanessa's number, the friend she'd been staying with upon her return from Africa, before she'd rented her room in the city and started going out with him. He contemplated what he would ask, then figured there was nothing to be said but the truth.

To the background roar of music and group conversation, Vanessa answered. No, she had not seen Leah in about a month. She knew even less about her movements than he. She made sympathetic noises for about twenty seconds when he indicated she might have left him. But her ideas about Leah's whereabouts were not helpful: Antarctica, Idaho, Brazil. The conversation broke off in background squeals and party laughter.

He was left alone in the darkened bedroom high up in a tower overlooking the Potomac. His dusty carry-on bag lay on the floor, filled with more dirty clothes. His den had been ransacked. His briefcase had partly spilled its contents onto the bed, including the fragmentary photo from Terezín. He had been in Czechoslovakia for thirty hours, and it was as though he'd been gone a month.

He mechanically went through the den, trying to determine if anything was missing. The "exterminator" had obviously just begun his search, for he hadn't made it to the bedroom, where Lhota's file on Emil still remained in a shirt box in the closet. But why had the intruder been so sloppy as to be on the scene when Robinson arrived home?

It all came down to how they had tracked him down and identified him. At first he thought it was his airline ticket, the Arab man following him in Prague. The Arab had seen him get on the Lufthansa flight to Frankfurt in Prague that morning. They must have gotten his cover name somehow—probably from the Inn of the Wandering Boar—then traced it in an airline computer and seen the uncorrected original flight record that had him arriving back in Washington the next day.

But it was under another alias that he had come back in, another layer of protection, to avoid triggering any U.S. government record of his departure from the country while on medical leave. So how had they gotten his real name and address? The only person he'd given his address to in the last three days was the limousine dispatcher at Dulles. Improbable that someone could have been sent to his apartment in the hour it took him to get home from the airport.

Had the dependable Hamza at Great Escapes botched it somehow, leaving his real identity on an invoice, a computer file? Robinson was working himself up into a belated fury, when his eye fell upon his carry-on bag. This tired bag, used on the trip because it was nondescript, suddenly mocked him in his misery.

Hadn't there been a name tag on this bag once? He couldn't immediately remember ever having written his name and address there, but then he'd bought the thing just after the divorce; who knows what he might have written? And as he stood there illuminated by the glow of the video terminal, he theorized he had written his current address in there two years ago, after his banishment from the White House basement and from Operations, thinking he'd never be sent on another covert mission as long as he lived. And it was this name tag that someone had snatched from him, either in Prague or in Frankfurt.

Then again, they might have been on him from the beginning. It might go all the way back to the breakfast with Lhota in Pettyville, or Darlene Scoggins' visit in December.

He tried to sleep, but the absence of Leah and his stupidity that led to the rifling of his apartment caused him to fall into a devastated hole that would not allow sleep. It all boiled together, the departure of Leah, someone breaking in.

What to do now? He had totally screwed up the case of Lhota. Should he chuck it, go find Leah instead? His excitement at getting closer to the mystery was now turning ominous, threatening. Leah was the most immediate problem, the stuff of life, of the future.

He wasn't given the opportunity to make a choice. Sometime late in the night, when he had finally fallen asleep, the phone rang.

A hissing silence waited there, the white electronic noise of the long-distance line, the whisper of fiber optics and satellite faces.

It was Leah. She would not tell him where she was, and she told him not to look for her.

"Come back," he said, trying to remain jovial but fighting an urge to accuse, to beg.

"No," she said. "Dan, you didn't want me there. You made your decision."

"Where are you?" he asked, and she would say only that she was in the mountains. He gathered by the sound of the line that it was the continental U.S., but far away.

"Can I write you?" he asked.

"I'll think about it," she said. "Right now I have to try some things on my own."

"I need you," he said into the hiss.

"I think you're just afraid," she said. "Forget about me for a while."

The wind of telecommunicated air continued for a time.

"Call me again soon," he asked.

"Maybe," she said. He took that, wanted more, asked another question, but she had said all she wanted to say; she was ending the conversation.

"Goodbye," she said. He made a response, but it was not intelligible; the phone went from that most tenuous connection to the brutal buzz of the hang-up.

He too hung up, and slumped into a kind of stunned stupor, his head whining with eleven hours spent on an aircraft, the wired feel of too much travel. The ice night sat deep on the capital, and the lights of cars on the bridges and parkways were fewer and farther between. He tried again to imagine how he had been identified and tracked down so quickly, but the whole thing was a fevered maze, and in his present state of jet lag it made him dizzier.

An indeterminate time later, the phone rang a second time, and he leapt for it.

He could hear what he thought was long-distance hiss.

"Leah," he said.

"You motherfucker," said a voice, certainly not Leah's. Instead, Robinson detected only enough to surmise it belonged to a man born in one of the lands touched by the Islamic sweep.

"Pardon me?" Robinson asked.

"You stay in your own business," said the man, "or you learn a very bad lesson."

"Hello?" Robinson asked. For the second time that evening, he was hung up on.

Had it indeed been long-distance, or a call from down the block on a cheap, badly connected phone? He laughed a moment, helplessly.

Doubly stunned, he let the whole thing fall to the floor, where, for a time, a recorded female voice said, If you need assistance, please consult your directory, followed by a high-pitched beeping, followed by total silence.

During the period of silence, he collected his thoughts enough to chain his front door and find in his dresser a long-unused pistol, which he loaded and placed under the bed within easy reach.

The pain of Leah's departure was still with him in the morning. In fact, it blocked out recollection of the break-in. But when he saw his den in the light of day, the anger of the night before became a slow dread at the violation of his home.

Should he call the police to report the break-in? He initially thought yes, but any mention of his employer would probably mean reporting it to FBI counterintelligence, and that would not be helpful now. Instead, he called an overpriced emergency locksmith service and had two new dead bolts installed on his front door by lunch-time.

While away, he'd received a letter from the CIA Medical Director's office, proposing a psychiatric interview early next week. He would have to make an appointment, to maintain the appearance of cooperation.

He pondered writing a note to Bob Yamamoto, urging him to say nothing of their Prague encounter, but then decided not to, thinking that would draw too much attention to a matter Yamamoto might have forgotten by now.

Then Robinson turned his attention to the material Lhota's fiancée had given him in December, together with the shreds gleaned during his trip to Prague.

He had the photo of Michalský and Emil taken at Theresienstadt/Terezín camp in 1942.

He had a letter to the Holocaust Survivors Council, describing Mrs. Alena Petchek Moskowitz's sighting of the "Angel of Theresienstadt" in the Hotel Camino Real in Guatemala City in 1982, after he had been reported killed in an Ethiopian plane crash in 1978.

He had the phrase "Veil / the face of God" in Lhota's handwriting on a postcard.

He dialed Mrs. Moskowitz in Key Biscayne. A message machine carried her husband's voice, saying they were spending the winter in California, recovering from her surgery. They were staying with their daughter, but gave no city or number. The message section had been overloaded, and so he could leave no message on their tape. With no other avenue open, he wrote out a letter and mailed it to the Key Biscayne address, asking that they contact him as soon as possible.

He called Raver, who was deep in negotiations with the sultanate of Brunei, a prime customer, and would have to call him back.

And then in early afternoon he drove out to the Agency for his psychiatric consultation, feeling as though a year, and not just a week, had passed since he was last there. As an afterthought, he took the pistol from his coat pocket and put it under the car seat.

"I suppose you think you're alone in what you see as your failure," Dr. Pauls was saying. "I know how you Operations types think."

Dr. Pauls was the chief Agency psychiatrist, and she was doing her best to be warm and collegial, even irreverent. But her office was just around the corner from Security, and the effort was futile. She was tall, restrained, fiftyish, with a slightly dusky complexion and a hint of guava lipstick, hazel eyes that could best be described as neither friendly nor hostile, a Michigan accent and brown hair back in a bun. Their conversations were slowed by her need to filter every comment through the screen of analysis. She wore a brown tweed skirt and a beige pullover sweater, and she sat in a small swivel chair such as a secretary or typist might use. He sat sinking into a Haitian-cotton sofa that had been draped with a South American Indian blanket. The bookshelves were stuffed with Rollo May and Fritz Perls. She had a small window opening onto the courtyard.

"But far from it," she added. "Many of your colleagues, at one or another time in their lives, have been in a similar situation. A stressful life, one of controlled duplicity and of manipulation. Takes its toll. You shouldn't be ashamed at all," she said. "Simply reaffirms you're human."

He said nothing and looked out into the bare trees, thin and sapless against a dim blue sky.

"Why don't you begin by telling me what prompted you to seek help on the outside?" And so he tersely summarized for her the reasons: disappointment with his career; a series of disturbing dreams; depression over loss of custody of his daughter. She nodded, asking what conclusions he and his therapist had reached. And he tried, as best he could, to recollect. She took notes, nodded sympathetically.

"Are you currently using any kind of antidepressants or tranquilizers?" she asked. He shook his head.

"No Equanil?" she asked, looking at her notes.

"No," he said.

She seemed unconvinced.

After nearly an hour had passed, she closed her notepad.

"Daniel," she said, "I see nothing at this point that would indicate you need to be institutionalized. Nor do I think you're ready to go back to the stresses of the work environment. What I would like to do is, for a period of, say, eight weeks, have three weekly sessions together, like we had today. So we can get to the root of this anxiety and help you clear it up. I see no reason why you couldn't go back to work soon. But what this is now is a time of rest and recuperation . . . of listening to your internal messages . . . and of learning to think about life and yourself in new ways."

He took that, not out of agreement, but simply to placate and disarm her and get this impediment out of the way. He didn't trust her; better said, he didn't trust how the institution would make use of her, even if she was well-meaning in her own right. All the promises in the world about right to privacy were arrayed against an entity that existed to break rules and violate the inviolate.

He wasn't comforted.

They shook hands, with an appointment set up for the following Monday to begin their weekly cycle. In leaving the building, he realized how much the encounter had depressed him, by making him think he was somehow dysfunctional. Seeing the familiar flow of Agency people in their routines, when he had been outside the flow, made him feel strange again, reminding him of childhood when he had been sick with the flu and away from school for two weeks, only to return to class as if his armor had been softened or taken away, so that it took several days before he seemed to be really back among the living.

He had been ashamed then of being sick. He felt that way now, again.

Lhota was far from his thoughts. In Lhota's place was Leah, drinking a bottle of beer on the sofa or taking a bath in the tub. He wanted Leah, for Leah could have pulled him up out of this valley. She would have mocked his colleagues and his routine, she would have told him he could be happy as a housepainter or a tugboat captain and to hell with the government.

He stopped on the way home to swim laps in an indoor pool near his apartment, and then went back home. How he wished he would find Leah there, in bed, or fixing something in the kitchen. He wondered how he would make it through this winter.

His heart jumped when he saw the message light on his answering machine flashing with a single call. He was so certain it was Leah that when he heard a male voice booming out of the message speaker he nearly smashed it.

It was Wilson Raver, with his Arizona twang.

"Meet me at Le Poof in Alexandria at seven-thirty. Hot women. And you're buying . . . old buddy."

Robinson was not in the mood. This was confirmed to him when he walked into the nouveau lushness of Le Poof that night to find a dozen aging singles in their hoarse hilarity—executive women in their business scarves and female neckties, heavy-jowled male counterparts with ties loosened and cheeks reddened by drink and tanning booth. Periodic drunken roars erupted from the drinkers in response to a televised basketball tournament.

Raver was slightly drunk and slapped Robinson hard on the back.

"Expecting the Boobsey twins any minute," he said. "Lobby for Aerial Technologies. Twenty-five. Experts in look down–shoot down guidance."

Raver rolled his eyes up and down, in a simulation, then swiveled his large pin-striped hips.

Robinson was given a huge Bloody Mary, since he was the thirteenth customer, whatever that meant. Its chemical odor was powerful and unappealing. Raver swilled his own beer, then brought his face about two inches away from Robinson's.

"Know what you're fucking with here?" Raver asked.

"What?" Robinson asked.

"Okay," said Raver, inhaling deeply for the air necessary to tell a long tale. "Užhok was easy enough. Ancient history. I thought, Let's call Hap McCracken. Hap's the best explosives man I ever knew. He did his last tour in Addis when Selassie was still in power, left the company early, when you and I were just babies. Why, you ask, him? Because I was thinking Czechoslovakia. Semtex, that greatest of all Czech exports. Emil the Czech. A connection. Are you with me?"

Robinson nodded.

"And it was a brilliant leap on my part. Hap remembered Emil . . . or at least he did when I mentioned the crash in Ethiopia. He says, and I quote, 'I think that was Terp's job.' "

"Terp?" Robinson asked.

"Frank Terpil," Raver said.

"I don't think so," said Robinson.

"Hold on," said Raver. "I asked what he meant. Hap says, 'The word was Terp blew him away clean.' "

"But that was in '78," said Robinson. "Terpil was already out of the company."

"Dan, I didn't say who he did it for. Hap just said Terp did it, for fun and profit."

"How did he do it?" Robinson asked.

"Well, Frank at that time was tight with the Libyans. He had a base down there in the desert. . . . Hell, he may still have it."

"I thought he was in prison."

"You can do lots from a prison cell," said Raver. "Anyway, Terp could have run an operation like that from Libya, a hop and a skip across Nubia to Abyssinia. Terp had a loyal net across the western ergs; maybe he had one in Ethiopia."

"The story was that the Eritreans shot the plane down," said Robinson.

"Good story," said Raver.

"So why would Terp do it from outside?" Robinson asked. "Who on the outside wanted Užhok dead? Who on the outside even knew who he was? Užhok was an invisible Warsaw Pact ghoul, on detail. International ramifications."

"Exactly," Raver agreed. "I can point a few fingers. First the Eritreans."

"Were we helping Eritrea?"

Raver gave his sweet maidenly smile.

"Maybe they were our Maoist bastards. Or two: Frank was entirely free lance, working for the Eritreans on his own."

"It doesn't really matter, though," said Robinson, "if Emil didn't die there. Did you ask about that? Could he have walked away?"

"No way. The plane made a big fireball north of Ras Dashan; no survivors. Took a chunk out of Mengistu's northern command—one general, three colonels, and your friend. Hap was adamant on that. He said that Užhok went down in flames, and it caused a stink all the way back to Moscow. So it looks like Lhota was wrong."

"Sounds that way," said Robinson. "But Lhota still got killed over something in Guatemala."

"People get killed there," said Raver. "Which brings me to my second point. You know how I love North Africa, the desert, the dry ergs. Clean emptiness, shifting alliances, betrayal in the screaming night. Good tribal politics. So different from the cucaracha circuit, which I told you I wouldn't touch. Well, I broke my rules to do you a favor. After Hap fizzled, I decided I would check out this Guatemalan death. I made a few calls."

The television had now been turned off, and a very aggressive jazz heard only in bars like this was now being pumped at them.

"Did you find anything?"

"I'm a bit rusty down there," continued Raver, "so I visit Bud Funkhouser over at Southern Air. Bud's flown every piece-a-shit route to every guerrilla peckerhead in Central America. I ask him very intelligently: 'Hey, Bud, anything funny happen in Guatemala lately? I'm asking because a Czech friend of a friend got his head blown off there a few months ago. This Czech was looking for another Czech who had some Warsaw Pact job and disappeared in Ethiopia and maybe reappeared in Guatemala four years later.' You think it sounds weird now, you should have heard it as I asked Bud. I was embarrassed, ready for him to laugh at me and throw me out, because Bud doesn't suffer fools and that's one of the stupidest questions I ever asked anybody. And Bud is just sitting there looking at me. I'm ready for him to laugh, I'm ready for him to cuss, whatever. And you know what he says?"

"What does he say?"

"He says, 'I don't fly to Guatemala.' And I said, 'What, you flew every inch of that country. You taught those monkeys how to fly. What do you mean?' And he says, 'I stay away from Guatemala.' This conversation was getting real uncomfortable. I said, 'Bud, why do you stay away? Since when? Why?' And he just looks out the window for a while. Needless to say, I was wondering what the fuck is going on. I said, 'Bud, did somebody scare you off? You got orders, what?' And then he says the damnedest thing."

"What did he say?"

" 'There was an event.' "

"What?" Robinson asked, irritated by the gush of conversation around them that had made it hard for him to hear.

" 'There was an event,' Bud said."

"What the hell does that mean?" Robinson asked. "What—a coup? A termination? An 'event'?"

" 'There was an event,' Bud said. 'I don't fly to Guatemala,' he said. I couldn't get anything else out of him. He looked like he was gonna cry or something. This was not good at all. And then he said, 'Rave, you touch that one and you pull back a stump.' Okay, I take that message very clear. Bud is a close associate at times, a good contact, and we've been together on several fine moneymaking ventures over the years. I value him. He's my best link to the cucaracha circuit. So end of conversation on Guatemala."

Robinson saw his own reflection, and that of Raver, in the bar mirror. They looked like photos that had been superimposed on the scene, because they just didn't belong. That was the curse of being a spook, or an ex-spook: You didn't belong anywhere, except on the run.

The restaurant adjacent to the bar was now filling up with a different crowd: marrieds, in some way without the ragged self-awareness that drove the bar people. A pair of blond young women in leather skirts were standing in the bar entryway. They were undoubtedly Raver's young friends from Aerial Technologies. They looked over expectantly, and Raver waved and gave them a "wait a minute" sign with his palm.

"Does this help you at all?" Raver asked.

"Not really," said Robinson. "Either Lhota was lying about what he was doing, or he was wrong, or crazy. Or Hap McCracken was mistaken and Emil wasn't killed in Ethiopia."

Raver shrugged.

"Guatemala thing is curious, though," said Robinson.

"It's all yours, friend," said Raver. "Hey, what was that phrase Lhota left behind?"

"Veil / the face of God."

"Some sort of code? Piece of a poem, song?"

"I don't have a clue," said Robinson.

On impulse, Robinson almost asked Raver to run a sweep of his apartment, to catch bugs or things more dangerous that might have been left the night before. But it was too soon to be this honest; that would raise questions in Raver's mind, such as why was Robinson going outside the Agency to get a sweep of his own home? Robinson decided not to say anything.

Raver's attention was wandering. Robinson saw that the prime part of the evening lay ahead for his friend, so he thanked him for his help. Raver beckoned the two girls over. He introduced them, but Robinson took his leave. He was in even less of a mood for frivolity than he had been before. The girls seemed not disappointed; they could sense he would be a drag, and they were there for fun.

Raver was already his old self again as Robinson exited the bar. He had one of the lobbyists on his lap, and his Arizona voice was booming out above the martial jazz playing on the sound system.

What on earth had Miroslav Lhota stumbled onto?

The jungle was filled with clusters of wild flowers and sweet-scented groves, and for the first time, far in the distance I saw the white peak of a volcano. Air clear as crystal, the transparent region . . .

—Carlos Fuentes, *Terra Nostra*

The Miami airport is a metaphor for our time: through its limited facility surges a flood of humanity without limit, so there are never enough lounge seats, never enough restaurants, never enough toilets, to accommodate the sheer gush of humanity in anything other than the cramped style of the refugee.

You must understand I hadn't the slightest interest in making this trip, it was my husband's idea, he is a true American, native born, he has that innocence and openness so many Americans have, being brought up in an atmosphere of innocence and trust, of people treating each other decently, of the happy ending, of the Fourth of July. . . .

The airport, like the city itself, is an awful no-man's-land between two cultures, this gateway to both worlds that in its human face now resembles Latin America more than North America, second-generation *cubanos* manning the checkout counters, ticket stands, and car rental desks, speaking more Spanish than English, the bulk of the passing human flood more Latin too, but mixed swirling with the plastic refulgence of North American marketing, the peppy decor and manufactured facilities, efficient gringo crowd-herding techniques, until you have a strange hybrid floating suspended between the two worlds, the two ideas.

I myself am the opposite, knowing the wicked ways of the outside world, having survived the war and the camp and come to the United States by choice and never having looked back to Czechoslovakia, for myself I would be entirely happy to remain all my days right here in the U.S.A., but he wanted us to go on a tour, he wanted to see ruins, Americans are so starved for the old since they have none of it, he fixed upon the idea of a trip to the Guatemalan ruins, and there was very little I could do to dissuade him. . . .

The flow headed north seems greater, brown and energetic people drawn away from disintegration into the safe haven of the colossus, refugees from the collapse of the sol and the cruzeiro and the cordoba, refugees from the fall of regimes and from the fallout of regicide, refugees from the collapsing feudal into the soft womb of materialism that is North America.

What can I say about the ruins themselves but that they were old? that there was a sadness about them, the emptiness of things lost and forgotten, a splendid kind of isolation in the sun-beaten jungle? But more honestly I should say I was on edge the entire time, I did not like being there so exposed in the jungle, I was concerned about an attack of some kind, my husband said Nonsense, he was wearing his Panama hat and safari shirt and Bermudas and binoculars, he said Nonsense as we trooped up and down pyramids, into imperial ball court and bathhouse and sacrificial chamber, Nonsense he said. . . .

But the flow the other way is significant too, first of returning refugees trying to take back with them as much of the northern world as they can, televisions and beeping video toys and vulgar appliances and mundane housewares, even bags of bulk cereal and candy strapped in groaning cardboard boxes, miserably heavy cargoes turning travel into the exodus, into a grinding effort of will, yet so strong the human need now for such goods that almost any indignity will be endured to acquire them, at a discount, benefit of exchange and tax rate differences.

And of course it was nonsense, no attack ever came, no screaming natives surged out of the woods or robbers or murderers, just a few Mayas trying to sell us postcards and trinkets, just watching us trooping up and down the pyramids of their forefathers, yet the feeling of dread lingered with me until we were in the capital city. . . .

And the northern salesmen and manufacturers' representatives on their way south to sell, bankers extending or servicing loans that will never be repaid, importers and narcotics brokers out to buy handicrafts and *pasta básica*, and the dewy blond *Wandervogeln* in blue jeans and duffel bags, refugees from their own post-industrial world, forsaking the safety and soullessness of America for the danger of the world outside, the outer world where things do not work, the world of fear and tradition, the world of mysticism and untamed landscape.

And there was Daniel Robinson, going to Guatemala for his own reasons, for the first time in years going out on his own name, on his own passport.

The hellacious frenzy of the airport was such that during his midday layover of three hours, he sat on an outdoor bench in a narrow garden strip between the passenger drop-off and the parking decks. It was a tiny island of verdure in the roaring arena of concrete around him, and he ate a sandwich and a yogurt there and read *Fodor's Guide to Central America.* He sat among two palm trees and several planters filled with acanthus and ficus trees. He tried to pretend he was away from the mess, but the screech of tires on the parking deck floor and periodic shrieking overflights of jets and the continual passage of car-rental shuttle vans repeatedly broke his concentration and his attempts at serenity.

Guatemala City itself brought back memories, an absurdity since I had never been there before, but it brought back memories of what it is like to be a prisoner, to be a few steps away from death, for that is what I saw as a girl in Europe and that is what I saw as we came into the city from the airport, I could see the look in people's eyes, a furtive quickness, the expectation of disaster and a sort of constant celebration when disaster did not come, this moment of life snatched from the jaws of death, no expectation of anything more than a squeaking by, a hope of slithering between the cracks, that is what I did as a girl and that is what they were doing, I did not like this memory at all. . . .

Midafternoon arrived, and the flight to Guatemala City was due to leave in an hour. He surrendered to reality and trudged back into the swirl of people inside the terminal, through the hordes of shoving passengers and clinging relatives at the security checkpoint, en route to the gate.

The plane was perhaps half full. On board, he was seated next to a young balding blond man in wire-rim glasses, khaki pants, and Hush Puppy shoes, with the air of nonprofit, of social work, about him. The man was reading a thick typed treatise on urban poverty in Guatemala City. Robinson thought of speaking, then let it wait.

Miraculously they were up and off only thirty minutes behind schedule, and soon after were making their crossing of the island of

Cuba. Robinson dozed and ate the dinner and read an in-flight magazine while his seatmate finally abandoned his reading and took off his glasses, in preparation for a nap.

And there is very little to report at all save those final minutes of our last day in the country, we had seen the ruins and toured the city and spent the night and sat by the pool until afternoon, finally coming down in the hotel elevator with our luggage, headed for the tour bus to the airport and flight home and I heard this breathing, this breathing that made me start, a deep tubercular guttural sound, it came from so long ago, this sound, of course the elevator was crowded, it was checkout time, I looked around and I recognized no one right away but then I saw a man, a tall gaunt man in a suit, with white ragged hair, the look of a professor, of a man shut away with his own ideas too long, it was his breathing I knew and I was almost overwhelmed and very nearly cried out, It is you, the anděl *of Terezín, the angel of my prison girlhood. . . .*

Strangely, the idea of Guatemala made him much more uneasy than a renegade trip to Prague, because he would be much blinder and more inept there; he knew little of the place, although he did speak rusty Spanish, because in the early 1970s a Kissinger decree had gone out that all officers had to have a "minor" expertise, and so he had supplemented his Czech experience with an assignment to the Cuban desk for eight months, drudgery for him because his heart was not in it: he carried the same prejudice, the same snobbery that all his Eastern European colleagues had, that Western Hemisphere Operations was a dumping ground for thugs and mediocrities who couldn't learn a hard language.

His work had been with "Fire Brigade," a program to counter lingering Cuban subversion in Latin America, the program's purpose being to funnel money to democratic leftists, anti-Communist student groups and newspapers, and ex-guerrillas who would renounce the armed struggle.

Robinson was racking his mind for the key. He had dealt superficially with a group in Guatemala, a network of farm cooperatives run by a priest. Robinson at first couldn't dredge up his name, but the program was called PAN—Programa de Acción Nacional. Then he remembered: Padre Elizondo Huidrobo, an industrious middle-aged ladino Jesuit priest earmarked by the CIA station as a good investment for the future; the good padre he'd met only once, when he'd traveled to Mexico City to deliver that first check from the

Edward Streeter Foundation, the cover for "Fire Brigade," to launch PAN to bring "bread and dignity to the most downtrodden."

And I did speak, I spoke to him in Czech, my tongue thick with not having formed those words in conversation in more than a year, I said, Angel, you are an Angel of Terezín, and I saw in his eyes and the quiver of his mouth that he understood and was afraid, yes, afraid of being recognized, even as he mumbled something in Spanish or French or even English, Perdón? *he asked, but I know the sound of a Czech* r, *then another man intervened, this one answering for him,* Señora, usted está equivocada, *we now had someone interpreting the Spanish into English, I said, You were one of the angels of the camp, and through the interpreter the gaunt man said, You are mistaken, the elevator was now open, we were out in the lobby, my husband had hold of my arm and this man was slowly moving away, still I insisted, It is you, it is you, and he was shaking his head,* No, señora, no, *he said, and the companion's last words to me as he shook his head and smiled at me were,* Cara de Dios, Cara de Dios, *he said, What is that? I asked, what is that? thinking perhaps he was using the Czech word for czar, only when this man was gone away was it explained to me the words meant Face of God, I have no idea what that was, a goodbye, such a strange goodbye, why he wished to keep his identity secret I do not know, but I am convinced he is the one we called Emil, Emil, and so I file this report so that those of us who survived that camp shall know that one of the good ones survived also, I hereby close this, Alena Petchek Moskowitz, 1000 Atlantic Way, Key Biscayne, Florida, October 4, 1982.*

He dozed and read, ate a meal and spoke some pleasantries with his seatmate. They talked about the weather they would find in the capital (springlike), what kind of work the fellow did (Ford Foundation), the politics now prevailing (a thin veneer of ballot box over bayonet), and the unique growth of Protestant fundamentalism there (the only Latin country where evangelicals might someday outnumber Catholics).

They encountered clouds not far south of Cuba, which cloaked the Caribbean for much of the trip . . . but when the clouds parted, they could see briefly into deep green canyons, misted promontories and summits, shreds of low-flying cloud torn on cliff as wild and untouched as Amazonia or New Guinea.

When the plane was over the high central Guatemalan plateau, it began its approach to the capital, the jungled abysses gone, replaced by rolling pastureland and mountain ridges, corrugated tin-roofed settlements and concrete highways conveying antiquated old buses, the same landscape, the same curious blend of tropic with desert and highland, one could find in the Mexican central valley and the high American Southwest, a low ceiling of rainless cloud hanging over the entire panorama, given a further gloom by approaching night.

The terminal itself was squat and dingy, tarmac dotted with combustion-stained DC-3s and a few Cessnas, which now made up the Fuerza Aérea Guatemalteca. The arrival of the Eastern flight from Miami was apparently the main event of the day, for a host of baggage handlers and mechanics looked as if just roused from a daylong wait, neither Guatemala nor its airport yet touched by the global surge in tourism and air travel.

The entry led down rubber-carpeted stairs into ersatz wood paneling and Immigration and Customs. Yellowed tourism posters dotted the walls: Indian market at Chichicastenango, Mayan ruins in Petén, Lago Atitlán. *Inmigración* Coronel López Díaz looked long and hard at Robinson's unofficial passport. Were Robinson here on official business and his affiliation known, this man would probably have swept him into a back room for a drink of *aguardiente* and a hymn of praise to America, to the Old Man and the CIA. But he was not; and so Coronel López Díaz treated entry into this sad haunted house of a country as a privilege cautiously granted, not an automatic right.

"Why you come to Guatemala?" he asked.

"Business. *Negocios.*"

"*¿Habla usted castellano?*"

"*Sí,*" Robinson answered.

"*¿Qué tipo de negocios?*"

"*Finanzas y inversiónes,*" answered Robinson.

"You are comin' to inves' in Guatemala?" he asked.

"Possibly," he said.

López Díaz nodded at that.

"Where you are estayin'?"

"Hopefully the Camino Real."

"Is a berry nice hotel," he said, grimacing slightly as if to say, I'm a Guatemalan *coronel* and I've lived here all my life and I can't afford to stay there.

"*¿Cuánto tiempo en Guatemala?*"

"*Dos semanas*," said Robinson.

Coronel López Díaz stamped his passport and meticulously wrote in "*14 días*." Next came *Aduanas*, where a young Mayan in uniform carefully opened everything, including a bottle of vitamin pills. Finally Robinson was through, into a waiting group of about a hundred expectant friends and family. The color black seemed to be in fashion, not the old *luto* of Spanish mourning but black polyester pantsuits and sport coats, and skirts on women, so that a new somberness crept in. And there was something in the faces, the bodies . . . a restraint and a physical heaviness unlike the lithe movement of the Afro-Hispanics of the Caribbean and Panama or the slim Indian race of the Andes or the Mexican mountains. This was something else.

Robinson was embraced by a taxi driver, who swept him toward an old waiting Volkswagen.

"Which hotel?" the man asked, grinning.

"Camino Real."

"You got a reservation?"

"No."

"Forget the Camino; its full. We'll go to the Huxley."

"Why's it full?"

"Big convention," the driver, whose name was Lucho, replied. "Christian Anti-Communist League. Your Senator Blisterson is guest of honor. Don't worry, I get you into the Huxley." He turned to him and winked. "Where in the States you from?"

"I'm British," Robinson said, wondering if he should be wary.

"Bullshit! You're a gringo."

Robinson inwardly flinched.

"I live in the States," Robinson improvised. "Near Washington. Have you visited there?"

"Hell, man, I lived there for nine years. Washington, D.C. I lived on Seventeenth Street, waited tables at La Fonda. Then Mamá got sick and I came back. I'll go back someday. Where you live?"

"Virginia."

"You CIA?" Lucho grinned ear to ear.

"Business," Robinson said. Lucho nodded. They wound through streets that Robinson had a hard time getting a fix on . . . then he realized the street lights were few and far between. He strained to see the passing cityscape through the falling darkness. Squat *roble* trees shrouded concrete corner stores and high-walled houses, occasional *bodegas* selling newspapers and candy. But few pedestrians walked the street.

Then they turned a corner and came upon a street-corner revival being led by a Guatemalan in tie, shouting out his witnessing into the megaphone. A rapt crowd of about fifty nodded quietly, then shouted periodic "*aleluyas!*" Lucho seemed to take no note of it.

"What does the bishop think about that?" Robinson asked. Lucho looked at him without comprehension, then a question animated his face.

"Hey, what happened to Jim and Tammy? You think they really stole all that stuff? What a show! Used to get it live here."

Lucho steered onto a broad roaring street lined with small industrial offices and *fábricas*, service stations. Another turn and they were at the Huxley, an unnecessarily tall edifice like its namesakes the world over.

Lucho was inside with his bags in an instant and called to a friend in the Huxley uniform. They consulted, then went to the reservations desk, manned by a young woman in black skirt and white blouse. She evinced a hostility fairly typical of public-contact workers in large institutions in the developing world. It was usually not, he had learned on his travels, directed at him personally. It was rather a learned habit, a safe starting point.

A discussion ensued, with shaking of female head. Finally Lucho waved Robinson over.

He was being booked in.

"You need a driver here?" Lucho asked.

"Thought I'd rent a car."

"Rip-off," said Lucho. "I can drive you all over. You want to go to Atitlán, I take you. Indian market, ruins, whatever."

Robinson didn't know.

"Take my card," Lucho said. "Call me anytime."

Robinson gave him a fairly large tip. The bellboy led Robinson down the corridor to the elevator. The modular blandness of the hotel, a global prototypical design for adaptation to Indianapolis or N'Djamena, had been localized by the installation of real parquet floors, popular in Latin America, together with cheap shiny replicas of Spanish colonial furniture. A depressing bar stood adjacent to an empty dining room staffed by three glowering effeminate waiters. The corridor was lined with junky displays of jewelry and overpriced imported doodads found all over the world. The interior of the Huxley smelled of gasoline, the smell coming from the floor wax, which was probably refinery waste.

His room was on the tenth floor, and he settled in. He looked out on the dark, surprisingly chill city from a tiny balcony. The low-roofed buildings opposite him had a squat mountain look to them, a hint of somewhere he'd seen before but couldn't peg. A few motorcycles whined up the streets around the hotel.

The dinner in the dining room was surprisingly good but diminished by the fact that he ate entirely alone. The waiters watched him take each bite, watched him chew and swallow, and whisked plates away the instant he was close to finishing. As a result, a very nice dinner with good Argentine wine shot by in about twenty minutes, and he was left with an evening to kill, since he was sure Padre Elizondo Huidrobo could not be contacted tonight.

He opted for a stroll around the block. This he had to repeat twice to the concierge, who insisted on calling a cab over as Robinson went out the door. No, Robinson said, he just wanted to walk. The walk was marred by the fact that the Huxley had stationed a private guard force at close intervals all the way around the hotel, and so it was as though he were conducting a military review. He alternately startled, baffled, and irritated the guards as he walked by.

For a Latin American capital, the streets were unusually dark and depopulated. He saw only two things of interest outside: a lively little dance club for *guatemaltecos*, where the twenty or so couples salsaed and merengued with abandon until they saw him watching, and then glared back; and a sinister-looking nightclub–strip joint called the Copacabana, which he wagered also served as a whorehouse. When he stuck his head in the door, a half-dozen bored prostitutes stood up, ready to assist. He backed out.

He returned to the hotel just in time to be swept up in the arrival ceremony of Senator W. A. Blisterson, who was bedding down here and not at the Camino Real. The senator himself and his diminutive wife, "Miss Minnie," were at the core of a phalanx of Guatemalan bodyguards carrying Uzis, followed by several wild-eyed aides from Capitol Hill. The goggle-eyed senator looked taciturn, but Miss Minnie, dressed as she might have been at a Baptist church social in Pettyville, was clearly frightened by the show of weaponry.

They rolled on and into the elevators.

After reading travel brochures in the lobby, Robinson went back to his room and turned on the television, just in time to see a sweat-soaked Reverend Donny Lunkard deliver a twenty-five-minute prayer.

Robinson turned everything off and went to bed before eleven.

"*Mi amigo Danilo,*" Padre Huidrobo said over the phone the next morning, claiming to remember the transactions of almost fifteen years before. "Why you are in my country?"

"Business," Robinson said. "I was hoping you'd let me take you to lunch."

"*Muy bien,*" the Padre said. "What you like—how about a good typical *Guatemalteco* meal?"

"Fine," said Robinson. Before lunch, he took a tour of the city, with Lucho as his driver. Guatemala City, like most Latin cities, had an ancient center core with a broad cobblestoned plaza fronting the Palacio Nacional, the symbolic seat of centralist power from which all flowed. For presidents and plotters, control of the palace and plaza and the presidential sash meant control of the fatherland. The place had been the site of scintillant inaugural ceremonies and of midnight coups with the sound of combat boots on cobblestones, wild Carnival celebration and the funereal commemoration of Easter, with heavy crosses borne and self-flagellation. Earthquake had shaken its foundations periodically. Passageways and colonnades reeked of urine. The neoclassical architecture, as in Prague, had been sooted gray by centuries of effluent from fires, buses, and trucks. But the medieval twists and turns of Slavic Europe gave way here, in the plaza at least, to a pre-Christian monumentalism both sinister and melancholic, echoes of the Inquisition still resounding in these alleyways, living remnants of a subjugated race now walking the margins of these same plazas.

The newer inner city had broad boulevards lined with firs and giant Norfolk Island pines, neoclassical residences that in some areas had slipped to become language academies and private clubs. The Teatro Nacional was a strange modernistic cement ocean liner on top of a hill. Street after street of peeling, dusty modern apartment blocks and offices, and clusters of *tiendas* selling cheap polyester clothes from Taiwan and El Salvador, made up the rest.

Aside from the colonial architectural gems, Guatemala City was a place that looked as if it had lost its way in more recent times. The form of life was much the same as elsewhere; but the guiding vision that had shaped it was secret, and neglectful.

Midday approached and, with it, Padre Huidrobo, who called for him in the Huxley lobby. The Padre, little over five feet tall, was rotund and bowlegged and walked leaning slightly forward, as though he were plowing into life. He was wearing a dusty black suit, obsidian sunglasses, and a wide-brim Panama hat that made him look like a cross between a plantation overseer and a blind man. Accompanied by a driver-bodyguard, he had a silver fringe of hair and a mustache—a luna moth that had landed on his upper lip. But most expressive were his eyes—which he exposed only when he took off his glasses to better scan the room: eyes totally round and able to expand to twice the size of normal eyes—and a mouth that was forever grinning, grimacing, gasping, or miming to exaggerated degree. It was if he was a silent-movie star playing to a huge half-blind audience, and the effect was both hilarious and bizarre.

"*Mí amigo Danilo*," he said twice, hesitantly, to the wrong people in the outer lobby. Finally Robinson caught his eye and the Padre shouted and gave a warm *abrazo*. He must have been seventy years old by now. Having heard how well PAN had done over the years, Robinson was surprised when the Padre took him to a very modest, unfinished cement home in a working-class suburb of the city called Montserrate. The Padre lived there with his younger sister, who was a widow. An Indian woman was preparing their lunch.

"Jus' because PAN has power doesn' mean I mus' live like Caesar!" said the Padre, laughing his guttural laugh and gripping Robinson's arm. "I am a modes' man. I know you invite me to lunch. But you are in my country, and it is my *responsabilidad*, and honor, to have you as my guest."

They sat on two stuffed vinyl-covered chairs and faced a concrete wall displaying the Padre's own watercolors of the Guatemalan *campo* in wooden frames.

"*Aguardiente*," the Padre said, and Robinson took a shot glass and the Padre toasted him.

"To your generous *ayuda* to the poor of Guatemala, and to PAN, that make our success of today *posible*."

The clear liquor, like its Mexican cousin, tequila, burned as it went down. The Padre proceeded to tell him that PAN had grown and prospered because it did not directly threaten the power structure, and because he and it had always remained devoutly apolitical.

"We have learn to be *diplomáticos*," he said, winking and crunching his shoulders in a kind of parody of servility. "I talk to everybody—General So-and-so, millionaire Whatzisname . . . We even talk with the *protestantes*."

"Padre, what do you think of them? All the *evangelistas?*"

The Padre screwed up his face in a look of deep seriousness, for it was clear this was a subject he had considered often.

"You know I come from some—*cómo se dice?*—bias," he said. "The Mother Church she shape me, form me. So I am always uncomfortable with those outside. But I will give to the *evangelistas* one thing: if they motivate my people, if they energize them, then that is good. This week we have the convention of the Kiwanis, next week the *Rotario*, then the *Leones*. En Guatemala all these groups are very *protestante* . . . they are teaching people business, work, organization, values of the *burguesía*. Dale Carnegie too . . . You may laugh, but all these *grupos—sectos*, shall we say?—are shaking off the passivity. This is something my church never do. The ones who take action are all *izquierdista* . . . like the Sandinistas, *teología de liberación*, et cetera. But this would not work in Guatemala." He screwed up his face and pouted his lips as if reaching for a weighty explanation, then made a throat-slitting gesture across his neck. His eyes popped wide open, and then he laughed uproariously. Robinson laughed too.

"*En Guatemala*," the Padre added, "the *sectos* are the real revolution. My little PAN is a small potato compared to them. We are a bit old-fashion. Between you and me, I think we have burn out. *Cooperativos* cannot compete with razzle-dazzle. Fly with the eagles, or escratch with the *gallinas!*"

And so went the luncheon conversation. Robinson was never able to get in more than a few words or a short question before the Padre held forth again, either during the drinks or during the excellent lunch afterward, served on a muddy patio behind the house.

After lunch, the Padre took Robinson back out to his car. Inexplicably, he gave the driver the afternoon off and insisted on driving himself. Both Robinson and the driver blanched at that thought but could not dissuade him.

"I want to take you and show you a PAN cooperative near here—one of the first, that your money from the *generoso* Edwar' Streeter Foundation make *posible.*"

He looked over at Robinson and winked. They drove for a time without speaking on the highway that led to the Pacific coast. The Padre turned up the radio, and then leaned over to him.

"Bueno. Por qué estás en Guatemala?" the Padre asked.

Robinson was a little taken aback at the direct tone of the question. Robinson had assumed that no one in this part of the world knew of the sources of the Edward Streeter Foundation's funds, even though it had leaked out during some of the Senate hearings on the CIA back in the 1970s. But the Padre seemed to be saying that he did.

"My friend, we mus' be very careful here," he said. "I exist between the *león* and the *tigre.* One is asleep, and the other is pickin' his teeth, so I'm the little mouse who do my work quietly. In that way I help the other little mice to a better life. But quiet, quiet, so the big boys won't pay much *atención* to me and gobble me up."

He grabbed Robinson's arm, chomped at the air, his eyes bulging, then laughed uproariously.

"My friend, we are winnin' the *lucha* for the *campesino, poco a poco.* We will make this a better country, inch by inch. But it is our curse to do it in Guatemala, where God choose to blink his eyes while he was flying over the beautiful world he build in seven days."

Robinson took a deep breath. "I'm here to find out what happened to a friend of mine who died last year in Guatemala."

The Padre raised his gray eyebrows and made a face.

"Who was your friend?"

"Morris Krámský. Born in Europe but lived in the U.S."

"Judío?"

Robinson shook his head. "Catholic."

"And why you come to Padre Huidrobo? Your people have contact in the security apparatus, *fuerzas armadas*, up to the President's chambermaid, *me imagino.*"

He raised his eyebrows and made a face at his own statement, then laughed.

"Because I can't trust my people and their contacts," said Robinson. "They—" Robinson didn't finish, and the Padre watched him expectantly.

"Ah ha. So you are runnin' a kind of . . . *investigación privada, digamos?*"

Robinson nodded. The Padre looked at the approaching highway and said nothing for a minute.

"Then you too are caught between the *león* and the *tigre*," he said. "My frien' Danilo, that is very dangerous to you. When I am with my *campesinos*, and when I talk to the press, and to you, I mus' put on a happy face, the face of a clown, to make people laugh and forget and think the world not so bad. But, Danilo . . . is very bad here. You know our own *Presidente* sleeps with pistols and *revolveres* under his pillow. . . . Yes, my friend, he and his lovely *señora* have enough guns in the presidential bedroom to start a *guerra civil.* And that is because he is in danger. He is our little show of democracy, and he sits on the tiger's nose. Everybody who is not part of the *tigre* is in danger."

They were winding down to a lower altitude, in a farming valley to the south of the capital. The hot, dry mountainsides dotted with century plants stretched up on either side of them.

"How did your friend die?"

"A hole was blown in his head. Some were saying it was suicide."

Padre Huidrobo smiled.

"Many foreigners come to Guatemala to commit suicide," he said. "Is our wonderful climate and low cos' of dyin'. A nice *funerario* cos' only two hundred dollars, complete with *orquesta*, last rites, embalming, hairdo. No police *investigaciónes* or trials. Where it happen?"

"Near San Carlos de Chixoy. They said he was on a hunting trip."

The Padre turned to look at him in amazement.

"What he was huntin'—*comunistas?* Did your friend have some funny business with the *guerrilleros?* Danilo, that *distrito* has been notorious for fighting and violence for ten years. *Muy aislada*, dense forest and mountains. No one go there unless they are lookin' for trouble. What was his business? Maybe he was supplying the *rebeldes?*"

Robinson shrugged. "It's possible, because he was in the sporting goods business and he might have been trading in guns. And it's also possible he was looking for someone. He'd long been in search of someone from his home country, a person from World War Two. He had been told this person had been seen in Guatemala."

"This mysterious person was a *criminal* of some sort?" the Padre asked. "A German, maybe? We used to have many *alemanes* . . . from the coffee days."

"Possibly; I don't know. Equally likely he was a Communist, a spy; I don't know."

They pulled over to the side of the road so that the Padre could buy a bunch of ripe bananas. He offered one to Robinson, then began peeling his own.

"The *plátano* is a wonderful fruit," he said. "So *honesto*. You peel and find this soft white *fruta*. Perhaps a bruise or two, but no surprises. Guatemala is not so simple. *Es un cementerio* . . . you dig, fearing what you will find."

The Padre also bought an afternoon newspaper from the capital. It announced a new summit of Central American leaders to be held in Managua, to discuss regional peace.

"Peace, peace," scoffed the Padre. "More die in this peace than in most wars. My hones' *consejo* would be to stay away from Chixoy. Is the mos' painful, mos' tragic part of this country. Thousands of *inocentes* die there while the beasts fight out their battle. You see what happen to your friend. You mus' open many graves to find the truth . . . if there is any at all to find."

"I know the danger," said Robinson. "Padre, Krámský was like a father to me. I owe it to his widow, and to his memory, to bring his killers to justice."

The Padre, as Robinson expected, was moved by this appeal to family and honor.

"As you wish. But, Danilo, you will not find *justicia* here. The word has been made a mockery. We Guatemalans mus' await *el día de la salvación* to find it. Here, the system of laws is in the hands of jackals and baboons, *gallinazas* sitting on the roof of the *Corte Supremo.* Do not be drawn into our battle, for all emerge with their honor, if not their souls, *comprometidos.* My compromise is to be a smilin' clown, carvin' out a little path for the *campesinos.* I have to take the knife to my own *vocabulario* . . . no '*socialismo*,' no '*comunismo*,' no 'social progress,' no '*reforma agraria*,' no 'human rights,' because any mention of them will bring down the *apocalipsis*. No, I speak in silly jokes about cooperation and self-help, because anything else brings *muerte* and *miseria*. This way, I postpone it a bit, hopin' a better day will come."

The Padre swerved to avoid hitting a trio of piglets that suddenly bolted into the highway. Looking in his rearview mirror, he saw all had survived.

"What more I can do for you than warn you *que no vayas?*" asked the Padre.

"Padre, I'm like a blind man in Guatemala. Perhaps you know someone who is knowledgeable about events in San Carlos de Chixoy, someone who could assist me?"

The Padre thought for a time, without speaking.

"I will give you the name of a good man in Huehuetenango, for that is as close as you may go alone. For a gringo to be in Huehue is a surprise; for a gringo to be in Chixoy can mean death. I do not know him, have never meet him. I have only hear of him. He, like all *hombres rectos* here, is in danger, and you will be in danger when you seek him. He is a journalist and a *novelista* and is the local monitor for *Amnistía Internacional*. I have no *garantía* he will speak to you. He will be immediately *sospechoso*, assuming you are up to no good. He is a very clever man—otherwise he would be dead—and I doubt you can fool him. But he more than any other is likely to speak to you the truth about your friend. If he knows it."

"What is his name?"

"Socrates Salazar."

"How do I find him?"

"Ask anyone in Huehue. They will direct you to him."

By this time they were driving up the approach to the first of PAN's cooperatives, funded with money from the bogus Edward Streeter Foundation almost fifteen years earlier. Daniel Robinson spent the remainder of that afternoon being shown the accidental fruits of his forgotten labors of many years before, surprised and embarrassed to find that this small bit of the treasure of the United States spewed into the covert battle had actually done some lasting good. He saw the cottages of the coffee driers, the medical clinic, the food service, and the elementary school run for the children of the workers. It gave him pause, because, of all the things he had ever initiated, only this seemed to have had any positive human impact, and only by the good works of the Padre: the rest had been swept away, vanished, gurgling down the gutters of time almost as if symbolizing the weakness of the United States itself—a profligacy, a gargantuan wastefulness and bumbling inability to focus on anything this small, but ultimately so important.

The next morning Robinson found himself in Lucho's "L'il Hoss" pickup truck headed north on the Pan American Highway, toward Mexico. He had been about to sign a car rental agreement with Hertz in the hotel lobby when Lucho had fallen upon him with such desperation, sweetened by his offer to undercut the car rental rate by about two hundred dollars, that Robinson had reluctantly given in.

"We *guatemaltecos* need foreign assistance real bad," said Lucho. "Hertz don't need your stinkin' money."

They stopped at a roadside *cantina* in a high mountain pass an hour outside the capital, where the warmth of the tropics had fallen away and it was cold enough to make a fire, as the *cantina* owners—a pair of Indian women of the Cakchikel tribe—had done. They sold Indian crafts, together with bundles of mountain herbs and dried red peppers hanging from the ceiling and bunches of fruit in baskets trucked up from the lowlands. The place, wrapped in the rising clouds of mountain mist, was serene and nicely removed from the nondescript sprawl of the capital, giving a sense of what the original Guatemala, before the ravages of modernity and unrest, might have been like.

As they descended from the pass into the valley that would lead them to Huehuetenango, Lucho pointed out the periodic sentry stands on the mountainsides, overlooking the highway, which Robinson had already noted.

"*Patrullas de Autodefensa Civil*," said Lucho.

The stands, often nothing more than a thatched hut or traffic kiosk in the weeds, were manned by young men with rifles.

"Lucas García created them," said Lucho. "*¡El gran hijo de puta!*

Ordered all the *campesinos* to give time as 'volunteers.' Protecting their cornfields against *comunistas.*"

Lucho looked over at him and gave a laugh. His Maya face was like a piece of exhumed pottery, with broad hook nose and a prominent muzzle of a mouth and straight obsidian hair that hung in a rock-star cut onto his forehead and shoulders. It was a face of a thousand years ago, not of a leader or conqueror but of a clever server, a face that might have toiled in the ceremonial centers at Tikal and Uaxactún, an acolyte to the high priests who were the rulers of a theocracy now swallowed by jungle. And in mockery of the vulgar transient era in which they now lived, Lucho wore a black T-shirt with a lurid phosphorescent auto-da-fé of a popular American television star gagging herself with her finger.

They wound on through valley and ravine, through countryside that could have been Colorado, forests of piñon and tumbling rivulets and mountainside fields of highland *maíz.* But the light was whiter than Colorado, an intensity noticeable even when a billowing cloud crossed the sun. This was truly the land of light, without the morose *sombra* of Northern Europe and North America.

As a reminder of the recent strife, they crossed a bridge under construction. "Reconstruction," corrected Lucho, for the twisted girders of the original, destroyed in a rebel bombing, lay by the riverbank. They ate a lunch of *cerveza* and *pipián*, the national dish, at a roadside café near San Cristóbal de Totonicapán, then continued on across the dusty central plateau toward Huehue. The beer made Lucho even more assertive than before. Rather than going straight into town, as Robinson wanted, Lucho insisted on taking a detour to the ruins of Zaculeu, a pyramidal shrine of the Mam people that had been restored in 1940 by the United Fruit Company as a "gift to the people of Guatemala."

"Ha," laughed Lucho, reading the inscription and watching Robinson's reaction. "They fucked the whole country and gave us a cement pyramid."

Robinson didn't say anything.

"United Fruit," continued Lucho, testing. "You gringos don't know about United Fruit, do you? Don't know your Secretary of State John Foster Dulles represented the company as a lawyer, that his crazy CIA brother Allen was on the board of directors, that Henry Cabot Lodge, your U.N. ambassador, was a big stockholder?

That's who overthrew Arbenz in 1954, United Fruit. It wasn't the *Estados Unidos*, it was the *Frutas Unidas*."

"I'd forgotten," said Robinson.

"Hell, man, I got a degree in Latin American studies at American U! I had to go to Washington to learn the truth about Guatemala, because you don't get it here. That's because the U.S. is a great country and Guatemala is a shithole. Hell, I love the U.S. Americans are great people. America is a great country. So why does it fuck around with Latin America?"

Robinson couldn't even begin to answer. Lucho nodded into the silence, wanting more.

"Pure *racismo*," said Lucho. "I think they do things to brown people they can't do to white people."

Robinson walked around the ruins for another five minutes. He looked off to the northeast, to the ragged green silhouette of the Sierra Cuchumatanes, and imagined that somewhere beyond them, where the billowing clouds cast profound shadow on the abyssal valleys of the north, lay the Indian village of San Carlos de Chixoy, where Miroslav Lhota had died almost four months before.

> On this site in 1525, the Spanish conquistador Pedro de Alvarado laid siege to Zaculeu, ceremonial center for the Mam nation. The Mam leaders, seeing the overwhelming force of the Spanish, concluded that they were *hijos del sol*—children of the sun—and that resistance was futile.

Lucho was sitting on one of the steps of the pyramid, facing west. The electric sun was falling all over him, and he smoked a cigarette. He had put on a set of Walkman headphones.

"Let's go to town," Robinson said. Lucho was now strangely silent, perhaps embarrassed at his previous outburst. They drove down the rutted dirt lane to the town of Huehuetenango, slowing periodically to pass Indian men and boys carrying loads of firewood, produce, and even groceries on their backs, secured to their foreheads by tump lines to lessen the load.

"This way of carrying goes back two thousand years," said Lucho. "Mayas didn't discover the wheel, and they've never been that comfortable with it."

The town itself, capital of the Departamento de Huehuetenango and center of the counterinsurgency operations in that province, was small and seemingly tranquil. The plaza was square, surrounded as in most colonial Ibero-American towns by colonnades with shops, *cantinas*, *bodegas*, and perhaps a *residencia* or two. But the scene was dominated by a Moorish–Art Deco bandshell. There was also a white stucco cathedral. The shrubbery in the park had been sculpted into animal shapes. *Palmas*, *piños*, and *naranja* trees dotted the neat expanse.

"Too quiet here," said Lucho, looking around him.

It was siesta time, and a slight but steady flow of people moved in the street: men in straw hats pushing bicycles; an Indian mother in chocolate shawl and striped tribal skirt with her tiny daughter; a Hispanic woman in pantsuit with purse. Puddles from an earlier rain spotted the street, and the sky held billowing cumulus clouds, with intervals of ultramarine blue sky. The breeze, like the day, came in curious intervening bursts of raw dampness followed by an arid heat, carrying smells of spices like *ají* and *pimienta*, smells that even had he been blind and deaf would have told Robinson he was in another world. The side streets meandered away from the plaza as little more than alleyways, thick-walled cement and stucco flat-roofed structures painted in avocado green and citron yellow, rust brown and Malaga red, colors born of a different aesthetic than the north's. The same hybrid of Moorish and Art Deco continued into the little *barrios* off the plaza, the smells of woodsmoke and urine and *pimienta* perfuming all.

This town, only one thousand miles from the U.S., felt more foreign than Prague or Tokyo ever would, the projection of another mind, another imagination entirely.

"Hotel Zaculeu is the best in town," said Lucho. Robinson assumed that meant expensive, until he found upon inquiring that two single rooms could be had for six dollars apiece. The foyer opened onto a courtyard that was a miniature of the plaza's park. The rooms, with tall double doors, were arranged on a tiled walkway around beds of flowers, birds in cages, colonnades hung with bougainvillea. The adjoining dining room, bare wooden floor with tables and straight-backed wooden chairs, looked unchanged for a hundred years.

"I like it," said Robinson. And he did. It reminded him why he had gone into the line of work he had chosen so many years before: the constant surprise, the constant awakening received from the alien.

Sitting in this modest little inn, he felt ashamed he had got caught up in things that now seemed so false. The small room was Spartan but adorned with local handicrafts—handwoven cloth, tin candlesticks, clay water pitchers. He was moved that people would provide this degree of service for six dollars, whereas back home, twenty times that much might have got a computer-printed "Thank you!" on the bottom of a receipt handed over by a surly desk clerk.

Something had been lost back home.

Robinson gave Lucho the afternoon off; Lucho looked grateful for the chance to sleep off the morning beer. Then Robinson inquired of the desk clerk how he might find Mr. Socrates Salazar.

She wrote out the address meticulously, and he scrutinized it as though it would take him an hour to find.

"*Dónde está?*" he asked, concerned.

She pointed out through the front door. It was just on the other side of the plaza, in a storefront, maybe one hundred fifty feet away. He could almost have talked to Salazar without leaving the hotel. This was the office of *El Heraldo de Huehuetenango*, the province's main newspaper. He laughed at his different experience of urban distances, and she laughed too.

Crossing the plaza, Robinson knocked on the louvered front door of the *Heraldo* and was puzzled when there was no reply. But of course, he thought, looking at his watch. Siesta. No one would be there for perhaps another hour.

So he sat in the park, watching the clouds pass over the sun, and the cerulean sky behind it all. Occasional children would come to stare at him from a distance, and then go on. He felt the warmth of the sunburst on his face, and the slight chill that would fall when a cloud came; he even dozed for a few minutes, although he could never completely let go enough to fall dead asleep in a public place, certainly not here. He went over to a *farmacía* that had remained open and bought some chewing gum. He overheard a conversation between the pharmacist's clerk and a half-deaf old Indian man about a rheumatism drug. The cost was three quetzales—about $1.30. The old man had only one quetzal, so he was nowhere close to having enough.

Robinson caught the eye of the clerk.

"*Yo lo pago,*" he said. She was surprised, but then agreed. The old man, looking sadly out onto the square, hadn't heard.

"*Señor,*" she said. "Your medicine."

The old man looked back in puzzlement at the medicine bottle in her outstretched hand.

"*¿Qué pasó?*" he asked.

"This man paid the difference," she said, pointing to Robinson. The old man looked at Robinson for the first time, in amazement, then he walked away as if insulted.

Back out on the plaza, Robinson realized the *Heraldo* door was open. He walked over and stuck his head in. An unusually tall, rawboned teenage boy was sitting at a desk, writing checks out of a huge antiquated draft book and making penned notations in an account ledger.

"*¿Con qué le puedo ayudar?*" the boy asked.

"*¿Está el Señor Socrates Salazar?*" Robinson asked. He knew the answer, for through the opened inner-office door he could see a pair of legs and shoes resting on the desk; the rest of the man was obscured.

"*Momentito,*" said the boy, going inside. Robinson heard him say a visitor was there. Who is he? Robinson heard the invisible man ask.

"*¿Quién es usted, señor?*" the boy asked, sticking his head out.

"*Yo soy Señor Daniel Robinson, de los Estados Unidos.*" The boy nodded and repeated everything, murdering the pronunciation of his name. *Bien*, he heard the invisible man say.

"*Adelante, señor,*" said the boy, indicating the doorway. Robinson went inside.

Socrates Salazar was not at all what he had expected. Not a typical Latin newspaper editor—blustering, dictatorial, ink-stained, scarred by the continual battle with the authorities—but rather a scholar. Robinson could see this by the books lining the shelves of the office: Bioy Casares, Carpentier, Lezama Lima, Sarmiento, Bernal Díaz. Two-hundred-year-old volumes of Central American history, Nicaraguan poetry. And the roar of the newspaper race, the cigarette smoke and stained coffee cups, were nowhere near him; the newsroom-pressroom, such as it was, was a block away.

Intersperced among the volumes were objets d'art and curios:

Quiche pottery, a meteorite from the high Sierra, a small print of *Guernica*, a framed certificate of recognition from Amnesty International in London.

"You must forgive me," said Socrates Salazar, gently, almost deferent. "My office is a mess; I'm caught up in a translation."

"Of what?" Robinson asked.

"Bowles, *The Sheltering Sky*. Salazar, *a sus ordenes*," he said, extending his hand.

Salazar was of medium height, and slight, with an almost boyish quality that came through despite the gray brush-cut hair. He wore blue jeans and loafers, and a plaid flannel work shirt.

"You speak English quite well," said Robinson, noticing Salazar's improbable mix of Indian nose and blue eyes. When his lips were closed, a hint of the upper front teeth, slightly crooked, was exposed. It further heightened his boyishness, and his charm. Salazar hardly nodded in acceptance of the compliment on his English, as though he had been told it many times, and by more important men than Daniel Robinson. There was also a sadness about him, a quietude and resignation that might have indicated vulnerability. But this man had managed somehow to survive here.

"I'm Daniel Robinson. I was sent to you by an associate in Guatemala City, who recommended you highly."

Salazar looked at him a bit quizzically, the light smile fading.

"Elizondo Huidrobo," continued Robinson. "He said you were a good man." Robinson thought he saw in Salazar's face a hint of disappointment, or was it distaste?

"That was . . . kind," said Salazar. "I have never had the pleasure of meeting him. But I read of his . . . activities."

Perhaps the two Guatemalans were on different sides of the political fence. Perhaps Padre Huidrobo was too much of an accommodationist.

"Can we speak freely here?" asked Robinson.

Salazar smiled, his eyes narrowing.

"If you are alluding to my secretary, his loyalty to me is unquestioning. He saw his entire family die in an attack by the Guatemalan Special Operations Command. Slaughtered with bayonets and flamethrowers."

Robinson nodded, embarrassed.

"And if you are concerned about listening devices and other James

Bond tricks, this is a developing country. The telephones barely work. I doubt our secret police could keep a bug working long enough to pick up anything more than my afternoon farts."

Salazar laughed harshly.

"And for what did Huidrobo recommend me?"

A small cracked picture of the overthrown reformer Jacobo Arbenz stood on the desk, taken in 1953 during his brief presidency. On the bookshelf was a picture of Ramsey Clark shaking hands with Socrates Salazar, probably in the 1970s.

"He said you might be of help in finding out what happened to a friend of mine who died here in Guatemala last September."

Silence followed, while Salazar looked down at the text he was translating. Robinson was surprised to see a face that had at first been so boyish and open suddenly convoluted. Salazar seemed to age, to mature, right before his eyes. It was this very unique face and its range of reflections that would have told him Salazar was unusual, even had nothing else been known about him.

"Are you an investigator of some kind?" Salazar asked.

"I'm in investment finance. I investigate investment opportunities. But I came here for personal reasons. To learn more about my friend's death."

Salazar closed the Bowles text and looked at him.

"What a devoted friend, to come thousands of miles to learn more about a friend's death."

"We were very close."

Salazar paused, observing. "I should say."

"He saved my life," said Robinson.

"Oh?"

"When I was a young businessman in Europe, I was an amateur mountain climber. He prevented my death."

Salazar seemed a touch skeptical. Robinson thought he even winked. The conversation stalled for a second, as if Salazar wanted to pursue this dubious issue of closeness, of a life being saved, but out of politeness and unfamiliarity would let it go.

Socrates Salazar looked away, and Robinson relaxed slightly.

"Will you have *un cafecito?*" Salazar asked.

"Yes, thank you."

"Tito. Dos cafecitos, por favor."

The tall boy in the outer office assented.

Salazar smiled with his original warmth.

"Could I see some identification?"

Robinson handed over his passport. The passport was brand new, crisp and unstamped, except for Guatemala's visa.

"I presume you have gone to the authorities?"

Robinson took a breath. "I haven't," he said.

"And why is that?"

"That's why I came to you. Because it's possible the authorities were involved in the death."

Salazar tapped his pencil on the desk.

"And what gives you reason to believe that?"

"Because of the locale, and the prevailing political climate there."

"Where did he die?"

"San Carlos de Chixoy."

"A long-standing area of rebel activity and counterinsurgency. Why would your friend have gone there, except for that?"

"He may have been jaguar hunting, he may have been searching for a missing person. As for the fighting, I just don't know; it's possible he was involved."

"Did your friend have some kind of sympathy for one of the parties in our conflict?"

"Possibly."

"With which side?"

"I don't know," said Robinson.

"What does that mean?"

"It means that at different stages in his life he had different sympathies. If he was to be believed in his most recent statements, he might have sympathized with the government."

Salazar's eyes were immobile.

"You imply he wasn't truthful?"

"Not at all. I've learned to be skeptical."

"As have I. But of your closest friend, whose death motivates you to travel thousands of miles to find out more?"

Robinson laughed. "I suppose I've been shaped by my profession."

"Which is . . ."

"Investment banking, as I said. In my profession, surfaces are often deceptive. We learn not to make an evaluation until we have accountants' sworn testimony."

"In business, yes. But close personal friendships?"

Salazar's eyebrows were raised, and he waited. A messenger boy in Indian poncho entered, leaving a parcel, and departed.

"Very well," said Salazar, as if to ease the heaviness of the silence. "I do not profess to understand the North American mind. I spent my foreign years in London—"

"An unusual choice for a *guatemalteco* . . ."

"You refer to our territorial dispute with England over Belize?"

He awaited a rejoinder from Robinson, but there was none.

"Where were we?" he said. "Oh, yes. Your friend's change of mind. So I gather he was a convert to the rightist cause, late in life?"

"He was a convert to democratic ideas, yes. As to whether he was a rightist, that depends on your use of the word and to his own inclinations, which in the last three or four years weren't always known to me."

"I won't get into a debate about labels. Had he been of the left earlier?"

"Yes."

"And he was a European?"

"Yes. A Czech."

Salazar cocked his head slightly.

"A refugee?"

"Yes."

"Refugee from socialist Czechoslovakia?"

"Yes. He became a Catholic activist in the 1960s and was finally allowed to leave in the 1970s." Robinson wondered if this aspect of Lhota's new cover identity wouldn't just confuse things.

"I'm at a disadvantage when it comes to Czechoslovakia," said Salazar. "It, like Guatemala, was so long out of the spotlight. Until the recent changes. Here as well as there, the darkness allows evil-doers to get away with more. What was his stated business in Guatemala, again?"

"He was supposedly hunting. Jaguars. And it was somewhat plausible, because he was a hunter, though not of such exotic game. And he was in the sporting goods business. But it is unlikely he would have come so far for game hunting alone."

"Might he have been in the weapons business?" Salazar asked. "I ask because Czechoslovakia supplied our popular militia back in 1954, before President Arbenz was overthrown."

"It's possible. Also possible that this other man he was searching for had some connection. This other person might have had a criminal or fugitive nature. It might have been a personal vendetta from long ago. Someone—"

"Was he searching for a German?"

"No; a Czech, as I understand it. Or actually a Ruthenian, from the Carpathian Ukraine section that once belonged to Czechoslovakia. Why do you ask?"

"Oh, because Guatemala has sometimes served as a haven for German fugitives. Our coffee plantations were once German-owned, and there are still many German families here, though their power is much diminished. Back to your friend . . . what was his name?"

"Morris Krámský."

Salazar turned and looked out through the huge French window that opened onto the alleyway off the plaza. A pair of boys were pitching coins to a line in the broken pavement. It was now late afternoon, and the sun was throwing a helianthin light onto the torn streamers of cloud that reached down from above, like arms of the exploding sun, still incandescent, fusion cooling but still under way. It must have been getting on toward six o'clock.

"Let me get this straight," said Salazar to his own faint reflection in the window glass. "Mr. Robinson is following the footsteps of a dead Czech rightist Catholic named Krámský, who had become a jaguar hunter and sporting goods dealer, and who in turn was looking for another Czech of possibly criminal nature, in a faraway corner of Guatemala, in a place where ten thousand innocents have died. People following other people, persons of vague portfolio, individuals in places where they are not supposed to be. Refugees, criminals, guns, hunters, secret vendettas."

In the corner of the room stood a single wooden table devoted to the tasks of newspaper editorship. It held back issues of *El Heraldo*, clippings, glossy photos, articles already typeset but not approved. Heaped up were press releases, newsletters from around the world, back copies of *Time*, *The Economist*, *The Nation*, *Excelsior*, *L'Humanité*. A front page bearing the censor's mark was framed on the wall.

"Was your friend an intelligence agent of some kind?" Salazar asked.

"I don't think so," said Robinson.

"And are you?" Salazar asked, watching him.

"No," said Robinson. "Are you?"

Salazar jerked his head back slightly and grinned.

"In Guatemala," he said, winking, "nothing is to be trusted."

Tito came in with the tray of coffees. It consisted of a thick black avatar of *café*, to which was added hot water from a pot. Tito went outside again.

"This matter reeks of intrigue," said Salazar, turning back to the exploding sunset sky and the window. Then he looked at Robinson.

"Intrigue," he repeated. "Señor Daniel Robinson *de los Estados Unidos*. I must say I am astonished you have come to me, rather than a lawyer or an investigator. My mind is running in a thousand directions, wondering who you really are and what your presence here means. . . ."

Robinson returned his stare, but too stiffly.

"My identity, on the other hand," continued Salazar, "is a matter of public record. I gather you know something of me, and you have concluded more during our talk. I am a writer, an editor, and a modest activist on human rights. I say publicly that I am apolitical, but that is silly, for in the context of Guatemala, to advocate human rights is a political act, an ideological one. Here in this humble part of the world, the human rights violated most often are those of the simple people who are born and toil and die an early death. Those are the human rights that matter most to me, if only because my energy and power are limited to this corner of the world, and the downtrodden here have so few defenders." He paused to light up a pipe, tamping in the tobacco.

"And then there are the human rights of rightist Czech refugee jaguar hunters who died looking for Czech fugitives, and of gringos who came looking for them. They are aberrations, they come from far away, they have no connection to this land, their allegiance is uncertain. As human beings, their rights must be considered . . . but in light of what contribution they themselves have made to the rights of their fellowmen."

He took a deep draw from the tobacco and looked at Robinson without smiling.

"Mr. Robinson, perhaps it has occurred to you to ask how someone like me has remained alive here. In part, it is because I have a chorus of defenders in places like New York and London who can unsettle our rulers with their squawks of indignation if I am jailed or harassed. Several times has this distant Greek chorus kept me from prison or death."

He took another draw from his pipe.

"But there are limits to the protective power of the chorus," he said. "That is because Socrates Salazar is not a name like Benigno Aquino or Archbishop Romero, because Guatemala is not in the spotlight like El Salvador, because I am not a writer of the stature of García Márquez. To exist without that added protection, I must also be clever. And I must be very careful.

"That is why I must ask that we end this conversation," said Salazar. "Certain things in your search intrigue me, as a journalist and a Guatemalan historian. But it is too much an affair of secrecy and foreigners, and I do not see it as the most valuable use of my time. I must choose my battles carefully, and I think that this one is yours, not mine."

Robinson's disappointment was great, and yet there was an underlay of relief, for this man had aroused his uncertainties and wariness. The only question was, without Salazar, how could he get to the truth about Lhota in anything less than a lifetime?

"Surely you understand my position?" Salazar continued. Robinson nodded. "And do you understand your own here? I think you do not. Yes, Guatemala is considered a democratic country now, because we have a civilian president for the first time in many years. I do not belittle that, for it has made the climate of life a little better for people like me. The kidnappings and gunshots are less frequent, the censorship less blatant. But the improvement is still superficial and cosmetic, for the President dare not make key military appointments, he still has no hand in the counterinsurgency, no death squads have been brought to justice, people here and there are still jerked off the street or shot. So let me make it clear: The longer you remain here, pursuing an investigation of such a patently sensitive nature, the likelihood of your coming also to harm, like your friend Mr. Krámský, is ever higher. At some point, I think it is overwhelming. I urge you to leave, and consider your friend one of the many murky casualties. Let him rest in peace."

"Should I take that as anything more than your personal warning?" asked Robinson.

Salazar's blue eyes were narrowed and flashing.

"To even think otherwise is to insult me gravely."

The *cafés* were finished, and Robinson rose to leave. He was searching in his head for how this man might help him in these final seconds together, and he came up with nothing. Salazar wanted Robinson out of town, and that was understandable.

Salazar also stood, although he did not escort him out. He stood, awaiting his departure.

"Don Socrates," said Robinson. "You asked me many questions. I'd like to ask you one."

Salazar shrugged.

"Does the phrase 'Veil / the face of God' have meaning for you?"

Salazar looked at him, confused.

"My friend left only a few cryptic notes behind before his death. One phrase was 'Veil / the face of God.' Does that mean anything to you?"

Salazar cocked his head, as if trying to understand. He seemed unsettled.

"What did your friend know about that?" asked Salazar. "The Cara de Dios?"

"He said nothing, other than to send me the phrase written on a postcard."

Salazar turned and looked back out the window that opened onto the side street. The brilliance of the flames above had faded, because a western cloud must have intervened; the clouds above were now shadowed and leaden, while the cracks of open sky revealed a waning eggshell blue.

"The Cara de Dios," Salazar said to himself. He seemed to have forgotten Robinson was even standing there.

"Don Socrates. Do you know something of it?"

Socrates Salazar turned back to him, smiling almost sadly. It seemed his face had come the full circle from their first meeting half an hour before.

"Yes," he said. "I know something of it."

Robinson waited a minute, expecting an answer.

"What do you know?"

"I know," Socrates Salazar said, closing the Paul Bowles text with finality, "that it does not exist."

"What?"

Salazar had only the smile. He then began gathering up some papers from the desk, into a battered briefcase.

"Where are you staying?" Salazar asked.

"At the Zaculeu."

"Will you be in tomorrow morning?"

"Why not tonight?"

"Not possible," said Don Socrates. "I must give a talk on Rubén Darío at the Academia tonight. It will take until perhaps ten or so, and I am very tired. I will come by for you at eight tomorrow and tell you how the Face of God does not exist."

Robinson walked out onto the perimeter of the plaza with Salazar. He was able to ask no further questions, for Salazar only smiled cryptically and took his evening leave. He left Robinson to make his way back to the Hotel Zaculeu, the tiled arch of its entryway now lit by an electric lamp orbited by a few early moths. Lucho was there, sober again, reading an old Madrid celebrity magazine stuffed with photos and gossip about Queen Sophia and King Juan Carlos. When Lucho asked where he had been and what had happened, Robinson begged off, to go into his room and take a quick nap and bath before dinner.

Prague, 1939

On the morning Herr Hitler first waved to us from the Prague Castle window, my homeland and city were blanketed with a snowfall so deep and white it was as though the time of the glaciers had returned and we humans would have to live out our lives tunneling through great dunes of frost, our beards glistening with primeval ice, our cheeks blazing from exposure to a cruel new world. I had made my way slowly on foot from my chambers to a long-scheduled ceremony of investiture for the latest graduating class of medical students from Karlova Universita, to be held by the Minister of Health in the Castle Great Hall. And it was only there, as the steel-helmeted panzer-brigade troops stopped us with their bayonets, that we fully appreciated our destiny was now in the hands of the Führer.

Strange as it may seem to those of us looking back, I suspect that to most of my countrymen on that morning it was of no great concern that the Fascist forces were triumphant. For the conquest—if you can call it that—of little Czecho-Slovakia had taken less than a working day, despite the fury of the March snowstorm. No, my colleagues and compatriots had stood almost as welcoming adorers, so awed were they by the German tanks and artillery rolling by, still polished and unfired, covered with crystalline snow, much more like a holiday military parade than an occupation. I am told there were pockets of resistance here and there, but from such unlikely champions of our national honor as the police in such and such a town, or the militia in some lost parish. The great Czech Army stayed in its barracks and came forth only to admire the beauty and efficiency of the German war machine as it streamed effortlessly past.

Because, you see, we Czecho-Slovaks had long been conditioned to foreign domination. After all, we had been sprung from the yoke of Austrian "bondage" only a bare twenty years before by the great moralist Woodrow Wilson in league with T. G. Masaryk; to be honest, in its later decades that imperial bondage had been quite benign. All of our senior civil service had been trained as Austro-Hungarian subalterns, all of our veteran politicians had cut their teeth in the protective womb of the Hapsburg monarchy; you need look no further than our sitting President at that time, the elderly Catholic Emil Hacha, who had spent most of his life in the service of the Hapsburg crown. And so that must have been on my countrymen's minds, they not terribly upset to be losing their independence, expecting a new but not entirely unbeneficial "partnership" with a more powerful neighboring state, this time speaking with the harsher Prussian accent rather than the Latin flow of the Austrians, but altogether quite similar to what we had known.

That Hitler was an Austrian made him almost a member of the family!

It had been foreordained in the Munich Agreement, at which time Britain threw us to the Nazi wolves. We had all known it would just be a matter of time; the surprise was that it took Hitler from the fall of 1938 until nearly the spring of 1939 to make his move. We had watched as the fragile fantasy that was our fairyland "republic" was once again subjected to the redrawing of borders, before Hitler ever moved the first tank. For the Vienna Award of late 1938 had already given great pieces of my native Slovakia back to Hungary. The Teschen industrial area of Bohemia had already been ceded to Poland. Ruthenia (or would you rather call it the "Carpathian Ukraine"?), out in the far east, had first been given something called "internal autonomy," but Hitler looked the other way when Hungary occupied it even as he was occupying the Czech lands. And on the eve of our own conquest, Hitler had smiled as my little native Slovakia broke away from Masaryk's twin state and became a "sovereign" republic with its own goose-stepping imitations of the Brown Shirts, called the "Hlinka Guard."

And it might have been a fatalistic sense too that our little interlude of independence was to be no more than that, an interlude, that we were small and weak and it was time to pay the piper and so we would have to defer to higher powers once again. As for myself, I had allowed the bourgeois comforts of two decades to dampen my own revolutionary fires, and so where in my youth I might have taken to the street with torch and carbine, now I was more an observer, watching with an almost perverse detachment to see what this historic event would do to my country and to me.

On that chill March morning, as I and my colleagues stood detained in the snowdrifts, it was quite by chance that Herr Hitler emerged from the third-story Castle balcony to receive the adulation of the Sudeten German welcoming committee. Standing beside me was the journalist František, whom I had long known from our common Party membership.

"Look how those Germans are fawning on him," František whispered to me. The group of welcoming Sudeten Germans was quite small and unimpressive, no more than a hundred: these, the sole representatives of the "oppressed" German minority Hitler had used as a pretext for the invasion.

"Do you know what I heard?" said František. "The Führer wanted to go visit the hundreds of German victims of Czech violence in the hospital this morning, only the Gestapo could find not a single German 'victim' anywhere."

"So what will he do?"

"They will keep him here this morning to meet with Hacha, then back to Germany in the afternoon. I understand some heads will roll over this one."

Standing a few yards from us was the young chief of the American legation, George Kennan, whom I had met several times. He was with a pair of junior aides, and they had clearly come up on foot, for Kennan's Packard limousine was nowhere to be seen.

"The Americans know where to be this morning," I said.

"Huh!" snorted František. "I count them almost as low as the British. Where are the great Wilsonian democrats, now that the Hitlerites occupy us? Where is this great undying brotherhood Masaryk told us of, which would safeguard our republic?"

"Wilson is dead," I replied.

At that moment Hitler emerged from behind the curtains of his window. He had apparently slept in the imperial suite.

"When did he get here?" I asked.

František coughed. "He came over by train and motorcar late yesterday, to inspect the job. I'm told he got here last night and moved in while our cabinet was meeting just down the hall. They didn't even know he was here.

"He had a snack of Prague ham and Plzeň beer before bed," František confided gravely.

The cheers and applause of the small German contingent sounded truly pathetic in the chill morning air. Even Hitler seemed to curl his upper lip in contempt.

"Oh, this is too rich," František gasped.

Hitler looked as though he had not slept well. There were circles under his eyes I could see even at that distance. He had on his uniform but did not wear his hat. His shock of black hair hung down and looked shiny with pomade from where I stood. His skin was singularly pallid and doughy. I immediately wondered about a thyroid imbalance.

After a perfunctory "*Sieg heil*," the Führer without a word turned and went back inside. The French doors were closed and the curtains drawn. The crowd immediately dispersed.

"Are you printing today?" I asked František.

"Václav was meeting with the Gestapo until after midnight," he replied. "I am assuming we will print, but under some kind of censorship."

František took his leave, and I walked back to my chambers. While there were a few German soldiers on the streets, the snowfall had had much more impact on the city than the invasion. Laborers were trudging to work an hour late, and shopkeepers were shoveling great heaps of snow from the sidewalks into the street, so that some semblance of business could be conducted.

Even I, lifelong enemy of fascism, found my thoughts wandering more to childhood adventures in the snow than to the German conquest. When I returned to my office, my secretary was just staggering in, caked with ice.

"I thought you would be at the Castle ceremony now," she said.

"It was canceled," I replied, going into my inner office.

"Because of the snow?" she asked.

"Because of Hitler," I replied.

Aktion Gitter, they called it, the rude end to our fantasy that this occupation would be gentle. Even as Hitler had waved from the balcony, a *Wehrmacht* officer was signing the order commanding the arrest of all suspected Czech Communists. But strangely enough, I was not worried. My heavens! Our Communist Party had received over a million votes in the election of 1938. We were the largest red party per capita in Europe, second only to the French in total numbers.

Were they going to arrest us all?

And they entrusted this operation in the beginning to our noble Czech police force, who hadn't ever bothered to register Communists.

My telephone rang that evening after I had returned home. It was František, this time breathless.

"They are arresting all suspected Party members and sympathizers," he gasped.

"Where are you?" I asked.

"At the Foreign Ministry."

"Come to my house immediately," I replied.

"But there are checkpoints now," he said. "They'll get me."

"Don't worry," I said, trying to calm him but secretly chilled by the news. "This will take the Nazis weeks, months. They're still finding their way to the pisspots.

"Stay close to the river," I added. "Don't take the main streets."

He hung up.

Out through my French doors, all seemed normal. My little courtyard garden of snow, my hollies hung over with white, my dead peonies given new blooms of white frost, all stood in frigid, pristine beauty. A small iced statue of Cupid posed above a frozen fish pond.

My valet, Josef, stood in the doorway.

"You have heard the news," he said.

Josef, my employee and confidant of twelve years, was a true Party stalwart, unshaken in his belief in the higher cause of the Revolution. In the absence of my beloved Loki, he had been as a brother to me.

"Yes," I replied. "How much petrol do we have in the car?"

My sudden turn of thought, now expressed aloud, startled me. He seemed already to have contemplated it.

"A full tank," he replied.

"What do you think, Josef? North, or east?"

"I should think they have the Polish border well patrolled, although we could cross somewhere in the Tatry, on foot. In springtime, though; not now."

"How about east?"

"Our risk of being caught is greater, until we enter Slovakia. All main highways will be controlled, though the disorder might work in our favor in Slovakia. We hear the Hungarians have moved into Ruthenia. Slovakia is of course now an 'independent' country. You have friends and family there, as I recall?"

"My poor old mother, among others. Any German troops in Slovakia?"

"No."

"For how long?"

"For a few weeks, at least. They are now digesting Moravia and Bohemia. It is quite possible, the way Tiso has capitulated, that Slovakia will not be occupied at all."

"My mother would be the first place they'd look. I do have old friends in Bratislava. We could go there."

"I would not recommend Bratislava," said Josef. "Too close to Austria, crawling with German Intelligence right now. And the Tiso government is not to be trusted. They could earn favor by turning over someone like you. I was thinking farther out in the country."

"Josef," I said sardonically, "how did we get ourselves into this fix? We should have flown the coop with people like the Masaryks, Beneš. I never thought Hitler would actually send in troops; he knew all he had to do was knit his brow and we would fall prostrate."

"I passed the Peček Palace today," he said. "The Gestapo seems to have taken it over. I was talking to Bohumil, the majordomo. Nazi pigs were clomping around in their snow-covered boots. Bohumil was thanking God he buried all the silverware and valuables out in the garden when the family left."

"How much snow did they get in the east?"

"I think twenty centimeters or so. The storm went down into the Carpathians, really heavy that way. Also bad in the Tatry, but it always is."

"How much snow on the ground up there?"

"At this time of year, with no thaw yet, they probably have at least a meter and a half on the ground, even three meters in the high passes and valleys."

"I think that would be a disaster," I said.

The clock struck half-past seven.

"Get me the map," I asked. Josef went out of the library, returned two minutes later, dusting snow off his lapels.

"We could go east," I said, "the north road, through Hradec Králové, then Šumperk, loop up to Ostrava and Bohumín. That would put us in Rybnik and Chorzów in Poland."

"If this is our plan," said Josef, "we should leave now. Every hour means the Germans are more consolidated, more in control. As for now, I'll wager there is hardly any kind of frontier between Slovakia and the Czech lands. We could cross easily."

" 'Now' meaning . . . ?"

"Meaning this evening. As soon as possible."

"I'm waiting on František," I said. "He's coming on foot. We'll certainly not leave till he is here. And I must think this through. My friends in the country are few, I haven't seen them in years. I have a cousin a few miles south of Ostrava. We would be conspicuous in the country. By leaving here in such haste, we will draw attention to ourselves, possibly touch off a search. After all, I am a Central Committee member."

Anna the cook brought in two steaming bowls of soup, small quartered salmon sandwiches. Josef and I ate in silence. I was actually quite excited with the idea of a mad dash to the Tatry. I'd not done anything like that in years. Hitler's invasion was serving to shake me out of the cozy bourgeois cocoon where I'd slumbered so comfortably.

Once in Poland, I thought, we shall make straight for the Ukrainian border, for Lvov. We shall cable Lavrenty Beria and arrange to go to Moscow.

We shall wait out this unfortunate time in Moscow.

I had never been to Moscow. The idea was quite intriguing.

"Tea, sir?" Anna asked.

"Yes," I replied. We shall have to practice up on our Russian, I thought. What an adventure.

The doorbell rang.

"That will be František," I said. Anna withdrew to answer the door. We heard it open, low voices, the sound of their approach.

I rose to greet František, full of myself. In through the library doors walked Anna, accompanied not by František but by four young, impossibly green Czech police cadets.

"Yes?" Josef said, rising to act as my intermediary.

"We seek Dr. Radan Michalský and one Josef Blažek."

"Yes," Josef replied.

"On orders of the German High Command, we have orders for your arrest, as known members of the Communist Party, on suspicion of subversive activities."

The spokesman nervously held out the arrest warrant and actually allowed the two of us to read it, which we did at great length.

"Come with us," he said after an interval.

"May I get my coat?" I asked.

"Yes," the senior cadet said, embarrassed that he might have made us go into the cold without clothing. Dressing, we walked out into the foyer, Anna following respectfully.

"Anna," I said with a flourish.

"Yes, sir?"

"Turn down my bed for the night," I replied. "I shall be home before ten."

"Very well," she said.

With four of our young countrymen, Josef and I went out into the snow. Politely we were escorted into the back of the police wagon and taken to police headquarters, a place of pinched faces and dirty walls, now supervised by Nazi officers, where we were grouped together with another three hundred men and women, shivering, our numbers overflowing out into the street. I saw František among them, and we exchanged nods. It was our small part of an operation that swept throughout the country that night, until the jails, the abilities of the police to process, were overwhelmed, until it seemed they would have to arrest the whole country itself.

The chilling thing was that our new masters seemed disposed, even able, to do it.

While *Aktion Gitter* came and went, and most of those arrested were released, that was not to be my fate. For some reason, I was considered a special risk, and so an assortment of orders and warrants handed down by the Nazi Command kept me in detention.

When the confusion of that first day and evening of the occupation had settled, it became clear to me that my continuing imprisonment, after the other Central Committee members were let go, meant I had somehow been betrayed. Imagine how I racked my brain during those agonizing days of solitude and waiting, those days of boredom that I thought could not help but have some negative impact on my health. Who, I thought, who of my comrades would have fingered me as someone worth considering a special risk? It was only upon the signing of the Molotov–von Ribbentrop Pact a few weeks later that I became convinced I had been betrayed by someone in the Soviet camp. None other, I decided, than the repugnant Rodion, who had undoubtedly concluded I was not trustworthy and so had taken this special opportunity of Nazi-Soviet collaboration to put me on ice.

What a choice I had been given in those years: to commit crimes for the overlords of Moscow, or to rot in a Fascist jail. I was above all a Czech Communist, yet that seemed not to be an option.

In those first two years of my incarceration just outside Prague, the *Reichsprotektor* of Moravia-Bohemia was an aristocratic German diplomat by the name of Konstantin von Neurath. He sent a personal note once, to "apologize" for my continued detention.

The note said the matter was quite out of Von Neurath's hands, being in the purview of the SS and the Gestapo, and that while he could ensure that I was civilly treated, I was in a special group of officials who were considered too great a risk to security and order to be released.

And so, while the Reich tried to figure out what to do with me, I languished.

Learning how to administer an instant empire apparently took more time than the Germans had originally planned. But I must add they were temperamentally better equipped to carry out the task than any others.

It was not until 1941 that I learned I was being moved again. This time, not to freedom but to a special new detention and transshipment camp being set up at Theresienstadt, also known by its Czech name, Terezín. This camp, the first of a planned network all across the Reich, was to be a model, where subversives, Jews, Gypsies, and others not a part of the new order would be sent, pending final resettlement. All but the Jews would be resettled in the Ukraine. Jews, we heard, would be transported to Madagascar.

The opening of the new camp, and my move, coincided with the replacement of von Neurath by Reinhard Heydrich, a young man rumored to be Himmler's—and Hitler's—favorite.

To give you a picture of Heydrich's abilities, this fellow, before ruling our conquered territory, had coordinated all the Reich's security and intelligence forces.

I was being detained more for being a Communist than for being a Jew, I was told.

What a comfort!

And so I was loaded on a railroad car and sent to that small town in west Bohemia that would be my home for the next two years.

I was issued my camp uniform and assigned to work as an orderly in the camp infirmary. For the first time since being a medical student, I was emptying bedpans and swabbing up puke. My home was a barracks, which I shared with twenty other male political prisoners, a cross-section of all those who had offended the Reich politically: Social Democrats, two clergymen, radical Czech nationalists, a minor poet, and a loud-mouthed organizer for a Plzeň brewers' union.

We got along fairly well. Two of the politicals I knew slightly, having seen them about town. A certain camaraderie grew up, and the situation, though certainly miserable, was in those early days not much different from military service by a conscript. I should add that this was in a "model" camp, so decreed by Reinhard Heydrich, and before the horrors that would later be exposed had occurred.

We knew this camp was important to Heydrich, because he made a personal inspection visit a few months after my arrival, in the fall of 1941. His stop was brief and I was kept at a distance, but I did take note of the frenzied preparations for the arrival of his emerald Daimler-Benz. Even the fearsome camp commandant, Joekl, had run about like a nervous bride in anticipation.

Had I known I would again cross paths with this Nazi viceroy, I would have paid more attention to him.

It was in the infirmary that I first became acquainted with the chief physician, Dr. Franz Hodl. Hodl was a mediocrity of a man, a sweaty little fellow with alcohol-reddened cheeks, who wore wool suits and a black homburg on his rounds, as if he were back in Munich. Clearly of the lower Munich bourgeoisie—I could pick it up in certain inflections he sought to paper over with ornate grammatical constructions—Hodl was a self-taught oenophile and a student of Brahms. I gathered these two affectations were acquired out of obligation rather than springing from any real interest. They were things that Hodl, an aspirant to upper-class acceptance, would need to have.

Hodl's knowledge of medicine was even less impressive. I observed bumbling and malpractice of the worst kind. The man could not even get in a hypodermic needle without drawing blood in five places or collapsing a vein, yet he insisted on doing it himself, so little did he respect his camp staff.

I had acquired a deft hypodermic technique after years of administering tranquilizers, oftentimes to unwilling patients, and so one day, when he and I were virtually alone in one of the wards, I quietly volunteered to assist.

"And what would you know about it?" he snapped, drawing back as if to slap me.

"As a physician and psycho-analyst of almost thirty years," I said, "I have done my share of injections."

That seemed to give him pause.

"What is your name?" he asked.

"Dr. Radan Michalský," I told him, expecting to be consigned to the brig. He screwed up his face.

"I recall reading several texts by someone of that name who had done research on addiction to . . . to . . ."

"Morphine," I replied.

"So you have read it too?"

"I wrote it, together with Milos Kouril," I said.

Hodl's eyebrows shot up like birds taking wing.

"Good heavens. And what are you doing in a place like this?"

In that comment Hodl showed he knew little of the identities of his uninvited guests.

"Apparently Communists are not in favor right now," I said.

He looked shocked.

"You? A red doctor?" He harumphed and cleared his throat. It was apparent his tiny brain was wrestling with that.

"Well, politics aside, it is good to have a fellow healer here with me."

He actually extended his hand in greeting, and then pulled it back when he realized what he was doing. But his pompousness seemed to fade. It was clear he knew his own limitations.

It was thus that our acquaintanceship, and the curious impact it had on my identity as a prisoner, began.

Not long after, I was even invited to his private quarters for lunch. Not officially, of course; he requisitioned me to wax the floors. But once in, surrounded by the overstuffed domesticity shipped from his home in Munich, with the curtains drawn to shut out the sights and sounds of the camp, and the Grundig gramophone playing his favorite Brahms, I was treated as a guest.

At that first luncheon, I met Fräulein Hodl, a puffed-up churchy busybody of a woman, who clearly did not approve of my being there. But after a sharp word from the doctor, she withdrew to her knitting and baking.

Hodl thought himself a connoisseur.

"You must try this Carpathian claret," he said to me during that first luncheon. He believed it to be one of the best wines in the Reich. I dutifully tasted, and found it one grade above table vinegar.

"This Bulgarian cabernet sauvignon is excellent," he said, and that I also tried, finding it sugary and malodorous. I took it as a further mark of Hodl's tenuous rank that he could obtain only wine from points south and east, whereas none of the acknowledged French or Italian vintages that the Reich counted within its dominion ever made it to Hodl's Theresienstadt cellars.

The clincher was a Romanian sauterne he raved about, which to me tasted like a tart's cheap perfume. It was so bad I wondered if there had not been a mistake in labeling.

"Good that you were assigned here," Hodl said at our second lunch, as if I were a colleague. "I am simply famished for some intelligent conversation."

"I consider you a friend," he said, inebriated, at our third.

I gradually concluded that Hodl, although a Nazi Party member of five years, had joined the National Socialists for opportunistic reasons. And the Party, casting about for faithful doctors to in help in the growing effort of conquest, had selected him to go to Theresienstadt.

It was clear that, aside from having me as a confidant, he hoped I might covertly advise him on the burden of running the camp's medical programs. While his specialty was urology, he had to administer the full range of medical services, from surgery to pathology.

Those luncheon interludes were farces that lifted me out of the drudgery of camp life and helped soften the gradual transition of the camp's atmosphere from fairly benign in the beginning to something darker. My barracks mates, rather than being angry or mistrustful of my friendship with Hodl, encouraged me to pursue it. They thought it would provide them with special understanding of how this camp worked and what lay ahead.

This quiet time I will remember as a peaceful interlude before the abominations that followed, an interval when a false feeling of relief lay softly on all those Czechs who had fallen under the shadow of the Fascist occupation.

My life in camp settled into a routine of menial day labor, and secret medical counseling and conversations with Hodl. His patients at that time were both the internees and the camp staff; that was the supreme evidence of his trust in me, that I could advise him on the treatment of Germans. But to remind me of where I was, the steel rails would groan periodically as trains pulled into the camp siding and were disgorged of their human cargoes, only to be rolled back out to points east and south. And there were the thundering noises of midnight departures, when those hundreds who had passed some time with us were sent north, to who knew what destiny beyond the Tatry, in Poland.

Hodl was really becoming quite attached to me, so desperate was he to maintain his image as a physician in this prison camp he was forced to administer. And I must say, although he was in the service of the Fascists, and a man of bourgeois inclination so stolid I wanted simply to kick him every day, in my own way I appreciated his friendship. First for the reason I have already alluded to: it offered brief respites from imprisonment. And a new incentive presented itself, which I did not turn away. No, bit by bit my acceptance of his invitations to come and take tea or sip crude Ploesti brandy (with a rank petroleum aftertaste that I am sure came from the oil fields there!) were motivated increasingly by my desire to be in the presence of a shining light that was like a beacon of another world, a world of beauty and happiness.

This beacon was his daughter, Ilse, a young girl of fifteen. God knows what had brought forth this blossom from such mediocre parents and in such an abominable place, but there she was. Prisoners would crane their necks out of barracks windows to watch her walk by, and she in her goodheartedness passed nuts and candies through the fence to the internees, who stood before her ashamed of their status as prisoners. At first the guards would tell her to move away, but she answered so directly and with such authority that it startled them into silence. And so it became accepted custom, the ministrations of this girl Ilse. I heard her question her own father as to why people were being treated in such a way, and she laughed at his pompous rationalizations as only a clear-minded child could. And she committed the ultimate blasphemy, suggesting that the guards themselves be locked up like cattle and the prisoners set free.

Her ministrations to the prisoners grew more bold and more generous, until she was smuggling meat from the family icebox and whole loaves of bread through the fence. Perhaps it was this that drew me to watch her with such interest. But then later I realized what it was, what was so fascinating. I saw her as the reincarnation of my long-lost Loki, and perhaps even my dead sister, Margret, as they would have been at age fifteen. I could imagine what kind of woman Ilse might become, if allowed to reach her heights. And unlike Loki, Ilse seemed to be free of any major traumas, other than an unconscious yearning to break free of the mediocrity of her parentage and the gestating horrors of our little camp.

"Oh, Michalský, what shall I do about Ilse?" lamented Hodl over Ukrainian vodka at one of our luncheons. "The poor thing is only fifteen. I can't send her away yet to boarding school. She is too young to be away from the good influence of father, mother, and home, wouldn't you agree? Imagine sending her out into the harsh world."

I gasped at the irony of this "home," the dreadful waiting room for the Nazi people-thresher to which we were all becoming too accustomed.

"But you should send her away," I said. And I learned that Fräulein Hodl had taken the same position, urging her husband to let their only daughter spend several years with emigrant relatives in either Brazil or South Africa. But the father was stupidly resisting.

To see Ilse in all her unfinished youth, on the verge of womanhood, still possessed of an innate childlike generosity, seemed to say a better human being slumbered in all of us, if only it could be allowed to awaken. Her curiosity was great, and she appeared quite intrigued by the fact that I was a Communist. She would repeatedly question me as to what that meant, saying she might like to become one, and in her naive expression of support for what I had learned over the years was a very complex set of values, she seemed much as I had been as a young student. I wanted to serve as her tutor, in fact, not just about communism but about many things. Yet I checked myself and held my tongue; I did not want to do her any harm in her father's or others' eyes.

So as the world went dark, soon there remained nothing of beauty in it but young Ilse, a candle flame in the cave of my, and her parents', mistakes, one lone childish voice saying what should have been the whole human chorus, a serene and pure note of the flute not yet fully drowned out by the groan of the rails and the barkings of the guard dogs, not yet overwhelmed by the cries of the imprisoned and the growls of their prison wardens: the light of freedom and the sound of truth, the noblest of our race's possibilities, even in that awful place not yet totally snuffed out.

Comida at the Hotel Zaculeu was to be served promptly at seven, but by seven-fifteen—all tables save one occupied with expectant diners—not even a glass of water had emerged from the *cocina*. But activity was under way there, for the swinging door would periodically open, and steaming kettles and boiling caldrons could be seen, as well as a staff nervously awaiting some signal.

The signal, apparently, was the arrival of a personage. His arrival was heard before it was seen, for his spurs and riding boots resounded on the dry wooden floor. Coming through the *comedor* doorway, the maker of this noise was a mountainside of olive-drab military bulk, a *general de brigada*, marked by the one-star insignia and a cluster of oak leaves, with a pompadour of wavy jet-black hair and a full black mustache garnishing a great head once ravaged by the most terrible burns. On this man's face were the keloid expanses of an unnamed war, a meteoric scarring almost planetary and geological. His eyes quickly swept the room, pausing for a second at Robinson and Lucho, and then fixed on his own table.

He was accompanied by a slender, fine-boned *coronel*, about forty, quite handsome, with the sharp Ibero-Arabic profile and black hair found only in southern Spain and northern Africa.

Together they seemed the two opposite male genetic poles of this culture.

As these two were seated, the kitchen doors burst open on cue, and waiters emerged bearing water glasses, salads, crudités, and breads.

"Big sticks," said Lucho, wolfing down the gravied *lomo*. "Probably Gordillo, the military commander of Huehue, and Villareal, the intelligence man. I heard about them in the bar."

They ate the yucca and gravied meat, and it was quite good, the kind of meal Robinson might have got from his grandmother in the California desert when he was a boy. The scarred heavy wooden tables had been taken from some feudal highland hacienda, and the embroidered lace place mats and white *servilletas* still carried a family monogram not belonging to the hotel.

At last it was time for *flan* and *café*. Robinson, unsettled because the scarred general had stared over at them several times, wanted to be gone, and so he was irritated when Lucho insisted on ordering dessert.

Finally Lucho was finished, and they were able to leave. Outside, a stellar highlands night had descended. The only clouds to see were billowing moonlit silver, over the distant Sierra de Cuchumatanes.

"You got a problem with the law?" Lucho asked.

Robinson shook his head. "Do you?"

"Everybody has a problem with the law in Huehue."

They walked once around the plaza, which was totally deserted, except for two Guatemalan Army sentries, smoking cigarettes, guarding the general's car. Lucho spoke to them as they passed but got only nods in response.

"I was talking to this fellow in the bar," said Lucho. "While you were napping. Town's still in shock from the *guerra civil* back in the early eighties. In most towns you see people out at night walking, talking, flirting. Latin people are that way. But in Huehue, people stay at home. Let's take a ride."

Lucho drove back up to the ruins, now lit a ghostly bone white by the moon, and so much more imposing than in daylight.

"You smoke?" Lucho asked.

Robinson shook his head, then realized Lucho was holding a joint. For no good reason, he assented.

In a few minutes Robinson was transported, the Quiché, the Maya, the insurgency, moving around him, unending war, a dark part of the world torn apart by tectonic movements of earth and man. The two of them smoked their way around the ruins, Lucho appearing here at one minute, there at another; Robinson was having a hard time keeping track of the driver's whereabouts.

The pyramid reposed fluorescent, opalescent, in the moonlight.

Lucho was singing off in the darkness, a ceremonial sound to it, and in a sudden flush of paranoia Robinson cursed himself for getting into this situation, powerfully stoned, totally passive and helpless, at the mercy of this landscape and history and cabdriver.

Then he realized Lucho was singing snatches of lyrics from a forgotten rock song about UFO sightings. Robinson sat on the luminescent pyramid and watched Lucho come toward him.

"*Hola, señor,*" said Lucho. "I got you figured out."

Robinson just sat there, inert. He would listen to anything, hypnotized by Lucho, who was swirling the lighted butt of the joint in a dervish-like circle.

"At first I said to myself, CIA. *Sí, hombre.*"

An idiotic cackle emerged from Robinson's mouth, flying heavily off into the ruins and the surrounding fields like a departing vulture.

"But then I figured not so. I figured, a guy with a problem. Written all over his face. A man with a serious problem."

Robinson stopped laughing and sat there, like protoplasm. He was a toadlike fixture on these steps and could remain there a thousand years.

"Hey, man, you got family?"

Robinson reflexively pulled out the dog-eared photo of his daughter, Shannon, this atavistic ritual of revelation with strangers acted out in bars far from home. Lucho lit it up with a flaming match, Polaroid hagiography shining in the pre-Columbian dark.

"*Muy bonita,*" he said. "And wife?"

Robinson shook his head, aware of the weight of his lips and face as he did so. Oh, this was all such a mistake.

"I do have a girlfriend," Robinson heard himself say. "Somewhere." It sounded maudlin to his own ears, and he started laughing vultures again.

"Yeah, I know how it is," said Lucho. "I had a girlfriend back in D.C. After I left, we wrote, talked on the phone, for years, she even came down here one time. But she hated it."

Robinson saw a meteor streak the northern sky with awesome clarity.

"You can understand why," he added. "Guatemala is at its best right now. Nobody within a mile of you. Then you can feel it, see it in its beauty."

Lucho was now stretched out on the ground, looking up at the sky. The sky itself seemed to be shifting slightly at the horizons, like an overlay not firmly in place, an observatory bowl, a construct.

"Why the fuck do we try to come back?" he said.

Robinson shook his head. It all sounded so terribly profound, he wanted to consider the statement at length, but he realized he was following Lucho to the pickup.

"Where we going?" Robinson asked.

"Guatemala."

They got in the pickup and drove back down to the main highway north, the vast expanse of the Central American cosmos spreading above them, Magellanic Clouds welling over the far-rising mountains, primordial stellar depths above. With the windows down, the frigid air surged over him and into his lungs so powerfully Robinson almost couldn't get his breath; he was being inflated by the wind, and he would have laughed yet again but couldn't push out the sound. The stars in the sky mingled with the distant stars of mountainside villages; it was hard to say where earth and sky stopped. The truck sailed out through dark space. Lucho was right: it was beautiful, held at a distance, right now.

Then they landed on another world, distantly related to, but altogether quite distinct from, his own. He knew the forms of things, but up close, their variations startled him. He was bathed in the nuclear glare of two service stations where the town road ran into the highway. Beyond them stood an Alamo-like truck stop of green cement called El Farolito, with a *cantina* that attracted truckers making the north-south trip to Mexico. Sinister Mexican-built rigs hand-painted with lurid desert scenes and nicknames like "El Gaucho" y "La Bestia" and "Queztalcoatl" stood parked in the dust, lit with necromantic arrays of red and yellow and green blinkers.

Robinson was having trouble walking. He told himself it was the changed gravity, the lighter atmosphere composed of a different gas. He was quite certain he placed his feet properly and continued on a direct course to the bar door, but an unsettling lag of nanoseconds occurred between impulse and execution. Inside, a pair of Mexican truckdrivers were flirting with a young Maya barmaid. Robinson and Lucho each drank a beer. Lucho left Robinson alone for a time, to talk to a man behind the *pensión* registration desk.

In Lucho's absence, Robinson savored every ghastly corner of the bar, its racks of *tequilas* and *mescales* and *aguardientes* and *anises de mono*, its life-giving elixirs and delicious poisons. All were bathed in a submarine green. He thought he saw the barmaid steal a glance at him.

Harshness, risk, danger . . . He was on the edge of the known world, the unrestricted possibility of evil right here, immediate. The thought gave him a thrill, and he considered for a moment: This is what is meant to be alive. The palpability of evil, the proximity of risk. The Maya maiden was saying something to him, an incantation. What are you saying? he thought. What are the chthonian roots of your words, what black memories do they key? He shivered a minute.

She was asking him it he needed another beer and he was sitting here going quietly crazy, now Lucho's acolytic face in his own, shoulder-length hair like a headdress.

"Man, let's get out of here," Lucho said. "Smells like puke."

Then they were in the pickup again, headed this time to the south.

"Now where we going?"

"Physical therapy," said Lucho.

They wound back through Huehue and up toward the northern mountains, the wall of the Cuchumatanes, as opening jaws of earth and a profusion of ebony sky engulfed them. Lhota had hunted and been hunted and died out there somewhere; particles of air that Lhota had breathed were probably in Robinson's own lungs right now. They pulled up through the town of Chiantla, Lucho peering into the darkness, trying to get his bearings, and finally turned into a rutted driveway. They approached a hacienda. Several other vehicles gathered like desert animals drinking at an oasis; two dark children played in the light of a single outdoor lamp.

Lucho led the way to the door; someone peered out through an eye slot, then admitted them. They stepped into a fog of ultraviolet light bounding off the phosphorescent teeth of a half-dozen boaed prostitutes, Ladina and Indian. A Maya girl with a multicolored spiked punk wig stood in a bikini. She came up to link arms with Robinson; Lucho had already become fused to an older Ladina woman in a sequined one-piece.

"Jesus," said Robinson.

"Jesus is over at the bar," said Lucho, his words exploding in a flash of phosphorescent teeth. Jesús was a rotund black bartender from the Caribbean coast, who danced from the waist down while his elbows, emerging from a blazing-white guayabera, rested on the countertop.

They all danced awhile to recorded *cumbias* and *merengues*. One other couple danced, a farmer and a fat woman in a nightgown. Wide sets of steps off the central dance floor led up to swinging doors and, beyond, the rooms of the girls. It was still early yet, and quiet.

"*Me llamo Inéz*," she said. "*¿Y cómo te llamas?*"

"Allen Dulles," he said.

"*¿Alan?*" she confirmed. "*Me gusta. Eres norteamericano?*"

"*No me acuerdo*," he said.

I do not remember where I'm from, he said, somewhere on the palpable edge of evil.

He swam in the music of *amor perdida*, of betrayal, of tears of blood and forbidden love in the shadow of the *palmeras*, but he never felt as if he really caught up to its rush, a half second behind, and always would be, on this planet so far from his own.

Someone killed my friend, he said, dipping her, swinging her.

"*¿Cómo?*" she chirped. "*No entiendo.*"

They killed him with his shirtsleeves rolled, he said.

"*Roldós? Me dijíste Roldós?*"

He bought her a drink, and Jesús winked, never stopping his hip-swaying *cumbia*, rub-a-dub-dub, knowing she drank only daiquiris, *gracias*, and he would drink anything now.

They danced down the corridors of time, twin stars in locked orbit, music of the spheres fading, all music fading.

I have a girlfriend I love very much, he felt compelled to say.

"*Amor*," she said, lightly pushing him. "*No seas pendejo.*"

The moments were becoming snapshots, each scene lit up by the pulse from the universal core, the source. Now at the bar; now in the hall; now in the room. And in between he was looking into a great black maw of nothingness, a thrashing black sea of night.

The boa, the bathing suit, came off. She was quite cute, little upturned nipples bouncing as she stepped around him on the cold floor. His pants were down, she was sucking him, he hadn't even had time to get his shoes and socks off.

I, O, I, O. He had a girlfriend somewhere, he loved his little girl, he was on the edge of evil and aliveness.

I, she said.

O, he said.

Someone killed my friend.

He burned with a fever, the blood was in his skin, and once again he was half a step behind, trying to catch up, holding her, spreading her.

The last O was barely out of his mouth before she jumped up and away, patting at herself, Kleenexes, a glimpse of the douching ceremony through a louvered bathroom door. He meanwhile lay on a cool serene shore, having crossed the desert and at last found water, a placid interval of peace.

A few moments passed, and she was by him, hand extended.

Diez quetzales, she said. *Diez;* she was less than the price of the hotel room. He wanted to rest a little while longer in the coolness, and paid her extra, so she killed time playing with her eyebrow pencil before the mirror. Then the time was truly up, and he went back outside, for a drink, courtesy of Jesús.

Jesús spoke with his feet and his hips, a true dancing fool. The man never stopped. Lucho was still out of sight somewhere. This parallel universe pulsed on to its own beat, unstoppable.

Aguardiente, he heard himself order.

Each sip was a crystalline fire, an elixir of magma that worked its way down into his chest and abdomen; he felt nothing but his own central maw as more men appeared in the club, and here came two in uniform, until he locked eyes with them and had no chance of escape. The burn-faced *general* and the *coronel* from the hotel nodded at him as though they were acquaintances. Oh, how he wanted Lucho to come back out, but Lucho was still cruising on that wave of blood, and he would have to go this one alone.

The *coronel* stood, summoning him; the *general* was already seated, coat off, hat removed and placed center table, Jesús doing a tableside rumba, ready to take their orders.

Robinson steered an elliptical course across the depths of the void, barstool to waiting chair.

"*General Gonzalo Gordillo*," said the *coronel*, indicating the *general*, who was still seated but whose hand was extending to be shaken. "*Y yo soy Villareal.*"

"Robinson," he responded, trying to take the *general*'s substantial paw, but the *general* was already looking past him.

"Mi amorcito," erupted Gordillo, now abruptly rising to kiss Inéz, who swept up, fresh from intercourse and douching, to wrap her boa around the *general*'s neck.

"Te presento Alan Roldós," said Inéz, indicating Robinson. Coronel Villareal looked confused.

"Sientense," gruffed the *general*, his meteored face highlighted by a sheen of sweat and oil, pulling Inéz down onto his lap, her flesh that had shared Robinson's and would soon share Gordillo's, if things took their course. Robinson pondered the symmetry of this, this circular transaction of energy and evil.

"¿Norteamericano?"

"Sí," said Robinson.

"Welcon to my contry. You hab alrethy got . . . getten . . ." The *general* was lost a minute, searching for the words.

"Gotten to know the lovely women of Guatemala?"

"¡Exacto!"

All three of the males, Robinson included, made a growling, affirmative, *cka-cka-cka* sound.

"¿Aguardiente?" the *general* asked.

Robinson accepted.

"¡Aguardiente para todos!"

Jesús was in full salsa, the liquid streaming from a bottle held high over his head, jerked expertly, firing beads of liquid in tumbling iridescent trajectory into waiting crystal snifters.

"My beautiful country," said the *general*, this poor malformed beast of a man, now bouncing Inéz on his knee.

Cka-cka-cka, they all said, Inéz trembling with the force of the *general*'s *cka*s. The tray of *aguardientes* hung in space, approaching, quivering to Jesús' beat; the *general* took his own into firing position, thick neck tensed, elbow level with chin, eyes locked onto the shot glass. Robinson prepared to drink his in conventional manner, but the *general* was offended, lower lip pouting out, hairy index finger wagging no-no.

"Así se hace," he said, popping it in with the flick of a wrist, past teeth, past tonsils, past well-worn uvula. "Hehhhhhh," he hissed, serpentlike, after the swallow, eyes bulging slightly, leonine melted head and oiled obsidian pompadour shaken by an inner tremor. Villareal followed, and then Robinson, remembering slivovitz and

vodka, Lhota, O my beloved old country, so many times drowned in the rites of the *zrnko víno.*

"*Más!*" commanded the *general*, clapping his hands, and Jesús was at it again. Lucho had come out of the back room now but hung in the shadows, not knowing what to do, and Robinson, held prisoner, could do nothing but envy his freedom.

"*Tienes que permitir que yo hable en mi idioma natal*," apologized the *general*, begging to be allowed to speak in his native tongue.

"*Por supuesto*," said Robinson. The world was coming in snapshots again, a whomp whomp whomp, everything seen at the end of a narrowing ever-lengthening charcoal-colored tube, long black sepulchral moments in between the flashes of light.

"So what brings you to my beautiful country some business some tourism some curiosity?" asked the *general*. "I love your own beautiful country because I served as military representative of my country to your country and must I say how I was hurt to hear how so many evildoers besmirched my people and my homeland they accused us of the most unspeakable infamies who are they to say what is wrong who are they to cast the first stone?"

Whomp: my now-dead friend lost in the heart of the blackest isthmian jungle, thrashing crashing through unmacheted walls of lianas and thorn, pursuing and now pursued, as far from the land of the Slavs as imaginable, Miro/slav, your name meaning celebration of peace, your shirtsleeves rolled and you falling dying alone and forgotten, the only father I ever had, a father who crossed over the line and made me what I am today, your blood of the steppes in the dark Central American volcanic soil out there beyond the black sierra, what happened to you, who can tell me who did it, how?

"Villareal and I often argue," the *general* was saying, "can a man be good if the system of laws be bad can the beauty of goodness blossom on the sewer scum and so as a result of the anarchy we must suffer *comunistas sectos narcotraficantes?*"

Whomp: my girlfriend departed from me out there into the cowboy freshness the uncorrupted rawness of the black western eventide, a land of sterile night mountains, a moonscape blessed with black waters, the prairie windscorched igneous metamorphic and sedimentary uplift called here the Sandia Peaks, there the Wind River Range, the Medicine Bow wilderness wilds, why did you leave now,

now of all times, leave me alone in the darkness of my aloneness, the cellar of my sadness, deserted?

"Because you must understand my friend what is your name again my friend Alan my country sad though it is was ironically built on a more humane tradition than yours ours was the tradition of evangelization of souls not the murderous extermination perpetrated by your legalistic English settlers who could not abide a red skin no to them it was much better to exterminate than to mix and so you feel you can throw the first stone because the statute of limitations has passed on all your crimes."

Whomp: my little girl lost in the black maw of the parting, torn from my side in the most unholy of unweddings, flesh of my flesh, half mine, the probable root of what Lucho meant when he said he got me figured out, he knows I got a problem, right, I got a problem with things falling away from me into blackness, the blackness bigger and bigger each time, an opening door, I'm supposed to go through and I won't because it is an exit no entry, an exit no entry, tearing all from me, from my side, unholy . . .

"Have a good time here my friend," said the *general*, "but please be careful because this wild land is like a bucking bronco and our destiny is to try and tame it how can I possibly be responsible for every corner of it much as I would like to be so be careful stay out of trouble and pardon me for saying so but are you ill?"

Whomp: Ten quetzales said a gyrating black Mosquito Cay of a face, black Jesus, brought by destiny and time from the black forest of the Yoruba to the black scorched cropover canefields of Barbados and then at last to the black tar sands of Puerto Barrios on the Laguna de Izabal, you black Jesus, come at last to collect.

"Ten quetzales"—or was it "Allen Dulles"?—said the *general*, "nothing to pay for a good time but my friend I'm worry about you look ill do you need some fresh air do you need to take a step outdoors out through the door to draw a nice deep breath of my rich Guatemalan air?"

Whomp: out through the *salida / no entrada* a view of Lucho the black-haired acolyte on the chalcedony steps of the temple, reading the Popol Vuh, my very own book of the dead, he knows I got a problem.

"*Jesús, ayudale a mi amigo.* He is ill."

And this at last is the moment of final implosion the collapsing of the universe of all matter and energy and space itself down into a black body so dense that one teaspoonful of matter weighs more than the planet earth, no light, no energy, no verification of its existence possible except for the ripping suction of light and heat and matter and space itself into the core, the down, the shrink, a pain of smashed quarks and fused neutrinos of crying bosons and splintering muons the compression of all reality and life the shrieking dolorous agonizing collapse his last thought was how can there be any existence at all beyond this?

The answer came in good ancient Mayan ceremonial fashion as in the most advanced astrophysics, just as Jesús and Lucho, being experts at this, managed to carry him through the *salida / no entrada:* once he was across the threshold, he felt free to release out of the black core of his final collapse and pain a sheer geyser of heat light and matter, he was free to pump out the remnants of all his corruption and failure in great laserlike shots in the parking lot, a geysering of the miserable failed remnants of all that had come before and been collapsed and reformulated for a second try, up and out it came, the violent pumping projectile vomiting that cleared it all out of him and, most mercifully, that cleared his mind.

Although Lucho kept saying fuck, fuck, as he drove them back to the hotel, concerned about this unwanted encounter with the jackbooted forces of order and oppression, Robinson was at peace. In the fullness of that peace he made it to the room and fell into the sweetest sleep imaginable, a coolness again on the stiff sheets, a rescue of sorts, even a deliverance.

In the sweetness of that reborn sensation he could not imagine that any harm at all would come to them, ever, ever, ever again.

"I doubt there are any other words you could have spoken that would have induced me to continue my conversations with you," said Socrates Salazar as they sat in his office the next morning. Robinson heard everything through the surreal haze of his hangover and post-purgation, also aware that his stomach, scorched by the *aguardiente*, had gone bad.

"But the Face of God is probably the most intriguing case I have seen in my work, both as a journalist and as an advocate for human rights. And when you said it, in connection with the death of your friend, and his very curious background, I had to suspend my concerns about you and your agenda here, in the hopes that you might help shed light on this mystery.

"I must add that neither you nor I will be able to find the answers to our respective questions if information is withheld, if agendas are concealed, as I still suspect in your case. Is that agreeable to you?"

Robinson nodded.

"When I said that the Face of God does not exist, I was alluding to my own frustration in tracking down its existence. The term Face of God is a popular reference to an evangelical Protestant group, known formally as Witnesses to the True Face of God, one of more than a thousand such denominations that operated in Guatemala in the last decade. It was a very small group, a splinter of the larger and fairly well-known Brethren of the Word of God, themselves the product of some abstruse doctrinal dispute that would make sense only to those who took part in it.

"But the tiny Face of God was different, quite secretive and clannish in their affairs, making groups like the Mormons look like publicists. Most surprising is the way the parent organization refers to the offspring, calling them satanists. At first glance that appears correct, but it is an oversimplification. For the Witnesses to the True Face of God had at some point concluded that God and Satan were not separate entities but two faces of the same deity—thus the True Face of God. They found some meager scriptural support for this—a phrase here, a psalm there—enough, in their minds, to justify this belief.

"In this case, the Face of God would have passed unnoticed, a very small fish in a sea dominated by such whales as the Mormons, Jehovah's Witnesses, PTL, Lunkard, and so on, but for a seminal event that briefly thrust it into the limelight. By the way, are you a religious man?"

Robinson shook his head as gingerly as possible.

"As best as I have been able to reconstruct, the Face of God had first been represented by a small office in Guatemala City beginning in 1981. This office did little other than show the flag, so to speak; I could find no witnesses to its activities, nor evidence of activity at that time, other than the opening of the office itself, until early in 1982. It was then that Witnesses to the True Face of God, as described in news stories, announced the opening of a hospital and clinic to treat the peasants in far northwest Huehuetenango and north Quiché. It was to be staffed with a team of foreign volunteer doctors from within the faith and would be supported by donations from overseas. It would meet all the requirements of the Ministry of Public Health and Social Welfare. It would have twenty-five beds and would begin operations in June 1982.

"Though generous in its objective, the announced clinic would have merited little attention except for the locale itself. The site was to be on land donated to the faith—by an unknown benefactor—about five miles northwest of the village of San Carlos de Chixoy. And as you are probably aware, that was in the heart of the guerrilla and counterinsurgency campaigns of that time, an area of sporadic combat, terrorist acts, and periodic anarchy, resulting as first one rebel group, then another, and finally the government forces, would take and then lose control of towns and highways. You must be aware that the guerrilla forces, though sometimes working in harmony, were a fragmented group themselves, including the Fuerzas Armadas Rebeldes, the Ejército Guerrillero de los Pobres, the Organización del Pueblo en Armas, and others, all following different doctrinal interpretations of the revolutionary faith according to Mao, Fidel, or even Hoxha."

Socrates' assistant, Tito, had brought in a tray of tea and fresh bread and butter, but Robinson declined, out of continuing nausea.

"The location itself, and the political climate of that time, indicated to some that the clinic, for whatever reason, had the attention of the national leadership at the highest levels. For as you will recall, at that time our government was controlled by a general who had converted to the evangelical faith himself and had elevated to high position several of his coreligionists, who themselves became involved in the counterinsurgency campaign, land reform, and social development. But whatever the intrigue behind its creation, little was heard or seen from Clínica Chixoy or the sponsoring Face of God for nearly a year. And then it burst onto my stage in a most grotesque manner."

Salazar opened a drawer and produced a file folder, slapping it on the desk.

"I was asked, on behalf of Amnesty, to investigate a possible atrocity which had occurred there.

"The only facts that all parties agreed on was that some seventy-four peasants from the village of San Carlos had perished in a fire at the clinic. This might not have attracted as much attention in your country, or even in mine, but for the fact that it included virtually the entire population of the village. Trying to determine anything at all beyond that, such as why the entire village was in the clinic, and how the fire had started, and how none of the seventy-four had managed to escape, simply opened a torrent of rumor, innuendo, and unverifiable accusation.

"The event was originally reported in *El Tiempo* of Guatemala City, April 14, 1983, as a mysterious accident that would be investigated by the proper authorities. *Tiempo* at that time reputedly had good sources within the Army High Command, although not necessarily with the Chief of State himself." Here Salazar opened the file of clippings and waved a few. "The next account was a message that evening, on Radio Liberación—pro-rebel, of course—charging that the government Special Operations command had surrounded the clinic and burned it, with all the peasants inside. It should be noted that none of the clinic staff, which I believe was entirely foreign, was killed or even injured, despite later claims to the contrary. Or I should say, if foreigners did indeed perish in the fire, their remains were not recovered. And I should add that my effort to pursue that point illuminated the either deceptive, or slipshod, nature of the record keeping of both the *clínica* and the Ministry of Health, which was supposed to be monitoring the clinic's work; no one in Guatemalan officialdom knew who precisely was working there.

"A third interpretation came in a communiqué on the national television news on April 17, quite closely controlled during that time by the Chief of State's office, which said the official investigation revealed the guerrillas were trying to divert attention from their own perpetration of the atrocity against the peasants, who had been chosen for this vicious punishment by virtue of their recent religious and political awakenings, which placed them in strong opposition to the earthly pursuits of the atheistic revolution.

"Amnesty was hesitant to tread into this one, because it had all the earmarks of some kind of ruse, or trap. That the rebels made the first accusation could be interpreted to lend a slight bit of credence to the government's being the perpetrators, confused by the fact that the army did leak the first news of an accident. But more so, all signs indicated to Amnesty that perhaps both sides were telling half-truths and that there was a third possibility: neither side knew who precisely had done the deed. That of course raised questions as to who had, if indeed it had been a deed and not an act of God. And there was the continuing question: why an entire village in a clinic?

"My fact-finding journey to the site did not happen until April 21. It was impeded by the initial refusal of the military commander to allow me safe passage. He claimed, and accurately so, that the region was a combat zone and unsafe. I had to make a journey to the capital to seek an audience with the dictatorship to allow me to go into the war zone. I was kept waiting there for three days. I accomplished little during those three days, except to pick up on several rumors that might or might not have had meaning. One was that the inspector general from the Ministry of Public Health had been trying to do an inspection of the clinic during the months of February and March, and was prevented from doing so. This inspector general, Doctora Rosalia Iribarne, was not without her own agenda. She was a devout Catholic, who had been vocally critical of the 'anti-progressive' work of the evangelist sects. She made no secret of her opposition to the dictatorship. And she seemed protected from removal from her post by the vocal support of the Archbishop and Catholic activists, who gathered around her as one of their few advocates within the government.

"Doctora Iribarne told me that she suspected collusion between the Special Operations command and the clinic itself in preventing her inspection visit. The official reason for the delays were Special Operations concerns that her safety could not be guaranteed and that no protective escort could be spared for her use. She said her interest in undertaking the inspection had been prompted by a rumor that cases of child sodomy and molestation had occurred there. Her interest was also piqued because of an account of some sort of a divine visitation in or near the village several months before. That, plus the fact that the clinic had not been inspected since its opening the previous June, and its uncertain operations in a combat zone, made an inspection essential.

"Finally my permission to visit the site of the tragedy was granted, without my ever seeing the junta. And it was accompanied by the announcement, given to me by a midlevel functionary of the Army High Command, that the staff of the clinic were being detained for violations of certification and safety codes. This functionary, one Casariego, also divulged that the affair had triggered a dispute in the High Command itself, with the Chief of State on one side and his cohorts on another. Apparently the Witnesses to the True Face of God, though long since separated from its parent church, the Brethren of the Word of God, might still be associated with it in people's minds, and with the Chief of State, himself a follower of a similarly named but totally unrelated denomination.

"I was torn at that point: whether to remain in the city and seek an interview with the detained clinic staff, who were being brought back to the capital, or go back to San Carlos de Chixoy. And so I asked a friend of mine there in the city to seek on my behalf to meet with the detained evangelist doctors, headed by a Dr. Dwayne McClatchy, while I went to the site.

"By the time I arrived in Huehue on April 20, early rains had struck. We left the next morning, taking the long unpaved road across the Sierra Cuchumatanes, winding the final arduous miles into the jungled wilderness where San Carlos is located.

"The village itself was deserted, a ghost town, and was being guarded by troops from the Special Operations command, the counterinsurgency force that technically falls under the control of the National Police but is commanded by an army major. Only after a loud argument between the Special Operations leadership and my Army High Command escort, including the brandishing of weapons, did the Special Operations troops grudgingly allow me access to the several modest adobe buildings and huts, but nothing beyond that. My army escorts had no information to impart, but they did enable me to speak to one young fellow from the Patrulla de Autodefensa Civil, a young Quiché conscript, who was terrified beyond speech. He himself had been through a grueling interrogation by the Special Operations command, and but for the fact that he had some knowledge of my reputation as an advocate on behalf of human rights in this unending war, I might have got nothing from him.

"When he relaxed, he told me he believed there were a few villagers who had not died at the clinic but had fled into the jungle or down to Huehue or perhaps across the border into Mexico. He had heard that contrary to the government account, the dead villagers had been in the *clínica* for some time and had not taken refuge there from the guerrillas at the last minute. He had heard of, and accepted as fact, the visitation of the Virgin Mary to the valley in March.

"From the village I went to the site of Clínica Chixoy itself. It was in cleared jungle, completely isolated, an eerie scene. Four army helicopters sat on a dirt landing strip to one side, rotors slowly turning. That the *clínica* possessed its own landing strip answered questions I had about how it might remain adequately supplied and stocked in such a remote area, but it also raised questions, because a landing strip frees one of the limitations of earth. A *general de división*—the highest rank we have in Guatemala—was in command, wearing camouflage garb, and he had about fifty men bivouacked there. He was friendly enough but able to do no more than answer with shrugs. He said he had only arrived on April 18. I got the distinct impression he had been involved in a firefight there, both because the troops were deployed in a defensive position and because I found some spent shell casings on the ground. When I asked him if that was true, he shrugged again. He did tell me Dr. McClatchy had been removed to Guatemala City on civilian charges. The other missionary staff of the clinic had presumably gone to the capital on their own. He had heard, but was uncertain, that the Witnesses to the True Face of God were either withdrawing or being expelled from Guatemala.

"I spoke with an army coroner about the bodies. He said off the record that he believed there were no Caucasians among the remains he had examined. His preliminary tests had turned up nothing overtly unusual, but the tests were hardly conclusive since the bodies had been burned to a crisp and had lain in the ruins for four days before his arrival. He was baffled by one fact, however: the position of the bodies indicated to him that virtually all, if not all, had died in reclining positions, as if sleeping or unconscious when the fire struck. He did not take that to mean they had been dead before they were burned, although that was possible; it was also possible they were physically restrained in the reclining position at the time of the fire, but he could find evidence of that in only three cases—burned leather straps. I was also allowed to speak with an accident-reconstruction specialist, an Israeli on detail to the army, who would not give me his name. That in itself may not be as mysterious as it sounds. Perhaps you know Israel has maintained close links to several Central American militaries, in appreciation for those countries' support for Israel on the diplomatic front. But they wish to keep the assistance quiet, since it often goes to unsavory types. This fellow said the site showed strong evidence of kerosene and napalm inundation, suggesting arson or firebombing or even flamethrower attack. He could make no guess as to the origin of the incendiary used.

"When I asked him if the army and Special Operations were in conflict on this matter, he nodded and laughed but would say nothing more.

"I must say I was surprised at my reaction to it all. I must preface that by saying I have been to a number of similar scenes, such as the scene of a purported guerrilla atrocity or a great government victory. They were usually staged by the Army High Command for the international press, and they all reeked of fabrication and public relations. Strange as it may seem, this one was disjointed and unrehearsed, as though I had squeezed in between some institutional cracks. Perhaps it was heightened by the fact that I was touring this thing alone, without a circus of reporters with microphones and cameras.

"I found myself believing the accounts of these men, who were part of an apparatus that had so often committed the unbelievable. I have undertaken many such investigations, and rarely do I even get to the interview stage; I'm often given written answers to questions, and I deal with low-level public relations lackeys. I am faced with obfuscations, lies, and the worst kind of slander. But I was being given an unusual degree of entry and access, and I do not know now why, nor did I then. I can only attribute it to the rift, or dissension, that was reportedly occurring in the *junta de gobierno* over this matter.

"At any rate, the rift quickly sealed, because two days later my colleague's request to interview Dr. McClatchy in the capital was denied by the Ministerio de Gobierno. Our attempts to locate any of the other medical staff from the clinic, who had reportedly traveled to Guatemala City, were to no avail. Doctora Iribarne from the Ministry of Health was my ally in this, and she made a goodhearted effort to extract some information; I think she might have made progress but for several events that swiftly swept Clínica Chixoy into oblivion: a horrendous battle between guerrillas and the army near Sacapulas in late April, a rainy-season scorched-earth policy by the army in Huehue and the north that drew international outrage, and then the swift collapse of the Chief of State's power, culminating in his overthrow in August. Despite all this, Doctora Iribarne was able to divine that some kind of deal had been worked out to allow the Face of God principals to be expelled from the country without facing charges—it was a deal in which the Catholic Church concurred, because although they were uncomfortable with the growth of the evangelicals, they were more uncomfortable with the precedent of religious personnel standing trial for political or criminal charges (it would have placed their own leftist activist priests in jeopardy, and were the authorities to start delving into matters such as priestly sodomy and child molestation . . . well, who can cast the first stone there?). This arrangement was possible because Dr. McClatchy and probably other of the foreign personnel of the *clínica* had registered themselves as ordained ministers in the Church of the Witnesses to the True Face of God.

"Although I was distracted by all these succeeding events, I still tried in my spare time to track down Dr. McClatchy and the others. Doctora Iribarne, though chastened by her Catholic superiors to drop her public pursuit of the affair, allowed me to see what files she had on the Face of God. They were sparse, and what I gleaned from them is copied here almost verbatim in my own notes, and I will make them available to you. I could not pursue every lead. But I did pursue every one of significance. For example, I contacted the U.S. Evangelical Coordinating Council in New Orleans about the supposed membership of the Witnesses; no such group was a member. I wrote to the post office boxes in Saint Kitts–Nevis and Switzerland given for the Witnesses' home address; the letters were returned to me three months later. After several calls and letters to the American Medical Association, I established that a Dr. Dwayne McClatchy of Oklahoma City had been a pediatrician member from 1930 until his death in 1965. The Brethren of the Word of God, the supposed parent organization to the Witnesses, based in Nashville, Tennessee, said that there had been a breakaway group of about four pastors and five hundred members in and around Anniston, Alabama, in 1971, calling themselves the Witnesses to the True Face of God, but to their knowledge the schismatics had disbanded by 1975. They had never heard of Dr. Dwayne McClatchy."

Socrates Salazar was now smiling, lighting up his pipe.

"That, Mr. Robinson, is why I say the Face of God does not exist."

Salazar paused a minute to take a call from his pressroom. Apparently the rotary press had broken down, and someone would have to drive to Guatemala City to get a part. He okayed the trip.

"Now it is your turn. I have told you all I know. You must tell me how your dead friend fits into this picture."

Robinson tried to make sense of the blur of words and memories of the last hour, the last year.

"My friend Krámský had long been obsessed with his search for a man he knew as Emil Užhok. In the early 1970s, while still in Czechoslovakia, he had wondered about the curious role this Emil played, for he had arrived with the Soviet troops when they invaded his country in 1968—"

"A rather bold obsession for a Catholic rights activist, as I believe you told me he was?"

Robinson paused a moment and sipped his tea, now cold.

"At that time Mr. Krámský was working for the Czechoslovak police."

Salazar couldn't help but smirk. "And the pro-Soviet Czech leadership asked this humble Catholic policeman Krámský to investigate this curious Mr. Emil, who had some tie to their own Soviet patrons?"

"Yes."

Salazar ran his hand through his hair. "Go on," he said.

"In the course of his research on this man, assassins twice nearly killed Mr. Krámský in Czechoslovakia. As a result, his superiors asked him to drop the search. Surmising that his investigation of Užhok had triggered these attacks, Mr. Krámský was now given the added incentive of finding out who had tried to kill him and why. This mysterious Mr. Emil had a position with the Warsaw Pact in Prague, and then was gone abroad for several years, and then returned to the Pact secretariat. Mr. Krámský was allowed to move to Vienna by his Czech patrons. He continued his search quietly. But another attempt on his life prompted him to seek asylum in the U.S., which he was given. He came to the U.S. in 1977."

"Quite a remarkable career for a Catholic activist policeman," said Salazar.

"I gather that Mr. Krámský's curiosity was both piqued and frustrated once again when he heard that in 1978 this Emil Užhok had been killed in Ethiopia in a plane crash. Krámský believed Emil was there on business related to the Warsaw Pact and the guerrilla war in Ethiopia."

"Ethiopia now," commented Salazar.

"The search lost some of its urgency, because this individual, whom he considered his blood enemy, was now seemingly dead. But it didn't stop. For he continued obsessively to research, at a distance, through exile groups and others, the possible motives this Emil and his protectors might have had for their attempts to kill him. He even had an ally back in Czechoslovakia who was helping."

Salazar was sketching on a pad.

"Then, apparently last year, a discovery renewed his sense of urgency. He learned that a Czech Jewish woman, an émigree to America who had been interned at the Terezín concentration camp as a child, saw a man in 1982 while on vacation in Guatemala City whom she thought to have been one of the men, a duo of doctor prisoners known as *anděl*—Czech for "angel"—whom she remembered as having helped children to escape from the camp. She was the only survivor of her family, and she had left the camp at age nine, in 1945. Anyway, she recognized this man some forty years later by his curious manner of breathing and speaking, which she remembered because it was so frightening to a child. A deep tubercular rasp."

"Did she speak to him?"

"Yes, she did. They were in the elevator together at the Hotel Camino Real in Guatemala City as she and her husband were rushing to catch the tour bus to the airport and the flight back to Miami. She felt so overcome she spoke to the stranger in Czech when they stepped into the lobby, calling him *anděl.* He seemed startled but then in Spanish asked her what she meant; a translation of the Spanish was required. She told her story rather excitedly there: the gentleman, now in his sixties, was not alone but was with several other people, who seemed impatient to leave—she remembered them as Caucasians—but he told her in Spanish she was mistaken. She insisted, in this garbled exchange of Czech, English, and Spanish; he replied, '*Cara de Dios,*' shaking his head, as he and his companions withdrew. She was confused, thinking he had said something about the czar, because Czech for 'czar' is *car.* She wrote the phrase down phonetically on the way to the airport, not making any sense of it, even after it was translated for her. She was so convinced of his identity, however, that she reported it to the Holocaust Survivors Council in Washington. And my friend learned all this from them."

Salazar continued sketching for a moment, then dropped the pencil and rubbed his temples. He looked at Robinson.

"It could have been a case of mistaken identity," Salazar said. "If so, your search has no connection to my riddle, other than to determine why your friend was killed here . . . if indeed he was killed. If, however, the man in the hotel was indeed 'Emil the angel' from the Terezín camp, later turned a mysterious figure in the employ of the Russians, then a thousand new questions arise. How did he go from death in a plane crash in Ethiopia to riding an elevator in Guatemala four years later? What was his relationship to the Face of God? And what was the Face of God itself?"

Robinson shook his head. Salazar paused a moment and lit up his pipe again. The January day was electric, irradiant and clear and warm, like a late-spring day in the United States. The dampness of morning had been burned away, and a steady stream of marketgoers passed Salazar's large window onto the side alley.

"My friend came to Guatemala probably not knowing what *Cara de Dios* signified," said Robinson, "but learned of it while here. He learned of the clinic while in the capital. His search then took him to San Carlos de Chixoy. He may have even thought he would find this man Emil still in the environs, or at least someone who could help him locate the man."

Salazar nodded, billowing a sweet smoke.

"And there he died," completed Salazar. "I think the only possible answer to any of this will come from learning more about his activities at San Carlos and the circumstances of his death."

"Surely it was recorded under some jurisdiction," said Robinson. "I briefly saw a file on it, back in the U.S. I think the national police were involved, and the army."

Salazar nodded, then got up for a minute and looked for an ashtray.

"I have dealt with both," said Salazar. "More easily with the police than the army. You will have to leave this to me; I'm known in this area, and a call from me is not so unusual as a call from a strange American."

"If the Face of God and this recent death are so sensitive, won't you draw attention by inquiring?"

Salazar laughed, a sort of bark that rang in Robinson's ears for a minute.

"You can rest assured I won't go to General Gordillo or the national police. I think we can glean even more from the lowest level . . . and it is there I have the best relationships."

"Could Gordillo be involved?"

Salazar smiled inexplicably. "I doubt it."

"Why?"

"Oh, simply a hunch. I know the man socially. He is quite complex."

"How so?" Robinson asked, immediately suspicious.

"He is one of the two best poets in Huehuetenango."

"The scar-faced general?"

"The very same. He won the Rubén Darío Prize nine years ago. I gather from your incredulity you have met him and make your judgment on appearance alone. Granted, he does wear the uniform. But even his scars have depth. He was not scarred while ordering some awful genocide. He was scarred as a child day laborer on a coffee plantation, when one of the curing vats boiled over. He has some sensitivity to the poor. Otherwise I don't think I could bear him, poetry notwithstanding. I gather he was sent here by the new regime, to turn over a new leaf with the peasantry."

A number of things were going through Robinson's mind, and he almost spoke.

"You must trust me," said Salazar, waving his hand. "I will come to you when I have something. In the meantime, go be an investor or whatever you are supposed to be."

They parted without shaking hands. Robinson went back to the hotel, where Lucho was waiting, ready to go exploring. Although Robinson would have liked to languish in bed all day, he took Salazar's advice and contacted a local real estate broker, a small potbellied attorney named Fuentes, who was missing a front tooth and wore a white guayabera stained by the dripped remnants of several meals. Dr. Fuentes was so astonished to have a possible client, and a foreign one he assumed had access to real capital, that he stumbled all over himself in preparing a massive tour of the entire province. And so the remainder of the day was given over to jostling rides to forgotten haciendas, any of which might have served as the basis for the artist colony–resort that Robinson was supposedly seeking to create. Robinson tried to stay awake through the droning blabbered narrative of Dr. Fuentes, who was a wellspring of genealogical information on this long-dead landowner and that land-rich widow, but the mix of *dons* and *doñas* was too much, and Robinson more than once felt himself slipping off into sleep, only to be jolted from it by a strategically placed pothole or a blast of Dr. Fuentes's awful breath in his face.

The only other time he came out of it was when he thought he recognized a face in the market at Sacapulas, a cleft-chinned Hispanic man with a widow's peak. The face startled him for a second, as he tried to place where he had seen it. Robinson was good with faces in a crowd, he always had been. Rationally he told himself it should not be a matter of concern. It was a random face he had seen in the town or perhaps even in one of the watering holes from the previous night's revels. But a fluttering, a skittering deep inside, told him the face was from elsewhere. Eventually he calmed, deciding he had seen the man in the town, one of the dozens loitering about the plaza. Only when he was back in his room at the Zaculeu hours later, half asleep, did this face come back and jerk him up out of slumber and into a full bout of panic. For Robinson feared, although he could not be positive, that he had seen this man in the corridor of his Virginia apartment building, the same man who had worn an exterminator's uniform and who had presumably ransacked his home. And who at a minimum knew his name, his address, and, most important, why he was in Guatemala.

In those parts, they call crossing the Cuchumatanes *caerse del filo*—falling off the edge. It is there the frosty summits begin their tumbling roll down into the viridian labyrinth of jungle canyon and savanna where the lost cities still stand, some uncovered and opened to a trickle of visitation, the others still slumbering beneath a coat of vegetation so thick they have become part of the earth once again. It is there at the edge that the springlike freshness of the sierra begins to slide into a selvatic heat and humidity like nothing so much as a fever of mother earth, a womb of primal civilization, a hothouse fever of exuberance and biology, a warmth promising the thrill of pleasure and disease and, in the case of what is now lost forever, death.

At the crest of the pass, the three travelers got a glimpse of the cascading tributaries that formed the headwaters of the great Río Usumacinta, winding in and out of the jungled pinnacles, tropic clouds torn on rain-forest parapets. This was where the tenuous human order administered from Huehue and the distant capital broke down, this was where memory faded into forgetfulness, into a blank slate of possibilities. A place of hiding; a place without authority. And down there somewhere lay the village of San Carlos de Chixoy, and a ruined *clínica*, and the spot where Miroslav Lhota, alias Morris Krámský, had died.

"I was able," said Socrates Salazar to Robinson and Lucho as they began their descent, "to find out that Mr. Krámský did attract attention, both in life and in death. He spent some time in these parts before he died."

"With whom?"

"That is what we will find out here. My inquiries told me what

I already suspected—this case has a strong component of intelligence."

He turned and looked at Robinson as he said that. Lucho of course was also listening, and he looked into his rearview mirror to get Robinson's reaction.

"I should tell you I think I'm being watched," Robinson said. Both Guatemalans turned to him.

"By whom?" Salazar asked.

"A man with a widow's peak. I've seen him several times here. The first day in the plaza, yesterday in the market at Sacapulas." He didn't add he'd first seen the man in Virginia.

Salazar pursed his lips.

"It could be anyone," Salazar finally said. "We will simply have to be careful."

Lucho was muttering to himself, apparently contemplating mutiny.

"Back to your dead friend," Salazar said. "What we will do is talk to the Patrulla de Autodefensa Civil in this area. The patrulla found your friend's body."

That would be done in the village of Taxoy, several miles upriver from San Carlos.

"Why not San Carlos?" asked Robinson.

"Because," said Salazar, "San Carlos does not exist anymore. We would be talking to lizards and jungle rats."

The day was warming up, and all the truck windows were down. Lucho was mopping his brow, both from the heat and from the strain of navigating an endless series of switchbacks and blind curves on a dirt road dusty from weeks without rain. In another half hour they pulled into Taxoy, itself no more than a cluster of adobe buildings where farm supplies and hardware were sold. Indians in tribal garb seemed startled at the arrival; they wore full white trousers that ended at the knee, red-and-white-striped serapes across their shoulders, and straw hats. Married men's hats were tied under their necks, while the ribbons of the bachelors' swung free.

Salazar went over and greeted them. Several recognized him, causing a hubbub of excitement. The reception was friendly, and more people came from inside the stores to see the valiant defender of the people Don Socrates and his "assistants," Don Lucho and Don Danilo. Soon Salazar had perhaps twelve men around him;

others stood admiring the truck and looking furtively in at Lucho and Robinson. Salazar finally thanked them for whatever information they had given.

"We will speak with a man named Juan Comalapa. He found the body of Mr. Krámský. By the way, everybody in town knows about this death."

They left Lucho and his truck in town where the driver had gathered a small crowd with today's offering from Lucho's collection of fluorescent T-shirts: the disembodied silver head of a transvestite rock star, floating on a sea of black. Robinson and Salazar began a climb up a footpath that wound into a highland jungle forest of mahogany and cypress, chonta palm and wild *café*. Yellow thrushes shot above them like quivers of arrows from tree to tree; iridescent dragonflies orbited in columns, while chlorophyll grasshoppers bounced across the damp mud path. The hut of Comalapa was about a thirty-minute hike. Several children from the village followed at a safe distance.

"The civil defense patrols were a silly idea," said Salazar. "Trying to get these peaceful people to take up arms against invisible Communists in the cornfields. But in a way, I suppose it is more humane to have them standing guard here than some desensitized conscript from far away. A local fellow is less likely to open fire on his neighbor. And in this particular case, they are about the only people I can trust. They are without guile and see me as their ally."

A little boy in tribal costume directed them to the hut of Juan Comalapa. A woman stood by a caldron strung over a wood fire; several chickens and a small pig rooted in the packed mud. The woman went inside to get Comalapa, who was sleeping off his previous night's duty on the patrol. He stumbled outside in his tribal pants, but shirtless: almost a petite man, though his arms and chest were corded with the effect of years of labor. While nervous, he greeted Salazar warmly. His wife admonished him to get inside and put on a shirt.

Salazar told Comalapa to take his time in getting ready, that they would wait there outside. And so Comalapa went about his wake-up toilet. His wife brought out tin mugs of mango juice, and they sat on upturned stumps and drank the juice.

"This is the way man was meant to live," Salazar said. The only manufactured items in view were the polyester pants of the wife, who clearly preferred them to her tribal skirts. She was barefooted, like everyone else they'd seen that morning.

"We are off the edge," Salazar said.

Beyond him, through the leafy canopy of the forest, great white thunderheads shimmered white and gold in the full winter tropic sun, looming out over Petén and the invisible Yucatán to the northeast. Three children stood on the path, looking at these visitors from another world.

"The place attracts fugitives and misfits," Salazar said. "One of our most famous guerrillas, Yon Sosa, passed through here on his escape to Mexico. He escaped the Guatemalans, but sad irony: the Mexican border patrol shot him on the other side. He was one of the best. Trained by your very own CIA at Fort Gulick in Panama when he was a teenage conscript in the army."

At last Comalapa was ready, and he sat down with the visitors. Yes, he had found the body of the gringo Krámský; he almost wished he hadn't. For it had touched off a torrent of visits from Huehue and then Guatemala City—delegations from the G-2 ("army intelligence," said Salazar), the Kaibiles (a Maya-named army counterinsurgency team), the Policía Militar Ambulante, even the United States. And each visiting delegation had questioned him, his family, his fellows on the *patrulla*.

"How did you find the body?" Salazar asked.

Comalapa replied that he was on his regular rounds in the southern part of the patrol zone, near the road back to Huehue. He had found the body on a path that leads from the road to a cluster of huts to the east, and from there on to the abandoned village of San Carlos de Chixoy.

"I thought the road was the only way to Chixoy."

"It was originally," replied Salazar, "but during the time of the insurgency the road was so heavily patrolled by the gun-happy army and Special Operations that the locals cut a path and took it to avoid being continually interrogated or shot at."

"Can we see the place?" Robinson asked.

"*Muy bien*," replied Comalapa. So off they trooped, taking a path that bypassed the village to the east and cut ten minutes off the trip to where Lhota fell. After a few minutes they came out of the forest and into a cleared area where *maíz*, *piña*, and *cano de azúcar* were being raised. The path wound through a grove of palms and then joined the eastward-heading path from the main road. They crossed the main road and headed into another overgrown field, presumably in the direction of San Carlos. After a mile or so, just at the western edge of a clump of mango trees, Comalapa stopped.

"*Aquí*," he said. He indicated a point on the path itself.

"Strange place for a suicide," said Robinson.

"Describe the body," asked Salazar in Spanish.

"*Se quedó así*," said Comalapa, actually lying down on the path. He lay with arms and legs fully extended and pistol hand up near his head.

"Do you believe the stranger killed himself?" Salazar asked in Mam dialect.

Comalapa got up, looked uncomfortable, cocked his head this way and that. Comalapa's re-creation squared with what Robinson remembered of the file photo he had seen at the Agency. Robinson turned in a slow circle, surveying the scene, imagining Miroslav Lhota's last minutes in this landscape so alien to him, being pursued.

"How long had he been dead when you found him?"

"*Todavía caliente*," said Comalapa, shaking his hand and fingers as if to indicate the body was hot to the touch. Where was he going, where was he coming from? Robinson asked himself. To the southwest stood the main road and the village; to the east, the small cluster of huts where this path led; and beyond, abandoned Chixoy.

"Did you hear the gunshot?" Salazar asked.

"*Quizás*," said Comalapa. He wasn't sure, because it had happened during a violent rainy-season thunderstorm, complete with bolts of lightning striking nearby. He might have heard an uncharacteristic crack.

"Was Señor Krámský seen with anyone during the time before he died?" Robinson asked in Spanish.

This touched off a rapid exchange in Mam between Salazar and Comalapa, Comalapa shaking his head in agitation. Robinson heard the words "gringos" and "G-2," words for which no Mam equivalent probably existed. The exchange lasted perhaps two minutes.

Robinson thought he heard the man say "Chixoy."

"Well," said Salazar after a pause. "We are getting close. This fellow has apparently been raked over the coals on this one. Mr. Krámský was looking for survivors of the fire at the *clínica*. And that entire subject, as Comalapa confirmed, is taboo. To be a survivor of the fire in 1983 is to be a potential witness to whatever happened. The message communicated by the authorities was that Chixoy was to be forgotten."

"Krámský must have found a survivor," Robinson said.

Salazar nodded. "I think he probably did. But the situation is sensitive. Mr. Krámský's death brought down a second avalanche of investigators, stirring up everyone's memory of Clínica Chixoy and the Face of God. This man claims the G-2 sent interrogators—that is serious business—and even the Americans."

"What were they asking?"

Salazar pulled up a shaft of sugarcane, broke it, and sucked at the nectar. Comalapa did the same.

"Some of them were asking most persistently about a book," said Salazar. "A diary, a book of some sort. Something Mr. Krámský had, or had stolen. Would you know anything about it?"

The journal, thought Robinson. Dr. Radan Michalský's journal from Terezín. Had Lhota brought it here with him? Was it somehow assisting him with his search for Emil?

"Did they find the book?" Robinson asked. As this was being relayed to Juan Comalapa and he shrugged in response, Robinson thought: Of course they didn't find it. They were still looking for it when thy came to Darlene Scoggins's house in North Carolina later in the fall.

At first Robinson rejected the possibility Lhota hd brought this much-sought-after journal to Guatemala. Why risk osing it in an alien environment such as this one, which he couldn't control, where he was at such disadvantages?

Yet the more Robinson thought, the more possible it seemed Lhota might have brought the microfilmed journal with him to Guatemala. Yes, it did make sense, in retrospect. Lhota had thought he would find the Angel of Terezín here; perhaps he intended to barter it for the truth, or use it as bait to attract Emil Užhok.

"Señor Comalapa," asked Robinson abruptly in Spanish, "do you know with whom the dead man spoke when he was here?"

Comalapa, who had been quite tranquil up until now, spat his cane juice onto the soil.

"*¡Ese hijo de puta comunista! Es el tipo que causó todo el problema.*"

Salazar was now intrigued and surprised.

"*¿Quién, señor? Quién es comunista?*"

"*Ese bastardo Gabriel López,*" answered Comalapa in Spanish. "He's the one who spent his time with the dead gringo." López, he continued, was a troublemaker. The village had made a mistake in letting him settle nearby.

"Was Señor López," asked Salazar in Spanish, "one of the survivors of San Carlos de Chixoy?"

"*Claro que sí. Puro comunista. Imaginate: un hombre que rechazo la visitación de la santíssima Virgen. Una desgracia.*"

Imagine, repeated Robinson: a man who denied the visitation of the holy Virgin. A disgrace.

"Did López live near here?" Salazar asked in Spanish.

"*Por supuesto,*" Comalapa spat, waving his arm in the direction of the small settlement that lay on the path to the abandoned San Carlos de Chixoy.

"Who might know where to find him?"

"*¡Esa putita allí!*" he answered, spitting on the path. "*Esa Margarita.*"

Salazar walked over to the agitated man. He put his arm around him in consolation. Comalapa cursed a few times in Mam, then seemed to relax. They spoke in the Indian tongue for a moment.

"Mr. Robinson," said Salazar. "Mr. Comalapa is tired. We rousted him out of bed after he was up all night on patrol. We are putting everyone at some risk by our meddling here. I think we should compensate him for his trouble and his generous help and send him on his way."

"Money?" Robinson asked, embarrassed.

"That might help."

"How much?" Robinson asked, prepared to give him twenty quetzales.

"No, no. Five will do."

Robinson gave the money to Comalapa, who bowed and started to back away. Salazar bade him farewell in Mam. Then Comalapa bowed again and left, almost running back down to his hut.

Salazar was shaking his head.

"I only wish the G-2 could hear these people talk. They only want to be left alone, they have no interest in ideology. *Comunistas!* The word has been so degraded in this country, this hemisphere."

Midday now reigned. The sun was at its zenith, throwing an electric white light over palm fronds and blades of grass. A lone gray

Brahma bull grazed in the overgrown field, its throat wattles swaying with each slow movement. Otherwise all life, including the insects, had taken refuge in the shade. Everything seemed to be drawing down, in preparation for the heat of the day.

Salazar mopped his brow. Then, without a word, he began striding up the path.

"To Margarita?" Robinson asked.

"Yes," the older man replied. They stepped from the blazing arena of sun into the cathedral of forest shelter, silently following the path that wound northeast and downhill, ever closer to the warmth of the past, ever farther off the edge.

They sat in the darkness of a thatched hut, one of several among the trees in this isolated spot. In a rear room, an elderly woman softly hummed Quiché songs as she worked a small hand loom, weaving a *lienzo*, and tended a baby in a crib made of a cardboard box filled with banana leaves. This was the same woman who had first told them Margarita was gone. Only after the insistence of Socrates Salazar did a slender young woman, probably half Maya and half Ladina, come out. She was taller than the older woman, her mother, and had an upturned nose and wavy auburn hair. She spoke softly but directly, responding to Salazar's questions.

"Gabriel López is my love," she said matter-of-factly, in Spanish. "We lived as man and wife; that is his son in the crib. He wanted to take me with him when he left, but I was too pregnant and the journey would have been too hard. We had been together for two years."

"Why did Gabriel leave?"

"To save his life. The men who killed the *gringo señor* would have killed him too. He only had a minute's warning. . . ." She looked up at the hut door, as if remembering. "They came here, just after he left; he had heard the gunshot. . . . He was worried. That was the last time I laid eyes on him. Last September."

Salazar lit up his pipe and rubbed his forehead. The smell of the imported tobacco smoke attracted Margarita's *mamá*, who got up from her weaving.

She and Salazar spoke in Mam. And then Salazar let her take several pulls on the pipe.

"Pardon my asking a sensitive question, *señorita*. But if that was the last time you saw Gabriel, how can you be sure he escaped?"

"I knew first when the bad men came here just after he left. They were asking for him. That told me they hadn't found him yet. And then when he wrote to me, weeks later. He wrote me first from Villahermosa in Mexico, using the words of love that only we used together. They were our secret words. And then he wrote me a letter. *My dearest love*, he said, *I want you and my little baby*, *who I have not yet seen*, *by my side. But for now I must keep my hiding place a secret*, *so they will not find me. They are of the devil*, he said. The letter came from New York, in December. Many *guatemaltecos* go to New York. It is also in Mexico, correct?"

"A bit beyond Mexico."

Now her deadpan tone had gone to quavering tearful recollection. She stopped a moment to dry her eyes and blow her nose.

"*Sen˜orita,*" Robinson interrupted in Spanish, "did you see the men who you think killed the gringo?"

"*Sí, por supuesto.* There were two. One, old and white. The other, Ladino and small."

Robinson, fumbling for words in Spanish, turned to Salazar.

"Ask her if the Ladino man had a widow's peak."

Salazar did so. The woman nodded in agreement.

"He ad eyes like a lizard," she said. "Gabriel did not know him. But he knew the other from the *clínica*—"

"Excuse me," interrupted Salazar. "*Señorita,* how did Gabriel see this man and tell you about him, if he left before they arrived that night?"

"But he did see them," she protested. "He saw them walking down the trail to our hut, after they left the gringo's body. They were lit up by lightning flashes, he said. Gabriel was watching from the forest. He is a careful man. He lived for many years in the forest. He knows its secrets."

"But excuse me again, *señorita.* How did he tell you these things if he never saw you again after he fled?"

"In his letter from New York. He said the man's face was lit up by flashes of lightning, a face of Xibalba, just as he had seen it on the night of the fire, lit by firelight. . . ."

"Xibalba," said Salazar in an aside to Robinson, "is the Maya underworld, the realm of evil."

"Gabriel knew the man," continued Margarita. "He knew him

from the *clínica*. This was the man both the dead gringo and Gabriel had been searching for. The man Gabriel had helped find. The firelit face of Xibalba, of evil.

"This was," she added, "el Doctor Emilio."

Emil, the Angel of Terezín.

Now the questions exploded into Robinson's mind. Emil the Angel had been in Guatemala as recently as September. Why had they chosen to meet Emil here? How had Lhota contacted him?

"*Señorita*," blurted Robinson, "why had they decided to meet the doctor here? Why not some other place—the capital, or elsewhere?"

"Because my Gabriel wanted it that way. He said Chixoy was our homeland, the capital would be dangerous and confusing. The *gringo señor* agreed."

Robinson could not get out the words fast enough.

"A book," said Robinson. "Did the dead *gringo señor* say anything about a book?"

"Yes," said Margarita. "A special book, hidden. But he told only Gabriel where it was. A secret."

"Do you know the hiding place?"

"I know only this," she said, pulling out a worn Bible. It held a scrap of paper with a meaningless entry.

Gtm/Utbta 3353 oul

Salazar took the paper, handed it to Robinson.

"Did anyone else find this?"

"*Sí*," she said, eyes downcast. "The two killers. They threatened us first. I had no choice but to tell them. The baby . . ." She began to cry.

"Did you know what the letters, numbers, meant?" Salazar asked.

"No," she said. "The killers shook me, asking me to tell them. I had no idea."

"Did you give the numbers to anyone else?" Robinson asked.

"I told the *investigadores* the killers wanted a book. But I gave these numbers to no one else."

"*Señorita*," Salazar asked, "is there some way we could find Dr. Emilio again? Do you remember how Gabriel first located him in the capital?"

She sat a moment, thinking.

"There was a name," she said. "A carton, a label from the burned *clínica* he saved. Among the things Gabriel took from the *clínica* years ago. He let the dead gringo see it all. And the gringo knew this was the way to find Dr. Emilio."

"Do you have those papers, *señorita?*"

"No," she said. "The killers took them all away."

"The name of the place, *señora.* Do you remember?"

"Alesa . . ."

"Pardon me?"

"Alesa," she replied.

"You know it?" Robinson asked Salazar. The Guatemalan shook his head.

"Perhaps an acronym for a company," Salazar said. "The letters *sa* could be an abbreviation for *sociedad anónima,* meaning 'incorporated.' "

"*Señorita,*" Robinson asked, "what were Gabriel and the gringo going to do when Dr. Emilio came out here to meet them? What would they do, with such an evil man?"

"They were going to take him as a hostage, in the ruins of Chixoy, a place Gabriel knew well," she said. "They would use him to bring some justice to the people who were wronged by this evil."

"So how did the plan fail?"

"Gabriel believed he was betrayed soon after they made the first call to Alesa. Dr. Emilio and the other man appeared three days early, and they came straight for the *gringo señor* and him. They knew right where to find Gabriel. Gabriel is known in these parts. He is the only survivor of the fire at the *clínica* who stayed nearby. He is known to the police, to many people in this village, who think him a troublemaker and wanted to see him gone. Dr. Emilio must have gone to the police or someone and found his name. The gringo was no problem to find; he was famous in this area. He ate the *salchichas;* he gave them to the children."

Lhota and his infernal sausages.

"You and your child were fortunate," said Salazar, "that harm did not come to you because of your relationship to Gabriel."

It was now midafternoon. The baby, Lázaro, had awakened, and Margarita nursed him.

"See. He has Gabriel's fierce eyes. The eyes of Xbalanque, of the jaguar deer."

Salazar lit up another bowlful of tobacco, catching the baby's attention for a moment with the flare of the match. A cloud had passed over the westward descent of the sun; there would be rain on the Pacific coast before sunset. *Mama* had moved onto the packed dirt outside the front door, to catch a soft breeze. She was peeling potatoes and shucking small ears of *maíz* to be boiled for dinner.

"*Señorita*," Salazar asked, "what did Gabriel tell you of the Clínica Chixoy? Was he a patient there? Did he perhaps see the fire that destroyed it and so many people?"

She was humming softly to the baby, to get it back to sleep.

"My Gabriel was in the beginning a believer. He was so glad to have the Cara de Dios here. He was a youth when they came—fourteen years old. He spent as much time with the *médicos* as he could. He worked for them, often as a volunteer, in exchange for a bowl of food. Then they hired him, to clean, to dig, to do errands. He dreamed of becoming a doctor himself. And he loved their faith . . . the singing of songs, the praying, the coming closer to God. He was a follower of the Cara de Dios."

The baby had fallen asleep, and she put it back in its crib of banana leaves.

"What changed him?"

She seemed perturbed, had difficulty forming the words.

"It began with the *visitación*. Gabriel is a believer. But when the *Virgen* appeared to the others in the valley, Gabriel doubted. He thought it was a trick of the underworld . . . a trick of Xibalba. He said everyone fell under a spell. He wanted to go for help . . . but he was terrified to leave, terrified of the evil he saw moving in the world."

"What did Gabriel tell you about the *visitación?*"

She was now trembling, agitated. Robinson could see she was torn—she still had not resolved whether Gabriel had been wrong to doubt the visitation.

"He would hardly speak of it to me. He said only that a figure came in a veil of raiment. The others saw the *Virgen;* he saw the face of X Kiq, the blood girl of the underworld."

"I know this is hard for you, *señorita*. But did he speak of the fire?"

"No. He said such an abomination should not be repeated in words. It is the way of his people. To speak terrible things—to name them before vengeance is done—means they will happen again."

"He told you nothing of the fire?"

"He said it was an abomination."

"Do you believe the *guerrillas* set it, *señorita?* Did they attack the people of Chixoy because they had become too close to the Cara de Dios, because they were now believers?"

"I don't know, *señor*."

"Or did the army do this thing to the people of Chixoy, thinking they had joined the guerrillas and must be punished?"

"I don't know," she repeated, head bowed. The silence of the tropical afternoon floated on the air, on the smells of drying earth and moldy vegetation.

"*Don* Socrates," she asked, "do you think harm will come to my Gabriel? Will he be punished for being an unbeliever?"

Salazar placed his hand on her forearm.

"*Señorita*, you know in your heart Gabriel is a good man. God knows this goodness in him. His danger is not from God but from man. And we will do what we can to help him. If we can find him."

She looked up.

"*Señorita*, you have spent much time with us. We will get to the truth of the wrong that has been done here and in Chixoy. I want you to know that if you feel in danger yourself, come to Huehue and you will be sheltered."

She broke into a brief smile.

"But now we must go," he said. "We will go to the place where Chixoy once stood, and to the *clínica*, and then we will be gone. But thank you for your help. We will bring justice."

Mama looked up from her potatoes, unconvinced. Salazar gave her his pouch of tobacco.

They all bowed, and Robinson and Salazar left. The two men walked for a time without speaking, on down the path to the abandoned village. The jungle was ever warmer and richer the farther they went, the stalks of the bananas dripping with moisture and bejeweled by army ants on maneuver. Here and there an orchid blossomed on a tree trunk. Thunder sounded to the west, an almost regular rumble.

"I begin to wonder if this puzzle has any solution," Salazar said. "Just as we near an answer, it evaporates into a new layer of questions and doubts. I fear we will never find Gabriel López or any other survivors. All their secrets are being taken to the grave. As for Alesa, that is a possibility. But I'm sure it will lead down some murky path which we don't have the resources to pursue."

"And Krámský's note?"

"It appears to be code. Could you shed some light?"

Robinson looked at it for a moment. *Gtm/Utbta 3353 oul.* Yes, it might have been code. In his communications with Lhota years before in Vienna, a written letter meant the immediately following letter in the alphabet, and written digits were the second succeeding digit. With a pencil he translated, in disappointment:

Hun/Vucub 1131 pvm

"You had a most unusual friendship," said Salazar.

"Does this mean something to you?"

"Yes. There is a myth in the Book of the Council of the Quiché Mayas—a work known to its authors as the Popol Vuh. Rather than a book, of course, it is an epic tale told in Mayan pictograms; the Mayans had no written language. The two brothers Hun Hunahpu and Vucub Hunahpu were defeated in a ball game with the rulers of the underworld and beheaded. But they were reborn through a rather strange fertilization. The same X Kiq, daughter of the underworld, whom Gabriel López saw instead of the *Virgen* went to look at the two heads hanging on a tree; one of them spit at her. The saliva hit her on the hand, and she became pregnant, bearing the sons Hunahpu and Xbalanque."

"And the numbers?"

"Quite by coincidence, I believe I know their meaning. The primary collection of the Popol Vuh material is at the Museo Popol Vuh, a fine collection given by Jorge and Ella Castillo and stored in the Edificio Galerías Reforma. That is where anyone would go looking for material on the Popol Vuh, and thus the letters 'pv' in the code. But the four digits and the final 'm' tell me it refers to a duplicate microfilm collection of the Popol and related reference materials I stumbled upon in the Biblioteca Nacional only last year. I found it quite by accident when I was doing some research on the Mayan sky goddess Ixchel for a collection of poetry. There is a little man sitting there napping, supposedly watching over the collection, but more likely guarding the microfilm reader, which would be worth more to a thief than the microfilms. Heaven knows how the collection came to be, or how your friend found it. So I would imagine if first you look up the Hunahpu brothers, then you search there for pictogram 1131, you will find either your journal or some other clue."

"But the girl said she told the killers about it. They probably found it months ago."

"I seriously doubt they could find it. Even if they were cryptologists and translated your code, they would require a knowledge of Maya mythology and a degree in Guatemalan library science to go any further. And if they deciphered the meaning of the name reference, they never would have found the microfilm collection. I don't think anyone has ever used it, except by accident, since there's no catalog reference to it anywhere. When you return to the capital, I suggest you drop by there."

They were now in a clearing of shoulder-high overgrowth and humped masses of vine. It was all that was left of San Carlos de Chixoy after nearly ten years of abandonment. It yielded nothing other than a sense of death and desolation. From there they continued on an obligatory hike to the site of the *clínica* ruins. Though it took them more than an hour to reach, they could see the site long before they got there, up on a curious cleared shoulder plateau of the northern face of the Cuchumatanes. Perhaps a defoliant had been used, for nothing grew in an area of several hundred acres except knee-high grass. The ground itself looked as though it had been landscaped. In that setting, the place had an almost strategic look; the runway, though broken with clumps of sawgrass and thistle, was substantial, conveying a sense of lost importance. Rusted barrels lay in the grass, presumably once fuel containers. In the ruins themselves—mostly intact white stucco walls with enduring black scorch marks—twisted black bed frames were garlanded with climbing selvatic vines. No roof survived. Several tropical rats scuttled away into holes where the concrete floor had buckled from the walls. The heat of the fire must have been intense, because nothing recognizable, beyond the heat-twisted metal bed frames, survived.

"And there we have it," said Salazar with finality. "About all I can say with certainty is that a terrible crime was committed. And that once again, powerless people have been treated as insects."

He stopped a moment to roll over a rusty barrel. A brilliant red *culebra* slithered away into the afternoon grass.

"And it is now time for our work together to come to an end," he added. "I have allowed you to use my good offices in the hopes that you would shed further light. Yet the opposite has happened. I hold no ill will; but I think a debt is owed here.

"In repayment I ask only this," said Salazar. "Our little horror is only one chapter in your story. For us it is the beginning and end; our horizons are here for you to see, while yours are global. I ask that when and if you do find the truth about this affair, you share it with me, no matter what the cost. So that we can at least pretend we are people of justice."

As if to punctuate the finality of what he had said, the ricocheted sound of a not-too-distant explosion bounced off the walls of the Cuchumatanes, the crash of a dynamite cymbal, an alien and disturbing sound in this panorama of earth and nature. It was a good ten seconds before the sound had fully played itself out in the jungled canyons and silence reigned again. But a column of black smoke snaked up into the sky several miles south, roughly from the direction where they'd started today's walk. The smoke was a reminder of the alienness of this sonic event. And the smoke was like a flare that caught Salazar's attention and drew them both back toward Taxoy, in an urgent, slow, but purposeful trot, knowing that what they would find would not be good.

At first it seemed the worst; Lucho's "L'il Hoss" had been separated into two significant portions about one hundred feet apart, while Lucho himself had been blown against the foot of a palm tree shading the Huehue-Taxoy road, where he was surrounded by a group of squatting peasants. But to the good, he survived because the bomb went off while he was napping in the ditch, waiting on his passengers to return. No one in the village knew anything at all, and Salazar thought it beyond the powers of anyone residing in this community to have engineered a car bomb.

"This was set in Huehue, or even back in Guatemala City," said Salazar. "No one up here would be able to work with timing fuses."

"Hey, Mr. CIA, who pays for my Hoss?" Lucho managed to ask from his bed of pain in the one-room village health clinic, despite a broken collarbone and lingering deafness and shock. Naturally, he carried no insurance on the vehicle. He rallied from his pain to demand some kind of payment from Robinson, who gave him all the cash he could spare and his phone number in Virginia. But for Robinson, the task now was, first, to get to the Biblioteca Nacional and find Dr. Radan Michalský's journal from Terezín, presumably hidden in the microfilm archives by Lhota; if he had time, to find out something about Alesa; and, that completed, to get out of Guatemala.

Salazar was nice enough to take on Lucho, but he would do no more on the Cara de Dios until he heard from Robinson.

After hitching a late-afternoon ride on a banana truck to Huehue, Robinson took an express minibus to the capital late that night, searching the shadows for the face of the man with the widow's peak. He spent a sleepless night at the Hotel Camino Real, door chained. The next morning, after anonymously determining that the Eastern flight out that afternoon had sufficient space to permit a departure without a reservation (he didn't want to trigger another bomb placement), he went to the Biblioteca.

The Biblioteca Nacional itself was gargantuan, befitting a nation ten times the size of this one, its grandiose cornices and friezes covered with soot and dust. And although the student library was jammed with young scholars, the remainder of the building was quite underutilized. Empty was a better word, and as Robinson went deeper into its confines, he felt less and less comfortable. The poorly lighted, often totally dark stacks could provide cover for all sorts of ill deeds. The dust was centuries old, and the floors and sagging wood shelves had possibly never had finish or paint. A number of dead bats and their dried droppings lay on the floor and on books; sparrows nesting among the rafters flitted in the gloom. He was sorry he was alone, wished he had Lucho or Salazar along for assistance.

But his discomfort gave way to satisfaction, for within fifteen minutes of locating the Popol Vuh shelf, he'd found an envelope with the Czech scribblings of Lhota and strips of microfilm holding the memoirs of Dr. Radan Michalský. The microfilmed journal was temporarily useless to him, because he did not read Slovak well. But he could see it consisted of a series of chronological entries, presumably written in Michalský's own hand: Vienna, 1909; Prague, 1926 and 1939; and Terezín, 1942 and 1943.

Also in the packet he found the roll of Terezín negatives Simona had smuggled out of the Czech Higher Party Archives. He held them up against a dim light and looked them over, but they were meaningless in their present state.

"*¿Señor, que haces?*" a wizened library guard called as Robinson walked toward the exit; he had seen Robinson put the envelope in his shirt pocket.

His breath shortening, Robinson tried to explain that the materials belonged to a friend of his who had accidentally left them there, not to the library.

The guard just looked at him, grinning strangely. Robinson had no idea what that meant. He began searching around for means of escape, ways he could immobilize this guard, the adrenaline starting to flow.

The man muttered something under his breath.

"*¿Cómo?*" Robinson asked.

"*Te los puedo alquilar*," said the guard.

The guard would be willing to "rent" Robinson the materials. They settled on a price of ten U.S. dollars. The guard then eagerly told Robinson to hide the envelope of microfilms in his shoe, to avoid the guards at the front door.

Robinson secreted the materials in his shoe, then continued on away from the Popol Vuh collection into the bowels of the library itself, in order to reach the main entrance on Parque Centenario, where he'd come in. On the left he could hear the muffled sound of a meeting or lecture in a closed hall as he passed. He paused a minute to try and make out what was being said, but could not.

And it was in that instant that he was ambushed, the person who had probably been there all along, watching his every move, now materializing like darkness brought to life. Robinson knew only that he was jumped and pulled up backward against an unbathed man, a forearm across his throat so fast and his own arm twisted back in such pain that he couldn't get the wind or the strength to throw the attacker. The tip of a body-warmed blade pressed against his jugular. And he could feel stubble-rimmed lips at his ear, enunciating a command.

"*Dámelo*," the man said, asking for what Robinson had. Robinson didn't even need to see him to know who it was or what he wanted. He could sense the widow's peak right against his own head, the knobby chest and arms doing what they had been trained to do. Stalling, Robinson tried to answer, but the forearm jerked tighter, gagging him. He could still throw them both onto the floor, risking at best a dislocated shoulder, a cut jugular almost as likely.

"Give it to me," the man repeated in English, his Caribbean Spanish accent coming through, and Robinson nodded as much as he could, hoping the man would think he had triumphed and would ease his grip. Robinson's eyes swept the scene, searching for some salvation, but there was none; the two of them were totally alone in sepulchral darkness. Robinson's corpse might lie here for days without being discovered except by scavengers. To buy time, he let his own body begin to go limp, as though he were defeated.

The nearby yet unseen meeting hall rumbled with muffled applause, mocking him. The attacker tightened momentarily, to gauge whether this sound posed a threat to his transaction. And when he apparently decided after a few seconds that it did not, neither one of them really registered what was happening as a pair of giant wooden doors facing them burst open and a phalanx of uniformed men—army, national police, MPs—came surging out. For a second or two, both sides faced each other in surprise.

It was at that moment that Robinson threw himself backward with full force, sending both of them crashing into a tottering bookshelf. And so it was that the entire row of moth-eaten volumes came crashing down on Robinson and his assailant, knocking them to the ground and momentarily blinding everyone in a blast of moldy dust, fluttering pages, and splintering wood.

That was followed by commands, shouts, pistols being drawn.

"*¡Qué haces!*" a whole team of MPs was shouting at them both, billy clubs waving, while a further crowd gathered behind the MPs.

A hand was on Robinson's arm, and it was not the attacker's. "*Señor*," a young MP was asking, "you are a touris'?" Robinson nodded. Widow's peak, the breath knocked out of him by a tumbling column of bound nineteenth-century Central American newspapers, was being arrested.

As Robinson was being helped up, a group of Guatemalan military brass pushed forward to see what the hell the commotion was. And so it was that Robinson found himself face-to-face with General Gonzalo Gordillo, Counterinsurgency Director for Huehuetenango Department, his cratered face contorted in a look of amazement.

"Es my fran Alan!" General Gordillo cried, gripping Robinson and shaking him with verve. "Es my wonerful contry trying to rob and murder you?"

Robinson couldn't say anything.

"You trying to esneak out early from my lecture?" General Gordillo asked, ending the question in a volley of *cka-cka-cka*s.

"I'm sorry?" Robinson asked.

"I geb a lecture on your wonerful Walt Whitman, to the Sociedad Literaria de Guatemala. Don't tell me you miss it?"

Robinson was speechless.

"I bring all my boys, so they will learn a little bit of culture." It was then Robinson realized all the army officers and MPs were clutching Spanish translations of *Leaves of Grass*.

"Who this *hijo de puta?*" Gordillo asked, motioning toward the man with the widow's peak, still dazed. "He try and rob you?"

Robinson nodded.

"*¿Bueno, señor, quién es usted?*" Gordillo gruffed, walking over to the prisoner, who did not answer. His pockets were emptied, papers produced.

"*¿Nombre?*" Gordillo barked, and four billy clubs vigorously whacked the detainee to speed a reply.

"García," the man finally muttered.

"García," repeated Gordillo. "You don' look like *guatemalteco* to me. *Guatemaltecos* don't have such bad manners, to rob poor touris'. Eh? *Hijo de puta?*" The questions were punctuated with more syncopated clubbing. One of the MPs said Mr. García's national identity card was not in order.

"Eh? You don' even smell *guatemalteco*," said Gordillo, walking around the restrained Señor García. "Eh? You come from Cuba? Eh? *Cubano?* Eh?"

Whap-whap-whap went the billy clubs on thighs, shoulders. Señor García was stoically silent.

"*Llévalo a la cárcel*," said Gordillo, throwing the identity card to the floor. And so Señor García was dragged off to the Central City Prison, to enter the machinations of the Guatemalan system of justice.

"*Bueno*, my fran Alan," said the general. "I take my boys now to eat fry . . . es . . . es . . ."

"Shrimp?" Robinson guessed.

"*¡Exacto!*" Gordillo laughed. "You come with us? Eh?"

"I would love to," Robinson answered. "But I'm returning home this afternoon. I don't have time."

"*Bueno.*" The general nodded. "You need *guardia? Hospital? Medicina?*"

Robinson shook his head.

"*Bueno*, my fran. *Vaya con Dios*, eh?" He laughed, and they shook hands, then exchanged an *abrazo*. And a great contingent of the Guatemalan Northern Command went rumbling off down the hallway, clutching volumes of Walt Whitman and leaving Robinson surrounded by wreckage and dust.

Calmly, he picked up "García's" identity card and put it in his pocket.

Then, once outside the library, Robinson stopped at a darkroom for a rush developing job on the Terezín negatives, paying extra to have the black-and-whites ready well in advance of his return to Miami that afternoon. Back in his room at the Camino Real, he checked the phone directory, then questioned the operator for a listing on anything called Alesa, but without success. He wondered if the young woman at Chixoy had remembered the name correctly.

Despite having General Gordillo as a sponsor, Robinson was so preoccupied with the potential threat behind every bookshelf, at the end of every corridor, that he didn't begin to relax until he was on the plane out over the Caribbean, Miami bound again. The fact that Senator Blisterson, Miss Minnie, and entourage were also on board gave little comfort. And it was only then that he had the time to scan the newly developed photos from Terezín, taken in 1941, when the camp was still under construction and not yet inhabited: photos of the motor pool; the mess hall; the guards' exercise field; the main loading dock; the power plant; each and every one of the guard towers from assorted angles; the inventory of gravel, coal, and lumber for use in camp construction and maintenance; the well; the individual barracks; the latrines. Finally he came upon the photo of Dr. Michalský and Emil Užhok, a portion of which Simona had given him in Prague.

Simona's suspicion that a third man had been excised from the photo was correct, for staring up at him now was a high Nazi official standing in full regalia, *posing* with the prison camp inmates.

Robinson was sitting in his seat considering that, photo before him, when recognition of the third man came to him . . . not unassisted.

"Dreadful man, you know," said Robinson's seatmate in British English. She was a jug-headed older woman, who had that know-it-all air of the empire about her. "Partisans did the world a service when they blew him up."

He knew that behind her comments, as with all of her type, armed with absolute Britannic certitude, was a probable wealth of knowledge, gleaned from direct experience, reading the newspapers of almost fifty years ago, the London blitz as a young girl.

The ragged edge of the tear in Simona's original photo fragment had been a mystery in itself, a blatant effort at concealment of something. Now Robinson was even more mystified, as he saw the embracing arm of a Nazi dignitary, which crossed from his portion of the photo to grace the shoulders of Dr. Michalský.

The British lady had said a name as she clucked over the photo, and it was still echoing in his head, one of those *H* names bunched together in a trinity awful to those who had been touched by them but which, because of Robinson's generation and relative youth, did not immediately conjure up for him an identity from the pantheon of the Third Reich. The name she had uttered he now remembered, prompted by the lightning-bolt insignia of the SS on this man's collar. This was the Führer's heir, his spiritual son, felled by those he was sent to rule.

Robinson remembered textbook photos and prehistoric film reels of that Gothic-cum-satanic ceremony, a ghastly maudlin funeral for a dark hero sent up to Valhalla, choreographed by the masters of Fascist spectacle, a bier, an altar, cinematic keening by the diseased father with the withered testicle who endlessly punished the world for his own deformity and weakness.

Decreeing a Czech village scorched from the face of the earth in biblical revenge for the murder of his Nazi heir, the fallen son, the man in the photo . . .

Reinhard Heydrich.

Terezín, 1942

'Tis I —Mephistopheles

My surprise summons to see the *Reichsprotektor* came without warning on a late-January morning in 1942. His emerald Daimler-Benz, which I had seen once before, during his fall visit, came this time passengerless, its balloon tires popping across the frozen, frosted ground. Even Joekl, the camp commandant, was stirred from his routine by its arrival, and was both publicly disappointed and privately relieved to learn that his boss, Heydrich, had remained behind in Prague.

I was making my morning rounds of bedpans and pisspots when Hodl burst in on me, all out of breath.

"Michalský!" he said. "He . . . Prague . . ."

"Hodl," I stammered, "what are you saying?"

"The *Protektor*," he answered, recovering. "He has sent his car and driver for you, to take you back to Prague."

My heart leapt, and yet none of this made any sense. Was I at last to be freed? Why was I, a lifelong Communist, now to be freed at the height of the destruction of the Czech Communist Party by the Nazi occupiers? My initial excitement gave way to dread, to the fear that perhaps this was my end.

Looking out the window, however, I did see the imperial Daimler awaiting me. Hardly a cattle car for shipment to the mysterious "resettlement centers" in Poland.

Perhaps something else did await me after all.

I was given a quarter hour to pack a small bag, Hodl clucking about me all the while.

"This is a godsend," he said, "the opportunity of a lifetime. You must make the most of it. They say the *Protektor* is Hitler's secret heir apparent. And he is reputed to be a genius."

Yet I could not imagine what the *Protektor* would want from me, a Slovak Communist prisoner of war with Jewish parentage. It made no sense.

With a growing sense of foreboding, I rode in grand style across the frozen hills of north Bohemia, the *Protektor*'s personal flags flying on the fenders. As we drove through villages like Litoměřice, people turned and peered inside to see the dreaded viceroy of Moravia-Bohemia.

Whenever we passed *Wehrmacht* and SS troops, they clicked their heels and raised their arms in the *Sieg heil* of the Reich. Then they saw the curious gray-bearded face of a Slovak psychiatrist, and they were mystified.

As was I. It was as though I were living some kind of perverse nightmare.

The driver, a square-headed corporal of the Waffen SS named Klein, spoke to me through the glass partition and told me fruits and sweets awaited me in a small cabinet.

I took and ate.

As we rode through the frozen lands of Bohemia, the wintry dreamscape passing before my baffled eyes, the white sky and the white snow all merging into a world without depth, without shadow, I had a sudden vision of myself as a child, on a skating party with the other children from the orphanage where I and my sister Margret spent part of our childhood. Now I realize I was doing more than simply remembering; as I drove through the wintry land in the motorcar of Hitler's viceroy on that frigid morning, I was *reliving* a distant event that even to this day causes me pain as does nothing else, a trauma-memory that I had thought long ago excised by psycho-analysis but was in fact simply repressed, stuffed down into the cellar of forgetfulness, and now coming forth to haunt and mock me at this most bizarre moment.

In my mind I could hear the orphanage master cautioning us not to venture onto thin ice. I, being several years older than my little sister, and certainly more adventurous at that age, was swept up in the euphoria of the snowy day and the party as, momentarily for-getting my otherwise careful vigilance and protection of her, I went off slipping and sliding with the older boys (I myself at that time was eight). My sister, rather shy by nature and certainly so since our arrival at the orphanage, went on her own explorations of the ice, alone.

Yes, dear reader, it is now time for you to learn the secret to which I alluded in my first entry, when I narrated the ritual acted out with the prostitute Lili in Vienna. To understand me and what direction my life has since taken, you must know I have felt no shock equal to that I experienced when, upon running with my friends to a corner of the lake to answer the cries of someone in distress, I realized my own Margret had fallen through and was thrashing in the frigid slushy water, in danger of drowning.

The desperate maneuverings, the fumblings, the inept rescue that finally brought her out, barely alive, followed swiftly by pneumonia and her death at the age of five, permanently seared me with pain and affected my relations with all people as only such an experience can do. For you see, I had carried as an injunction in my young heart a commandment my mother imparted to me on the steps of the failing Slovak farm where our family had made its last stand. As she sent us away from the wretched household that could no longer feed us and the stepfather who did not wish to keep us, to a new life as orphans in Bratislava, she had begged me to serve as Margret's protector and champion in the absence of a parent; this above all I was to do. And I had taken Mother at her word, I had committed myself to guide and protect this young soul through a dark world, thinking it was within my powers as an eight-year-old to do so. To see her now waxen, lying in the tiny coffin, was proof of my failure, of my complicity in her death. This is no kind of injury for such a young one to bear; in those times, we were already scarred with fears and uncertainties, about where the next day's bread would come from, or whether we would fall into the clutches of some terrible foster parent. Indeed, Margret's deepest fear had been that we would be separated, as we had been from our widowed and remarried mother. I had promised her that it would never happen, and had meant it.

And so as I rode in Hitler's hearse I relived Margret's funeral, I could see Mama brought in from the country by the awful news on a wintry day much like this one, crying in black, while the remnants of our shattered family circled round us. I saw a splintered pastiche of my own recurring dreams of that time, when Margret was reaching out to me from beyond the shroud of death. As always, I was skating alone, under a luminous sky, across the ice. And Margret would rise up out of the frozen lake, clutching at me, shrieking, Save me, brother, save me! And I would feel her icy hands grabbing at my wrists, my neck, I sobbing all the while, half tempted to plunge into the icy depths with her.

In my auto-analysis at Bratislava after my return from Vienna, my great mentor, analyst, and teacher, Jaroslav Stuchlík, had helped me face up to my guilt over her death and, I thought, to shed the tendency to avoid emotional attachments for fear that I would fail someone in time of need.

"My young Radan," Stuchlík said to me, "you must forever guard against your impulse to shield yourself in ice armor, where you and Margret are forever protected from pain. You must remain open—in fact, seek love—or you will be as dead as she."

My breakthrough with Stuchlík in 1912 had indeed ended the dream, and I had accepted my guilt about my sister's death. And, I told myself, my revolutionary politics were my own way of giving love, for I would rescue my fellow men from the kind of world that had produced such pain and misfortune.

My God, such a memory!

It left me limp and shaking. The two-hour drive from Terezín flew by like two minutes, as I rolled in my childhood pain; before I knew it, we were turning up the driveway that led to Zámek Panenské-Břežany, which the *Protektor* had taken as his own. Twelve miles from Prague, surrounded by woods and parklands, it was built as a replica of one of the châteaux of the Loire, a classic example of the high Gothic style. It was possible to imagine that knights in its forests still dreamed of the Grail, and troubadours still wandered the shadowed paths.

An SS guard met me at the door and took me into the *Protektor*'s working office, a parlor that had been furnished with all the latest communications equipment, telephones and shortwave radios tying him directly to SS bases in Prague, Brno, Bratislava, Munich, Vienna, Paris, and Berlin headquarters. A stenographer sat by his great desk, which had belonged to the Hapsburg counts and, before them, to the Holy Roman baronates.

The *Protektor* was deep in a conversation with Berlin, and although he spoke softly I knew it was with someone of the highest rank, someone with whom only he could communicate. Still my thoughts were with Margret, though other things were tumbling through.

Heydrich turned in his chair, nodded in my direction, continued talking. His hair was close-cut in the Prussian style. He was still a young man, less than forty, with a curiously elongated face and body and a long nose, broken at the bridge, which dominated his face. His eyes were small and quite close together, but startling in their glassy blueness. It was a horse face, and yet not unattractive.

But the most incongruous feature of all was the voice, the crackling high-pitched croak of a boy just entering adolescence. The sound he made, even when whispering, was nothing so much as a goat sound; I could see why his nickname as a youth had been *die Ziege*—the goat.

"Sergeant," said Heydrich, cupping his hand over the receiver, "show the *Doktor* to his quarters."

He resumed talking as I was escorted away.

I was taken up the circular castle staircase to a suite certainly as large as one I might have found at Hradčany, and much better heated, for the Reich had installed electrical coil heaters driven by small fans. The room was warm and inviting, albeit with the odor of hot heating coils instead of firewood and ash.

A uniformed SS chambermaid came in and said she would draw my bath.

I had not had a proper tub bath since my arrest nearly three years before.

While I waited, seated on the bed with its Viennese crinoline spread and overstuffed pillows, I sampled fruits on a silver tray by the bedside. There were even Viennese chocolates and a portion of Sacher torte tied with a red ribbon. The opulence of all this made Hodl's shabby provisions seem some kind of cheap parody of power.

My bath was ready.

While I languished in it, I watched the profuse black hair of my legs and chest wave like seaweed, and my long-dormant phallus lolling like some kind of limp moray in the shifting reef currents. Remarkably, while three years' detention had taken their toll in other ways, I had lost the fifteen pounds of flab my successful Prague practice and bourgeois existence had given me, and so I was surprisingly trim for a man of my age and lack of exercise. The hairy muscularity I had inherited from my grandfather Levy was still reasonably intact.

The gloom I had felt during the ride began to lift slightly. In fact, I felt like a virile young man again, if only for an hour. I reveled in a proper room and unbarred windows and a real feather bed, as opposed to the various utilitarian and even malign articles of furniture, food, and clothing with which I had been tortured these last three years.

On the bed I found a note from the *Protektor*'s office, telling me he would receive me for libations at seven, followed by dinner at eight. Just as I read that, the chambermaid brought me a wheeled cart bearing lunch: duckling à la orange, fresh juniper berries, a French Sauterne, and Bavarian cream cakes.

After lunch I slept and, sleeping, dreamed of many things: of young Ilse the idealist, and my long-lost Loki, and my sister, Margret, and of Lou Salomé, who now would have been more than eighty years old, probably in the exile of senility or even dead; I did not know.

I luxuriated in the warmth, and the memories.

The *Protektor* had not yet arrived in the library at seven, and so I had a moment to examine myself in the borrowed suit I had found in the closet, which fit reasonably well (though the sleeves were a bit too short). But no matter, for I had not worn a proper suit in three years, and in my eyes, it might as well have been a cutaway.

The *Protektor* came in, this time in dress black uniform with a silver-and-red swastika and the ever-present lightning-bolt insignia of the SS.

"I am glad you could come," he said, continuing this polite fiction that I was not a prisoner and he not my jailer. "Unfortunately, my wife, Lina, and our children are on vacation in Berlin. I am sorry they could not be here."

He walked over to the fire and tossed on a log.

"But perhaps in their absence we shall be able to speak more frankly, and at length," he added.

I had no response.

"Did you find everything to your liking?" he asked. As he did so, he stroked the bridge of his nose and examined me with his blue eyes, I all the while searching for the clues that would explain this puzzle of a man to me.

"Of course," I said. Behind him, I was straining to read the titles of books that the prior owner, the Nestomice sugar millionaire Bloch-Blauer, had left behind—all the comedies of Molière, the adventures of Robert Louis Stevenson, the plays of Tirso de Molina and Calderón de la Barca, Shakespeare, Chekhov. And there were political works, by Friedric Engels and Schopenhauer, John Stuart Mill and Disraeli, the *Memoirs* of Clemenceau . . . books I knew to have been banned or burned in Berlin.

He seemed to read my thoughts, for he smiled slightly.

"You are wondering why I have invited you here," he said more than asked.

A steward served us an excellent claret.

"I am trying to decide what to do with you," he said, and sipped the wine. I joined him.

"What are the options?" I asked, my heart pounding, out of fear, confusion.

"One of the most tiresome aspects of this job," he said, "is working off the backlog of nondecisions left by my ineffectual predecessor, von Neurath. Decisions about security, about order . . .

"And about prisoners," he added.

"We can't have people stacking up like cordwood around here," he said.

"The option I first chose, and which I have not yet carried out, was to have you executed."

My heart contracted, my gut was hard and trembling.

"This is a magnificent library, is it not?" he asked rhetorically, waving his hand around him. And I agreed, for it was. The tall Gothic windows looked out on the frosty Central European night, and the gaslights gave it warmth, a night promise and mystery that only such a library can have.

"I think it appropriate I meet a man such as you in a place like this," he said. "This library symbolizes all the best that the human mind can create. The repository of ideas, timeless ideas, all the twists and turns of logic and of illogic, of discovery and error and fantasy, that we as a race have made.

"We are creators, and captives of, ideas," he said. "Do you not agree?"

I agreed with the obvious.

He reached onto a shelf and pulled out a volume of Aristotle, in the Greek.

"Imagine the symmetry of the Greek world, the form-perfectness of its architecture, its sunlit harmony, the marble logic of its thought."

Then he took down a jeweled leatherbound translation of the *Thousand and One Arabian Nights.*

"And the desert mania, the magic cave that is the prime symbol of the Arabian world, the searching for the oasis . . . While we, sons of the northern marauders, wanderers in the forest, the night forest of our dark Europe, are now called by destiny . . ."

Did this "we" he spoke of include me? I wondered.

He stroked his nose again, turned, and in the half-light and silence, an impetuous thought, based on a rumor I must have heard and ignored back in the camp, came bubbling out of my subconscious.

This man, I thought to myself, is part Jewish, as am I.

Why did I think this? Was it an intuitive leap, or a total error on my part?

He must have seen my face lighting up with some kind of realization, for he examined me closely.

"I can see . . . you are a student of Spengler," I blurted.

His face tightened a bit, and I feared I had insulted him. Should I have used the word "student"?

"Better let us say a reader of Spengler," he said. "He has written only half a book."

"I beg your pardon?" I asked, thinking he had read only Part One.

"He wallows in the decline of the old West," said Heydrich. "But he does not write of the rebirth of the new West.

"He is too much in love with death," said Heydrich. "As are so many of my compatriots. This is something I must struggle with daily. This nihilist death wish."

I was totally intrigued now. Uncertain how he was using these terms, whom he meant by his "compatriots," I thought it best to remain silent.

"Death is the beginning of new life, is it not?" he asked. "Why stop at the funeral, rather than carry on to the rebirth?"

I was lost.

"I could have had you destroyed," he said. "And the conventional logic would have told me to do that. You, a Communist. More than that, one of the founders of your nation's Party, a lifelong struggler for its ends. Intelligent, a confidant of powerful members of the international Bolshevik movement. You, for example, are a friend of Lavrenty Beria, are you not?"

This is it, I thought. He wishes to interrogate me about the Czech movement. But of course! What else would he want of me? I felt a sinking sensation. The room began to go dull. They must have found that infernal thank-you note from Beria in my files.

"I have never met the man," I muttered. "I did a favor for his legation many years ago."

Heydrich only smiled.

"This is not an interrogation," he said. "Your friendship with Beria, whether you tell me the truth or lie, is of little importance. You are a clever man. Do not dissemble about your politics, for you have given your life to them.

"As have I," he added.

"You and I have that in common," he said.

"We are prepared to die for our politics, are we not?"

This condescension from a Fascist made me burn.

"Yes." I nodded, inwardly hoping I would not be put to the test. For in me, the life wish was still stronger.

"Yes, the conventional crude wisdom would have told me to eliminate you, for you are dangerous. This impulse to blot out all that is dangerous is something with which I battle every day. I struggle with the lesser minds of my movement, those who would lay waste everything of value. These crude men who share the swastika are in their own way dangerous, and although we fight under the same banner, they are my adversaries. They are people who would burn books."

I was now more perplexed than ever. I felt I was being drawn into things I wished to have no knowledge of. He appeared to be attacking his own leaders, committing treason with each new idea.

I wanted to respond in some way. But as a psycho-analyst, I could not overlook the possibility that he might as much be conversing with himself as with me.

I would not risk closing this opening he was making.

He was in the grip of the numinous.

"Rather than destroy the dangerous, which is what you are," he mused, "why not harness it, and you? After all, the Reich has prospered this long by channeling dangerous forces into manageable structures. We have animated the masses with a vision, we have unleashed powers that lesser men might fear and fall victim to. Thus far we have prospered."

At this point the great doors to the dining hall were opened, to reveal a carved baronial table suited for fifty but set for two, illuminated by two dozen candles and the original Bohemian chandeliers, not yet converted to gas or electricity but still studded with shining candle flames.

As we stepped into the dining room, I felt as though I were six hundred years in the past, with the end of the Crusades almost recent enough to be remembered. The empire was still at its height in my fantasy, Hradčany a place of ideas and intrigue.

Two glasses of champagne were poured.

Reinhard Heydrich, the *Reichsprotektor* of Moravia-Bohemia, raised his glass in toast.

"To the dangerous," he said.

I answered his toast.

The first course, pâté de foie gras garnished with fresh parsley and asparagus, was brought in. Then Heydrich nodded for the white-coated waiters to withdraw, and they did.

"You are Slovak by birth," he said, his first allusion to my nationality. "With your curious blend of Ukrainian mysticism and the sentimentality of your Hungarian overlords. A tiny bit of a race, a fluttering leaf tossed on the continental winds, like a dozen others of Middle Europe. A tiny lost tribe . . . considered by the Führer to be non-Aryan; though not an enemy, yet perhaps resentful enough to subvert the Aryan nation, and so a danger."

I said nothing.

"You are also a dangerous man because you are a practitioner of a forbidden science, the dark science of the mind, the cult of Freud and of sexuality."

Heydrich smiled as he said this, as though it were all ironical, a joke whereby he and I were secretly mocking those who describe it so. I simply did not know what to make of him. I did not trust him in the slightest.

"I am told," he said, "that you provided your comrades with psycho-analytic portraits of some of the Czech leadership. Is it true?"

I coughed and shifted my position, without answering.

"What kind of portrait would you paint of our Hitler?" he asked, winking.

Ah ha! I thought. He wants insights into Hitler's mind.

"I would not venture any kind of opinion," I replied.

What perverse impulse prompted me to then say what I did?

"You have overlooked the most dangerous thing about me."

Heydrich was surprised to find me suddenly taking the initiative. His face showed a bit of contempt.

"And what is that?" he asked.

"That I am a Jew," I replied. "That would seem to be the most dangerous part of me."

Heydrich was clearly unsettled. Perhaps he felt some anger at having been interrupted—for though he was speaking to me as if in conversation, it was clear he was in control—but something else was at work.

"Of what consequence is that?" he blurted, without calculation.

In that instant I was even more convinced I had intuited his secret. He was so unsettled he took a few seconds to recompose his thoughts. This was the little boy whom his schoolmates used to mock for being a Jew; this much I now remembered I had heard whispered of him from my camp colleagues.

"But why are we afraid of danger?" he asked incongruously, returning to his previous subject. The numinosity I had noted earlier began to flow back into his features, and I could see that some inner part of his soul had been activated by this entire conversation.

"We are not afraid of the Führer, are we? And the Führer is truly dangerous, is he not?"

There was no way I was going to answer that particular question.

"Yes, you can admit it to me," Heydrich hissed. "He is an adolescent, a preadolescent in conqueror's clothing, an infantile destructive force that could consume us all, a tyrannical infant who has physically matured but carries those awful traits to this day. His is a crude mind, a vulgar mind, but as terrible in its soarings as only the unchanneled preadolescent mind can be.

"That," Heydrich said, "is why he has prospered. This dangerous force is present in all of us, and he articulates it for us, he awakens us. In his blind, uncomprehending way, he gives life to this movement, through his death wish, his delusions."

My head reeled. I felt I was being drawn into some kind of plot, even though I was the blood enemy of my coconspirator.

I was still waiting for him to pump me for a psycho-analytical portrait of the Führer.

"This is why he must be channeled," said Heydrich, "saved from himself. We would not let a fire burn uncontrolled across the landscape, would we? No, we would restrict it to the fireplace, to the furnace, to the boiler room. But neither would we try to live without fire.

"The Führer, and his elemental force," said Heydrich, "must be channeled by more rational minds. To let this fire burn out in a suicidal flash would be a disservice to human history."

The doors opened, the pâté de foie gras and empty glasses were retired, and a course of Parisian sorbet, followed by smoked Carpathian boar, potatoes au gratin, and a red claret from the vineyards of Mouton-Cadet, was laid out before us.

"When I was first considering whether to have you executed," Heydrich said, cutting into the boar, "I asked the Gestapo in Prague to send me every file on you they had. As a result, I received several large cartons of documents, including materials sent by our Vienna and Bratislava branches.

"You have been quite a prolific man," he said, and I laughed slightly at this.

"You know Freud has died, do you not?" he asked, almost solicitously.

"Yes. He died in 1939 in London."

"He wisely fled west," said Heydrich. "Ironic, though, that this great genius would have so jeopardized his fragile health by the trauma of exile, and end up dying so soon after arriving in his new home.

"It was as if it were destined," said Heydrich, "as if his time were past. I understand that you and he had a falling-out early on."

"Yes," I answered, surprised to have this brought up so many years later, in this setting. "Many fell out with Freud."

"But of course," said Heydrich. "His was an absolute and unbending control of his movement. He could not tolerate those who would stray from his rigid path. Witness how the brilliant Jung was abused."

Inwardly, I rebelled at the thought that this Fascist could have any understanding of the inner struggles of the psycho-analytic movement.

"You seem to have read some of the literature of the field," I said. He nodded, perhaps pleased that I was at last acknowledging he was superficially conversant with my profession.

"There was an unfortunate time in my life," he said, "when I was a young man at the beginning of my career. I had nearly completed my studies as a naval cadet, only to be discharged because of false allegations of libertinism."

I noticed how his body stiffened and his face furrowed even now with memories of that painful time.

"Being compelled to give up the navy was the worst defeat that has ever befallen me. I and everyone else had been convinced I was intended for a brilliant naval career.

"After my discharge, there was a long interval when I could not find any gainful employment. I was engaged to be married to my beloved Lina, but that had to be postponed due to the false accusation of scandal, and my future was truly dark. This was before destiny had called me to serve the Reich, and the SS.

"At one point I was even tempted by suicide. I considered ending a life which had been unfairly cheated by the Fates.

"It was at this time that I read voraciously at the public libraries in Hamburg. Having spent most of my previous education mastering the various military and naval sciences, all for naught, it seemed, I was most attracted to the mystic Jung. Even to this day, I believe our failure to attract him to our cause was because of our blundering. I saw all sorts of applications of his ideas to areas outside that narrow field.

"In particular I remember reading Jungian interpretations of our great European epics, such as the Grail legend and the Song of Roland."

In the silence that followed, my mind raced, trying to make sense of this contradiction across from me. Was all this a deliberate deception by a powerful agent of the Fascist juggernaut, a seduction based on utter falsehood, an attempt to humanize the inhuman? Or was he indeed the secret plotter against crude Hitlerism, the literate jail warden taking a prisoner into his confidence?

I could no longer contain my curiosity.

"Have you not," I asked, "taken a terrible risk by bringing me, a prisoner of war, here? Drawing me into your thoughts this way? Describing Hitler as dangerous? Showing yourself familiar with thinkers whose works have long since been banned as decadent and subversive?"

Heydrich laughed quietly.

"As for you," he said, "I have taken no risk. In the eyes of the Reich, you are nothing more than the enemy. Who would believe anything you repeated of our conversation, or would even believe it had taken place, if they had not witnessed you here?"

I could see his point.

"And as for my cause," he said, "I am not a friend of its cruder manifestations."

"But what does that mean?" I protested. "Is it not one movement?"

He sighed, wiped his mouth, placed his napkin in the plate to indicate he was finished with that course.

"It is one movement, of which we are all a part, just as the brain and the foot are part of one body. Both are essential to the operation of the whole."

Our dessert, brought in at that point, consisted of fresh Spanish strawberries served in flaming brandy, then doused with dollops of Swiss ice cream.

"Yet you cannot equate the roles that the two play," he added, "for the foot can be done without, albeit painfully. The brain cannot be done without, but it requires the brawn of the cruder foot to carry out its tasks.

"Dr. Michalský, our movement arose out of the free-floating manias of our Führer. These were deep archetypal yearnings that lay latent in the masses but which when articulated by him were known by the millions of the race to be true, to be grounded in a blood truth. Because of him, the movement was born and prospered. Because of him, a daring campaign of world conquest, destined to create a new civilization surpassing the empires of Rome and Egypt a thousandfold, has begun. And it is destined to succeed.

"But, Dr. Michalský, I am different. Whereas Hitler is the powerful id driving this force, I and others like me—we are few, but enough—will serve as its ego. We will control its excesses, bring order to its disorder, and consolidate its gains.

"And we will take it to heights that the cruder minds among us never dreamed of.

"We will change the destiny of our race."

"What world," I asked, "do you envision?"

"It is a world," replied Heydrich, "where each will be assigned a task according to his abilities and destiny. Rather than being wasted and drained by the debilitating conflicts of past history, in our imperium the languishing and unfulfilled masses will at last find the society for which they have long hungered—a restored harmony of leader and follower, which existed in times long past, in the Aryan and Nordic and Slavic tribes of Europe's primeval dawn, in the great empires of Babylon, Genghis Khan, Egypt, in the city-states of Greece; but which has been destroyed by the so-called progressive reforms of the last five centuries, thoughts wrapped in the false and cheap tinsel of 'democracy,' 'freedom,' 'equality,' 'independence,' and the like, which have set the common man 'free' only to find misery, despair, a loss of meaning and direction, leading to decay, disorder, false revolution. Our healthy man—our worker—will be restored to the role he has subconsciously longed for, working in support of the dreams and visions of the true leader, the Führer, reveling in the glories and achievements of his masters, ready to follow their lead when summoned."

I pondered the way he spoke of the "worker." It confirmed in my mind that he was the driving force behind a phenomenon that we in the Czech Communist Party had never expected and were now seeing: under the German occupation, the Nazis were drawing surprising new support from the Czech working classes and even from our own Party. They were co-opting our Communist vocabulary and programs, and now our supporters. I had read of our erstwhile German comrade Ernst Torgler, who had gone over to the Nazis and was now supposedly advising Heydrich on how to portray the "National Socialists" as the true defenders of the working class.

"Imagine the Thousand Year Reich, if you will," resumed Heydrich. "All the silly nation-states of the past wiped away and reunited with the Aryan heartland, following the leadership of the superior Aryan civilization as we conquer the great frontiers before us: perfection of the human body through genetic and biological engineering, through research now being done by the great Dr. Josef Mengele; the conquest of the riches of the earth, through a partnership with our great industrial enterprises such as I. G. Farben, to open up the treasure house of our planet, now languishing beneath stinking jungles and inept stewards; the conquest and colonization of the moon and planets and worlds orbiting distant stars, with Dr. Werner von Braun and his brilliant rocketeers showing us the way; and finally, *Doktor*, the conquest of the secrets of the mind, through the development and use of new techniques and psychotropic substances from our Germanic pharmaceutical laboratories, unequaled throughout the world.

"We will be the stewards of a Pax Germanicus and the creators of an entire new civilization and race, a race no longer populated by flawed mankind but living at a level we can only imagine now, the rebirth of the beings you and I read of in our childhood myths, the rebirth of the Titans, half gods and half men, the heroes of Valhalla, freed of disease, of fear, of poverty and restraint. . . .

"Even as the workers toil in fulfillment of this great task, their leaders will live as demigods, with all the energies and collective powers of mankind at their disposal, ready to produce, to build, and to lay waste when that is needed.

"This steward class, the new Aryans, the supermen, will live as the misnamed 'democrats' of Athens once did, a small elite of the endowed, freed from the more mundane tasks to contemplate and test the very limits of human creation and achievement; and just as in ancient Athens, their glory at the summit will be supported by the guided labors of the working classes at the foot of the Acropolis.

"In a rational and systematic application of Darwinian selection, the weak, the diseased, the inferior, the unhealthy, the perverted, the evil, and the unclean will gradually and systematically be set aside, until only the purest, the quintessence of humanity, will remain."

Reinhard Heydrich rose from his finished dessert to show me back into the library. The huge oaken doors that might have dated from the time of Barbarossa were swung open, to reveal a fire burned down to glistening rubiate coals, coloring the leather bindings of the library with the tones of a furnace, of flames and heat and combustion. As Heydrich stood there in the doorway, his long-nosed pallor gave way to an internal glow. Inexplicably he looked decades older yet somehow more physically powerful. His whole aspect was changed.

"Why," I asked as I rose and traversed the length of the dining room to the library doors, feeling the huge fire's heat even at this distance, "why have you elected to tell me, a lowly Slovak psychiatrist and a Jew, a Communist and a prisoner, all of this? Why have you chosen to share these ideas, which might be grounds for your removal from office or even arrest for harboring thoughts of treason, with me, being entirely suspect and, as you have said, dangerous? Why have I been selected to be the beneficiary of these forbidden outpourings?"

Silhouetted in the glow of the coals, the shelves and high windows of the timeless Gothic library behind him, Heydrich stood holding in his hand the carafe of port wine, which shone too with the tones of the fire until it looked like some alchemist's potion.

"Because, my dear Dr. Michalský," said Heydrich, ushering me into the library and closing the doors behind us until the only sound was that of the crackling embers and his low North German voice, "you are one of us.

"I have known from the first time I read of your youthful works, and your expulsion from Freud's movement, that you and I are of one mind, and that you will lend your abilities to our common effort; that you will not forgo the opportunity to be a part of the making of history."

We were now truly alone in the library, after the *Protektor* had poured us each a port wine and asked the stewards to leave us for the evening. Heydrich himself threw three new logs on the fire, and the hot coals beneath quickly ignited the dry Bohemian oak cut the summer before.

"Will you have some *Blutkäse?*" Heydrich said to me as he stoked the fire. He pointed to the blood pudding on a small table. Although I declined, he spooned himself a portion and eagerly ate it.

"I spent the better part of a day culling through your file. The more I read, the more fascinated I was by your development, by ycur unique youthful ideas regarding manipulation and control of the human personality using the methods of Dr. Freud.

"I was intrigued too because I learned that your comrades had commissioned you to draw psychological profiles of those your movement wished to influence or subvert. I gather the Americans have undertaken similar studies of our own leaders—the Führer, among others. From your own perspective, how would you describe the psycho-analytic makeup of our Führer?"

I was truly hesitant to say anything. Although I could well imagine what the Americans might say—a paranoid delusional psychopath, just for starters—I was not about to voice such an opinion with his heir apparent.

"*Doktor*," insisted Heydrich, "are you afraid to tell me you think he is insane?"

I said nothing, looking down at the rich Persian carpet.

"Of course he is," said Heydrich. "In the conventional definition of the sane, he is unstable, tormented, in the grips of what you would call delusions.

"And yet," said Heydrich, "the only difference between the lunatic and the conqueror is whether or not one succeeds, is it not? What would Christ have become, had not millions been seduced into following his cult down through the years? He would have been a dirt-covered fool, a desert wanderer."

I did not want to argue with this dubious logic, for I did not want to enter his game.

"Is that what you want of me, to psycho-analyze your Führer?" I finally asked, as Heydrich stood sipping his wine before the fire, swallowing his *Blutkäse*. I reexamined this strange elongated man, silhouetted there by the fire's backlight: his lengthy hooked nose, his equine face and the small eyes relatively close together, the incongruity of his squeaking pubescent voice.

He truly was goatlike—a bizarre goat-man.

"Dr. Michalský," he said, "you are a tragic man, an unfinished man. A man whose greatest dream, born in the hot fires of youth, was set aside by the petty demands of our bourgeois societies, a genius forced to abandon his vision and content himself with making a living and serving his comrades.

"I am offering you the opportunity to finish what you only barely began . . . to carry out your research on the control and manipulation of the mind.

"I am offering the research situation that very few men on earth have ever been able to enjoy. I am offering you the opportunity to resume your research abandoned so long ago. To resume it in an environment where no silly law or medical code will constrain you, where the only constraints will be your ability to conceive and carry out, and where all the vast resources of the Reich shall be at your disposal.

"I am offering you the ability to determine once and for all if the human personality and mind can be reshaped using the lessons of psycho-analytic theory, as you and I believe they can. This research shall be done for the greater glory of the Reich, but more so, for the realization of a new age of mankind, a rationalization and regimentation of the disorderly tribal structures by which we have lived up until now, the transformation of the human race into a productive whole, a single being-ass fulfilling the race dreams of the most brilliant minds on earth.

"For now, to satisfy the formalities of the Reich and to avoid attracting undue attention, all credit for your research shall go to a German doctor. But you have my solemn word that as soon as you achieve success, I shall ensure that the world knows it was your genius which was responsible. Your methods will be duly attributed to you, and you will be elevated to your just position as one of the greatest minds in human history."

"And if I fail?" I asked.

The *Protektor* sipped his wine, then walked across the room to one of the bookshelves.

"You will not fail," the *Protektor* said with finality.

I digested that for a moment. I must admit, the whole affair was ending differently than I expected; so intoxicated was I by the wine, by the luxury after years of privation, by the attentions of this perplexing and supremely powerful man, that I wanted to know more.

"And if I refuse?"

The *Protektor* considered that for a moment, twirling the wine goblet in his hand like a crystal baton. The firelight flashed in its revolutions.

Then, in a quick movement, he threw the glass the length of the room until it shattered into a thousand pieces in the fire and was consumed.

"I will carry out my original decision and have you destroyed," he said in an almost offhanded, even tired, way.

"Dr. Michalský," said Heydrich, breaking a lengthy reverie marked only by the popping of the fire. "Do you use cocaine?"

I was taken aback by this question.

"Do you mean as part of my therapeutic method? Yes, I once did, particularly in the 1920s. Freud himself introduced me to its use."

Heydrich erupted in that curious goat laugh.

"I do not mean for therapy. I mean for diversion . . . for enlightenment and pleasure."

I was flustered for a moment.

"Yes, I have experimented with it. I would not have felt comfortable prescribing it for a patient otherwise. I tried it in my youthful days in Vienna. Although not since."

Heydrich was half seated, half reclined, on a gilt divan perpendicular to the hearth. He rose again, walked to the bookshelves, brought over from a lower cabinet a violin case. While he took out a violin, his real objective was a small snuffbox of the Viennese style, which he opened. He extracted a small vial of white powder, which I assumed was the drug.

"Will you join me?" he asked.

I assented.

After he took it nasally, using a small spoon, I followed.

It had been a full three decades since my last use of this drug. The powder immediately burned the inner linings of my nose and sinuses, and I sneezed a violent sneeze that shook the whole room.

Then came the long-forgotten euphoria, the dilation of blood vessels and the orgasmic physical ecstasy of the drug.

Heydrich himself was also euphoric, coming out of the first impact and standing up.

He took the violin and bow, and to my amazement began to play. I instantly recognized Bach's "Chaconne," from Partita #2 in D minor for unaccompanied violin, surely one of the most difficult violin pieces ever composed, which he was playing from memory and, to my albeit intoxicated ear, flawlessly.

I rode with him on that curious flight produced by strings and bow, but this time in touch with the celestial. The clear tones of the strings produced beams of light in my mind's eye, a music of the spheres which I had not fully appreciated until this minute. I felt myself transported.

It was now well on toward midnight, and through the blackened study windows I could see the moonlight as it fell on the snowy fields and warrens of frozen Bohemia.

The violin recital seemed to last for hours, and yet when it was over, I could not recapture its splendor, its beauty . . . not even a single note of that magnificence. I began to wonder if I had even heard it at all, whether instead I had been in the grips of the cocaine.

"Come," said the *Protektor*, rising abruptly.

Staggering, I followed him out through the opened doors into the central hallway.

The sentries on duty stirred from their torpor and jumped to attention.

Heydrich ignored them, threw open a closet, and took out greatcoats for us both.

"Where is the car?" he barked, his speech slurred.

"I will call for it," a young corporal responded, but Heydrich did not wait, instead stumbling outside into the blustering wind of the January night.

The Daimler was already coming toward us, but illuminated by its approaching headlights, Heydrich blocked the way and forced it to stop short of the entrance. The loyal Klein, sleepy but eager for duty, jumped out.

"I will drive!" Heydrich bellowed. The driver seemed prepared for this and surrendered the car and keys. I joined the *Protektor* in the front seat.

We careened through the night, as the trees swirled before a powerful arctic wind coming out of the northeast. The moon's ice light spread over the frozen landscape, a polar moon, one meant for the raised nape hairs of the silver wolf.

Heydrich turned the huge car down a side road made rough by once-slushy tire tracks now frozen hard as rock. Then we pulled out into a wide treeless expanse which was soon confirmed to be an airfield.

Several transport aircraft were parked by the main hangar, but Heydrich drove right up to a black Messerschmitt fighter plane, apart from the rest. This, I surmised, was the experimental model we had heard of, given to Heydrich for his personal use.

The drowsing guards flashed a light in his face, then jumped to attention.

"We are going up!" Heydrich cried over the roar of the wind.

"But, sir, this gale is terrible," a young man shouted. "We told Munich to cancel the nine o'clock resupply flight."

"Get me the ground crew!" Heydrich rasped, waving him away. In seconds they were there, fueling and starting the engine, while we watched from the warmth of the car.

Then we were being assisted into the cockpit, which had been equipped with two seats abreast.

"Do you fly often?" Heydrich asked as the canopy was lowered.

"My first in a fighter," I was able to stammer.

Heydrich snorted, and then took us lurching out to the end of the runway. The field landing lights had just been thrown on, and their parallel lines stretched away toward the eastern forest, converging in the distance.

In the roar of the engine and propeller, we thundered down the runway and were soon up in a violent sea of air that thrashed with demonic life, with unseen conflict I thought would shake off our wings.

Unafraid, totally in his element, this beast-man took us nearly straight up, the fire and sparks flying from the exhaust ports on the sides of the engine.

"Ha ha!" shrieked Heydrich in his goat ry, pulling us straight toward stellar Aldebaran and the ice-white moon.

Up and up we went, the engine shrieking like some devilish creature aiming for that unreachable moon. Below us, the earth spread away, the moon glinting from the snow-covered roofs of the farmhouses, from the parapets of the *Protektor*'s looming Gothic castle, from the little towns of Kladno and Rakovník, Slaný and Kralupy. And beyond shimmered the lights of Gothic Prague itself, only twelve miles away. Farther was the glow of Plzeň.

To the north, enormous pools of light sat on the horizon.

"What a rare treat," shouted Heydrich. "To celebrate some victory on the Eastern front, the blackout has been canceled tonight . . ."

"What is there?" I cried, pointing at the horizon glows, like false sunrises.

"The great cities of the Fatherland!" cried Heydrich. "See the lights of Dresden and Leipzig," he shouted over the roar of the engine. "And beyond, the greatest glow of them all, Mother Berlin, the new world-city!"

The visibility was unlimited that night, so that coupled with the clear skies and snow-covered ground, it seemed as if all the continent were at our feet. To the northeast I could see silhouetted the jagged hills of the Polish border, and beyond, the lights of what must have been Breslau, all stretching on and on into the frosted mists of Byelorussia, the Ukraine, Carpathia.

It was overwhelming.

"See the heart of the Reich, of the new Aryan imperium!" Heydrich cried. "Mitteleuropa, the Aryan heartland!" he shouted, taking us into a vicious spin in which moon, earth, light, and darkness all swirled together.

"See our Reich as it expands to the four corners of the globe," he roared, still in the grips of the cocaine, yet fully able to master this machine as if it was an extension of his own body.

"Come with us, *Doktor*," shouted Heydrich, "come with us and help us build a new race!

"Join us!" shouted Heydrich as we plummeted toward what must have been the German frontier. "And live as a god!

"As a god!" he repeated. Above us were all the stars of the firmament, stripped free of the glare and haze of day, of clouds or any impediment whatsoever. I saw space for what it was—an opening vastness, a depth without end, an immensity so enormous that it could not even be comprehended, yet this man and his colleagues were bent on conquering it.

"Will you join us?" he asked me, his small eyes now alight with fire. "Will you?"

The earth was at my feet, the heavens were opening up before me. I was in the grip of a powerful drug and a dark satanic wind, and although much of me was repelled by this man and everything he stood for, it was almost as if a deeper part of myself wanted to answer him: perhaps the id itself wished to speak. I found my mouth attempting to form words my mind could not have conceived.

Over the roar of the hellish engine, while sparks and flames flew at either side and a trail of moonlit smoke and ice fell away behind us like the tail of a comet, I wanted to shout:

"I will! I will do as you ask!"

Only with the shock of that impulse did I begin to awaken from his spell, only then did I regard my compliancy and near-seduction with horror, realizing that only a hairbreadth had separated me from answering just as he wanted.

Washington

Washington: now, for him, at the lowest ebb of late winter afternoon, only the fossil shrine of forgotten Enlightenment ideas, patriotic struggles, blood obsessions. A coral reef of a city, furred with leafless trees. Seen from above, an encrusted heart of monuments, rimmed with exurban mirrored boxes, desolate plazas, suburban temples of commerce surrounded by a feeding frenzy of autos.

How ironic that even as the old adversary of the East was collapsing, this heart of the winner had no fire to it, except in the rush of money. Was that why there was so little celebration in the victory city, at the end of the Forty-five Years' War? No crowds massing in squares, no ticker tape, no proud boys coming home. Instead, only the abstract designs of finance, a rarefied, esoteric opening up of new Eastern markets, the hemorrhagic bailout of ambassadors into investment banking, grabbing for a few more goods, higher income, better job.

Peace, order, business. There were no ideas, no passions, no screaming mass visions, left in his people, or the enemy. There was no God left, there was no patriotism left, there was no danger. And yet, in that was the danger. For this steady state in the affairs of men could not last.

He felt dread, a dread deep in his gut. He felt the whole thing would blow apart very soon, maybe this year, maybe in five. And also, in his gut, he carried a biological memory of his tropical trip, an intestinal vengeance that had made the flight back from Guatemala particularly miserable. He had lain like a refugee next to the men's room door in the Miami airport, waiting for the next assault, unable to find a proper chair, tasting a bit of the squalor of destitution, misery, disenfranchisement.

Now he was home. The answering machine was jammed with

calls from the Agency: first the friendly voice of Dr. Pauls, then her less friendly and more concerned voice, each succeeding message with ever-rising timbre, warning, urgency. Someone from the Medical Office had even come to visit him, leaving a note. He called the Medical Office, hoping to head off more serious consequences.

"I've been in Florida," he told Dr. Pauls. Which was true, as far as it went. But why, why had he not told anyone where he was? That was why Security had been told of his temporary disappearance.

"I've been in Florida," he repeated to a secretary in Security, when she told him Ruthie Lowenson was out. He heard the slightest catch in his own voice, which Ruthie of all people would have heard. Damn, he thought, he couldn't do a polygraph right now if they wanted one. He just couldn't do it without coming apart. And then what would happen? Those long interrogations as they circle and zero in, those baboons from the FBI, three at a time, a tag team, good cop–bad cop strategies. Maybe even some criminal charges. After all, if they'd been on him closely enough, they had enough circumstantial evidence to at least get him on insubordination.

And he called his ex-wife, who commanded him to take care of Shannon for two weeks; she had to go to a seminar in Palo Alto. This certainly was not the best time for him to be a father, but what could he tell her?

He picked up Shannon from Three Bears Childworld, then got her sometime nanny from El Salvador, who lived in Arlington, one Lupe Diezcanseco.

"Where were you, Daddy?" Shannon asked.

"I went to Florida," he said, without thinking.

"Did you go to Disney World without me?" she quavered, ready to brim with tears and injury.

No, no, he said; he went to check on an old friend who was sick.

"Lupe," he asked, "do you know any *guatemaltecos?*"

"Eh?" she inhaled. "*Muy mala gente.*"

He didn't have time for these national rivalries. "Have you ever been to New York?"

"*¡Qué horror!*"

"Have you?"

She had once, it was too big, the Salvadorans there were *otro tipo.* The Central American nationalities didn't cluster residentially in New York. She knew of Guatemalans in Queens, in Westchester County, in the Bronx. In D.C., they lived in Adams-Morgan and a few in northern Virginia. The upshot was he had virtually no way of finding Gabriel López.

They arrived on his floor in his apartment building, to find a woman waiting in the corridor to greet them. The woman was Ruthie Lowenson.

"Hi, Dan," she said.

"Hi, Ruthie," he said. "I'm kind of busy right now."

She smiled that institutional smile that told him virtually nothing could make him too busy to attend to the matter at hand.

"What's the matter, Daddy?"

"Nothing," he said. "This is a friend of mine." He looked back at Ruthie. She was unyielding.

"I'm going to have to talk to her for a few minutes," he continued. Ruthie nodded, as if to confirm the time frame.

"Shannon, you're just as cute as your daddy says," said Ruthie. Shannon didn't believe her. Lupe took Shannon inside, and Robinson rode the elevator back downstairs with Ruthie. They went and sat in her 1984 Chevrolet Caprice, which had the look of a fleet car: no white sidewalls, no FM radio, bench seats with a soured vinyl smell. Its old-car stink, the life it symbolized, depressed him. Why did people live this way? Where was beauty, harmony?

"Everything okay, Dan?" she asked.

"Fine," he said.

"Where were you?"

"Miami."

"Why?"

"Why not?"

She lowered her head a little. The smile was fading.

"You know how some in the building get upset when people go away and don't tell anyone where they are."

"I left the message on my machine."

A bit more of the smile went. Ruthie smelled of different things. He detected a utilitarian perfume, the sizing of her new London Fog, a hint of a Whopper burger on her breath.

"You didn't call us and tell us," she said.

"People go away on vacation all the time without telling you," he said.

"Not people on medical leave."

"I'm sorry."

"This isn't like you," she said.

"I've never been on medical leave before," he said.

"You're resisting."

"Fuck you," he said.

The smile was gone now, yielding to her steely side, the side that enabled people to serve as police, prison guards, live-animal laboratory testers, airline ticket clerks. Beyond parental, it was the enforcer in us all, running right up to the line on the other side of which stood the wrongdoer, the criminal. This was no kind of life.

"What's up, Dan? Hostility is the surest sign of concealment."

"Hostility is the surest sign of hostility," he said. "I'm on medical leave, Ruthie. I don't exist anymore. Am I supposed to sit here and rot while you decide what to do with me?"

"You're still on the payroll. You know the rules. The Agency is very generous and very lenient when you play by the rules."

"I never played by the rules before," he said.

"You never blew it before. When you blow it, they get out the rulebook."

They paused for an interval. The windows of the car were steaming up seriously. It made him nervous. She noted that.

"Are you high?"

He laughed. His laughter formed exhaust jets in the frigid air, brief white streaks like gunsmoke.

"What did you do in Florida?" she asked.

"I sat on the beach and got a tan."

"With your shirt on?"

"What?"

"Your tan line stops at your lower neck."

"Yes, with my shirt on," he said.

"Where did you stay?"

"Ruthie."

"Where did you stay?"

"Miami Beach."

"This isn't you."

"I've changed," he said.

"I liked the old Dan more."

"So did I," he said.

"So why did you blow it?"

He shook his head.

"You said you did the drugs and therapy because of the marriage, the career. Was there more?"

"No," he said.

"Don't resist, Dan. I don't like to see it. I know all the profiles."

"Could we turn on the heat?" he said.

She started the car, turned on the heat. Fortunately the engine was still warm, and the dry heat shot out in a furnace flood, smelling of old ductwork, internal leaks, and mold. This was the car of a single government woman, a woman without grace or style.

"Why Miami?"

"Because it's warm," he said.

"Miami's been cloudy all week," she said.

"It was sunny and hot as hell," he said.

That was a test, and for the moment, he passed. She would check the Miami weather when she got back to her office.

"Name of hotel?" she said.

"Huxley," he said.

"Which one?"

"Miami Beach," he said.

"I hope so," she said.

"Why?"

"We can check it out," she said.

"No you can't," he said.

"Why?" she asked.

"I used another name. I paid cash."

She was shaking her head, the new London Fog crackling and brushing. He reached over and pulled the defroster switch, so the foggy windows would clear. He felt exposed.

"Looking for somebody?" she asked.

He rolled his eyes.

"We can do this nice and informally, between you and me, or we can do it formally and with lawyers," she said.

"Do what?" he shouted. "Ask me about a suntan in Miami? What do you want, Ruthie? I'm kicked out, they'll never put me back on anything of substance, I'm a stressed man, I've got the shits, I'm supposed to be baby-sitting. What do you want?"

"The shits?"

He sighed. "A stomach virus."

He felt as if she were doing X-rays on him.

"I can put a tail on you," she said.

"You already have," he said.

That gave her some pause.

"No I haven't," she said. "Who would be tailing you, Dan?"

"I don't know," he said. "Some little Latino. Who is he—from the Miami station?"

"We've put no tail on you," she said. "Why would we put a tail on you before now?"

"You tell me," he said.

"It's not mine," she said. "Tails are serious. We've had no cause, before now."

"And why now?" he said.

"Because you stopped playing by the rules," she said.

"Give me"—he sighed—"a scenario for Daniel Robinson, disgruntled secret agent. A worst case."

"You know the worst. Cashing in. Going over."

He laughed the same laugh he'd laughed in the ruins of Zaculeu, only now, in the car, it almost blew out their ears.

"I'm a real prize," he said. "No promotion in four years, stuck on the Czech desk, in Intelligence no less, kicked out of the White House, kicked out of Operations, a glorifed clerk."

"You know they'll jump at anything, and you're the profile," she said. "They jumped for Ed Howard, the biggest turkey of all time, just a trainee. But look at you . . . the White House basement, you handled Lhota, you have a résumé."

She stopped a minute, took a breath. This seemed to be unsettling her almost as much as him. While she was having her own nightmares, night was now coming down fast onto the parking lot, onto the bleak edifice, onto the frozen lifeless forestlands of the riverbank where he lived, the river rimming the city of ideas frozen in stone. Down on the freeway, a red stream of light flowed south and away, an oncoming stream of white came up from the airport.

"Put a tail on me," he said. "I could use the company. Tap my phone. Make me feel loved again."

She exhaled. She was looking straight ahead. He thought she was shaking a little. She was probably still fighting it internally, fighting the slightest emotional attachment to the old Dan, the penitent confessor of ten years. People were starting to come home from work. Cars were parking around them and nearby; Robinson's neighbors looked in at them in curiosity.

"I have no choice," she said, as if to herself. "I'm going to have to run a full field on you."

"Run a full field on me," he said. "Sift through my travel vouchers, cables, dirty napkins, desk blotters. Call the NSA for my phone call transcripts back to 1968. Sift, sort, sniff, search. Second-guess me. I'm Danielovich Robinsenko. Give our fellow assholes something to do, so we won't get our budget cut. The world is changing, Ruthie. We aren't needed anymore, but don't give our bosses time to think about it. Stay busy. Generate activity, scenarios, threats, worst cases. Write a good horror story."

She was ready to go.

"And do me a favor," he said. "Find my girlfriend."

A little interest stirred.

"I think the KGB has her prisoner somewhere in the Rocky Mountain states. I'm horny and lonely."

"You bastard," she said.

"It's been fun," he said. "Ruthie, you're the best. America thanks you."

"Goodbye," she said, taking off the parking brake. He got out, barely closing the door before she gunned the engine and squealed out of the lot. He laughed a minute there in the enclosing fin de siècle night, before he began to shiver, shiver almost uncontrollably, with the overpowering impulse to cry, cry . . . oh, he wanted to cry, but he could not.

He thought as he went in the lobby door that someone was watching him, a face, a phantom with a widow's peak out in the dark. Maybe only his spirit guide, maybe only his shadow self, just out of sight, always behind him, unseeable but getting closer, closer, so close the back of his neck was tingling.

There *was* a verifiable tail on Robinson the next morning when he went downstairs and got in his car, a real gumshoe, gray suit, FBI written all over him and his vehicle. He followed Robinson to a microfilm xerography service in Arlington, where they both waited an hour and a half while Dr. Michalský's journal was enlarged and copied, the two of them eyeing each other, fleet car engine running, frozen exhaust billowing.

Robinson went over to the car and knocked on the window. The guy cracked the window.

"Dan Robinson," he said, trying to stick his hand inside for a shake and failing. The guy just looked at him, chewing gum, but ready to pull his gun if he had to. Robinson shrugged, went back inside, paid for his copies, deducing they had nothing on him yet, this was just Ruthie's vengeance and she had no search warrants or orders for his arrest.

Then Robinson drove over to a contract Slovak translator he knew in War City, Mrs. Tiso, the old woman whining when he asked for a rush job; he offered double her standard rate. This latest round of expenses prompted him to tabulate in his head how much of his own money he had spent so far in this free-lance obsessive search:

Six thousand dollars.

He calculated that if the FBI really wanted, they could get someone over to look at the translator's Xerox copy later that day, but then who would ever be able to figure out what it was?

This tail was certainly a drag; still, it might serve as some protection. Ruthie, he believed, was telling the truth; widow's peak was somebody else's. The gumshoe, if he didn't fall asleep, might be a convenient bodyguard.

Then to the question of Ruthie herself. This was nothing more than her bureaucratic bluffing, he decided. She couldn't arrest him until she had evidence of some crime being committed. And he had committed no crime, other than the trip to Prague, which she couldn't possibly yet know about and might never uncover, overloaded as she and her shrinking staff were. The gumshoe was there to turn up some quick evidence of criminal activity or treason—and Robinson wouldn't give it to him.

Robinson went back home and had lunch with Shannon and Lupe. The meal was interrupted by the phone. It was Wilson Raver, of all people. He wanted to meet for a bite.

"I'm already having lunch," Robinson said, not yet ready to talk to Raver.

"We'll have dessert," said Raver, his voice with an edge to it.

"What's up, Rave?"

Raver wouldn't say. They would meet in an hour at Hilarity House in Old Towne. Robinson finished his lunch with Shannon, read her a story, then went back to the car, the empty blue sky whitening up with western filmy cloud, ground still frozen hard.

The FBI tail followed him onto the Founding Fathers Freeway. God, this guy was bad, thought Robinson. Should he try an evasive? But that would just upset Ruthie more. He drove carefully, then down through the pastel phony colonial clutter of Old Towne gift shoppes and bric-a-brac outlets to the Hilarity, a riverfront nighttime pickup spot now reeking with that rancid beer smell of the morning after. He was glad he'd eaten at home.

Raver was there, in a huge stained sweatshirt and army-issue camouflage fatigues. He looked uncharacteristically spooked, ashen circles under eyes, orange tan of a week ago gone, faded into standard urban pallor. With him was a short, mustachioed man in a blue warm-up suit, a man smelling of synthetic musk.

The FBI tail had conspicuously come inside and sat down in a corner booth.

"Who's the gumshoe?" Raver asked.

"I think he's my tail," Robinson said. "Rave, this is why I was hesitant to meet today."

"Explain it to my attorney," said Raver, introducing his companion as Horenstein.

"Attorney?" Robinson asked.

"Tail?" Raver asked.

An interval of discomfort followed.

"You didn't tell me you were being canned," Raver said.

"I'm not being canned," said Robinson.

"You're out on your ass," said Raver.

"I'm on medical leave," Robinson said.

"Medical leave," echoed Raver, giving it a pansyish lilt. "You're flat on your ass."

Robinson wanted to protest, but the essential truth of Raver's assessment could not be disputed.

"They fluttered me," said Robinson. "I'd been going to a therapist. Some drugs, some uppers. It upset them."

Color was coming into Raver's cheeks, but it was the color of anger, of bile and rage, and it was not pleasing to the eye.

"Hey, pal, it upsets me too. I run my business right on the line. I have to stay clean; I stay out of the spotlight. I can't do my kind of work with a federal audience. What if they put a tail on me, tap my lines?"

Raver interrupted himself to intercept a beer off a passing tray.

"This why you called? They tap you?"

Raver didn't say anything, but he and Mr. Horenstein looked at each other.

"No, that isn't why I called," said Raver. "I called because someone's messing with me."

"Messing with you?"

"You heard me."

"How?"

Raver was watching him, seemed to be considering an issue internally.

"Who, Rave? The FBI?"

"No, not the FBI."

"Who, Rave? What are they doing?"

Robinson caught a glimpse of a lump in Mr. Horenstein's sweatshirt, and instinctively he went for it with his hand, grasping a small tape recorder, recording.

"What's this?" asked Robinson.

"Just talk normal," said Horenstein.

"We're buds, Rave. What's this shit?"

"This shit is, phone calls in the middle of the night that say things like, Hey, motherfucka, bend over and kiss yo' ass goodbye. Click. Or, Hey, pus-face, know where yo' son is tonight? Click. Or, Scream, scream, scream. Click. Or, sound of loading of pistol, cocking of pistol, bang. Click."

"You getting that?"

Raver nodded, eyes luminous.

"Tell anybody?"

"I've told my lawyer."

"How about the police, the FBI?"

Raver looked at Mr. Horenstein.

"I advise my client," said Mr. Horenstein, "the kinda business he's in, he sticks his fat cock out witha feds, they chop it off."

Robinson could see Mr. Horenstein liked to salt his legal advice with sexual imagery.

"So you take extra precautions and wait for their next move," said Robinson. "You try and find out who this is."

Raver looked at him through eyes hard, puffed from the other side of forty.

"I take precautions, Dan. I'm in the security business. And doing so did not keep my faithful German shepherd, Errol, from being doused with high-performance gasoline and set afire, to run around my town-house patio until he dropped."

Now Robinson too had a beer, but he could not yet drink it.

"Nor did my precautions keep someone from throwing a jar of live bees in through the window of my poor old mother's Phoenix nursing home room and stinging her to the lowest depths of hell. She was convulsing for two hours straight."

Robinson was speechless. Raver exhaled.

"I too have a tail," Raver said. "Not so steady as yours, Dan, nor so clean-cut. Comes and goes. Of the night."

"FBI?"

"A Shiite look about him."

"Shiite? Persian?"

"I'm guessing Omani."

"An Omani tail?"

"You know the type. Displaced Arab lumpen. Little beard, thin and wiry, thirties. Tight suit. You see them cruising porno shops on Forty-second Street, ululating in the Moulin Rouge in Paris, fueled by centuries of sexual repression."

Robinson sipped his beer. He looked over at his own tail, who was reading a book.

"Your Arab sounds familiar," volunteered Robinson. "I think I saw him."

"Where?"

Robinson didn't answer, not with a tape recorder running.

"Who you working for, Robeson?" asked Horenstein. "What's this crap?"

Horenstein pronounced his name like the black singer's. Robinson tried to laugh, but the sound was dry and weak.

"It's like I told Rave. It's just me alone, on a personal. Trying to find out what happened to Miroslav Lhota, why the Agency won't come clean, follow it up."

"Been making dirty phone calls at night?" Horenstein asked.

Robinson felt the loose despair of someone falsely accused and yet without the resources to refute, the molasses swim of seeping guilt, the fugitive in the child's dream who tries to run from the beast and finds his legs melting in cinematic slow motion.

"Why would I do that?"

"Maybe you're a loon, Robeson," said Horenstein. "Why'd you go to the shrink?"

This should have made him mad, but it just sent him down; he went down to the mat and couldn't come back up.

"Hey, Robeson," said Horenstein. "I think anybody tries to end-run the company on this kinda shit don't need a shrink, he needs a straitjacket."

"Where the hell were you the last week?" said Raver. "I came by about twenty times."

"I was traveling," said Robinson.

"Where?"

"Guatemala," said Robinson. As he finished saying it, Raver's graveyard smile came back, the same smile he used when describing his incinerated dog.

"You inta some kinda drug dealing?" Horenstein asked. "Nobody fucks around down there, unless drugs or guns."

Robinson didn't answer.

"Uh huh," said Raver finally, nodding his head, looking down at the table. "All things converge," he continued. "I had for no rational reason concluded that my own sudden personal troubles stemmed not so much from my business or past sins but from my talk with you and my calls to old Bud Funkhouser and Hap McCracken and our conversation about the country of Guatemala and crashes in Ethiopia. You remember them?"

"You spoke of Bud. He won't touch Guatemala anymore, you said."

Raver nodded.

"Why do you think it's connected?"

Raver sighed, finishing the beer.

"Nothing I can rationally explain," Raver said. "A thing of first hunches, a flash, free association—first thing popping into the mind. As in: Nasty phone call, mind racing, Dan and Bud and Ethiopia and Guatemala. Next nasty call, the rush of incredulity, then Dan and Bud and Ethiopia and Guatemala. Oh, I thought of my ex-wife as perpetrator, I thought of a chick in Bethesda I displeased in January, I thought of a customer in Kuwait who sued me four years ago. But always back to you and Hap and Bud and Guatemala. I thought of you all when I saw Errol flame out. You. And Bud. And Hap. And Guatemala."

Robinson was so astonished by all this that it was just not sinking in. Or perhaps it was the inane setting, the pickup bar by day, above their heads a soap opera unfolding on a television that would normally carry football to nighttime drinkers. It seemed maudlin this minute, not sinister.

"Hap came up with some new info about the crash," Raver intoned, reaching into a basket of ancient bread sticks and drumming one on the table.

"I'm listening."

"Maybe your Czech Emil didn't die in that crash," said Raver. "Hap called me back; he'd suddenly recalled gossip from '78 about somebody being spirited from Ethiopia out through Djibouti and then onto a flight to Brazil."

"Brazil."

"Brazil, via Baghdad," said Raver.

"Whose flight?" asked Robinson.

"It was a Brazilian flight, according to Hap. But Terp arranged it."

"Terpil again? He set up Emil's crash in the first place, right?"

"So we heard."

"So the crash and the escape flight went together? Terp operations?"

"A package, seemingly," Raver said. "Terp did the bombing at Ras Dashan, two weeks later Terp ran some fake ID papers and a ghost on a Brazilian contract flight out of Djibouti. Emil rose from the dead."

Raver had now built a small log cabin out of bread sticks, which he would periodically knock to ruins with the back of his hand.

"Who would Terp have run this for?" Robinson asked. "Why? Was it him alone?"

"Christ, I don't know, I don't care, I don't want to know," said Raver. "The burning question is, who's fucking with me? Is it you? Or is dead Emil haunting me?"

"Honestly, Rave," said Robinson. "I didn't do that stuff to you.

And I'd have leveled about being canned from the beginning, but I wanted some proof about Lhota first; you wouldn't take me seriously otherwise. I couldn't let them bury Lhota this way. He was a hero, he put his life on the line in Vienna while Langley fucked around, they've reamed him again, and I want them to pay for it this time. You've got to trust me."

Raver trembled slightly, if that was the right word for a beer-swollen ex-ranger, one of the brightest yet still unafraid of physical violence, hungering for it, for the crash, the collision, the wake-me-up I'm-alive full-body blow.

"It's my opinion," said Horenstein to Raver, "that Mr. Robeson wantsa go offa cliff, we let him. But no way we let him dick us over."

"Dan's a friend, and I believe him," said Raver to Horenstein, then turned back to Robinson. "I trust you as much as I trust anybody. I'm plenty pissed the way you went about it. You sucked me into your personal bullshit, and I'd like to tickle you with a flame-thrower. But these people killed my dog and hurt my mother. Utter wickedness. I do battle with wickedness. I'll smite them hip and thigh."

Robinson felt the first rush of comradeship, of relief from aloneness, course through him. Horenstein was shaking his head.

"Time's short," said Robinson, looking over at the gumshoe on the other side of the room, who was slightly curious. Then he looked at Mr. Horenstein and the tape recorder's bulge.

"Rave, turn off the tape," Robinson asked.

"Art, turn off the fucking tape," said Raver.

Mr. Horenstein turned off the tape recorder.

"We've got to talk to Bud Funkhouser," said Robinson. "I know he's stonewalling for his own good reasons, but we can compel."

Raver was nodding strangely.

"Rave, we've got to put some pressure on him, because he knows important things. I've come from Guatemala. There was an event, as Bud told you. In 1983. An evangelical group known as the Face of God was connected to the slaughter of a whole village. The 'face of God' in Lhota's phrase, Rave. Maybe Lhota was onto it for the wrong reasons, maybe Lhota was stumbling onto things he had no understanding of. But now I have the journal Lhota said was the key, that narrated what happened at Terezín and would explain all subsequent things."

Raver was still nodding.

"Rave, I'd have told you this before, but you'd have thought me insane. The world's coming apart, new worlds form out of the wreckage. Vacuums can't persist, they fill; all energy must go somewhere, and it flows right here underneath us. Bones stick up—a glint here, a flash there. Terezín, Lhota's murder, crash in Ethiopia, massacre in Guatemala . . . Our only limitation is time, Rave."

Raver looked almost sad.

"Wickedness," he said.

"Rave, we've got to get to Bud Funkhouser. Now."

"This I already concluded," said Raver, smiling in that ghoulish way again.

"So let's go," said Robinson. "Where's his office? Dulles?"

"He's not there," said Raver.

"Where is he?" said Robinson.

"He's dead, Dan," said Raver.

Clouds now covered the winter sun, and the Potomac was like the river Styx, dark and metallic, the trees dead. The restaurant smelled like a Greyhound bus, that reeking cleanser they use when someone's ill. On the television, a woman was shrieking in despair because her baby had been stillborn. A man back in the bathroom was hawking up a terrible amount of phlegm.

"He's dead?" Robinson repeated.

Raver nodded.

"How?"

Raver nodded again, almost apologetically.

"They got Bud where he would have wanted, in his Piper at Centreville Field. Airborne, actually, just getting up into the sky. It was in the papers, the Fairfax paper anyway. Little FAA investigation under way. Don't touch it, Bud said. Remember, Dan? Don't touch it, he said? Bud was a pro."

Robinson had nothing to say.

"We've got hold of a whopper," said Raver.

"Hun and Vucub Hunahpu," said Robinson.

Raver cocked his head in question.

"The Mayan Hunahpu brothers, dragged down into the underworld, then reborn."

Raver was smiling, beatifically.

"Old Czech *kouzelnictvi*," said Robinson, "screaming evil in high-noon forest, day-bright time of madness."

Raver ordered another beer.

"Are we crazy?" Robinson asked.

"Personally, I think so," said Horenstein. "You, Robeson, because you're a company man acting like the private sector. And you, Wilson, for even sittin' here listening to this shit. You got a business to run, alimony to pay. I say you break up this friendship real fast."

Raver was drawing a Kandinskyesque design with his pencil on the tablecloth.

"We're in danger," said Raver.

"Agreed," said Robinson.

"Exposure?" Raver asked.

"Daughter," said Robinson. Raver nodded in agreement.

"And you?"

"Mom, I suppose. My boy Shep at Staunton Military Academy."

"Rave, you do need some kind of institutional protection," said Robinson. "I think maybe you should go to the police, keep me out of it. That way you're inside."

"This cowboy's in no position to be coming inside," said Horenstein. "Cowboys they don't like. I saw how they treated Waldo Duberstein, just after I went inna private practice in '81. Waldo was pissing and moaning, he said Qaddafi was out to get him. FBI knew alla bout it. And Waldo ends up dead in his basement. Wha'd he expect? they sez after. Brought it on himself, they sez. We got higher priorities than protecting private American crooks in foreign funny business."

"Forget the FBI. How about Alexandria police?" Robinson said. "Say he goes and says he's being extorted, he needs protection?"

"You can be dead before they fill out alla forms. Plus, when you get inna national security anything, they shit. They call Uncle Sugar."

"So keep national security out of it."

"First question they ask," Horenstein said, "where do ya work, whadaya do for a living, Mr. Raver? Oh, well, I sell a little electric fence to the Red Chinese. And oh, I do a little pistol training in Jordan. They'll turn this over to the FBI in two minutes. And then you're stomped by a bunch of flatfoot gorillas."

"Back to this event in Guatemala, this village," said Raver. "Veil / the face of God, wasn't it? What about veil?"

"Veil I don't know," said Robinson. "The Virgin came down from the sky, Rave. Whole village saw her. All but about one of them died in a holocaust a couple months later. The survivor is hiding out somewhere in New York."

"Virgin, no less."

"Or X Kiq, blood girl of the underworld, depending on your faith."

Raver continued with his sketching. The FBI agent was just dying to get a shotgun mike.

"Veil mean anything to you?" Raver asked Horenstein. The lawyer shrugged.

"Let's find a nice tropic island, a place to live out our final days," said Raver. He was getting drunk, listing slightly, spraying with his words, but his mind hadn't slowed a bit.

"Back to you, Dan," said Raver. "Where do you go from here?"

"I get my ducks in a row, and then I take it in—the Inspector General, or the Senate if I have to. I get this journal translated, then we haul in Emil. The guy has killed at least seventy-five people, Lhota included. If he's still working for the Pact, then we goddam nail him and them too. Since when does the company walk away when its people get killed? I don't care about *perestroika*—we'll get him."

"Pathetic," said Horenstein. "Inspector General, he says. This guvmint laughs when its people get killed. Russians shot our army observer in East Germany couple a years ago, sorry, nobody even remembers his name. Forget that shit; you, sir, are in a big mess already. Lookit this guy over here watchin' us. Feds already got a dick up your ass."

"Right. But this is just Ruthie Lowenson throwing her weight around. She doesn't know anything. She's pissed because I took a powder for a week without telling her. Rave, they don't have anything on me yet, other than they put me on medical leave two weeks ago. My big crime is going to a shrink and not telling."

"But that's bull," interrupted Raver. "It's not going to take long to hook you up with Lhota somehow. If she's ordered a tail, she's running a full field on you right now. They'll get something. They'll get your trip to Guatemala, phone calls to Lhota, something. It'll come up, sooner than you think. All this running your own back channel. Then you're marked. I remember Ruthie. She'll sniff you out. She's a ferret."

"Amen," said Horenstein.

"I agree," said Robinson. "But she's got bigger problems than me. Security is so fucked up: the budget cuts, the layoffs. She can't run it all by herself. She's on about twelve priority cases right now; I'm just a curiosity to her. I've still got leeway."

Horenstein made a grunting sound. The barmaid brought them a large basket of fried chicken strips. They had been sitting under one of those infrared heating elements until the flesh was hard as wood.

"As devil's advocate, I have an idea," said Horenstein. "Robeson, suppose I calla company for ya. I have some ties, I can try and smooth things out. Emotional stress, blah blah. Made a mistake, old friend killed, you resign effective yesterday, you sign a piece of paper, lips forever sealed about Lorta or whatzisname. Wilson can give ya some dough to tide ya over, help find a job. But come clean with them, drop this free-lance thing right now."

"Not yet," said Robinson. "Not until I can blow them open. The Lhota case was closed up tight, no flex. It's fixed. I thought they were protecting the defector resettlement budget; now, with this massacre in Guatemala, who knows?"

"Guatemala is special," mused Raver. "Used to be our kind of place. Then came Carter and human rights, finger-pointing, lots of colonels with hurt feelings. They went their own way, hooked up with the Israelis and the Taiwanese and the South Koreans—and I know what you're thinking, but nobody tells any of that trio what to do. I bump up against them all the time; they're the tail wagging our whimpering dog. But back to Guatemala. Obviously what happened is somebody fucked up, somebody high up in Guatemala let in a Czech subversive unit under cover of the Face of God and they were embarrassed and we just don't want to rub their faces in it. Or, the evil empire has collapsed and it's all ancient history and who cares? That makes sense. In 1982 and '83 Central America was hot; El Salvador was on the ropes, Nicaragua was being very uncooperative, Guatemala seemed on the verge, and so maybe the Slavs tried something far out to push things along. When it didn't work, a fire was held. Now the world has rolled over, the Russians can't even shut up Yeltsin, much less overthrow Guatemala, we're gonna let bygones be bygones."

"They saw the Virgin."

"Christ, people see the Virgin every day. I see Art's point. This is out of hand. This has gone well beyond Guatemala, wouldn't you say? Now we're talking interior actions. The interior has been violated. My mother was convulsing."

"Not yet," said Robinson. "Not until we have more and can blow them off their asses with some proof. The company already thinks I'm crazy. I'm out on a mental. Even if they know the truth, this is a perfect excuse for a padded cell. And, Rave, I'm compromised."

"How compromised?" Raver belched more than asked.

"I took a trip to Prague right after they canned me. . . . I know what you're thinking, but it was to run down some of Lhota's stuff. I was in and out in two days, clean, mission accomplished."

Horenstein made a moaning noise.

"Brilliant," said Raver.

"It was crazy. I was crazy. It was my way of saying fuck you to the Agency. You've been on the street ten years, Rave, free agent. I was festering inside. It's a whole new crew, Garibaldi et al. They pursue the President's agenda, they write fiction for Congress. They think I'm crazy and/or compromised, and for all they know, you work for the Ayatollah, so I can't go to them yet."

"Wilson," said Horenstein, "this changesa whole picture. I say we let Mr. Robinson row his own boat. I cut you outa this clean—he's the perpetrator, you're an unwitting accomplice. We call the CIA this afternoon. Good Citizenship Award."

Raver got up to take a piss. The FBI was on full alert, watching closely from his booth. Robinson watched the television. The President and the First Lady were in a news break, having a birthday party for handicapped children in the East Room; anti-*perestroika* riots raged in Novosibirsk; an airliner had crashed into the ground outside Tokyo. And then the weeping mother of the stillborn child was back on again, contemplating suicide. Shimmering makeup and luxuriant hair styling had replaced the stylized facial expressions of D. W. Griffith's silent productions, but otherwise American melodrama had made no progress in seventy years.

Raver sat back down.

"We aren't calling the CIA," he said. "I don't turn in friends."

"Don't be a prick," said Horenstein. "This is your living, your rep at stake. For all you know, he's onna Czech payroll and now he's dicked you in."

"Shut up, Art," said Raver.

"Then may I pull out?" asked Horenstein. "You guys are acting crazy. A felony has been committed here, and I rather stay out. I gotta make a living, I gotta talk to these people and do business. I ain't goin' up against John Martin on this one; I see how he chewed up the Pollards, Whitworth, Pelton. No, thank you."

"Art, I'm gonna puke," said Raver. "What felony?"

"Robeson went into a Warsaw Pact country."

"What Warsaw Pact country?"

"Czechoslovakia."

"Aw, its cheesy as hell," said Raver. "There's no Pact anymore; all the Slobbovias'll be like Yugoslavia, not even on the list. Shit, Art, he's got a case for a whistle-blower's countersuit. Or the Inspector General. Say there's been a CIA murder cover-up. Show some balls."

"Whistle-blowers, my ass. There's no fucking whistles in national security. CIA Inspector General oughta be shakin' his ass on Fourteenth Street—he's the biggest whore in D.C."

"I'm not talking forever. I say we all together stall them a little while. So he can get his papers together."

"So whadaya do in the meantime?" asked Horenstein.

"We stay private sector," Raver said. "We diminish exposure. We're talking some expenditure."

"But can we protect?" Robinson asked.

"Of course we can protect. I know the best."

"Who?"

"The best."

"Who?"

"Some Africans."

"What kind?"

"The very best. We can put them on you, on me, on your daughter."

"Where do they hail from, Rave? What kind of Africans on me, my daughter?"

"Experienced Africans. Tested in battle. Victorious."

"Rave."

"We're talking Ugandans. British-trained. Sandridge. Unquestioned loyalty."

Robinson was shaking his head. "Rave."

"Tested, tried, true blue. Without fear. They look horror in the face and laugh. They handle Uzis, knives, hand-to-hand. The best."

"You're trying to avoid telling me they're alumni of Idi Amin."

Confirmation rang in Raver's laughter.

"Graduates of Idi Amin Academy on me, my daughter? Rave, I can't do that. I'll lose visitation rights. I don't want murderers around my little girl."

"Hush that talk," said Rave. "Half that stuff never happened, and the other half was done by Amin personally. He was a hands-on kind of murderer. These people are blood loyal. They appreciate me greatly. I got them green cards, got them off the watch list. They're eternally grateful."

"No," said Robinson. "They go to the highest bidder. They could be turned in fifteen seconds. We're dealing with something with great and variegated tentacles, and you want to hire Idi Amin's bodyguards?"

"You cowboys is crazy," said Horenstein. Raver was laughing in spite of himself.

"This is rubbish," said Robinson. "An utter last resort: How about you meet your Shiite demon face-to-face? See what they want to call it off. Open a back channel. Make a deal."

Raver was really laughing now, loudly and deeply; the empty bar shook with it. The five other people present watched. It was disturbing.

"What they've done to me is not a prelude to dealmaking or back channels," said Raver. "This is kitty toying with the canary before engulfment. This is sprinkling salt and pepper on the evening dinner. This is sadism for sadism's sake. There is no dealmaking to be made, in their mind. They think they are firmly and utterly in control. They are teasing before they snuff. Foreplay. Classic *hashashin*. No sweet oblivion for the victim; this is the communication of a message, to be carried into the hereafter and right up to Allah for judgment. A fatal awareness. I've seen this, Dan. I've seen it in the Sudan, Kurdistan, Mauritania."

The television reported the stock market had dropped 243 points in fourteen seconds. Approximately $370 billion in net worth of

American enterprise had gone into the ether. A special commission was being convened in New York. Recommendations were to be drawn up.

"So we're agreed?" Raver said. "I can put my boys to work?"

Robinson said nothing. This thing was acquiring its own insane inevitability. Protection? But of course. And the only people in the world who could do it were Idi Amin's ex-bodyguards.

"I'm agreeing to nothing," said Robinson. "Paint me a picture first."

Raver smiled the smile of imminent victory.

"We circle the wagons, set up a hardened base. Your place, mine, mobile, airborne, whatever. I have access to it all. Your little girl under twenty-four-hour armed guard, either with us or in a safe house, out of harm's way. You and I together."

"And then what?"

"And then we wait."

"What do we wait for? Bankruptcy? All this is out of pocket, Rave. I can't fund an airborne hardened base."

"Calm down. Our credit is lenient. We wait for them to show their hand. We wait until we find out a little more about who we're dealing with. We sit down and compare notes about what you found in Guatemala, the sequence of events, Bud's death. We factor it all in. We do some adversary modeling. You've been running this whole thing seat of the pants. I'd never run anything for a client this way."

"What's to model?" said Robinson. "Lhota was shot in Guatemala, tracking the Angel of Terezín. The Angel died in a plane crash in 1978 in Ethiopia, rose again in 1982 in Guatemala, working for the Face of God. The Virgin came down from heaven and there was a massacre in San Carlos de Chixoy in 1983. Face of God doesn't exist, except in some clippings and a shipping label from Alisa or Alesa or Elisa or some such."

Raver had lowered his head, so the look was coming out from under his black brows. It was a glance of utmost seriousness. He was exuding an odor of metabolized beer, a milky odor, the rheumy scent of a serious drinker. The organism of the body could take only so much of this alcoholic flushing without cell walls becoming distended, genetic messages slightly altered. Robinson could see that Raver would have a potato nose tinted by the flush of a million shattered capillaries by the time he was fifty. His black hair would thin away, revealing ever more of the pale sunless scalp beneath. If Raver didn't die of an act of violence, he would keep on drinking and eating and lifting weights until someday a massive explosion of aorta would come, he would keel over like a great buffalo on the dying prairie, and he would be down, probably by age sixty-five. He was marked for collision.

"Alesa," said Raver. The FBI agent was reading the paper again. The agent was balding; he probably lived with his wife and kids way the hell out in Virginia and commuted two hours each way to FBI headquarters. What kinds of lives were he, Robinson, Raver leading? This transience, this coffee-fueled pilgrimage through life? This politico-military purgatory?

"Out of the mouths of babes," said Raver.

"What?" asked Robinson.

"I know Alesa," said Raver.

"What?"

"A curious breed. Unique genealogy."

The midafternoon roar of jets taking off and landing at National had begun out over the river, a daily ebb and flow of turbine whine and fading explosion that punctuated all lives here, the roar, the roar, a stream of thunderous sound and kerosene exhaust tracing the path of the river below—deliberate, someone had told him, in case of crash, so the errant plane would come down into the river and not into *USA Today* headquarters, certainly not into the Pentagon, no, out into the river, the roar, the roar, America's nightfall heralded by explosive roar.

"Alesa broke away from a thing called Crescent Export. French and Mideast roots, Iraqi, work in the Kurdish war in the fifties and sixties. Always heard there was big opium trading too. But who knows. Started brokering Brazilian weapons to the Iraqis in the seventies, Latin money came in later, Brazilian mostly, and the Latin stuff spun off," said Raver. "Tight, clannish. Boutique."

"What kind of boutique?"

"Cutting edge, always small-scale. Site neutralization. I knew they had some Third World airline security contracts back in the mid-eighties. Hijacked airliners. Bring-'em-out-alive stuff."

"So what does it mean?"

Where did these jets go, and was all this coming and going necessary? Robinson watched the planes out over the water, banking furiously, missing the bridges, up, up. This hotdogging wasn't necessary, this screaming heft of titanium and steel, all this violence to move a bunch of loudmouthed congressmen back to their constituencies for some glad-handing, with their attendant symbiotic minions and more venal parasites, this historic grossness, this waste.

"Roots in the desert, but they spread their wings and moved west. I had some contact with them once, a contract with the Salvadoran Army. Hostage rescue, urban combat. I was very peripheral."

All this enormous infrastructure built up to support the movement of fat asses and their opinions to and from the grass roots, the ultimate motive being to dip into a bit of the federal gush. The car rental agencies, the mildewed motel rooms in War City, the soulless bars with plastic wagon wheels and polyurethane tabletops, all manned by people without history, people lost in universal ignorance and condemned to repeat the mistakes of the past. Loudmouths, contractors, contract servicers, skimmers, getting, grabbing, in, out, a streaming that reduced humans to energy, to sheer force, negating more and more the need for bodies, we would become just heads on stalks with wide limber spatulate hands for the tapping of keyboards and cathode-compatible pale shaded eyes, heads without bodies, pure energy.

"So where would you find them? That's how Lhota contacted Emil to set up the rendezvous in Guatemala, through Alesa."

"In Panama, probably," said Raver. "Things come a bit clearer."

A few people had come into the bar: War City types, military-industrial salesmen down for a late-afternoon swill. The nature of the place was changing. Soap operas were over, and reruns now gabbled above, *Bachelor Father* into *Lost in Space*, *Lost in Space* into *Flipper*, gabble gabble, the cheap refulgent electronic gush streaming over them and out into the depths of exploding space.

"How so?"

"Hard to say. Every entity has its personality. Definite feeling, ethos, to them. You know what I mean? Alesa was cultish. Oh, I picked up some drug vibes too. Very cultish and Arab-tribal. Not like everybody else the Salvadors were using. Uncle Sugar was paying all Salvador's bills, so the contractors usually had to be approved. That meant lots of retired Langley people were dipping in; the Intercontinental bar looked like old times at Langley. A lot of our old friends let go during the Peanut days were down there, ex–senior case officers and Ops people like Leslie Mowbray, contracting as liaison to trade unions, newspapers. More hearts and minds, but all private sector. That's why I was so surprised to see Alesa. They didn't belong."

"You're saying Alesa was on our contractor list in Salvador?"

"I don't know it for a fact," said Raver, "but I think the way the money was flowing from AID and IMET to the Salvador treasury and then out to the contractors, there had to be some kind of sign-off. No, I don't know if Alesa was paid with U.S.-originated funds. But we were on the same hostage project. You know IMET, right?"

"The Pentagon foreign aid fund. What's Alesa stand for?"

"Agencia Licenciada de Exportación, S.A."

The afternoon drinkers were filling up the chairs at the bar, they were creating a line, a Maginot line of paramilitary banter, heads just sticking up above the trenches. These were dark days for the big-ticket items that go bang, and these salesmen would bury their troubles in drink.

"What do you think, Rave?"

Rave was standing up, brushing himself off, a whole new aspect to him. Was there a glow, an aura, a numinosity sparking up out of the despair?

"I think Bud Funkhouser was too scared to talk about what he saw in Guatemala. I bet Bud flew for Alesa in Guatemala. Bud has now been scared to death."

Roar, roar, the afternoon roar.

"Think upon this, Dan. All things do converge."

Aircraft pilots and passengers who were taking off at that time rose from a gray colorless earth through a filmy layer of thickening cirrostratus that resembled nothing so much as the layers of the atmosphere of a liquigaseous planet, like Jupiter. Defined layers, ice crystals, shades of blue, gray, white. But once the travelers broke through into clear air, they looked down on the cloud tops arranged in an eerie scalloped symmetry, in transverse waves that stretched all the way from the southern Appalachians to well off the coast of Nova Scotia, a distance of almost two thousand miles.

To those who saw it, the view was both beautiful and disturbing. In canonical times, such a formation might have portended a change, a cosmic message. But in this day and age, it was a function of air temperature, of jet-stream direction and flow, of the polar air mass position. The sense of destiny that had governed human affairs for millennia was gone; now mankind was as much at the mercy of the universe as the first sentient being who had looked up at the sky.

"What is veil?" Raver asked.

"Veil," Robinson said. "Veil."

How winter can go on and on, in that grim pull from Presidents' Day to Easter. At last January is torn off the calendar, and earth makes its free fall into the void of February with no signs of life or warmth, only alternating blasts of ice and rain, low scudding clouds, and rattling trees that look dead for a hundred years. Supposedly the days are getting longer, supposedly the sun's rays are falling more directly, but when the days bring only rain or snow and the earth lies wrapped in roiling clouds of the apocalypse, how can you tell?

Robinson left his daughter and her nanny, Lupe, in the care of two strapping Ugandans, Oliver and Milton. His own personal bodyguard and driver was to be one Godfrey. He gathered that Godfrey and Oliver were cousins. Last names he did not remember, but they were authentically African. Godfrey was soft-spoken, having studied briefly on government scholarship at the London School of Economics before being called back to serve on Idi Amin Dada's personal guard force. Milton had driven a cab in New York for two years after the fall of Idi, before hooking up with Wilson Raver. They seemed like nice enough fellows, although they wouldn't say much about their former employer. Robinson gathered that their loyalty to Amin had been tribal, not personal. Well, wasn't that comforting?

The tasks remaining to him were formidable. Raver's questions of Bud Funkhouser had certainly touched on an exposed nerve in the labyrinths of covert action. Some linkage existed to Lhota's death and through that to all the attendant phenomena—Czechoslovakia, the Face of God, massacres in Guatemala, Alesa—but cause and effect were still not clear. The involvement of Alesa was clearly of great importance. But how in his present position of internal exile and surveillance could he find out anything else about it?

And there was Veil, now standing alone, looking like the name of an operation, a program, a plan. Was it the plan to conceal the activities of the Face of God in Guatemala? Or was it an operation Lhota had been involved in? And whose was it?

Alesa was now providing a path directly to Emil Užhok. Lhota had pursued that track and was now dead, probably dead at their hands. And Alesa was most likely the perpetrator of the indignities now visited upon poor Wilson Raver, the bombing of Lucho's pickup in Taxoy, the tailing of Robinson himself in Czechoslovakia and Guatemala.

And he could not ignore Ruthie, in her dogged way now retracing his steps using all the powers at her command, assisted by the fact that he had been exceedingly casual in his movements, almost deliberately so.

He and Raver decided a direct approach to Alesa was out of the question until they knew more. Raver would handle Alesa when the time came: they were his kind of people.

How to find out more about Alesa, without approaching or arousing them further? The Agency, the most natural avenue, was out, certainly in his present status as medical reject becoming security risk. Quite likely very few in the Agency knew anything about Alesa, or at least no one he would have access to. He had worked there himself until two weeks earlier and had never heard anything of it. It certainly had nothing to do with Czechoslovakia.

How to find out, then? He racked his brain. And he kept coming up with only three possibilities.

The easiest and least likely to succeed was through an unclassified data service he knew in Arlington. It was a glorified interlibrary net, using only published data. Might Alesa pop up there? He'd try, but he doubted it.

The most inviting was Beth Bodenhorn, his ex–CIA classmate now on the Senate Intelligence Committee staff. He'd talked to her briefly in the fall about Lhota's case, months back, before Darlene Scoggins had passed on Lhota's little bag of clues. Maybe Alesa would mean something to her. Beth was a friend, and she was reasonably trustworthy, though with different loyalties.

But who was he kidding? What loyalties did he have now?

One other viable possibility existed. He'd toyed with this one at the time he first called Beth—Preem in the White House. He'd been

Robinson's understudy on the National Security Council, supposedly on a temporary assignment like Robinson, a real sleeper of a poli-sci doctoral candidate, straight out of the University of Illinois at Carbondale. Preem was the kind of guy who had announced to his eleventh-grade homeroom that he'd be President of the United States someday, while everybody honed their spitballs to hit his greasy forehead. But miraculously Preem had done what Robinson had not: he had impressed somebody over there in the imperial basement and stayed on, extending his detail indefinitely. And as for his homeroom boast, he *had* made it to the White House.

He was a pleasant enough fellow, now revealed to be ambitious in that classic Washington way, the old suck-up, kick-down tradition. But one on one, he'd always been under Robinson's spell; Robinson concluded it was a physical whammy, Preem's fear of people who might pop him if pushed, people who used their bodies more than just as a conveyance for their heads. He was astonished to find Robinson had actually been in Operations, once did karate. He'd seemed a bit in awe of Robinson in that period of overlap when Robinson was showing him the ropes in the White House basement. Preem would be only about thirty now, some kind of world record for youthful advancement.

Robinson called Beth's office first. Her secretary informed him she was traveling with a codel—a congressional delegation—in China and wouldn't be back for another ten days. That eliminated her for the moment.

He called Preem at the White House, dialing his own former number, which had been burned forever into his memory. It was late morning.

"Mr. Preem's line," came the secretarial response. Impressive; never in his two years there had Robinson rated a secretary. She was screening for her boss, and he gave his name, gambling it would have enough shock value to blow him in the door.

"Lawrence Preem," came the sudden response.

"What's with this Lawrence shit? A budding Kissinger?"

A periodic of mechanical social laughter followed.

"Robinson," Preem said, sounding totally off balance to be hearing from his predecessor.

"The very same. How goes my successor?"

"What a surprise, Daniel. How are you?"

A new pomposity rang in this voice.

"Oh, moldering in the same spot. I hear good things about you."

Preem was always a sucker for praise, an easy stroke.

"What are you now?" asked Robinson. "SES 17 or something?"

"Ha ha," said Preem, not answering, meaning he had in fact gotten some kind of enormous promotion and didn't want to talk about it.

"Larry, can you get together with me?" Robinson asked, abruptly.

There was the slightest silence. This was truly a cold call.

"Surely, Daniel. What, a beer or something?"

"How about I come by?"

"Here?" Preem said.

"Yeah, Larry. Some very quiet business stuff."

Preem made the sounds of looking at his calendar.

"Maybe late in the week," he said. "We're redoing the annual threat assess."

"Hmm," Robinson said. "It maybe can't wait. How about late today?"

Preem exhaled, a bit pressed.

"It'll have to be very late," he said. "After six."

"The old hours still hold, I see."

"Daniel, we've proposed putting in a little bank of apartments down here. That way they can have us twenty-four hours. Yes, come by at six."

"Don't forget to call the gate. I don't have my pass anymore."

"Of course," he said. "I'm writing myself a note here. Call gate for Dan Robinson. What's your social security number?"

Robinson gave it, wondering how thorough Ruthie had been.

"Very good. See you at six. It'll have to be brief."

"Appreciated," said Robinson. "Till six."

This boy now sounded like a young American don. Well, the task was done. The White House at six.

The remainder of the day was spent reading the portions so far translated of Michalský's journal, watching television, seeing instant replay of the President of the United States being bitten on the hand by a little girl in a community center in the Bronx, the stock market up 182 points, consulting briefly with Raver on the phone, lunching with Lupe and Shannon.

After lunch, he and Shannon spent some time playing with her Cutesy L'il Horseys in the living room. Robinson had been astonished at the childish love and affection these bizarre little toys engendered. He tended to view toys through the lens of his own childhood: he remembered zoomorphic stuffed dogs and teddy bears. These grotesque equine figures were made of some antibiological polymer that glowed in the dark, like chunks of cadmium or yellowcake uranium, and in their syndicated television series and their marketed accessory games they were forever involved in a horsey version of thermonuclear warfare with their nemesis, Lord Thraxor, barely winning by virtue of a Goodly Skyshield that they shot over the sky from their manes, not unlike the strategy behind SDI. How could a child hug them, talk to them, want to sleep with them so close by?

Matters had come to a head about six months before, when he tried to wean her away from them and back to old-fashioned, Beatrix Potterish toys. The flash point was Miss Horsey Highhooves, the Queen of the Herd, who Robinson had blurted out looked like a baboon, not a horse.

"She's not a baboon!" Shannon said, tears forming in her eyes, when she didn't even know what a baboon was. And so he had made one of those concessions of parenthood: not only would the Cutesy L'il Horseys remain, but he would embrace them as his own, joining in their horsey games and never again making acerbic observations about something sacred to the child mind.

After they played with the horseys, the two of them acted out a primeval drama that dated back to when Shannon had been a crawler. He got down on all fours and played the Daddy Cow, while she was the Baby Cow. They mooed and moved across the carpet. But she liked an edge to this one now, for after a moment or two of bucolic mooing and circling, she began to push him to turn sinister.

"Be the monster," she asked, and he hesitated a moment, seemingly out of aversion to such a wicked proposal, but really to heighten the suspense. And so after a moment of deceptive mooing and grazing, he obliged her, pouncing on her with a carnivorous roar, triggering her squeals of horror and delight.

Then it was naptime, and he took her into her room and they sat together on the bed, where he read her a story. At the same time he was noticing how much she'd grown in the last six months: some kind of critical line had been passed, and she was getting tall and leggy. The fat was gone, as well as that milky little breath kids have at a young age. Now she too could have adult-powered bad breath.

Once she was asleep, he gradually slipped to the door to escape and pursue his own project again. But he had a twinge, as he prepared to close the door behind her . . . a sense of time rushing by, a sense of guilt at having messed up her childhood by his own mistakes, a sense of not spending enough time with her, for it could never be recaptured. When he let this feeling come out, it was sometimes too much to bear. Today he fought it down.

In midafternoon he and Godfrey went outside. Inexplicably, the FBI had disappeared, nowhere to be seen. Robinson turned, scanning the lot, the landscape, the distant banks of apartment windows, each of which might contain telephoto lens, shotgun mike.

This was ominous.

First they drove to the Slovak translator and picked up more of Michalský's manuscript. The old woman, Mrs. Tiso, was furious to be working under such pressure, but she needed the money.

Then they drove to a data service in War City, that jerry-built suburban cluster spawned by pure Pentagon slopover. This hollow place, slapped up in the most soulless way during the Old Man's epoch of rearmament—without sidewalks, badly fastened panels of reflective plastic paneling occasionally falling to the earth, great cowflops of hardened cement dumped in midstreet by a forgotten contractor, no street level at all actually, since everything flowed from underground parking lots, not a tree in sight—seemed particularly desolate that afternoon. The end of the greatest defense spend of all time was falling hard here. Office space was going begging.

A very shapely black woman helped him in his brief quest. Neither Alesa nor Veil, which he submitted on impulse, brought any reference at all, except a bill to him for $96.78 for computer time.

Robinson took that opportunity to make a call from a pay phone to Ruthie in Security. One day an FBI tail on them, the next day not . . . It was a silly charade, and he wanted to sound off to her about it.

It was then that he learned, to his astonishment, that Ruthie Lowenson had herself been RIFed, as of a day ago.

"They can't do that," Robinson said to the secretary, who sounded as though she had just been hired. But they could in fact do it, although the young lady volunteered that Ruthie was suing the Agency.

"She was real upset," the girl said. In the background was the noise of even greater chaos than when he had been fluttered two weeks before. It sounded as though the office itself was being dismantled. Workmen were arguing about who would pick up a box, and heavy furniture was being dragged across the floor.

Assuming Ruthie's layoff was true, it would mean her incipient investigation of him would probably be sidetracked, at least for a time. It might be a ruse . . . yet that seemed unnecessary, overdramatic. Security didn't work that way.

Robinson felt a momentary sense of reprieve as Godfrey drove him across the Imperial Bridge into the quickening pace of the victory city itself, betwixt the concrete champions of the Republic, muscle-chested charioteers, gateway to the new Rome! They orbited the Lincoln Memorial, shot up to Pennsylvania Avenue, running against the sundown outward flow of humanity. Hail, O Columbia! Federal straphangers gagged the entrances to the Metro, while lobbyists' limos circled blocks or stood double-parked, billowing their clouds of frosty exhaust. Then they passed the haunted house of the Old EOB, concrete barriers in full force, making the final awesome approach to the House of White. A chill went through him as he remembered the two years he had spent working here, the horror of failure, the screaming adrenaline rush, the crisis high. A small gaggle of people waited at the Secret Service window, IDs and driver's licenses being passed through to gain precious admittance, fighting the tide of escapees coming out.

The place itself stood as the target of dozens of electroluminescent wands aimed up from the shrubbery so that even at this time of nearly full winter black not a shadow darkened its facade, not even a color, leaving untempered the totality of its white lightness produced by relucent vapor floods, a solid chunk of light onto which neoclassical porticoes, windows, cornices, and scrollwork had been affixed, a white-dwarf plantation house of luciferin light standing in its own parhelion, this corona of continental energy, this imperial aurora polaris.

Godfrey dropped him at the gate and was forced to circle the block like the rest. As Robinson stood awaiting the go-ahead to enter, while his social security number ricocheted through the computers of the Secret Service and the FBI and No Such Agency, the suspense of his getting in was superseded by another thought, framed as a statement, welling up from down inside, an observation that gave him the strangest feeling, a limp numbness, an implausibility.

It was with him as the White House gatekeeper gave the high sign and opened the electric gate for him after ten long minutes, overshadowing his relief at getting inside. It was with him as he walked through the West Wing limo parking lot to the White House basement door, showed his temporary pass to a Marine guard, nineteen and ready to die for God and country, or at least for the right to consume ample brew and party without limit, the right to go apeshit, *semper fi!* The observation was this, and this alone:

What a strange turn of fate and irony to be finishing up Lhota's quest not on the shadowy margins of the world, not in some sepulchral basement in Prague or some chthonian village in Guatemala, but right here in this most illuminated and conspicuous of places, this point of light so incandescent that all within its reach were suffused, a place of no privacy but rather a place of total attention and focus, where not a bush, not a rock, not a desk or a dustball on the carpet, was long allowed to follow its own spontaneous destiny, all instead bending to a central, dominant, plan.

The familiar basement corridors, carpeted in royal blue. The jaunty, take-charge feel, the gallery of photo glory, the ubiquitous musty basement reek. Skinhead cryptographers, flattop communicators, paramilitary chic. Knowing glances, the telepathic look that said, Are you one of us, we who control the world?

Then he saw Bob Yamamoto coming down the hall. They hadn't encountered each other since the lobby of the Inn of the Wandering Boar in Prague weeks before. Bob this time said nothing, but they nodded to each other, the nod of insiders privileged to be in the White House, the knowing nod of two careers on the upward track. Being here after so many years triggered Robinson's memories of rising at four-thirty so as to be on the job at six every morning, never home before ten on a noncrisis day, and then the devouring maelstrom of the crisis itself, everything going to hell, people on that crisis high because this is what they wanted, this is why we're all here, isn't it, egos tumescent, tempers snapping, clandestine assignations between staff assistants and classified encryption secretaries in bathrooms and dark offices; as they worked late, they imagined they were managing the crisis, television cameras and media personalities gathering out on the lawn to reinforce this distended view of themselves. He remembered measuring the depth of a crisis by the installation of temporary phone lines, the temporary lines waxing and waning with the crisis. . . .

Don't forget to eat, old Walter Runge had once told him before his suicide. *Sleep you can do without and food you think you can too, but after about fourteen hours something happens, you're sitting there doing a three* A.M. *briefing and the blood sugar changes, you see stars, you hallucinate, you black out or start retching in front of the Prez and make a fool of yourself, you blow your chance with the man. . . .*

The corridor photo gallery was still there, but most all the photos featuring the epoch of the Old Man had been taken down because the Successor President had let the word go forth: enough is enough. And so up went an astonishing array of impressive shots of the Successor with a panoply of world leaders, shots taken during his deputyhood and probably at funerals of state but so what, they were impressive, he had a lot of contacts. The Successor had trained for this for twenty-five years.

The Situation Room still stood in all its muted glory, small, nothing so much as an American suburban basement den with a bank vault door, its oiled teak table accommodating only eight at a time in Brazilian leather chairs to talk and view maps, battle plans, body counts, while the lesser lights hovered outside the locked vault door, the plexiglas communications center where phone calls, telexes, satellite commands, could be shot to just about anywhere in the world.

All in the past, so long ago to him now . . .

Robinson's own successor, Lawrence Preem, received him sitting down. Preem had a senior manager's office in the basement, just down the hall from the Situation Room; he had a leather sofa; he had the obligatory constellation of signed framed handshake shots with the Old Man (to convey roots and history), the Successor (to convey present connection), the Secretary of State (to convey breadth of reach); he had three color monitors, showing Ted Turner, Associated Press, Sky Channel. Preem had done well.

"Well, well, well," Preem said like a pompous fifty-year-old, having pretended to read until several seconds after Robinson entered. He extended his hand.

"Good to see you," said Robinson, shaking the hand, just slightly moist, with long pale fingers, tufts of black hair on the knuckles.

Robinson could see that in the best Washington tradition, Preem had recreated himself. Gone were the oiled lifeless hair, the gunmetal plastic-and-stainless-steel glasses, the stovepipe corduroys, the roseate acne. In their place reposed the new Lawrence Preem. His glasses had become contact lenses, for at intervals Preem blinked widely, apparently out of fear the lenses would slide up into his eye sockets. His hair had been cut starkly short to compensate for the bald crown emerging, so that he looked like a stylish monk. His acne had been stripped or sandblasted away, giving him a slightly overdone vermilion glow. He wore a tailored blue suit (sans jacket), a shirt so white it was nearly fluorescent and so starched as to be calcified, a gold tiepin pulling the points of the collar together below the tie. A gold watch glistened on the wrist. European tassel loafers had been buffed and glazed to an impossible sheen. Preem had been engaging in bodybuilding, for the beginnings of pectorals showed through the shirt. The onetime bulge of sedentary hips and midsection had disappeared, and now Preem emanated the disturbing anorexic aura of one holding the genetic body in check, keeping the dead self hidden within the new, recreated shell.

A febrility of movement, a turn of word, a gesture, completed the picture for him. In short, Lawrence Preem had quite obviously become influential. He might also have become insane.

"You've done well," said Robinson, looking around. "I couldn't even get a hot plate for my cubicle."

"Heh heh heh," said Preem. "Things have changed a little since you left."

"I see."

"So how is the Agency?" Preem asked, already telling with a glance he didn't really want to know, he didn't care, it was a dead end of faceless gnomes such as he himself had once been, before he found this place, the center, the holy font of re-creation, which had enabled him to blossom, to burst forth and be reborn, lustrous, illuminated, endowed.

"Dark days at the Agency," said Robinson. "Drones, caretakers, people without compasses."

"How well you put it, Daniel," said Preem. "You so know how to capture it."

Preem even moved differently. He swept his arms, he stroked the air. Had he taken some kind of lessons in how to talk?

"Tell me, Larry, what do you do now? Are you off Czechoslovakia and Poland?"

Preem was shaking his head in mock sadness. He had a prominent nose, receding chin, a horsey mouth like the House of Windsor clan. A face out of Goya, a genetic courtier, a Cardinal Mazarin. How had Robinson not seen it all before, latent, waiting to bloom?

"Daniel, you got such a bum deal. When you were here, Eastern Europe was a graveyard. It was sad. Those dreadful old commissars. Husák. Honecker. Kádár. Jaruzelski. And then, not long after you left, the dam broke. The great rollback. Oh, Daniel, it was so exciting around here. Twenty-hour days, the President in and out constantly, the meetings, the briefings. I was so fortunate. So fortunate."

"Visibility," said Robinson. "Face time with the bosses."

"What can I say?" said Preem, shrugging. His collar was so tight it was able to distend flesh on his anorexic neck. Preem was wearing one of those powerful musks, a wash of reconstituted pheromones so strong no hint of his own living organism penetrated its blast wave.

"So what do you do now?"

"Well," said Preem, almost blushing. "They gave me the whole thing."

"What? The whole Pact?"

"They gave me the common European home, Daniel. Portugal to Gorky."

Robinson was impressed in spite of himself. This job hadn't even existed back in his days. Maybe Preem *would* be President someday.

"I couldn't have done it without my predecessor," Preem said. "You taught me everything I know."

"Not everything," said Robinson.

"You are the best damned field man our government has, Daniel."

Knowing it came from someone who thought fieldwork was the end of life as we know it, Robinson was insulted by the compliment. He didn't like being condescended to by this sentient lizard. A monster had been born. Preem would coil around the legs and arms of the throne, becoming the imagination of the state itself.

"Enough chitchat, Larry," said Robinson. He could tell Preem didn't like the old moniker, and so he would continue using it. "I've got a little business problem; I thought maybe you in the basement could help me."

Preem's head was cocked, poised.

"You remember Miroslav Lhota?"

Preem nodded, eyes slightly glazed.

"Larry, he was my boy in Vienna. We brought him out in '77. He helped us blow the Czechs out of Vienna. They resettled him in North Carolina. Anyway, he was killed in Guatemala last fall. He'd gone AWOL or some such."

Preem was rubbing his forehead. "Have I heard something about this before?" he asked rhetorically. "I think I have, vaguely."

"You should have," Robinson said. "Anyway, I've been running a check on the whys and wherefores. Little backchannel thing. Very quiet. I've about got it knocked."

Preem had the earnest grimace of someone trying to bring himself down to this tiny level, the field level, the micro.

"My boy left behind a few little snippets. I've got them all put away except for one. May have been a Defense or AID contractor in Salvador. Ever heard of anything called Alesa?"

Preem looked down at his desk a minute, then up into the air.

"Maybe, but it means nothing right off. To be honest, we've farmed so much of the military and covert stuff back over to the Agency and Joint Chiefs since the old days, we don't do much micromanagement. They have bean counters who know tanks, fighter wings, bagmen, better than I."

"So they've taken the mil out of your pol?"

Something in Preem's grimace told him that the hard stuff had been taken away against his will. Perhaps Preem wasn't invincible. And good thing; he didn't know dick about weapons or operations.

"Quite honestly, Daniel, this job is too big. We're working with the new Czech parties, the Soviet spin-off industries, Hungarian fiber optics. I'm much more into economics than I ever wanted to be. This whole thing is economic, not military or covert. I spend much more time talking to bond daddies from Wall Street than armchair generals and station chiefs."

"I hope we still have a few."

"Generals? Of course we do; it's just that the spotlight is off the military. They've got to wind that whole show down and hold hands with all their collapsing contractors. I sympathize for them; lots of jobs lost. It won't help the President in those districts. I'd love to bring Grumman and Lockheed into Eastern Europe somehow, to ease the shock. But the action over there just isn't in aerospace. Daniel, we're teaching our Slavic friends how to keep books, not build space shuttles."

This was not good. Robinson had assumed the National Security Council would know about Alesa if anybody would.

"Can you give somebody over at Defense a call?" Robinson pushed.

"Why don't you? Call up their contracts office."

"Larry, you know how they hate Langley. They've hated us since time immemorial. Call 'em for me."

"They hardly love us either."

"They don't love you, but they fear you."

"I don't want to burn up what little capital I have over there with a cold call to some general about this," Preem said. "It'll look funny. They're terribly paranoid as it is. They assume the White House intends to cut them to zero on everything. And if Alesa is nothing, it'll make me look like an idiot."

"May be a total bust. But there's some tie to Lhota's death."

"I don't touch Central America," said Preem. "I abhor the whole region."

"I understand, Larry. It's off the map again."

They were at an impasse. Maybe this thing would have to wait until Beth came back from China. Maybe there was nothing to be done.

"How about somebody else in the building? Who's on Central America now?"

Preem looked as though he had gas pains at the very mention.

"Some Republican from Miami, a Cubano."

"Right winger?"

"Is there any other kind? We barely speak."

"How about military stuff? Who's the liaison?"

"They've got these colonels for each region, and then several issue specialists. We nod to each other in the hallway. They sit in the weekly staff meetings, drink coffee, eat lots of doughnuts in the mess. Totally worthless. You could try them, but I'm sure they all left at four-thirty."

"How about the Interagency Net? Let's punch it up on the screen."

Preem was shaking his head and waving his arms in protest.

"That could take all night, and we'd never find it. Plus IN doesn't exist anymore. They call it AL."

"So punch up AL."

Preem was balking.

"Punch it up, Larry, and I'm gone."

"You've got AL at Langley."

"There's only one, in the Director's office. They've got a waiting list a month long, I'll go on a log, it's too public."

Preem was exhaling.

"Piss," he said in surrender, turning to his screen. With irritation, he banged out a query for a global search for Alesa, possible contractor with Department of Defense or USAID, any reference. He looked at his watch.

"A global search can take half an hour," he said. "And like I said, we've got the threat assess."

"Just think, Larry. You might solve a murder right here. Screw the threat assess. No one reads it anyway."

Preem pursed his lips. The screen had already changed.

No reference exists to (ALESA). Do you wish to continue?

There was a moment of indecision as Preem argued for turning off the machine and Robinson nearly acquiesced, only at the last second, out of desperation, asking for a search for Veil.

Veil, typed Preem, any references.

In the succeeding minutes, Preem and the computer conversed about his national security authorization passcode, his full name, his social security number, his place and date of birth, his mother's maiden name, and his mother's date of birth. Then the telephone rang.

"Piss," said Preem. "A worker bee out at NSA has to call me and personally verify all this. I go on another log. Thank you so much, Daniel."

Robinson smiled. Preem spoke with the person at NSA for a time. Finally authorization to continue was given.

> (One) reference to (veil) exists. For that, enter (VISION/Ares/veil).

"Oh," said Preem.

"What?"

"VISION I've heard of."

"I have too," said Robinson, trying to remain nonchalant, a race in his heart now, the oxygen just not enough to fill the opening veins and increased rush. "I had to do some think-piece essays on Czech dissident groups, labor unions, that kind of bullshit. But that was two years ago. Vanished into the void."

"Blue sky. Futurist contingency planning, European theater. Worst-case stuff."

"Why don't I know more?"

"Daniel, as with everything we do, few people know more than one little piece. I just have a slight knowledge of the pol and econ, and that from a distance. It's all subcontracted."

"What about Veil?"

"It's probably military, but I never heard of it. Like I said, I don't do military."

Preem punched the keyboard. The screen said:

> VISION is a tasking document of the highest order.
> (CIC autho/SECDEF implement)
>
> VISION/Ares anticipates/creates
> SECDEF policy and programs for
> ex/em/proj mil outcomes.

"Blue sky stuff."

"Sounds like Rand Corporation bull," said Robinson, trying to lighten the moment, keep Preem moving. "They've probably been paid fifteen million to jerk off this crap. What's ex/em/proj?"

"Existing, emerging, projected."

Preem entered VISION/Ares/veil on the keyboard. The screen said:

> Ares and subgroups (veil, sonic, primus) drive
> cost-effective avant-garde,

experimental, and
humanistic tactical methodologies:
local to zonal (ie,
site-focused), w/o deterrence or
parallel, exempt from ex/em/proj
treaty, presuming tech/tac
modal synergy.
Response: URGENT RETURN
Eur/asia crisis models: ie, shift allegiance,
on-site civil/mil intermingle, unstable-hostile
site/periph public.

"All military contingency," said Preem.

"This has got to be Rand bullshit," said Robinson. "Humanistic tactical methodologies? On-site intermingling?"

"They have their own vocabulary."

"What's this stuff?" asked Robinson. "What are they talking about? Pull up more on Veil."

Preem asked for more on Veil. The screen said:

No other reference to (veil) exists. Do you wish to continue?

"End of story," chirped Preem, pleased that this quest was over. He was conspicuously looking at his watch.

"Larry," said Robinson, getting up, "it's been wonderful. I guess I'll go see the Secretary of Defense."

Preem looked victorious. He stood up yet remained behind the desk.

"Larry," said Robinson, from the doorway, "if you hear of anything on your own, let me know."

Preem smiled but said nothing. Robinson turned and went back down the corridor, past the Situation Room, things now settling into their eventide slower pace. Some of the offices were still lit, but only workaholics like Preem and the nighttime technical crew were actually working.

Robinson walked back out to the gatehouse, turned in his temporary pass, and stepped through the electric gate. Godfrey was hugging the curb over in front of the EOB, and when he saw Robinson, he shot up, tires squealing, to make the pickup.

Winter nightwinds were assaulting them with arid crystal breath, picking up dust off the avenue and carrying a smell of the pole and jet exhaust and desolate expanses of hard surface, while just across the street, some poor bearded devils were holding up a hundred-foot-long wind-inflated banner made from bedsheets, fulminating about the end, the end of this world coming, these poor frozen ragbags growing old as they waited for the incoming first strike, the firing of the nuclear quiver, *It will be on Your head the destruction of manKind. . . .*

Just as Robinson was getting into the car, he locked eyes momentarily with a passing driver, as one does sometimes for no conscious reason, an unadulterated stare freed of normal inhibitions by the fly-by nature of the encounter, speed, we will never see each other again. From an unconscious lock-on to a conscious recognition took him only a second or two, but it was enough time for the car to have passed on, heading east on Pennsylvania Avenue.

"Him!" shouted Robinson to Godfrey. "Follow him!" at last aware it was Señor García, the Latino man with the widow's peak who'd broken into his Virginia apartment, who'd attacked him in Guatemala, and who had apparently freed himself from a Guatemala City prison. And so Godfrey took him at his word, squealing tires so violently that the Capitol Police were no doubt alerted, triggering his subsequent ticketing. The vehicle carrying that man was only four or five cars ahead of them in the evening traffic now, one of those small, disposable vehicles, an Escort or a Taurus or some such, white and nondescript.

And behind them, the flashing red light of the police, attracted by Godfrey's flamboyant driving.

"You're going to have to stop," shouted Robinson.

"I can get him," Godfrey shouted.

"Stop, Godfrey, let him go—we'll all be in prison."

And so they were forced to pull over and surrender Godfrey's license (expired) and Robinson's registration. They made Godfrey take a breathalyzer test. Finally, his license confiscated, Godfrey sat sullenly in the passenger seat as Robinson drove.

No conversation occurred as he drove aimlessly down Pennsylvania Avenue and up Capitol Hill, turning east at First Street and on past the Supreme Court and Library of Congress on the left, the Capitol on the right. Earnest young megalomaniacs were leaving their staff jobs, everyone trying to look like Joseph P. Kennedy II, who was trying to look like his dead father and uncles, shocks of uncut hair, ties loosened from button-down collars, top button open, paper-chase chic. They were all going to bars to drink beer, seek urgent sex, and have issue-oriented discussions. Dark February night held everything fast in its grip, blustering wind out of the Great Lakes, whirling arid flurries in salutation of the victor, yes, the lore of ancient federal power and forgotten victory, the hollow roar of America in its old age.

Terezín, 1942

The events of that January night lingered with me the next day as a dream in daylight, as if I had been in the grip of some midwinter spell of darkness and evil. This was what I told myself the morning after, to avoid the deeper and more horrible truth: that my near agreement to become a collaborator had come from some deep well within myself: the fulfillment of a black longing for vindication, glory, and recognition. The facade of my supposed selflessness, my service to the Communist revolution, was blown away, to reveal the truth—I was an egoist, a self-promoter, a grandiose and deluded man. I was pathetically resentful and bitter over how my exalted revolution and party had done little but use me like a sop. I had allowed Heydrich's appeal to my vanities to overwhelm my own good sense. I had almost been bought by a soft bed, a hot bath, and a nice dinner in a stolen castle.

May you all pay witness to how close I came to ignominy!

And yet . . . was I simply bouncing off the walls of the ridiculous milieu in which we all found ourselves in those years—a world where there were only two choices: either an honorable but certain death, or a dishonorable life of collaboration and crime? Although I was not yet a religious man, it was as if the time of Satan on earth had come, the regime of darkness, and all who wanted to survive had to make a pact with him. There was to be no possibility of honor in survival.

That morning after, when I rose from my drugged slumber at Panenské-Břežany, I immediately voiced my refusal to cooperate to the *Reichsprotektor*, who sat in his office taking calls from all across his domain. Without responding, he dialed the SS office in Paris, and when the connection was made, called me over to the phone.

"This person is known to you," he said. Baffled, I listened into the crackling roar of the radiophone, the hiss and shortwave whine of a thousand miles between here and Paris. Paris for me was the other side of the universe, a place of light, in my mind still free of this dark reign. But what foolishness—Paris had fallen in 1940, and it was one more administrative garrison of the conquering wave.

I could only hear a woman sobbing.

"Hello," I said. "Hello, who is there?"

"Radan," came the answer, across fifteen years and a thousand miles. After a confused period of stammered words, I realized it was my beloved Loki, my long-lost love, who had fled from me and torn out a piece of my heart.

"Loki," I cried. "Where are you?"

She could barely be heard, her words lost in the electrified noise of distant sunspots, exploding stars.

"Radan, do nothing they ask. Take no account of me—"

Her statement was cut short by the sound of a blow, a scuffle, and her subsequent moaning, deliberately amplified into my ear.

Could it really be she? Was this some trick?

"She was arrested four months ago for underground activities in Paris," said Heydrich. "She is suspected of poisoning one of my best lieutenants."

The *Reichsprotektor* reported this without emotion.

Praise be to Loki! She had made the choice! She was honorable. All this time the *Reichsprotektor* was watching my reaction, assessing what ties I still felt to her and whether she might be used as leverage against me. It was in that instant that an impetuous, seductive thought sprang from my mind to my lips.

"There is only one way I can attempt to carry out what you proposed to me last night," I said. "As you know, I am a lifelong Communist. My mind is steeped in the values of the Revolution; it is the structure within which I function. I can undertake an experiment in psycho-social reconstruction only if I am allowed to pursue my original plan."

"And what is that?" he asked.

"I can do it only if I am able to indoctrinate my subjects in Communistic ethics, ideals, and objectives."

He considered that for a moment, stroking the bridge of his nose.

"And upon completion of the experiment," I said, "the subjects must be given safe passage to a neutral or Allied country." I could not believe my own impertinence! I was fully reconciled to his rejection, and my own execution. As for Loki and her fate, she had made her choice of righteousness long ago; it was almost obscene that I be given the right to determine the fate of this saint on earth.

Heydrich got up from his desk, deep in thought. He walked to one of the great windows and gazed out. The German chuckled to himself several times, as if at a private joke.

"As you wish," he said. "This of course shall require that you speak of this project to no one but your immediate staff at Terezín. Hodl shall be our intermediary. And of course, you shall have to keep a regular and detailed journal of your research and experimentation, submitted to me alone."

"What guarantees do I have?" I asked.

"As much as any of us has," he said.

"I should like to have it on paper," I said. And so a typist was called in and typed out our dictated agreement, only a paragraph in length. The *Reichsprotektor* and I signed and dated it, in her presence.

I was now dumbfounded. He had agreed. And then the doubts rushed in on me. The whole idea was preposterous. Why had I even said it? This horrendous proposition was forcing me to face up to the absurd theories of my own youth. Psycho-social regeneration? Had I believed in that once? Revolution? Had I been ready to give my life for it? It all sounded so silly and embarrassing now. And in the most ridiculous irony of all, I would now be compelled to do what I had once yearned to do—with Nazi sponsorship, no less!

As I was driven back to Terezín, I searched my brain madly, madly, for some way to pull a shred of redemption out of this horrid game. If I could somehow use my position to rescue those unfortunates who, like me, had fallen into the Nazi clutches . . . If I could use my new position of some small power to do a bit of good . . .

The *Reichsprotektor* had told me to communicate to him through Hodl. Through Hodl I could order supplies, pharmaceuticals and such equipment as I needed. As far as I could tell, I had no budget per se—it was to be charged to Heydrich's SS account, which seemed to be nothing more than a direct pipeline to the ocean of Nazi resources.

Upon my return, I found Hodl had already been called by Heydrich, and he was ready to go to work. While I turned over and over in my mind what to do, I kept Hodl busy by having him initiate contact with the big German pharmaceutical firms. I had heard talk of the lysergic acid diethylamide discoveries by a Swiss team at Sandoz, which induced schizophrenic reactions, but I was certain the Germans had been at work on the same things. They had already stumbled upon the hallucinogen "Ecstasy." I was convinced others were out there to be had. And I was right. Hodl, calling on behalf of the *Reichsprotektor*, was able to find several promising programs at those paragons of scientific research and selfless dedication to the relief of suffering and the uplift of mankind, the great pharmaceutical and chemical houses which are all household names to you, dear reader, through the marketing of headache powders and cough syrups.

Aside from drugs, of course, I would need subjects. At first the idea made me nauseous. How would I designate who would be "chosen" to be the subject of my experimentation? The power of life and death is hard enough for doctors and judges to exercise in peacetime; in this satanic new world, the burden would be horrendous. And it was then that the first inklings of my plan to bring something good out of this foulness began to take shape. Yes. I would need subjects. The more the better. Might I be so brazen as to designate all the inmates of Terezín as subjects? And might I be so brazen as to engage them in long-drawn-out innocuous experiments that would spare their lives for a time, while I hatched some other scheme to get them out of this prison?

But the *Reichsprotektor* would have none of that, I concluded. There were limits to what I could do. I would have to focus and restrict this somehow, lest the whole scheme blow up in my face and result in more suffering for the innocents. I would have to keep my scheme believable.

Still, as I organized the mechanics of this "experiment," a thousand devious ideas continued to rush to the fore in my imagination. Could I connive to give all the subjects placebos and perhaps enlist them in a hoax of deception and theatrics? Could I count on my "subjects" to evidence a complete personality reconstruction when asked to do so? Could I drag this on and on, for years? Could I say that my program needed a minimum of five years to come to fruition? Was there any chance the Allies could turn the tide and win this war?

Well, there was no way I could decide all these things now. The correct course would emerge in good time. In the meantime, I would appear deep in research, hardly a free moment to explain anything to Hodl. I would apply myself to the task of plan, organization, execution. I would appeal to the self-importance and insecurity of our medical director.

As winter wore on, I was asked more and more frequently who my staff would be. Did I need more personnel, from Berlin, from the various universities of the Reich? Did I need nurses, orderlies, equipment specialists, and so on?

It was at this time that a most fateful thing occurred. I knew that I could not carry out this scheme alone, as it was growing ever more complicated; I did need some kind of trustworthy, qualified assistance, even while I planned. And so as I was deciding to cast about for a deputy of some sort, destiny presented the ideal candidate.

This young man was a Czech citizen, an internee like myself. By the sheerest coincidence, it seemed, he was a former student at Karlova Universita in Prague, where I myself had been teaching until my incarceration. Though he was not a psychiatrist, or even a physician, he had studied pharmacology until his arrest, and so was unusually qualified for our current assignment. These things in themselves would have made him the natural choice.

But on top of all that, this person was a fellow Communist.

In that environment, however, we all had to be careful. For our captors were not above putting in infiltrators and informers, even in such an unlikely place for subversion. And in the absence of any way to independently verify his antecedents and background, I interviewed him more extensively than I might have otherwise. I asked about friends, contacts, Party work. And he recounted all easily and naturally, perhaps put off a bit by my clinical interest. We had mutual acquaintances. He filled me in on the whereabouts on this fellow and that so-and-so. Vasil had gone to the partisan armies with Ludvík Svoboda in Moscow; my valet, Josef Blažek, had died in prison. He himself had been a free man until six months before, when he had been fingered by an informer as one of the planners of a university strike against the occupation.

On and on I questioned. How much I wanted the assistance of my cellmates, some of whom were also Party members and experienced in this kind of thing. But a price I had to pay for my new assignment was separation from them, and their subsequent scorn. They saw me as a collaborator pure and simple; and there was no way I could tell them otherwise.

The newcomer passed all the tests, and in no way could I justify my hesitation in taking this young fellow as my assistant. Would I prefer someone forced on me by the Reich—some German sycophant, some Nazi spy? I really had no choice.

I was hesitating, I decided, simply because I did not like him. It was an aversion, I concluded, triggered by the most superficial physical characteristics. Oh, I suppose he was comely enough, to a girl: taller than average, sharp-jawed, quite slender, with a small mustache that gave him a priggish air. Though he was from a family of village shopkeepers in Ruthenia, he was not classic Ruthenian, possessing none of the sturdy peasant build; I speculated he might have some blood from the German diaspora. Maybe I, a Jew and a Slovak, felt uncomfortable from that standpoint. And there were his eyes, which I found singularly devoid of any dance or light; instead, there was a heaviness, a leaden staring that did not necessarily indicate low intelligence but rather reflected an incompleteness of spirit. Perhaps it was the absence of a sense of humor in him; I do not remember him ever laughing, or even smiling, for that matter. And finally there was the question of his breath. It was foul to me, so that I could not stand to have him near me as we worked.

But that was it: small reason to turn down a job applicant otherwise ideally suited. It was not as though I could run a classified ad. And so I went ahead and offered him the job as my assistant, without explaining the nature of my work in any detail. When he agreed, I obtained Hodl's swift permission. And so he was hired, separated like me from the other prisoners and sent to live in our own private barracks at the east end of the camp.

His name was Emil Užhok. Would that I had followed my original instincts and sent him on his way. But events in that time marched to their own crazy design. It was a time of darkness and sinister order moving on the disorder, and quite possibly no matter what I had done, he or someone like him would have emerged to fill the same role in this drama. Such was the pull of darkness in those days; it was flowing on a cosmic level, and things on the human plane simply fulfilled its twisted plan.

This is how they came to call us, Emil Užhok and I, the Angels of Terezín:

A decree went forth to all families at Theresienstadt, bound for the murky resettlement centers north of the Tatry in Prussia and Poland, that safe passage out of the Reich would be given to all young children who were accepted into a special educational program. If the anxious parents were not persuaded of the credibility of their prison wardens, then they had the curious figures of the bearded Jewish inmate and his young assistant, who served as intermediaries.

How, in the face of dark horror and the yawning void, the human mind will struggle to believe the best is still possible! These poor parents, ready to give up their children in the dream they would have a life of freedom somewhere, created hope out of hopelessness. I was moved to see them jump at the chance.

And how I could sympathize! For I myself had succumbed to the same phenomenon, the same denial, the same deception of self. I had fooled myself into thinking that I could cheat the inexorable denouement of this morality play, this cosmic lesson being taught all humankind; I believed I could trick destiny.

What a pitiful fool I was!

First, the whole issue of the bogus treatment. At the start, I had twenty-four bright-eyed young boys and girls in my custody, and what a heart-wrenching panorama of Central European childhood were they. From all across my homeland and beyond, they spoke with the different accents of Olomouc and Hodonin, Piešt'any and Prešov, young chatterboxes, improbably bringing into this loathsome atmosphere a rush of childish fun and gaiety. It was at this time that I regretted most strongly my own destiny of bachelorhood and lack of offspring, and I felt welling up in me a paternalistic concern for my "students," more powerful than I had anticipated.

I had assumed I would be able to coach my young charges to act according to my script, and that I would be able to manipulate the supplies of psychotropics and hallucinogens, keeping everyone either on placebos or on innocuous sedative doses until the larger part of the scheme could be developed. But I had not bargained on the tenacious efficiency and scrutiny of my German support staff, who took an immediate and undue interest in the inventories of hallucinogens, my records of therapies and regimens, my notes of progress and outcome. The most difficult was the young reptile who supervised the incoming shipments of pharmaceuticals. His name was Hauptmann, and he had that Germanic thoroughness and attention to detail that was dispatching half of humanity to its ruin. He immediately suspected me of manipulation of the supplies, for he noticed an inordinate drain on the placebo stock, and hounded me for my treatment books so that he could verify the supply, or report a theft.

And then there was the question of Emil Užhok. He became nearly as tenacious on the subject of the gyrating stocks of placebos, sedatives, and hallucinogens as was Hauptmann, equally determined to resolve this mystery. And so I was forced to confide in him sooner than I intended—I had wanted to gauge his loyalty to my scheme. He seemed startled that I was attempting to deceive the Reich; but then he consented to assist me.

I could see the end coming. Although Užhok was on my side, and together we could do more dirty work than I could carry out on my own, the thing would be exposed soon. And so I was confronted with the possibility of actually having to administer significant doses to these children.

And then came the arrival of the equipment itself. The best in galvanic electroshock apparatus, an excellent phonograph and sound system for the transmission of commands and rote memorization, transparency projectors and film projectors and screens, together with an assortment of more medieval implements: straitjackets and strap-down tables from your standard German insane asylum of the day, devices that brought home to me the horror of what I was expected to do.

My God, could I carry on this masquerade?

As I spent the evenings of the spring searching my soul, watching the bursting of the dogwoods and birches, the blossoming of the lilies and tulips and crocuses, a renewal of life and nature in this wretched time of darkness, I would hear the laughter of the children in their barracks house as they teased each other into sleep. For the first time in my soulless life I found myself praying to a God I had never acknowledged, the God of my Jewish forefathers, the God of justice and retribution, seeking some guidance out of the net that was winding tighter. Never in my life had I felt more strongly in the grip of Satan and darkness, as I walked the muddy ground of our little enclave, hearing the groaning of the trains coming in from the south, the thunder of the locomotives headed north, the barking of the dogs and the somber silence of an imprisoned people waiting, waiting for the next shoe to drop.

Where, where were we all being borne?

And in my pocket the envelope carrying the piece of paper, a contract I had negotiated with a Nazi prince, allowing safe passage of these young children, whether the experiment succeeded or failed: I had his word and this piece of paper that guaranteed their safety.

You can imagine, then, how I thought there was a merciful God in heaven when we received the word, fresh from the radios of the camp guards overheard by the inmates and passed through the incredible telegraph of wagging tongues, that the very same Reinhard Heydrich had been blown into the next world by a bomb placed by Czech partisans on the day he was leaving his assignment as Czech *Reichsprotektor* to return to Hitler's side, where he was to be groomed for ever higher and more powerful positions.

Yes, this man in his supreme confidence had been driving in a convertible without armed guard on his way out of Panenské-Břežany until, at a bend in the road, the partisans had tossed the bomb right into his back seat. Not an instant death but a painful several days of rising fever and infection, impossible wounds, and gradual demise. I needn't recount for you what the history books will show: how the Führer so mourned his heir and was so enraged by this affront that he killed every man in the Czech town of Lidice and deported every woman and child residing there.

That will all seem bizarre to you if you did not live these events, appearing almost unbelievable at your distance. But at that time, we did not have such perspective. And so it was that my initial thanks to God for carrying out this vengeance was followed by the realization that it meant not the fall of the Nazis and the end of my rendezvous with darkness but only the loss of one man. And that was followed by my fears that perhaps the one to come in Heydrich's place would be worse, having no knowledge of our little agreement and certainly no obligation to honor it.

And so we were thrown into another limbo, an uncertainty on top of uncertainties. Were we to continue with this secret project that as far as I know Heydrich had concealed from his colleagues and superiors? What would the Nazi overlords think of this Freudian training project for young Communists of the future, being conducted by a Jewish Communist prisoner on young Jewish and Gypsy children who would be guaranteed safe passage out of the Reich?

My uncertainty fell into an inescapable desperate dread when I was informed through Hodl that the Nazi Command had been informed of the existence of the experiment and wished to have a firsthand inspection of its progress.

The dread fell into horror when I learned that the inspector would be Heinrich Himmler himself, Heydrich's superior and second only to Hitler, the second most powerful man in their foul empire, and that he would be arriving within a few days to take personal charge of this most bizarre and irregular state of affairs.

Horror heaped upon horror. . . . Our headlong descent into darkness seemed now to accelerate, and there was not a single thing upon which I could depend for escape.

On the June night before Himmler's arrival, I took my customary walk around the grounds to try and formulate some sort of coherent plan, some way to head off or at least ameliorate the exposure I thought would surely come. It was a splendid summer night, one of those in the Bohemian summer solstice when all the world is soft and alive, when the air dances with the fragrances of rebirth, of youth, when the day is so long and the winter darkness seems forever banished to its hidden dungeon. What a mockery nature made of our collapsing human order!

Even the wretched camp of Theresienstadt had a softness about it. The guard dogs frolicked among themselves in their pen, perhaps agitated by a bitch in heat; the guards themselves were vying for the attentions of young Ilse, who would have nothing to do with these thugs; the inmate children found little games to play in the dirt of their enclosures. I could hear the folk songs of Slovakia and Moravia rising from a barracks here, an outbuilding there, and if one softened one's eyes a bit, we might all have been in some rural retreat, some rustic holiday camp to take fresh air and cast off the cares of the city.

It was getting on toward ten o'clock, and the only coherent strategy I could formulate was to say to our overlords that the "project" had not yet had time to make any meaningful breakthroughs. But what rubbish! What assurance did I have that Heinrich Himmler would consider this whole operation anything other than pure treason—the subsidized training of young Communists by a Communist Jew? And there was the agreement to allow the young participants safe passage out of the Reich even if the experiment was a failure. I decided that would be my final defense, if it looked as if the experiment would be terminated. I would present the document to Himmler and demand its fulfillment, saying the experiment was ended.

At first that gave me some comfort.

But suppose Himmler did not honor this agreement made by his immediate subordinate, now dead? All he had to do was tear it up. It might be the worst strategy of all to present the agreement to him. Better to give it to someone who might still be intimidated by the signature of Reinhard Heydrich—an inferior, like Hodl. Yes, that was my ace in the hole. He would be the one.

But the whole thing was a house of cards, and it was already collapsing. My little stratagems were preposterous, and one puff of Nazi air could blow them all away.

My deliberations were interrupted when I saw a soft light coming from within the little offices that Užhok and I used to store the pharmaceuticals. The offices were at the near end of the building that also housed the barracks where the children slept.

We normally closed and locked the office at seven in the evening at the latest. Why was it lit?

Immediately suspecting some wrongdoing, and wondering whom I might find there, and what they would be up to, I crept closer and stood next to the window, which had been curtained so that nothing more than a slight glow of light came out at the edges. But I could hear a low voice, talking nonsense.

It was Emil Užhok, giving some kind of command, or directions.

I crept stealthily to the door and turned the knob. But it had been locked from inside. By good fortune, I had the key with me, and I slowly turned it, so as not to make any noise. Luck was with me; I swung the door open soundlessly.

The next task was to approach the inner office, where Emil was, without making the new Bohemian pine floors squeak. This was a superhuman feat; it took me nearly ten minutes just to creep to the inner door, only twelve feet from where I'd started.

At last I stood there, trembling. I turned that knob at a glacial pace, making sure that Emil had not locked it as well. And he had not.

In one quick movement I swung open the door and confronted him. But what I beheld so contradicted what I had expected to find—him rifling the files or manipulating the stocks of drugs—that I was struck speechless for a few seconds.

Emil Užhok was sitting cross-legged on my desk, lit not by the soft glow of the single lamp I used to make my journal entries but by an arrangement of candles there on the desk and below him on the floor. He was stark naked, his clothes folded neatly on the floor by the chair. That in itself would have been extraordinary, because I had never thought of him without his clothes, which, even though they were the camp-issue gray, still managed to complete his air of an asexual small-town pharmacologist. I had never seen him expose himself in any way, as he had always bathed at the communal showers late at night, when no one else was there, in an almost obsessive way.

More shocking to me, however, was that four of the children—two boys and two girls, also naked—were holding down a fifth boy from our experimental group, a little Slovakian Gypsy boy named Silviu. Some sexual act had already been performed, for both Silviu and Emil were flushed and Emil was still in a state of erection. But most repugnant of all was that Emil held a syringe, with which, presumably, he intended to withdraw blood from the young boy, to add to that already in a chalice on the desk, an element in some ceremony I did not even wish to imagine.

"What is this outrage?" I was able to say, scattering the children, save Silviu, who stood trembling until I brought him to me. I took the little boy, terrified beyond sobs, and tried to assuage his pain and confusion, but my skills with children under normal circumstances were poor at best, and in this case I simply did not know what to do, so I made meaningless parental noises, like There, there, it was all a bad dream, while Emil had time to dress himself completely and run from the office.

My first concern was Silviu, and I spent nearly an hour with him in the outer office, singing to him nursery rhymes my own mother sang to me years ago, before I took him into the barracks, gave him a sedative, and laid him down to sleep.

Then I returned to my own quarters, which I shared with the

despicable Užhok. And he was there in bed, feigning slumber. I threw on the light and shook him. He took a swing at me, cursing me.

"You swine," I hissed. "What compelled you? How long has this been going on?"

"Shut up, you old fool," he said.

"You are vermin," I said. "I shall report you to Hodl and have you taken to the brig tomorrow."

He sneered, totally unrepentant. I was taken aback by his confidence and hostility, as if he had planned for this whole development.

"And if you do so, I shall denounce you to Himmler himself, for undermining the Reich's project."

"You wouldn't dare," I said. "You were an accomplice."

But I feared he would. And in the eyes of the Reich, my betrayal would be a thousand times worse than a simple case of pederasty. His offense would be lost in the uproar over mine.

But there was no way I could succumb to this kind of blackmail. By acquiescing, I would be leaving these children exposed to his abuses.

We lay on opposite sides of the room, neither one of us asleep, perhaps thinking the same thoughts. And my conclusion was that I had no choice but to kill him. I fantasized about doing it that night, striking while the iron was hot, before Himmler arrived.

I wondered if Emil had come to the same conclusion.

But how would I, a man nearing sixty years old, subdue this youth of only twenty-three or so? Although he was hardly an athlete, he was lean and in good health.

I had no weapons at my disposal. The only way I would be able to do it was to poison him. And a poison I could fabricate from my ingredients in the project inventory; or at least a sedative strong enough to allow me to smother or choke him.

But then another thought struck me. Emil Užhok the pharmacologist would most certainly know better than I how to fabricate a poison. And so I could trust no cup of coffee, no glass of water. I could not allow myself to sleep in his presence, lest he inject me with a toxin before I could even wake up.

The future stretched black ahead of me, an unending stream of tortures and impossible choices.

Gradually I came to the conclusion that the current state of murderous hatred between us could not be maintained without his attempting to kill me. And so I decided to offer an olive branch, saying I had been too hasty. This way I might lower his guard and make him more vulnerable to my own treachery.

I prayed to God, asking why I had been put in such a position.

And as the sleepless night wore on toward dawn, with its impending visit of the Deputy Führer, a thousand other thoughts flooded through me. I could not erase the image of him seated there on the desk, perpetrating his deed. Perhaps part of my outrage stemmed from the fact that the act reminded me of my own emotional truncation, my guilt about Margret, which drove me to seek forgiveness from prostitutes: a flaw that had prevented my normal relationship with any woman, a deep-seated obsession that had prompted me to lead the life of a bachelor and an academic. And that in turn triggered my mournful speculation about the nature of love and sexuality themselves, and how a force created for the renewal of life could flow off into such abominable directions. In a way, these wickednesses seemed metaphors for the disintegration of our world, for the misdirection of human creativity and enterprise into murder and tyranny.

Dawn approached. At last I could hear Emil deep in sleep. And so, shaking with fatigue and with the import of what I was about to do, I rose and went to pick up a large stone that we used to prop open the door during the very hottest of nights. I would use this stone to crush his skull.

But just as I lifted the stone from the door, he woke bolt upright.

"What are you doing?" he demanded.

"There was a draft," I said, closing the door with a desolate push. "The dawn air is damp, and I don't want to take the grippe."

He wasn't convinced.

"Listen," I said to him, hating myself for even having to pretend. "As long as you are awake, you must forgive my hastiness of last night. Your activity . . . was not the worst. Let me work with you, to subdue it."

He snorted with contempt. As with many pederasts, I gathered, he saw no other way of life that would give him such pleasure.

"I'm sorry I insulted you," I said. "Accept my apology."

He said nothing but seemed skeptical. The best I could hope for was that with the passage of time, his distrust would fade. I certainly had no expectation—or desire—that he would take me up on my offer of treatment.

And then it was morning, a resplendent June morning in Bohemia, nature bursting with life, nature triumphant. Shortly after breakfast we could hear the roar of the motorcycles escorting the motorcade of Heinrich Himmler, coming up from Prague, where he had spent the night. And within a few moments he was being shown the camp, led about by Joekl, the commandant. Himmler was a puffed-up man, shiny like a boiled egg, not nearly so exotic as his dead subordinate, with a sternness about him, a prudish kind of disdain, that reminded me of a schoolmaster or a priggish preacher, his spectacles glinting in the sun as he looked this way and that, striding in his SS regalia, his knee boots touching the pounded dirt paths of our humble camp. And strangely, the hundreds of inmates were allowed to come out of the barracks and workhouses and look at this personage as he passed . . . as close as they would ever come to the demonic force that had brought them, brought us, to this wretched point in human history. Strangely, not a sound came from them—not an insult, not a jeer, not a breath of sound. It was as though they had been struck dumb.

Only when a single woman, in an accent of far eastern Slovakia, begged in German for mercy for her children did a small chorus of pathetic petitions come from the ranks, and it moved in waves through the masses gathered at the fence.

Save our children, they whispered in German, to eerie effect. Himmler was taken aback for a minute, and he scowled. Then, with a leather-gloved hand, he beckoned to Joekl, and the bayonets came out and were jabbing at the wire barrier, which brought the brief outburst to a halt and sent the gathered crowds, gasping, back toward their barracks, retreating in undulant ripples like the tendrils of an anemone threatened by attack.

Then, before we knew it, Joekl was calling to Hodl, and Hodl was beckoning me to escort them over to the project. We walked away from the main camp and into our small compound, and Hodl was jabbering something about the vision of the great Reinhard Heydrich, a statement I did not think too diplomatic since I was never convinced Himmler liked Heydrich as much as Hitler did: perhaps he had feared this young protégé and was just as glad he was dead.

It all happened so fast, our entry into the offices, the production of files, documents, reports, and journals. Himmler would bark a question, and I would struggle to answer, but before I'd gotten out five words he was asking another, and it became a mockery of a meeting, him seated at my desk, papers being brought to him, SS secretaries and minions repeating his questions, shouting to me as if they thought I was an imbecile, in a cacophony of crude power.

The whole thing might have lasted five minutes. For a silent moment he rifled through my report books, the way a vacant housewife would look at a Berlin fashion magazine. Then he plopped it all down at his side. We awaited his pronouncement.

"This is a waste," he said. "I wish Heydrich had consulted with the rest of us. We can make better use of your time."

He looked directly at me.

"You are the Jew doctor?" he asked.

I replied in the affirmative.

"Your project continues," he said, "but you shall make some changes here."

And it was then that he outlined our new direction, our new purpose, our new calling for the greater glory of the Reich's sciences and intellectual achievement. It was then that he set out a whole new orientation and approach, a project that had only the most rudimentary affinity with what we had been doing—or saying we were doing—all those months. He described parallel experiments and research being done in other places, ticking off names of our fellow detention camps in Germany and Austria and Poland; he rattled them off as an industrialist would list his branch offices.

And in a matter of a minute or two he outlined a purpose and an approach for us that was so horrific and abominable, such an abuse of the words science and research, such a crime against humankind, that I had no choice but to refuse to have anything to do with it, right there, on the spot—a total refusal for which I was fully prepared, even eager, to die, and through the vehemence of which I caused embarrassment to Hodl, irritation on the part of Himmler, and a devilish glee in young Emil Užhok, the opening he had been seeking, his moment to move from the shadows into the limelight, the magic intersection of destiny and personality where he now found himself, Emil Užhok slavishly volunteering to carry out eagerly what I so utterly repudiated.

When Robinson and Godfrey returned to the apartment, pandemonium had broken loose. Shannon was shouting about a man, Milton and Oliver were shouting in a tribal tongue to Godfrey, Lupe was crossing herself and praying to the Virgen de San Salvador.

"We catch that little motherfucker," shouted Godfrey, his clipped English slipping into tribal patois, and then Milton and Oliver took up the chant: "We catch him, we catch him." They had caught a slender dark man sneaking around in the hallway and had very nearly beaten him to death, and they had him tied up in the guest bedroom.

"What the hell?" said Robinson as he was swept along by this human tide to the back bedroom, where a Central American man sat bound and gagged in the corner, the victim of Ugandan interrogation techniques. He could barely open his eyes. Shannon was trying to look inside the room, and Lupe was holding her in the hallway. "*Jesucristo*, this is no kind of a place for a little child," wailed Lupe.

They did not have the man with the widow's peak; it was someone else, a stranger. And it was only after a few muttered comments from the captive that Robinson realized the man at his feet was Gabriel López of San Carlos de Chixoy, the lone survivor of the holocaust at Clínica Chixoy, and that he had come down from Yonkers, New York, with Robinson's name and address, bequeathed to him by the late Lhota many months before in Guatemala. Whereupon Robinson went on a tirade at his Ugandan enforcers, telling them this guy was on our side, he was a good guy, he was needed to find the bad guys. At that, the Ugandans sulked off back to the den to watch *Entertainment Tonight!* and mutter in their native tongue.

Gabriel López was a Mam with some Ladino parentage, a handsome young man and a nice counterpart to his fiancée back in Guatemala. Though no match for the Ugandans, he had a physical assurance even while bound and gagged, a slight surliness that might have come from ethnic distrust learned over the years. He worked as a busboy in a Yonkers restaurant.

"Señor Krámský told me you would help," López whispered in Spanish, regaining his composure slowly as Lupe fed him some tea laced with rum and daubed at his bruises with a washcloth. Apparently no bones had been broken. But Shannon had heard all sorts of noises through the bedroom wall, and the whole affair would someday be recounted to his ex-wife, and Robinson didn't want to think about what the consequences would be.

Before they could converse further, Robinson was called to the door to speak with the president of the condominium association, Mr. Herbster.

"I . . . don't know quite how to phrase this," Herbster began, "but some of the other members have registered complaints about the comings and goings here. . . ." He was craning his neck to better see into the den, where two of the Ugandans remained, while Milton stood guard at the door.

"Are you now employing a personal guard force?" Herbster asked. Robinson moved out into the hall and pulled the door closed behind him.

"I entirely apologize," said Robinson. "These are friends of friends, in the process of moving here to Washington, and I agreed to put them up for a night or two. They'll be here just a few days longer."

Mr. Herbster seemed unconvinced.

"There was talk about weapons being brandished."

"I'll speak to them," he said. "They've just come in from Africa, terrible tribal bloodshed. No excuse, however. I'll speak to them."

"We don't want any tribal bloodshed here at Riverview Towers," said Herbster. "I'll have to call the police if anything further happens."

"It won't," said Robinson.

Back inside, Robinson returned to the back room. Lupe handed him a message: a Señorita Bodihone had called. Beth Bodenhorn back from China so soon? He took the piece of paper, with Lupe's strange scrawl and block letters. Shannon had drawn a cat there that looked to be in the throes of electrification.

Gabriel López volunteered the same information his fiancée, Margarita, had already supplied. He had fled the men who killed Lhota in San Carlos, but he feared they were going to hunt him down eventually; Lhota had told him Daniel Robinson would know how to protect him. He would also be a good help in finding Dr. Emilio, the perpetrator of all this evil.

Robinson was interrupted again, by the telephone. He told Lupe to take the message, but she returned to say that Mr. Raver insisted on talking to him.

Robinson took the call in the den.

"We've got to talk," Raver said.

"Things are popping here," Robinson answered.

"As they are everywhere. Listen, I've got some information on our favorite overseas contractor."

"Who?"

"Alesa, who else?"

They agreed to talk late that night, at Robinson's, as soon as Raver could extricate himself from the office. Then Robinson went back to the guest room, to hear Gabriel López's account of the divine visitation of March 17, 1983, and the massacre four weeks later.

The Chixoy people say that each dawn comes to their homeland as their first day dawned at the beginning of time. The cries of the macaw, the chattering of the sparrows and parakeets high up in the foliage, the skyborne mists torn on the forest parapets, all announce the birth of man. And the first light, shimmering in the million jewels of forest dew, the remnants of the dark night's rain, the sweet odors of earth and leaf and virgin sky, ring with welcome for the newborn world.

The Chixoy men awaken and spend the first minutes of the day recounting the dreams of the night. Who came to them in the dreamworld, what memories they have of the journeys of their spirits through the night, their wanderings in the underworld. The telling is marked by a shivering thrilled thanks that the night has passed, that day has come, that Itzamna is climbing the sky and warming the world once again. The cooking fires are lit, the men who hunt go into the forest, those who are building are already trimming and shaping the dead saplings for use, and the children run in and out of the huts, laughing, chattering in harmony with the birds.

In earlier times, Chixoy men were one with the world and were able to communicate with all things around them . . . with the chonta palm, with the cypress by the river, with the monkey and the parrot and even the jaguar, emissary of the underworld. Although that time is lost, destroyed forever by the time of troubles and the killing and the crying and the forgetting of how things were, sometimes the Chixoy men, alone in the forest, try to regain that skill, softly talking and listening to all around them.

On the morning of the visitation, Gabriel López was doing just that, taking the forest path up to the clear mountain spring, where he would fill the buckets for the day's needs. Then he would leave for the *clínica,* where he would hang about, hoping for some odd job from the Cara de Dios. He had only just arrived at the spring and was kneeling by the clear pool to fill the bucket when a thunderous roar came out of the northern sky, a sound like a terrible wind as it approaches through the trees, the sound of a distant storm. But the sun was glinting in powerfully from the east, and there was no question of storm today.

He ran to the clearing beyond the pool, so that in the northern sky he could see a glow, outshining even the sun, with a halo, a great white ball in the sky growing larger, the first roar fading into a steady sound, of rushing water, of wind, of things heavenly and far distant. He could see people in the village below running out of their huts and could hear them shouting. The ball became enormous and was coming at the village, and at him, with a terrible speed. People were frightened, falling on their knees in fear. And as he too fell to his knees the cloud and its tendrils were all around him, a glowing white fog that shone with the light of the sun above, flowing in and out of the trees, turning the morning into an eerie reflection of the dreamworld.

He was overcome by a smell of cinnamon, a spice he knew from the market only, for special festival days, and to this day he associates the visitation with the smell of cinnamon. As the smell filled his lungs, he laid himself to rest on the ground, soothed as he had never been before. And only then, as he lay on his back on the forest earth, did he see a form coming through the mist, through the forest canopy above him.

He saw a face, a woman, he saw what he thought at first was She, and he wanted to pray out in thanks and reverence to her merciful holiness, but he could not even move his lips, he could barely formulate the thoughts in his own mind. He fell into the deepest swoon, losing sense for a time of who he was and where he was, knowing only the rich fragrance. He was a little boy, he was a sparrow, he wandered in the *clínica* at the foot of the tall elders who had seen the true face of God.

She was above him, a face in the sky, and her face was wrapped in an aureole of gold and for a time he was comforted, yes, it was She. But as he watched, She changed, her beatific smile turned into a scowl, and then her eyes glowed with a fire that was not heavenly. He saw her teeth like fangs of the jaguar and he wanted to cry out, he wanted to cry but he could not even form the words. He was compelled to lie there like a rat and suffer her indignities.

She grew and She swelled, her hair was a tangle of flames, and he thought She was speaking directly to him at times: was She cursing him, or was it the wind in the palms? Who can this be, who has come to torment us this way, and he concluded it was none other than X Kiq, blood girl of the underworld. Her face was flaming red, She gave off such heat that She burned his skin and blinded him, She spewed out the worst obscenities and licked at him with the tongue of a serpent, he felt her hot breath on him, burning him, drying him.

She was horrid to behold, and yet he could do nothing but lie there in her grip. She dared him to make love to her like a man, and he shrank from her touch, and when he did, She laughed and mocked him and spewed bile and burned him with her breath, She sent the insects of the forest, the *escarabajos* and the *hormigas* and the *cienpies* and the *zancudos*, the *abejas* and the *avispas* and the *aranas*, to torment him, to tickle him and bite him with itching fire and, yes, to sting him without mercy, crawling into his ears and over his burning eyes, yes, even onto his tongue, and they tunneled into his shorts and stung him in his most private parts and still he could not even cry out.

What a horror She was! He had no sense of time, it seemed time had stopped, and yet it was growing darker, cooler, before he realized She had gone from him. Could it really be night, had he lain there all day? But indeed he had, it was dark, She was gone, and pale

Ixchel hung in the sky, cool and paraselene, soothing him. Yet he waited a long time before he got up, so fearful was he She might return. Slowly he rose, his skin burned and swollen from stings and bites, he felt dizzy and breathless, and before he knew it he had fallen back down in a faint. But the growing chill of the forest revived him and drove him to try again, and so he succeeded, stumbling downhill for a few steps at a time, resting against palm trunks until he could take the next steps.

Strange lights were flashing in the village, and so he crept along the margins of the bush, trying to make sense of it. He could see white shrouded figures moving, ghosts or angels swinging their beams of light to and fro. In their flashes he could see a few of the villagers up, like himself, but many still lay where they had fallen, and the shrouded figures crouched over them.

Presentación María was being helped by one, she was sobbing and she called out as if to an angel, were they going to take her up to heaven? No reply was given, only the white shrouds moving in the darkness and the light, and Gabriel was held back by fear in the darkness. Old Papa Tutlán was also up, crying, asking what had befallen them all, and it was then Gabriel heard a voice in reply.

"You have seen the true face of God," said the voice, a voice unearthly and thunderous, and yet so familiar to him that he wondered if it was indeed the voice of God replying. But no, on second thought it sounded as if it was coming from a radio. It was a voice he knew, an everyday voice, yet the alteration helped it escape him for a moment. But Papa Tutlán did not believe he had seen God, he said he had seen all the dead of ten thousand years rise up out of the earth and torment him with their loneliness, he had seen not heaven but hell. And so the voice replied to him, Question not the awful ways of God, saying those words he had heard before, and now he knew the voice, he recognized Dr. Emilio from the *clínica*, Dr. Emilio was speaking from within one of the angel shrouds.

It was Gabriel's first instinct to run to the doctor, for he knew him well, Dr. Emilio was one of the senior elders of the Cara de Dios. But Gabriel did not, he held back, held there by a fear that he could not explain. He was afraid of this event, he was afraid to see his people strewn on the ground like leaves after a storm, sobbing like infants, he was afraid of these figures moving in their midst.

So he held back and watched. The shrouded figures moved from hut to hut, bending over the fallen Chixoy people, ministering to them. And gradually the Chixoy came back to life, some deliriously happy, others speechless with fear, others lost in a kind of stupor he had seen only in the very old or those about to die. These last ones were helped back to their dwellings, where the strange cries lasted well into the night. And when the next morning came, people walked about in a daze, some talking excitedly, others lost in their own thoughts.

And quickly the Chixoy people broke into two groups. The larger one believed they had seen the Blessed Virgin or God himself or the heavenly host in the sky, and they were astonished and horrified to hear the accounts of others—dead rising from the earth, visions of the underworld, an earth covered with blood, the dark jaguar himself reigning over not only the night but the day—until those who had had the evil visions were compelled to keep to themselves. But a change had come over everyone; they were quick to quarrel, and all were afflicted with the most vivid, horrific dreams and memories. Some people relived the fateful day, others were awakened screaming by new terrors.

During this time Gabriel spent much time alone in the forest, trying to find an answer. And the only answer he could find was in his own aloneness. A few days earlier he might have been drawn to the *clínica* and the saintly doctors, but after what he had seen that first night, he did not trust them. Only he had recognized the voice of Dr. Emilio coming from the angelic shroud; the others either did not recall or thought it the voice of an angel, or of a dream.

Gabriel was at odds with his own father, who swore at him and called him a blasphemer for daring to question the vision of the Virgin. His father even took him and shook him madly, striking him in the face, the first time that had ever been done; in his father's eyes Gabriel saw the eyes of a murderer. And so he spent much time alone.

It was by virtue of his exile in the forest that he survived the night of the killings. Some weeks after the visitation, he found the atmosphere in the town especially disturbing. Screaming nightmares had begun to affect the townspeople in broad daylight, and several of them had to be restrained for fear they would do injury to themselves or others. The bizarre screams of their torments had become almost normal in the town; even Gabriel had got used to them. But after a particularly violent fight with his father in the afternoon, when the older man picked up a knife and swung it at him, it was as if the scales fell off Gabriel's eyes and he fully appreciated the evil spell that had fallen on San Carlos de Chixoy. Despondent, he went out into the hills beyond the mountain spring. The night was moonless and dark, with heavy clouds hanging over the valley and yet no promise of rain, only distant thunder. It was upon his return late that night that he learned a group of the villagers had set upon the eight who were "nonbelievers," including two young girls and old Papa Tutlán, and killed them with machetes.

This was horrendous. Gabriel suspected that his own father had taken part in the murders, and so he vowed to live in the forest, trusting no one. It was not long after that that the elders from the *clínica* came and took all the townspeople away with them in the *clínica*'s trucks. He journeyed up the forest path to the *clínica*, and keeping low to the ground so as not to be seen, he could hear the eerie cries of his people as they would ring out sporadically from within the *clínica*. Once again he thought of going to Dr. Emilio, but no one could be trusted now; everyone was in the grip of the spell.

For weeks his whole people were kept there. And he noticed that the elders of the Face of God, rather than going about their healing routines as before, now stood guard and watched the hills, or sat about playing cards.

Finally the spell was completed in the most horrible way. About a month after the visitation, when the chorus of the villagers' screams and shouts had become almost constant—a single unending cry of horror and torment—a plane flew in and landed. The elders set about unloading the supplies themselves; they no longer had the villagers to help. And boxes and barrels were loaded off and taken by truck to the *clínica*.

That night Gabriel observed a terrible quarrel, in a language he could not understand. He heard shouts and saw the pilot of the plane struggling with Dr. Emilio. It was then that the elders drew weapons, the first weapons he had seen with these people he had once worshiped as saints, and they forced the pilot back onto the plane. He took off and never returned.

At nightfall, the elders were engaged in feverish activity, emptying barrels around the building. Then he watched as Dr. Emilio and the others set the building afire and stood back, watching it as it burned, hearing the cries of the poor souls left within. The sight of this was so awful to Gabriel that he never fully recovered. But at the same time, one of the elders had spotted Gabriel watching in the firelight; he led a group with guns into the night, shining their lights and shooting bullets into the brush blindly. Gabriel used every ounce of strength left in him to withdraw into the far hills, and there he stayed for a night and a day, until he was sure they had given up their pursuit.

It was from there that he saw the elders preparing their departure, and the arrival of the helicopters of the army and the dread Kaibiles, sent to instill fear in the people. And it was then that he made his way up to the town of Taxoy, where he told a villager some of what had happened. But he was treated there as an outcast. And only when he met Margarita did he begin to reveal any of what he had seen. The dreams and memories came to him without warning, and still do; he dedicated his life to trying to find Dr. Emilio and punish him for this curse he had brought upon his homeland, and upon the people of Chixoy.

Robinson and Raver sat in the darkened den, bathed in cathode ray, the soundless LANDSAT images of the Weather Channel flickering over them, jet streams blowing according to divine plan, tornadoes raking the trailer parks of the Southeast, a polar outbreak in the upper Midwest that would kill thousands of cattle exposed to its blasts tonight, a great cyclonic formation out in the Gulf of Alaska throwing terrible snows into the Olympic and Cascade ranges, so unusual for this late in the winter, this climate of America at the end of history.

Raver heard what Gabriel López had had to say, and he was deep in thought, looking out on the invisible winds raking the capital grid. He wore a stained football jersey, army ranger pants, and black combat boots, he was swilling beer, and alcoholic visions danced in his head.

"I found the Face of God on the scope," he said. "I was asking around about Alesa, being oh so discreet, you know, so as not to stomp around with my size thirteen brogans like I did before. No, this time stealthy as an Indian brave."

"So what's the tie?" Robinson asked.

"Alesa bought the Face of God," Raver said, belching from deep in the diaphragm.

"They bought it?"

"Lock, stock, and barrel," he said.

"Why?"

The Ugandans were playing a card game in the dining room, and a dispute had erupted. Godfrey accused Milton of cheating, and a glass was thrown. Lupe ran into the dining room to berate them for disturbing Shannon, asleep in the guest bedroom.

"Alesa was looking for a Latin research arm. Face of God was for sale, so they bought it."

"What? Are churches on the market now? Is there some kind of for-sale list of sects?"

Raver was shrugging. "Hey, I didn't create this world. Maybe they have trade journals or something."

"So who sold it? Who sold it to them?"

"This is where it gets funny," he said.

"Who?"

"We did."

"We who?"

"We the company, Dan. Oh, I exaggerate. We brokered the deal. We knew both parties, we saw a fit, we put them together."

"Why?" Robinson asked.

"I gather it was to be used to help our side in the various Latino struggles. Just a standard cover operation, one of the Chief's dreams. But then we didn't need it, or plans changed. They were probably worried about the National Council of Churches. Don't act so surprised. You're a big boy now."

Lupe was in the kitchen, listening to a salsa station from Arlington. The song was called "La Casa de Fernando," and it celebrated a party that had gone on for twelve hours. The song threatened to run a close second in duration. Robinson called out to Lupe.

"And there's more," said Raver as soon as Fernando was silenced.

"Shoot," said Robinson.

"I was inquiring with my Alesa source about Dr. Dracula—"

"Užhok."

"Yes. And—"

"Who's your source?"

"Bubba Huffstetler."

"Wasn't he in prison?"

"That was bullshit. He never set foot in South Africa."

"What about all that evidence? He broke the embargo. What was he selling to the police—pistols?"

"Look, you want to debate South Africa or find out about Užhok? Bubba moves in those circles, the jobs nobody will take. There's some overlap."

Robinson went to the kitchen to ask Lupe for a sandwich. The wind was blowing horribly.

"Do you want something to eat?" Robinson asked, back in the den.

"I'm full as a tick, thank you. Anyway, I was asking about the good Father Užhok, did he perhaps work for Alesa, blah blah. And Bubba says, No, but it sounds like somebody else."

"Who?"

"He says, Sounds like this guy I met at a seminar on Derivative Tech."

"What's that?"

"Spin-offs, mostly from Star Wars. Pentagon's supposed to be controlling it, but this stuff is bandied about like Sally's underpants. Anyway, he said this fellow was a strange one—and for Bubba to say that, that's a lot. Name tag read something like Dr. Eduardo Villagran, Saint Kitts Med School or some such. But he was pure Slav, pure Carpathia. With this sepulchral voice, a cavern speaking. Show was out at Los Alamos, tight security."

"So how did Bubba the ex-felon get in?"

"Maybe he knew somebody. DIA controlled the access."

"And they're letting in felons and Slavic spics? It sounds like a joke."

"You're so cynical. I know what we both think of DIA. They cut out articles on Soviet planes that we planted in *Aviation Week* and have their secretaries retype them as classified, and they win Meritorious Honor Awards. That's the dumb as shit theory: Uncle Sugar is a bloated rotting retard who can't control access to his own asshole. But maybe Dr. Emilio knew somebody."

"So why was he there? What did they talk about?"

"Bubba thought it might have been about cost-per-kill."

"I don't want to know."

"It's an ugly world we live in. Cost-per-kill is important in this day and age. Sharp pencils and calculators are out, everybody's cutting corners. People want to adapt; they've got to make a living just like you and me."

"Translate."

"Finding new ways to project freedom's force, but for pennies. Everything's on the table now. A nuke, even a carrier, is no good at handling systemic breakdowns, urban combat. Smart people are scrambling, trying to save something out of the dribbling fountain of SDI. There's no line of Soviet garbage-can tanks coming across Rhine-Westphalia anymore, no incoming wave of SS-20s; it's creepy stuff."

"Like?"

"Germans, Japanese. Can you believe that? Serious adults worrying about the Axis. Invasion stuff. No more hold the line, we are a defensive alliance. Now, behind-the-lines insertions—I mean behind *our* lines, or what used to be ours."

Lupe was throwing dishes into the dishwasher with a horrific fervor, a crashing and smashing of metal and glass, making conversation and even thought difficult. The din continued.

"Lupe," he shouted, "*no podemos conversar.*"

A brief silence reigned.

"This could fit in with Veil," said Robinson.

"What's Veil?"

"I was in the White House today, Veil came rising up out of the computer. So much jargon; I don't know. But it's contingency. 'Tech/tac synergy.' 'Humanistic methodologies.' 'Local to zonal.' Does this mean anything?"

"Wait a minute," said Raver. "If you had to go all the way to the White House to find out about Veil, how had Lhota heard of it?"

"I can only guess," said Robinson. "Soviets must have learned of Veil by tracking Emil, a mole, somehow. The way the KGB is hemorrhaging these days, and the way Lhota kept networking with his former cohorts, he must have pulled it out of one of them."

"You hope," said Raver.

"I hope," said Robinson.

Now the noise came from outside. Apparently the wind was so strong that a piece of the building, a gutter or a cable, had come loose, and it went rattling past the window.

"I can sketch a scenario," said Raver.

"Sketch away."

"The Face of God was doing more than dark rites in Guatemala."

"Research," said Robinson.

"Some kind of mass hallucination," Raver said.

"Or something," said Robinson.

"Are we talking psywar?"

"Utter crap," said Robinson.

"All those Indians are dead."

"They were burned up by napalm and gasoline."

"But the screaming, the mood alteration. Why burn them?" Raver asked.

The wind outside was so strong Robinson could see the wide glass panes of the picture windows bulging. Had they better be concerned? Would this wall of glass explode in on them?

"Do you feel a draft?" Robinson asked.

"Lordy," said Raver. "There's a forty-mile-an-hour Canadian blaster outside. I feel six drafts."

Robinson looked around to see if one of the windows hadn't been sealed properly.

Shannon's bedroom door drifted open just as Lupe screamed from the rear of the apartment. In fact, they were nearly one event. A scream is like a door opening in the face, he thought as he watched it happen—and hers was long and dolorous, the cry of Latin Catholic horror and loss, of the cruelty of the world, of life is cheap and what will we do? Robinson saw Shannon still asleep in the half-darkness as he ran by her door, but how she could sleep through the lamentation of Lupe was awesome. Farther on, in the room where Gabriel had been recovering, Lupe was bent over him, shaking, unable to get her breath in the clutching continuing intake of a powerful sob triggered by his passing from this world, the departure of his soul.

And now Raver was there, already calculating trajectories, firepower, kill angle. The left rear of Gabriel López's head had blown out across the pillow in a roseate nimbus of matter, and his face was marked by the most serene smile, a horrid contradiction of the end. The tiny window in that bedroom was marked with a minute entry hole and spidery shatter marks around it, where lead had passed through glass, and Robinson was astonished they hadn't heard any of this.

"Walther silencer," said Raver, over at the hole, window now slid open, looking outside. "Dan, it was fired from about a foot outside."

They both walked to the window, looking down the hundred and twenty-foot sheer drop to the ground, another sixty feet up to the roof. There were no balconies or fire escapes or even decent mortar joints to provide any access at all.

"Ay," cried Lupe, and Robinson was more in tune with her than with Raver. First he pulled the bedroom door closed, so that Shannon wouldn't see; and then the wave swept through him, the sucking away of breath into the darkness, the opening up of lung and aorta, the *ahh* as the synaptical connection was made and he ran on to make sure his baby was intact: her window was larger than Gabriel's, and they had stupidly assumed the windows were safe; for anyone to get a shot at them twelve floors up on that hillside south of Arlington Cemetery, the marksman would have to be shooting either from aircraft, which the Air Force and Secret Service monitored around here like hawks, or from the top of the Washington Monument, three miles away—how absurd; more sensible to worry about pythons coming through the heat ducts or poison in the Pop-Tarts.

"Security is never total," Peri^Meter liked to say.

He burst through her door and she was motionless and he ran to her and the clonk as his hand came up against her torso was obscene: this was no daughter but a mummy; he turned it over to see its Kewpie doll eyes ogling up at him, wretched, ghastly, hollow. He had no daughter there but a large, vulgar doll that must have come from some dreadful carnival or some Third World workshop, and as he picked it up the head fell bouncing to the floor, again with that awful clonk.

"Auuch," a retching sound, was all he could do.

Now Raver was in the doorway, and he slowly came over to Robinson as if to console him, but to complete the disorder he pushed Robinson stumbling into the bathroom, wrenching Robinson's neck and knocking the wind out of him, and now Robinson started the instinctive attack, he was ready to kill Wilson Raver in rage and horror.

"Calm it, boy," snarled Raver, trying to restrain him ranger-style. "That mother . . . coulda been a bomb."

"Ay," shrieked Lupe. "Aaaa," shrieked the Ugandans, crashing into one another in the hallway, looking in horror at what they thought was Shannon's head on the floor, then gathering reverently for a few seconds round Gabriel López's head wound, before they went running out into the corridor, Oliver and Milton searching for access to the roof, Godfrey taking the elevator to the parking lot.

"Uhh." Robinson gagged again.

"Easy," said Raver.

It was out of his hands now, the tumbling into the vortex. He swooned, he wondered if he had wanted this all along, where had he thought it would end? Beyond the thunderous pain of the loss was another idea forming, a message repeating itself inside his head, some kind of final electro-organic response to this kind of thing:

There was no way he could live on.

"Steady," said Raver, reading his mind.

"*Dios nos protege*," implored Lupe.

Around him swirled a tornado of pain and outrage, a stripping away of virtually every part of his personality except the parental animal response: in this darkened tunnel with God and Satan, nothing else existed, a universe of blood morality and unspeakable evil. . . .

"There are ways," said Raver, still holding him.

His little child swept away, swept away, off into the whirling night, swallowed up, sucked out a window into the darkness that he himself had generated—he had provoked this, and if he did not bring her back unharmed he would kill himself forthwith. Swiftly, utterly, brooking no dissent.

A strange peace began to descend over him.

Raver was over at the doll carcass, his own face covered with a dish towel, nudging at the doll's body with a fireplace poker.

"If it was something nasty—i.e., bacterial—we're all dead."

Raver extracted a small piece of paper from the body and by skillful manipulation of the poker unfurled it.

"I've broken every rule of the bomb squad," he said.

Robinson really had nothing to say.

Raver shook his head with disgust, looked at Robinson, and was silent. Robinson walked over. The note said, in typescript,

All freezes now. If you take any action whatsoever, it won't be just Dolly's head coming off.

Milton was back, to report nothing untoward from the roof. Now Lupe was attempting to take in the second event, but it was as if she had vented all her passion on Gabriel's death. Her reaction to Shannon's departure seemed rather one of simple astonishment, silently marveling at the logistics.

"A message from beyond the stars," said Raver, after a moment's silence.

Dark, dark blew the winds. It was the weather; the weather had taken her. Strange things happened with violent changes of barometric pressure, mood swings, wars, suicides. It was the air, the tumbling isobars. A space had opened up.

And still the simple message from inside him, the escape hatch that would take him into the dark as well, the way out. This, this was his only solace.

The Ugandan searchers could not find a single clue to anything, other than a single rappeling hook up on the roof, the iridescent sheen of its electrolytic weatherproofing untouched by any age or use, brand spanking new, perhaps a fingerprint or two on it, but who cared, who cared: it was the hook that took his baby.

Dark, dark . . . We are drawn onward by what we do not wish to find but have sought since our race was born.

The night was not ended. Many things had to play themselves out in the fulfillment of their own plan.

Gabriel López had to be disposed of. In no way could his murder in Robinson's apartment be explained in a plausible way, and so measures were taken to remove the body.

Milton and Raver had a source who could provide a burstproof body bag, Vietnam surplus. The next morning they would return with a delivery van and remove the bag, concealed within a cardboard packing carton for a stereo home entertainment unit that Robinson had left over from his move into this apartment. The box would be placed in a rental storage compartment, where temperatures hovering in the twenties would keep the body inconspicuous for a few days, until they determined a permanent solution.

Then there was the issue of Beth Bodenhorn and the Senate. Robinson would now have to decide whether or not to speak with her at all and thus risk angering these persecutors who seemed to know his movements and now held his daughter. This decision he would leave until the next day.

There was the very large issue of the search for Alesa and the truth. Raver had been surprisingly understanding of Robinson's desire to bring the whole quest to a screaming halt and to do nothing whatsoever that would further endanger his daughter. In fact, Raver too seemed content to wait.

"They have to get in touch with us," Raver had said, as if that would make everything all right. In fact, Raver was perversely optimistic. Shannon was worth nothing to the kidnappers dead, he reasoned. And they hadn't used several opportunities to kill Robinson himself, so they wanted him alive, albeit neutralized. Perhaps, theorized Raver, these people did not want to risk more attention being directed their way by murdering an American CIA employee. Killing Lhota had been one thing, a fairly easy death to obscure; popping Robinson would be more difficult.

"Rave," Robinson had countered, "you and I both know a thousand and one ways to make me have an accident or die an untimely but explainable. Let's make it a heart attack. Or a wreck. Fire. Suicide. Mugging. Stroke. Forty-two-year-olds have strokes."

"Hush up," said Raver. "Accidents take time to set up. These people don't have time."

The more Raver reasoned, the more optimistic he got.

"They can't wait long to do business," he said. "They know kidnapping will draw attention pretty soon. We'll be hearing.

"These people are protecting a vested interest," Raver continued, growing more expansive. "We have humbly scared the piss out of them."

There was the issue of Ruthie Lowenson, and the FBI, and all that. Should they reappear, Robinson would have to intercede to call off their own tailing of him, lest they also endanger Shannon. In no way could Robinson trust the FBI to crack this thing or rescue his daughter. On the other hand, they might not even believe his daughter had been kidnapped when he told them, and might continue with their plodding pursuit, and so reap the whirlwind.

He sat in the dark, strategizing, thinking he wouldn't even try to go to bed tonight, because he would never fall asleep, and upon saying just that he did fall asleep, over a period of what seemed six hours he dreamed the wretched dream that had spared him in recent days but now came back with a renewed vengeance: he dreamed of his mother in the Bakersfield trailer, and she was in the doorway to the other room, yellow light silhouetting her, trailer smell of blankets and dirty clothes and enclosed cooking odors, she was a dark figure moving against a yellow background, she was saying something to him, pointing, crying, both of them were crying in unison, he with her, at last she was going to tell him something, why she had come back to him this way all these years and why she wouldn't let him alone—

He was torn from it by the telephone, seeing by the clock he had slept for seven minutes.

The call was as if from another universe. It was his departed girlfriend Leah, calling him from what sounded like a tavern or roadhouse, the background thumping to the sound of Ernest Tubb and then Roy Acuff and then Conway Twitty; she was in the heart of the West, drunk.

"How are you doing?" she asked, punctuating the question with laughter that confirmed she was drunk and implied that perhaps now she was ready to resume a friendship with him.

"I am not good," he said in a cadaverous, but honest, tone.

He wondered if they had tapped his phone.

"What's wrong?" she asked, not wanting to be brought down.

"Shannon," he said.

"Funny you should mention Shannon," Leah said. She recounted a dream she had had a few days before, in which Shannon had made a guest appearance. Shannon had been dressed in a shimmering coat of white and gold, and she was walking through a green field.

Robinson didn't want to speculate about its meaning, and then he was crying.

"What's wrong?" she repeated.

"Tell me where you are," he asked.

"Either Idaho or Wyoming," she said.

"That's a start," he said, heartened slightly. "Coming home?"

"This is home now," she said.

The electronic hiss intervened.

"Why don't you come out and see me?" she said.

"Oh, baby, I'd love to," he said. "I'll come as soon as I can."

"I miss you," she said.

"Same," he said. "I've got to get off the line. News about Shannon. Give me your number."

She laughed. "I'll give you my area code," she said.

He looked off into the night.

"Three o seven," she said. He looked at the telephone directory map: Wyoming.

"I'll call back soon," she said.

"Call me anytime," he said. "I'll come on wings of love."

She hung up, and he was in the dark again. Pinkish ground-lit cumulus clouds were breaking across the moon, being blown out into the Atlantic by a monstrous high pressure centered over Hudson Bay. The lights of the victory city flickered and blinked as the branches of dead trees were violently whipped along a northwest-southeast pattern. It was the breath of the pole itself, the very frosted nadir of earth.

And then the phone rang again, and trembling, he lifted the receiver.

"Daddy," he heard Shannon say, her voice undercut by a cellular telephone whine.

"Daddy . . . I'm afraid," she said, and her voice was pulsing, riding some kind of oscillating radio wave, a slow but steady pulse, about two seconds from peak to valley.

"Shannon, baby," he managed to say, "where are you?"

She cried, and the cry rose and fell with the atmosphere, broken by an occasional burst of static. She was moving away from him into space.

"Daddy," she said, crying.

What was left of his daughter was riding the waves of the universe, moving away from him at record speed, wavelength being increased by the velocity of departure.

"Are you okay, sweetie?" he asked.

"Yes," she said. At first he thought car, they had her in a car and were heading away, but the bursts of electromagnetic noise told him distance and speed, they told him aircraft: they had her on a plane flying into that apocalyptic night.

Just as he was able to muster enough breath and sense to ask her a meaningful question, such as Where are you, or Who has you, Shannon was gone, the link broken, nothing left but him alone on the dead field of earth, the solid here and now victorious over the invisible air, he worldbound, she soaring into sky.

But the torture was not over, for the phone rang again. He jumped to it, thinking Shannon's captors had softened, allowing an extended conversation.

"Robinson," the female voice said. He knew it too well; it wasn't Shannon but his ex-wife, Jackie Frankowski, phoning from her conference in Palo Alto. She was the only woman on earth who called him Robinson, and the last person on earth he wanted to hear from right now.

"Yes," he managed to say.

"Robinson," she said, "have you had your damned phone off the hook? I've called about ten times."

He couldn't even formulate a response.

"Sorry," he said. "Everybody in the world called."

She sighed audibly. "Look, I know it's late, but I miss my baby. Peep in and see if she's awake."

"Jesus," he said. "It's two in the morning here."

"I know," she said, actually sheepish. "But maybe she's awake."

He felt ill.

"Just go see," she said.

He agreed, and walked to the bed where Shannon had been only two hours earlier, before being snatched out the window by someone using a rappeling hook. He tiptoed back.

"She's asleep," he said.

"Shit," she said. "Hell, go ahead and wake her."

"Oh," he managed to groan. "She's tired, Jackie. Tomorrow."

He could hear her muttering.

"Is she sick?"

"No," he said.

"Are you sick?"

"No," he said.

"You sound sick."

He grunted.

"Okay," she said. "I'm calling tomorrow night. Have her by the phone at eight o'clock your time, five mine. I'm calling."

"Will do."

"I'm calling," she said. He hung up.

The full moon shone on the glacial surface of the winter river, a featureless flat plain between rimlands of dead willow and oak. Except for the thrashing trees and shuddering windowpanes, the earth's atmosphere might have been gone altogether, giving a glimpse of the world to come—polar, darkened, all matter and energy locked in the deepest sleep imaginable.

The next morning he decided, as he waited for another call from Shannon, to risk a conversation with Beth. At first she said she would try and see him late that week, because she was pressed by business at the Senate. Senator McMahon's violent attack of diarrhea had ended prematurely his visit to the People's Republic, and the Air Force had flown him back in a state of severe dehydration. Beth was designated to accompany him home, together with an Air Force doctor.

"He insisted on eating from street vendors," she rasped into the phone. "His parents had been missionaries in Shanghai, and he remembered his boyhood, and so he wolfed it all down. I'm sure it's amoebic at the very minimum. Or shigella. At least it's not a heart attack. . . . When he had the pains after fighting with Blisterson, I was sure it was his heart."

"Fighting with Blisterson?"

"Christ," she said. "We were in the Forbidden City, three of the Central Committee receiving us. Blisterson immediately began hollering at them about abortion, he called them murderers, he said he was going to cut off our military aid package over Chinese abortion. McMahon told him to shut up, old W.A. kept on going. One of the Chinese was fumbling at his Mao jacket; I thought he was going for a pistol. We're talking veterans of the Long March here. McMahon told him to shut up again, and Blisterson turned on McMahon and called him a godless baby-murderer. McMahon threw a punch. He decked W. A. Blisterson right there in front of the Chinese."

Swearing a life-or-death situation, Robinson finally won a promise from her to meet with him at the Cubicle Inn in Arlington that afternoon. It was close to home and would allow him to run by and pick up the remainder of Dr. Michalský's journal.

As far as Robinson could tell, the FBI had faded into the woodwork. He felt strangely exposed as he moved around the suburbs, even though he had Oliver along. Oliver sat at a discreet distance while Robinson waited for Beth in the deserted Cubicle coffee shop. Milton guarded the car.

Eventually Beth burst into the modular concrete gloom.

"What is so goddamned important?" she said, dropping her satchel to the floor.

"Remember our chat of last fall?" he asked. Beth shone out at him through her Waspo-Aryan face, an unshadowed face, a Germano-American countenance with pushed-in teeth and the nose desired by this culture, her blond hair cut in a tennis player's shag. In the face and upper body she looked athletic and lean, but she was cursed with a waist, posterior, and thighs that had widened beyond control. Not that she hadn't tried to prevent the thickening; she jogged, lifted weights, sat in a sauna, swam laps, and danced. But genetics were triumphant here, and she tried to divert attention from them with her frenzied talking, broken by paroxysms of self-directed laughter.

"I can't . . . Oh, yes. Your friend. Dead in . . . Mexico, was it?"

"Guatemala," he said. "I've found much more. I'm very close."

She was looking at her datebook, reading a stapled sheaf of pink telephone messages, scribbling notes to herself.

"I'm listening," she said.

"Lhota was tracking a supposedly dead Czech KGB man, who had resurfaced in Guatemala. With a bogus evangelical group that apparently was doing some kind of weapons research. They incinerated a whole peasant village in 1983."

"The Czechs did this?" Her tone of voice indicated polite conversation more than any real interest. Nineteen eighty-three was a long time ago in Washington terms.

"I don't think so, Beth. As many trails lead to us as to them. Apparently the Agency had these people on contract in El Salvador, maybe in Guatemala too."

She just looked at him. For an instant, he thought it was a look of condescension that said, This is getting a bit strange. Urgent phone calls. Life or death.

"Lhota was tracking down several clues, which he left behind for me. Have you ever heard of anything called Veil?"

She paused a minute, seemed lost in thought.

"How about Vision/Ares/veil?"

"Whoa," she said, crystalline blue eyes widening. She was frozen in the act of putting a breath mint into her mouth.

Oliver was looking much too conspicuous in his neighboring booth, resembling nothing so much as an African hit man eating a piece of cheesecake and wearing a suit.

"Whoa what?" he said.

"We don't talk about that in the Cubicle Inn," she said.

"You've heard of it?"

"Of course," she said. "How did you?"

"Through Lhota," he said.

She had cocked her head slightly and had the beginnings of a bizarre smile.

"You're telling me this defector died with 'Veil' on his lips?"

"He wrote it on a postcard and mailed it the day he died," Robinson said.

Beth was actually uncomfortable. She was looking around the room, and he thought he saw her hesitate a minute as she glanced at Oliver, who swiftly averted his eyes.

"Saying those words can get you arrested," she said.

"What words?" he said.

"Those three words," she said.

"What—Vision/Ares/veil?" he said.

She grimaced.

"Am I having a sucrose rush, or did this conversation just get more interesting?" he asked.

"I'm going to have to run," she said, snapping her purse shut.

"Oh, no you don't," he said.

"I'm sorry?" she said, with sharpness. She's scuttling for cover, he thought; she sees a sinking ship.

"Beth, someone with some connection to those words—Veil and Vision—has just kidnapped my little girl and killed a Guatemalan who survived the massacre in 1983. Beth, this murdering happened last night, about a mile from here. You've got to assist me."

Her lips were pursed, and she was taking deep breaths. Never in all his life had he seen Beth Bodenhorn with her lips pursed and taking deep breaths.

"Beth, they kidnapped my baby and they killed about seventy-four people in Guatemala and they killed Lhota in September and one more last night."

She was still making an attempt to get going.

"Beth," he said. "Beth."

"Who's that black man?" she asked.

"He's working for me," he said.

"I've really got to go," she said.

"Beth," he said.

"Please," she said. She was up, looking desperately around the room.

He nodded to Oliver. They both also stood. She began walking to the door.

"Beth," he said. "Beth."

She was walking more briskly.

"Beth," he said. "They have my little girl."

She was about to run for the registration desk when Robinson caught her hand and let her feel, through his jacket, the barrel of his pistol.

"Let's go outside," he said. Her eyes were closed. The cashier didn't even look up from her tabloid.

They were out in the parking lot. Patriots Parkway roared in the background with the going-home noise, a chinook blast of carbon monoxide and slapping tires, another nightfall, the capital rush.

He assisted her into his car. He had Oliver and Milton stand outside.

"All I want to know is what you know, Beth."

"This is wrong, Dan," she said. "This is wrong."

"Tell me," he said. He was scanning the lot, the hotel, the horizon, for someone watching.

"I play by the rules," she said, losing her voice.

He smiled.

"Rules never went beyond water's edge anyway," he said. "Now there's no edge, Beth."

She looked so sad, and she began to cry. How could one cry about these sorts of things? Save crying, he thought, for loved ones, for life, for the earth.

"You know I'll have to report you," she said, then visibly regretted it.

He smiled again.

"Beth, they have my daughter."

"God," she said, following it with an interval of intense guttural sobbing. He let her cry for a minute. He sensed this was some kind of barrier she would have to pass through.

"Beth, this is all true," he said. "I hate to do it this way, but I can't entrust my little girl's health to due process and the system of checks and balances."

The sun was setting, roseate and frigid, in the west. The hotel looked virtually empty. The loss of defense contracts had fallen heavy in this neighborhood.

"This town is bad," he said. "We start to believe this bullshit. We lose sight . . ."

She was blowing her nose loudly into a handkerchief. Oliver and Milton were edgy, scanning, wanting to be moving again. Milton flinched when a great sheet of that morning's newspaper came blowing around a corner of the building, looking like a manta ray in its death throes. The radio was on, but stuck between stations, broadcasting a soft crackle. The windows were slightly fogged.

Beth sighed, a sigh of grief and resignation.

"Only the other side would want to know about Vision and Veil," she said.

He laughed, but it rang harshly in the Saab.

"Talk to me," he said.

"Just a contingency," she said. "May never be used."

"I'm hearing invasion," he said.

She shook her head.

"Who we invading, Beth?"

She was shaking her head.

"Are we looking to reoccupy Germany? The Ukraine? What's this crazy stuff?"

She was rubbing her temples, trying to modulate her breathing.

"No one knows what's going to happen," she said, almost to herself.

"What?" he said.

"Fragmentation," she said. "Moving so fast everywhere, Dan. No control."

"Make sense, Beth. This is hallucinatory."

"First, we don't think he's going to make it," she said. "We know, we've seen all the numbers, the projections, the GNP. Total economic breakdown in Moscow, a real risk of mass starvation in about five years . . . Warlords on the steppes. Imagine, some Ukrainian general seizing all those sites in his territory. Or Byelorussia. Or Russia itself. Civil war right on top of the silos. A fascist Russian ayatollah."

"You're talking Soviets," he said. "Us neutralizing their nuke sites?"

"Or whatever," she said. "Disorder reigns. The Director laid it out for us beautifully: 1914, 1939, all over again. The Soviet collapse pulls all the Slobbovias down with it . . . and then the Germans and then everybody. A powerful fascist pull develops in the East Germans, some harmonizing in Bavaria and Schleswig-Holstein. The Federal Republic barely tolerates us right now, our two hundred thousand soldier boys, our F-16s crashing into kindergartens, our tactical nuke Lances, Honest Johns. We were the conquering force. They've deferred to us for almost fifty years. Messianic arrogant people, as messianic as we are, but squelched for centuries. Festering guilt, force-fed films of Auschwitz, never again. Horrid mix."

"So we have to be ready to go in again?"

"Of course. If only to save a NATO nuclear site, or our boys in the barracks, from screaming German hippies turned fascists. Or maybe to reoccupy. Maybe to keep the Germans out of Gdansk. We couldn't believe the velocity of reunification. Both CIA stations overwhelmed."

She paused a moment to breathe, blow her nose.

"Same goes for Japan," she said. "Eurasian black hole sucks them in. Or the Mideast really falls apart, à la Saddam Hussein, revolution in Saudi, Israel firing nukes, Egypt upside down. Then the world market pops, Tokyo goes down the tubes. Could be our bases. Or they could rearm in three weeks. Forget all this about 'our dear trading partners, they're just like us.' They aren't. Fifty years ago they were worshiping an emperor and committing kamikaze. Field's wide open for them now."

The engine of the car had been running all this time, but a change in its rhythm, caused by carburetor problems or bad gasoline, sent a tremor through them.

"Does the Senate know this?"

Beth began laughing, her voice still hoarse from the sobbing of minutes before.

"Only the leadership," she said. "That was the deal. The Wall falling elated the liberals. And scared the hawks, including our Chairman and your President and your Director. Then Saddam Hussein scared everybody with all those human shields. This is the deal. Overall defense gets cut, but the administration gets to develop these crash new programs for the worst case. And nobody admits to anything."

"Beth, there was no gossip, no hearing, no news coverage I ever saw. This is crazy stuff."

"Of course it's crazy. World is crazy. Empires falling in fifteen minutes, continental mood swings. Vision has all been done with winks and nods, private prayer breakfasts, golf at Congressional. It's only a year old. I bet only twenty people on earth know the whole thing. I only know because the Senator trusts me with everything, my Agency background, the mystique. Almost all the strategic planning has been given to contractors. They figure security is better in Palo Alto than the Pentagon. Morale is so bad at the Pentagon, they couldn't be trusted. Old generals in the dark corridors, crying in their napalm. This is all new stuff. Veil and the others are clean-sweep new technologies, low-cost stuff. Cheap cheap cheap. Nonlethal. It's hidden in the budget. It's just contingency, Dan. It may never be used."

"What technologies?" he asked.

"We don't know, and we don't want to know. Disciplines are overlapping: nuke with laser, laser with EMP, electronics with chemical. It's not bad work, Dan. Humanistic technology, that was the understanding. We don't want to blow people away like the bad old days. Nukes, howitzers, napalm, are bad PR for democracy. Grenada and Panama were awful messes, too many bodies for Congress. Iraq could have been the worst carnage since the killing fields. We're talking control of urban areas, sites, intermingling, lines blurred. America riding the chaos."

A small black boy came wandering out of the motel, carrying a bundle of newspapers. He walked straight toward the car. Milton cocked his pistol.

"God," said Beth.

"Easy," said Robinson.

Oliver moved away from the car, to head the boy off. The little boy asked him if he wanted a copy of the *Washington Times*. Oliver paid him, took the paper, then shooed him away. The boy ran off from the parking lot through a stand of bare Lombardy poplars to an adjacent convenience store.

"Help me," said Robinson. "Dead Lhota, my little girl, are part of this."

"This is all there is to tell," she said, almost apologizing. "The leadership's only barely aware. That was the understanding."

"Lhota was killed in Guatemala," Robinson said. "Face of God killed seventy-four, plus one. Oh, one more last night. Kidnapping my baby. Does this sound like humanistic technologies? Help me."

"I don't know. Maybe it's a contractor, or ties to a contractor, maybe one of ours. Maybe the research was going on long before Vision was actually authorized, maybe somebody screwed up in 1983 and they want to keep it quiet. Paths have been crossed, lines tangled. Your Czech boy Lhota, and now you, pissed off somebody with ties to somebody, this other KGB Czech. But I can guarantee you, in the current climate, no little sideshow Guatemalan massacre is going to derail it. Jesus, Dan, Ceausescu and his wife killed hundreds, Deng blew away three thousand. The Chairman said he hadn't seen this kind of unity and concern on the Hill since 1941."

"It has to be one of our contractors," Robinson said. "Garibaldi was keeping Lhota's death quiet; he must have known there was a link to Veil. Shit, he and the Director saw to it that I, FBI counterintelligence, never got into Guatemala. What's left of CIA Security did it."

"Then Garibaldi just went up in my estimation. I knew he was connected. This makes sense, of course. You know how the political appointees work. They're the only ones the White House will trust with this kind of stuff. Hell, Veil probably goes back to the Old Man's term. That would explain your massacre in '83."

He sat there, almost laughing. But the reaction was really more spasmodic—a kind of rhythmic convulsion, somewhere between retching and spasm.

The sun was now down, day only a luminous western glow that shone gilded at the horizon line, then climbed through the darkening colors of the nightfall spectrum, from yellow to bronze to heliotrope, and thence into magenta and full blue, blue into indigo, indigo into the black beyond. . . .

"Do you believe me?" Robinson asked.

She sighed and scowled, furrowing her Teutonic brow.

"I suppose I do. So what if I do? You'd need ten reams of evidence and a special prosecutor to even start anything. The Senate leadership agreed to things like Veil; the liberals are busy cutting the stupid MXs and B-2s; it'll be a while before they sour enough to do hearings on something this small in dollar terms. Dan, Vision is cheap cheap. Both the Dems and the Republican leadership are clued in. And besides, if this massacre was in '83, that predates Vision; it's weird ancient history. Do you know how many people we have going up and down the Capitol hallways saying the CIA bombards their brainwaves, DoD tested neutron bombs in their backyard?"

"I have this Czech doctor's journal from Terezín concentration camp; it's being translated," said Robinson. "They were into some kind of psychological manipulation as far back as 1942. A photo of the same guy—Emil Užhok—with Reinhard Heydrich, the Nazi viceroy. Some off-the-record detailing the linkage from the Nazis to the KGB to Frank Terpil to Face of God to a Mideastern contractor named Alesa to Langley. I think DIA even let this Czech go to a DoD seminar out in Los Alamos last year; he was talking cocktail talk about cost-per-kill."

Milton was now relaxed enough to begin skimming the *Times*. He rattled it open and flat with a loud pop, audible inside the car.

"The best . . ." She paused a minute. "The best you could do would be to get somebody in the House to raise it, some gadfly, maybe a little coverage, get it in the Congressional Record. Short of that, surface it in the press. But it's wild, esoteric. Mainstream press probably wouldn't go."

She pointed to Milton's newspaper.

"On second thought, the *Times* might take it. But whoever did, the minute anything led to Vision or Veil—and the link seems strong here—administration would come stomping all over it, court orders, restraining orders. Look what they did with Frank Snepp."

"I can't believe Larry Preem didn't know more about this," Robinson said. "He works for them."

"He's almost totally on economics now. This was given to DoD," she said.

There was an interval, marked only by the engine, the heater, and Milton rattling the newspaper.

"This is all moot anyway," he said quietly. "The minute anybody made a sound about it in public, they'd kill my baby."

The engine was laboring again.

"What would you do?" Robinson asked her.

She studied that one a minute, uncomfortable with this burden.

"I'd go to the FBI," she said. "At least that way you're inside."

"Vision, Veil's inside," he said. "I can't trust gumshoes to deal with these kidnappers. The kidnappers seem to know my movements; they'd pop Shannon at the first sign. They aren't scared of the pussy FBI."

"This is—" she started to say. Then she just sat there for a time, literally unable to speak.

Night, night was falling again, all across the riverine zone where these things transpired, a land of floodplain and muddy plateau descending from the last gasp of the Appalachians just a few miles upriver of where they were, a rocky violent zone falling into flat frozen mud, now all overlaid with old ice, old snow, old atmosphere.

In parting, Beth put her hand on his hand, and wished him luck, and said she would pray for him. When she said again he should take it up with the FBI, he actually did laugh, wondering if they would put up pictures of Emil Užhok in the post offices of America, former war criminal, former KGB operative, later evangelical physician, wanted for '83 massacre of seventy-four in Guatemala, murder of two more, possible kidnapping, complete with front and profile shots, slim youth at Terezín, now gray hair on lupine spectral Carpathian face, reward for knowledge leading to capture, $50,000.

Milton drove them back home, through the darkening winter night.

The message had come, by the time he got home, in the form of a messengered parcel. Lupe, now in a near-catatonic state, had been afraid to even touch it, so it had rested in the center of the foyer floor until Wilson Raver, having arrived before Robinson returned (with the final translated section of Dr. Michalský's journal), gambled it was not a bomb and opened the parcel, to find a manila envelope addressed to Robinson, and an audiotape cassette.

The cassette was unlabeled, made of cheap yellow plastic. It appeared foreign.

"Lebanese, probably," Raver said, fingering it and smacking his lips with a kissing sound on the shaft of a large Cuban cigar. "They have a big recording industry."

Raver was now listening as the message was played back.

He and Robinson spent some time focusing on the voice itself. It began by narrating in English, from memory, the story of Ali Baba and the Forty Thieves. It sounded as if it had come through two or three levels of electronic modification, taking on more and more of the character of computer-generated tones and less of human sound. Yet at the base, certain vocal signatures remained: a sigh here, a slight cough there, a pause to swallow or take breath.

The voice was male. The reader was someone on the far side of forty years of age. Hints of accents came through, inflections, snippets of non-English syntax and structure. Robinson thought he heard the popping *x* of Xhosa; Raver picked up on a soft Baltic *u*. But these two were so disparate as to be meaningless in forming any kind of profile of the speaker.

Their concentration was shifted by a change in the program, away from the monotonous recitation.

The change was a shriek, which at first sounded like an electronic malfunction. But no, as the noise persisted, it became clear it was human, the sound of a child's pain. Robinson had a flashing image of the time Shannon at age two had fallen onto a coffee table and cut a gash in her forehead, just above the eye, the blood, the open cut, racing to the doctor, where they tied her into something called a papoose, she was awake and screaming the whole time they stitched her, tied into the straitjacket, and the needle and thread being pulled through her forehead. Robinson and his ex-wife had gone out into the hallway and sobbed.

"Mr. Robinson," began the recorded message.

"You were instructed to freeze. You yet have pursued your activities. We brook no violation of rules."

That was followed by a strange metallic plea.

"Help me, Daddy."

Robinson in a downward tumbling of thoughts was certain it was Shannon.

A pause in the message followed, as if the producers had anticipated a period of shock and grief.

They were correct. Robinson spun close to the edge. Needle and thread being pulled through his child. If all goes well, said the doctor, she won't have any kind of scar at all. The way a child heals is miraculous.

The original speaker returned, but Robinson had trouble following it. He was searching between words for whole lives, panoramas. Everything had mystic significance.

The man said something about a ticket enclosed for a particular flight, passport, in the name of Arthur Thomas Chambers. More data followed: a flight tomorrow to Tucson via Denver, a rental car reserved in your new name, drive directly to the Corncob Airport Chalet, 7060 South Tucson Boulevard. Remain in your room, the man said, where further instructions will come.

"You inform no one of your travel. Your associate Raver is to withdraw with his stooges to home, and remain. If you violate these instructions, punishment of your daughter will be swift. You are to travel alone. You are to bring with you all documentation regarding your little operation and all related matters. Include all photocopies or duplicates. These are to be exchanged for your daughter.

I repeat. You are observed in every. If you are followed or aided. Punishment. Swift.

Then followed a period of more metallic crying. Shannon. That abruptly ended, cutting into the original underlay recording, an Arab romantic ballad, the eerie sound of the oud and the melancholy frenzy of Islamic love restrained. Robinson saw his child in some white-slave bazaar, Berber men in djellabas poking at her, feeling her hair, her skin.

"Don't assume it to be true," Raver said indecently fast, triggering a violent explosion that discharged much of the foulness that had been lying latent these last few minutes, days. Raver took Robinson's first punch, then dodged away, looking apologetic.

"This is bullshit," Raver persisted, desperate. "Pure psychotorture. They did it to heighten the paranoia, the fear. They don't know your every move."

"Shut," said Robinson. "That was Shannon crying. Get out."

Raver protested, but he seemed weakened.

"Away."

"At least let me wire you," Raver said. "A location transmitter in pocket change."

Raver was already fumbling in his duffel bag for such a device, which he found and placed on a coffee table.

"Go," said Robinson.

"You dance to their tune, you're dead," said Raver.

"Then I'm dead," said Robinson, pushing the heavier man to the door. He barked to Lupe, Milton, Oliver, and Godfrey to go. They were confused.

Then the whole group was out in the hallway, jostling, protesting. Mr. Herbster watched all from the elevator banks.

As Raver continued arguing, Robinson shut and locked the door. For the first time in many days he was completely alone in his own home, and there he sat riding the dark, with cassette, passport, ticket, and Arizona driver's license for one Arthur Thomas Chambers.

Getting Raver and crew out of the apartment was therapeutic, helping him to clear his head. Yes, yes, Raver was absolutely right: to go it alone would run the risk of almost certain demise for himself. But to attempt to deceive Alesa or run some maneuver carried an even greater risk to Shannon, almost total. Shannon was at risk right this minute, and would be until he did as they told. At that point, the risk to her would drop, if only slightly.

In his mind, that was why there was just no other choice. Maybe it was ludicrous, playing the 98 percent risk to himself, should he agree to their demands, against the lower 92 percent risk to Shannon if her father did as her captors asked. It was Robinson who was the threat to them and their contract, not Shannon.

He would just have to shoot for that pathetic 8 percent for his daughter, the 8 percent chance that with their demands satisfied, Alesa would have mercy on this innocent little child.

In his head, when it came to a choice between Shannon and Constitution or Old Glory or whatever it was, there was no choice at all.

He was positively certain he did not sleep a wink in the intervening thirteen hours, as he waited to go to the airport. Rather he sat in the heart of the dark swirl, single-mindedly focusing on an act, perhaps the last he would ever commit. He felt many parts of his humanity falling away, so all that was left was the embodiment of an impulse, a pure reflex, a response clean and harsh. He was so focused he didn't even take the call as his girlfriend Leah rang, and he screened her words without emotion, hearing her give him her long-withheld whereabouts. She wanted him to come out to Pinedale, Wyoming, where she was working as a waitress at the Badlander Grill.

He similarly listened without emotion to the voice of his ex-wife coming from the answering machine, as she called not once, not twice, but five times, enraged that Robinson had failed to have Shannon at the phone as they had agreed. By the final call, she was threatening to fly home early and get her daughter.

The world beyond the glass lay moonless and black, a planet far from heat and light.

And his child lay under an Arab moon, being fed dates, her wounds salved with olive oil and cinnamon.

Terezín, 1943

Thy wings beat so near, O Azrael,
O bright angel of death!

God came to me in my time of solitary, at last breaking the brittle pane through which I had seen all world and life and what purpose we had here in our time on earth, yes, the experience of a glass breaking, a darkly tinted pane that had filtered out all color and so much of the light of the wondrous world in which we are blessed to spend our time in human form, in an explosion of rebirth I saw all as perhaps I had not seen since I was a small infant in a little nursery in Bratislava, the clip-clops of horses' hooves on the cobblestones, the smells of the Danube coming up, the cries of my brothers and sisters, whom I had long since renounced, the sounds of humanity from which I had divorced myself even as I swore I had given my life to the liberation of humanity, yes, the light of the wondrous sun dancing on the moisture and the bird's beak and even the lowly weed and the grub, all was majesty, all was brilliant, all in the glory of God's love, which I accepted again after a lonely journey of so many years.

God first came to me as I lay in a pool of my own blood, after perhaps my third or was it my fifth or maybe my seventh beating at the hand of my torturer and life instructor, Ganz, the beatings coming with some regularity, for a while on a Monday-Wednesday-Friday schedule, then shifting sometimes when there was a holiday to Tuesday and Thursday, there might even be a lull of a full week when Ganz was sick with the grippe and couldn't find a replacement, at the end of which he would faithfully return and make up for lost time with an extra-vigorous kicking and a most emphatic punching or lashing, these visits calculated to take me across entire vistas of pain and misery but never to give me the mercy of death, no, never to send me beyond the vale but to keep me here in this classroom of punishment and vengeance, a purgation I knew I must have before I was fit to make the passage to the other side.

Did I hate this man, this heavyset beer hall brawler from Bavaria, with a dueling sword scar across his cheek and tattoos of a worker's pastimes on his forearms, this man smelling of bratwurst and beer, always in a guard's uniform but somehow escaping the efficient SS laundries, this man ever in need of a bath, did I hate him? No, I decided, I did not, I saw his pummelings and punchings and kickings as something I had long deserved, though my tissues and organism cried out in an agony of pain, in my heart, yes, I knew this was my justice, and I lay examining all the wretchedness of my life and my work thanks to the efficiency and dedication of his labors.

And it was then, when I lay as low as any human can, in that throbbing foggy zone where the mind is still aware of itself as distinct from the floor and the air but when the world is shrunk down by sickness and pain to just those few feet around you and the rushing universe of fevered thought inside the head, that I was aware of something else coming to me, another presence, not me, not my tiny cell of six by nine feet down in some damp forgotten corner of the camp, not a metal pot to shit and piss in and an identical pot that came once a day with a vomitous gruel, not Ganz come to beat me or any other human being, no, this presence came to me as a coolness, a cool breath, and a music of lightness, an almost harmonic smiling presence that came and moved over me and took away some of the pain.

And then God would come to me in many ways: in the breeze that blew through the tiny hole of a barred window, in a cockroach that would scuttle under the metal door that restrained me, a mouse that would scurry to tickle the lobe of my ear, or a beam of light playing from a crack in the stone wall, sending a luminous shaft of fulgurant power and symmetry in a stroking line, to hit the ground and spread fanning and widening across the dirt floor, or in a fine descending raiment of celestial snowflakes blown in on winter's breath, slowly turning and descending to me, to fall on my sores and my wounds, to caress them with cold. In all these things did I see God, and for all these things did I thrill and give thanks.

But most magnificent of all was his appearance in the fury of my fever, a fever that must have kept me there in its grip for many days, at last did He come and reveal himself to me as a wondrous bird fluttering in the window, a magnificent goldfinch who spent the better part of a day and night with me, perched first on the windowsill and then later on the floor, standing and watching over me as I shook and quaked with the tremors of some infection, some bacterial battle, whether my ulcerated back or my chancrous legs or my festering forearms, the source of the fever no longer mattered, it and I were all parts of the world.

O my God, I cried out, tell me, tell me what I have done to deserve this, and at first He laughed, He chirped the most wondrous trilling song, He was not cruel but He did point out to me the error of my ways. Where, where have I gone wrong? I implored, and again He answered with the most splendid trilling symphony, leaving me to ponder its meaning for more than an hour. And when I would give Him no peace, begging, begging for Him to tell me how I had gone wrong, He answered to me the only time He ever took the voice of a human, He spoke in a woman's voice, an even, clear, and majestic woman's words, a harmonic and even-timbred voice, and this is what God said:

"You learn what you have lost by now looking around you. You now see the raindrop, and the cool earth beneath your cheek, and the cockroach and the light beam, which are only several of my manifestations. This was your error, and now your lesson: To see what is before you, to breathe in each molecule of life, to think not of humanity but of the man beside you; to help this one, to help that one, and fly not into the imaginary spaces where your brain would take you."

And what is this thing, this closeness and immediacy, I asked, this thing that I have lost?

And the goldfinch said, Why, this is love.

Kickings, beatings, the rage of fever, and the majesty of God's visits, this was my life, these were my final days on earth. When I asked God if it was time for me to die, the sun rays and the water droplets and the goldfinch all laughed together, No, no, they said, your time is not yet here.

And so I spent that year mostly as a horizontal thing, a thing flat on the earth, feeling earth grow warm with summer and stony with winter, the play of moisture out of sky and out of ground, each and every cell of my body singing with pain and then the splendor of pain released, this was my world and my lesson in my final days, the penance of a fool and of a criminal, of a man who had forgotten he was a man, of a man who had forgotten God and was now reminded, of a man who realized he was nothing without God, and who looked for some way, some final way, to serve Him while he still had time to do so. . . .

On that final morning they came for me, earth sang with the melancholy grandeur of a Bohemian autumn, that time of year when the first frost is in the air but nature still runs with the pace of high summer, apples bursting with color and nectar, the polychromatic glory of the leaves turning their colors of flame and fire, the blood quickening with the approach of winter and new tasks of survival.

How appropriate that on that morning of our ignominy as a race, God's splendrous creation should salute us in this way. Was it mockery of our evil, or a message for the next millennium, a showing of the way of beauty and truth that might be pursued the other side of the flames?

I do not know.

All I know is that after more than a year in the solitary enclosure of my lonely cell, that fifty-four square feet of space that had been my home and existence for a year, someone new came to me. Or should I say someone I had not seen in a long time, which made his visit seem new. In reality, I would rather never have laid eyes upon him again. But such was not to be.

Oh, my hated guard and persecutor Ganz did come, yet not to beat and torture me that day but to admit Emil Užhok, my onetime minion and subordinate.

And how this young man had changed, under the challenge of his new duties. First, to appearance. He seemed older and more mature, no longer callow but moving with an odious but palpable sense of authority, his own variation of manhood. He had begun to clip his hair like the small-town pharmacist he might have been in another era and not like the drifting Communist student who had come to me; more precisely he cut his hair now in the Nazi style, shaved at the temples and well up onto the head, leaving only the crown slightly longer, a severe and martial way of grooming. Coupled with that were his changes in garb. He wore a medical coat, an abuse in itself since he was not a physician but a pharmacologist and entitled only to wear the pestle of that profession. But in our upside-down world, such distinctions dance to the whimsy of the powers that be, and they made him a physician. More loathsome than all was the insignia he now wore, the cursed lightning bolts of the SS itself, where you or I might have worn the old school pin or some piece of jewelry of sentimental value or an award received at Sunday school long ago.

He was one of them.

The most bizarre change of all was his voice, which was unrecognizable now. The flat voice of a small-town Ruthenian I'd known was now a horrendous gargling, a guttural thunder that did not even sound human.

"My God, man, what has happened to your voice?" I asked, unable to restrain myself.

"I suffered an accident," he said, caught off guard by my impudence.

"What kind of accident?" I persisted.

"Of a laboratory nature," he said.

I saw no signs of visible wounds to the neck, so I was forced to theorize that it was of a chemical origin, a massive trauma to the lungs and larynx caused not by simple ingestion of an acid (which wouldn't have been marked by this kind of vocal distortion) but rather by gaseous inhalation.

No matter: Emil Užhok's new voice and haircut were not the main event of the day. I was marched to a military car, and from there driven to the west end of the camp, a place where I had never before been.

We passed the barracks I had once known by name, the frame storage houses for all the poor souls brought to Theresienstadt. And I could see the slack-jawed occupants gathered there, gazing out of the barred windows with a look of illness and starvation, a degraded look I had not ever before seen there, but seen only in places of pestilence and famine, such as the far reaches of Slovakia after the end of the Great War, when famine swept those distant outlands of the collapsing empire and the inhabitants had come so close to the next world.

Were people now being starved as well as imprisoned here?

We continued on my journey of remembrance and discovery.

We drove out to an open field, a pasture one supposed might

have been used for the drill practice of the guards or the private parades and ceremonies, such as they were, of the Nazis.

The field was broken at regular intervals by wide swaths of freshly turned soil, to give it the banded look of a zebra's back.

Had some crop been planted here? I thought. Winter wheat or barley? Some experimental horticulture? It seemed so out of character.

It was only when my dull brain made other connections—the ratatat-tat of the riflery I'd heard periodically, the squalid and comatose look of the prisoners I'd just seen, the spectral presence of death herself—that I surmised this was a field of execution.

I felt strangely comforted in that.

At last, I thought, my day has come. They will do away with me here.

It was fall, with the rich odors of leaf and field, of falling fruit and the approaching frost; sounds carried on that clear air that never again would be so rich.

I breathed my last, drinking it in, wishing it all farewell. The flies and bees of summer knew too that death was coming, and they flew madly about in their final frenzy, drinking it all in like me, as I said goodbye to Loki and Ilse and Lou Salomé, to my poor old mother, whether dead or alive—to all the tumbling memories of this time on physical earth we call life, painful though it is, but always seducing us with those final brief seconds of beauty to try and hang on, on, one last moment. . . .

The undersides of the deep green grass were furled as the fall breezes blew over them. Great billowing white clouds came over from Germany, and I thought, We shall have clear weather on my day of dying.

But the day was to prove more complicated than that. As we sat there, a convoy of trucks came from the east side of the camp, where the troops were garrisoned. As I watched in some confusion, nearly a hundred men were assembled just to our front, the whole expanse of the field spreading before us.

They were setting up rows of military equipment—small field howitzers, aimed out at the field.

Had they brought me out here not to be killed but to watch a silly manuever?

It was then that I heard a totally dissonant sound, the sound of angelic voices drifting up on the wind from behind me. The sound was so lustrous and light that I thought for a moment it came from the heavenly host themselves, the angels arrived to carry me away, floating in on that clear autumn breeze that thrilled, that carried the tinge of melancholy and death but was drenched in the enormous beauty of nature.

They were singing a song of my childhood, *"U Hlupák,"* "The Dunce." They sang of this silly goose who has lost his way, and they sang it in rounds, in astonishing harmony.

I looked back and was moved.

Coming to us, marched along by only a half-dozen guards, were my precious children, the two dozen children who had been given to me to save, my little lambs. They were being marched out here in their nightgowns and pajamas, in this chill fall breeze, and they were singing with singular joy and clarity, and I was moved to tears.

I counted them, looked at how they had grown over this last year . . . little Pika and Rada the Gypsy and Vasil and even sad Silviu, who might have suffered the tortures of hell at Emil's hands but did not show it on that wondrous morning of death's release.

They sang, with the sound of youth and rebirth, the crystal innocence of the unspoiled, the good that we can be if only we will throw off the curse of ungodliness, of the beastly impulses of our minds unguided by the divine.

These innocents were marched out onto the field below us and arranged there in rows. They continued singing, in rounds, in delicious harmony.

The import became clear.

"My God," I gasped. "Have you brought them here to shoot them?"

Emil Užhok's eyes were lit by that devilish fire of the epoch; he was grinning.

"No, you fool, we have not brought them here to shoot them. This is graduation day."

I did not think I could look, nor live any longer. The singing continued, and why those men let it go on I cannot imagine. Perhaps they were so deadened to everything that they did not hear it at all. Or perhaps the children were not singing, except in my own febrile mind.

For the thousandth time my prayers rose up to heaven. But they had never before been answered, and today of all days, the possibilities of intervention were nil. The power of evil in that place was too strong, it flowed too powerfully in all of us.

The sun was rising into glorious fall morning.

As I stood numbly, I saw the troops putting on suits, masks, all-enclosing insectoid helmets. These things I had not seen except in accounts of the Great War, the trench warfare that had bled our continent of its young manhood.

It was then I bolted from the car, shouting out in great rasping sobs.

"Run, my children!" I cried. "They mean to kill you!"

Those young faces looked at me with curiosity, as if I were speaking a foreign language.

They smiled beatifically.

Užhok and Ganz were on me instantly, the brute relishing another excuse for a beating but withholding the favor of an execution.

"Kill me right here," I gasped. "What have you done to them?"

"I've tranquilized them, idiot," said Užhok. "Your fear won't touch them."

I could not make a sound, restrained as I was by my persecutor Ganz, his boot on my neck.

Inexplicably, the troops then fitted the children with similar masks and suits, as if to protect them from the assault.

This was some kind of dreadful experiment, I guessed, using them as fodder. I prayed for time to stop, but it would not.

When all was ready, a bayonet was dropped, the firing signal began. And rising into the morning breeze loomed a lurid cinnamon veil of chemical gas, a mockery of the colors of nature, which washed over them. This was an obscenity, something come up out of the most perverse imagination possible.

The shimmering crimson veil swept over our children, and for an instant they stood, seemingly impervious.

Perhaps, I thought, they would be spared.

But then they began to strip off their helmets and masks, almost as if in a frenzy to break free. And it was then the full power of the gas hit them, and they fell like flowers, field of little flowers falling, dying. It was a curiously silent collective death, the sound of their breath being taken away from them.

All I heard was a collective sigh, and then it was over.

"Your soul shall be cursed to eternity for this," I managed to choke at Užhok. "What did you do, give them defective equipment?"

"You have seen our success," Užhok said. "Doctor, do you remember prodalin-12? It was a psycho-active known to induce claustrophobia. We found that in aerosol form it can penetrate any gas mask or filter. So we combined it with the toxin sarin, which must be inhaled in sufficient quantities to take effect."

A part of me had been murdered.

"We shall revolutionize combat in the east, as Himmler requested," Užhok said.

As the fallen flowers were gathered up, presumably for inspection and further "research," I was taken back to my cell. And it was there that they let me live another brief while.

What was the impulse that had brought about such a project? Though when I witnessed the act I was at some psychic distance, believing I had shed responsibility nearly a year before, in those final hours of meditation I realized I had been as much of the process as Emil Užhok or Hitler or the beast who detonated the gas. My inclination to control the human mind and bend it to external guidance had given rise to this abomination. I had been proud to be a Czech Communist, a humanitarian, an anti-Fascist, a citizen of the world, and yet my work and fascism were as entwined as rock and ivy, for they arose from common manias. In our model of force, we had eliminated love from the formula and had tried to fill this void with violence against the very human soul.

What a wretched discovery, for someone who as a young man dreamed of setting mankind free of its shackles and breaking open the prison gates of oppression forever. I was forced to look once again, in revulsion, at the consequences of my life and labors.

A final day and night on earth, time for further contemplation. To live with the vision of such a wretched deed was a death in itself. The soul of no man—not mine, nor even of those drones who perpetrated the act—can long exist with such a memory. For me, perhaps release could come with real death; for them, I do not know. I do not know the depths of the forgiveness of the Almighty.

As I write these words, they come for me a second time. If my prayers are to be answered, it will be my turn at last to die. I cannot know this, but for this have I prayed. As a testament to the horror of man without love, I shall leave this journal and hope that it survives somehow, to a better day, as a dark memory and warning to the new world, the world that I cannot know but can only pray will follow this epoch of darkness.

Your servant in God,
Radan Anton Michalský

Psychiatrists say that the symptoms of schizophrenia can be induced by simple lack of sleep over extended periods. Daniel Robinson was not balanced as he packed his single canvas bag with the photos from Terezín, the microfilmed journal of Dr. Radan Michalský and its one photocopy and its translation into English, which he had not yet fully read, the scraps of paper from Darlene Scoggins that had started the whole thing, plus ticket stubs and credit charge slips from Guatemala and the trip to Prague, his own passport, the false papers given him by his pursuers.

He had given up balance, for balance was no longer of value.

Briefly he wondered who Arthur Thomas Chambers was. More than likely Chambers was dead and had been brought back to life for this transaction.

As an afterthought, he put a set of underwear and a toothbrush into the mass of papers. The ringing of the phone jolted him, and he nearly answered, but again remembered that Daniel Robinson didn't matter anymore, and so he listened to the machine as the voice came through.

"Sir, this is Claude at the front desk. Two men just come in saying they were FBI. They're on their way up."

Well. All was coming full circle. Either they were going to flutter him, or perhaps Ruthie had turned up enough in her search—the trip to Prague on Agency papers, the talk with Larry Preem, even a betrayal by Beth Bodenhorn—to warrant arrest.

This was not acceptable. It was an impedance and would have to be removed.

He took the pistol and holster and put on his jacket over them, snatching the bag.

He was out in the hall. The elevator had not yet arrived.

Robinson took the service stairway. The stairway was unadorned gritty concrete, the poured concrete walls preserving the board marks of the wooden forms into which this cement had been poured maybe twenty years before. While the outer building had aged, the carpet bald, the walls smudged, the halls filled with the stink of confined cooking smells and human retreat, this hidden stairwell looked new as the day it was built, a chamber of unfinished possibility, frozen in time.

The stairwell led down to the laundry room. From there a service door led to a desolate area at the building's side, where the Dumpsters stood. He would depart that way if he had to.

As he descended, he heard another door open onto the stairway, below. He heard it, suffered a spasm, controlled himself. People hardly ever came into this stairway. Still it was possible a tenant or service man had; perhaps the affair was benign.

But this person was not coming up. Robinson paused a minute, wondering if he was mistaken. Maybe the person had exited, not entered. He was now on the sixth floor, and this had happened at about the third.

The FBI would have come in from one. The doorman hadn't said anything about coming up the service entrance. But then, the doorman wouldn't have gone into that much detail, would he?

Thousands of thoughts shot by in sparks, cells through his veins, arcs across the synapses.

He got to three, and no one was there. He continued on down, the laundry entrance now in sight. And it was there that a fresh-faced young man stepped out to greet him, spawning an instant of confusion while they locked eyes, a moment of assessment.

With a gasp, Robinson raised his pistol and shot the man in the face. The roar of the pistol through the stairwell was thunderous; Robinson thought for a second he had shot himself. It nearly blew his own ears out, and he was dazed.

Briefly there on the stairs, Robinson held a mental picture of the man smiling, his mouth beginning to open, as if to ask a friendly question: directions, time of day, quarters for a washing machine? But it was in the past, and the young man, who was probably an FBI agent though Robinson would never be sure, had fallen back into the laundry room, onto a dryer. A projectile spray of blood and solids had settled on a basket of folded clean sheets behind him.

Robinson floated to the outside door and was fumbling. He turned the knob, and turned again madly, missing three times, the damned thing nearly coming off in his hand. As he kicked madly and began a frenzied breathless cursing, it opened with a groan as if it hadn't been used in four years.

The Dumpsters were heaped with snow.

Running down across the field of deep but melting snow toward the line of trees, he was aware of leaving a textbook set of footprints. He looked back once, expecting a pursuer, a shot from a window, but none ever came.

He made it to the trees, pistol still in hand. The trees broke through into a cheap low-rise office park that had the look of World War II prefabrication buried beneath its paint and remodeling, and from there onto a nondescript street. He ran along the street, downhill, toward the floodplain of the river, aware that he was making a periodic grunting noise, some kind of primal cry.

The street faded away into an access road and then ran under the Founding Fathers Freeway. Cars were rushing by him in unnerving fashion. But of course it was rush hour; cars would do that. The infernal morning rush, the American rush. He came under the freeway and looked out on the sea of the Pentagon parking lot.

The secretaries and the colonels were making their way to the great necropolis itself, adorned with the antennae, the helipads, the dishes, and the sensors, looking like the most sinister prison imaginable.

For a lengthy time he ran across the oceanic parking lot, which he'd read was the largest on earth. The distance he covered was about a mile and a half on the lot alone.

It was now 8:25. His flight left at 9:10. He had planned on driving to the airport under his own power.

Why the rush? He laughed sickly. He'd never known a plane to leave on time in his life.

Excuse me, a young man was saying. Does this stairwell go up to the third floor? I think the elevator is broken.

Robinson was still running as he stumbled through the commuter crowds coming off the Virginia buses to transfer to the Metro. He thought a minute about taking the Metro to the airport, but no, no, it was too unpredictable.

And he ran careening into a grandmotherly lady, a sweet-faced old Southern lady probably on her way to DAR headquarters in the city, a lady left here from the time when Virginia had been a Southern place, of men wearing hats and talking about land deals in front of the churches on Sunday morning, people asking you who your mother's people were, this poor old thing left behind to fight her way alone through the federal gush at the end of history. He knocked her to the pavement. Two men shouted at him. A distant Pentagon policeman seemed to look his way but then walked in the other direction.

Robinson was making for the little cab stand at the river end of the Metro station. A lone cab stood there, its North African driver outside, smoking a cigarette.

"National," Robinson shouted.

"I'm on break," the driver said.

"Big big tip," roared Robinson, fumbling for tens, fanning them.

The Algerian grudgingly got inside.

They wound through the parking lot. Two helicopters were orbiting the lot, over near the underpass he'd run through, but they might have been normal traffic. The driver slowly wound his way out of the lot, then made their way to Manifest Destiny Drive and the Founding Fathers Freeway, running south.

Excuse me, said this young man in the stairwell. Got change for a dollar?

The traffic was heavy but fast. They came off the airport ramp. As a precaution, Robinson got out at the Delta entrance, paid a twenty for a five-dollar ride, then plowed through the inside crowd to get to United. He left his pistol, still warm, wrapped in toilet paper in a bathroom wastebin. Then he navigated the metal detector, the gate, the line of people boarding. He must have looked a sight, for the stewardesses withheld their customary greetings and, silently, watched him pass as if he were an embarrassment. Or perhaps he was imagining it all; he didn't know for sure.

Not until they were somewhere over Indianapolis did Robinson realize he had been trembling for hours, a steady, spasmodic thing, like the chill of a flu. And it was only then, the national heartland spreading out into white grids, that he achieved some semblance of relaxation, a wired torpor that would break every time he allowed himself to think about what he had just done, what he had yet to do.

Excuse me, the young man said in the stairwell. Is this the way to the storage room?

Climatic zones, time zones, seismic zones, and zones of history, all passed below him.

The aircraft's passage described a nearly straight line following the thirty-ninth parallel, from National Airport in Arlington, Virginia, to Stapleton International in Denver, Colorado.

The Allegheny mountains and plateau, the Wabash, Mississippi, and Republican alluvial plains, and the Smoky Hills of west Kansas were crossed. Land that had taken three hundred years to subjugate and settle was covered in three hours twelve minutes.

The Front Range of the Rockies, that majestic uplift topped with eternal snows which many have called the "roof of America," was appropriately arctic and glacial as the pilot found his Denver runway locator out over the sagebrush emptiness where the Great Plains die away. On that clear midday, with a minimum of atmospheric suspension, visibility was unlimited, and the great mountain range rolled north and lordly into the Teton vault of Wyoming, south into the mystic blue rounds of the Sangre de Cristos of New Mexico.

Planes were changed there at Denver. Then the second leg of the flight began, curving just to the south of Mount Elbert to avoid afternoon solar convection, then crossing the Colorado Plateau in its many and continuing subfeatures, heading ever south-southwest, crossing briefly into New Mexico northwest of Farmington, then on into Arizona just north of Roof Butte. The Mogollon Plateau was similarly clear and grand, with unspoiled views of the Petrified Forest and the Painted Desert, the Little Colorado Gorge and the frosted edge of the Mogollon Rim itself near Show Low.

In Navajo County, on the Fort Apache Indian Reservation, a small Apache boy playing in the snow east of Cibecue watched the southwest passage of the aircraft at 32,000 feet, its hydrogen dioxide contrails billowing behind with singular fullness and clarity against the cobalt winter sky. He wondered what made that happen.

Then on descending, abeam Phoenix but remaining well to the east of that congestion, the aircraft made its final approach on the Tucson prime locator.

Landing was achieved shortly thereafter, and Robinson proceeded to the car rental counter and then on to the Corncob Airport Chalet. He checked in. He sat in his room, calling out only once, to order a dinner from room service.

He sat there until about 9:15 in the evening, when the phone rang.

The man on the line told him to drive his car the following morning south on I-19 until he reached the town of Nogales. There he was to park and lock the car in the lot of the Giant Genie grocery store. He was to walk to the Mexican border crossing and cross on foot as close to 10:45 in the morning as possible.

Then, in Mexico, he was to continue on foot down the main street of Heroica Nogales, turning left on Calle Segunda. Half a block down on the left, he was to turn into a small bar known as Cantina Fronteriza.

He was to arrive there about eleven in the morning. If he had time, he was to sit down and order a beer.

Then, at 11:15, he was to go into the toilet and wait there for further instructions.

He said he would do all these things.

His daughter was put briefly on the phone and said in a very small voice, "Hi, Daddy." Then she hung up.

Night came and waned, the sun of the next day showed its first edge. He was on the road by 7:30, the highway following the dry valley of the Santa Cruz River to its headwaters somewhere in the mountains of north Mexico. Arizona, unaware it was about to be swallowed by an alien world, sang its last, American refulgence unmitigated. Shopping plazas had been gouged out of arroyos, retirement suburbs laid waste to the serendipity of God's creation. Everywhere the monumental cut across the fragile land, what could have been a subtle beauty turned into a panorama without risk or randomness.

Only in Nogales itself did the aesthetic of the other world begin to show itself, and only barely so. Whole streets were given over to selling televisions and refrigerators to people from the other side, so it too was a distorted place, a place of the suction.

He bought a newspaper and coffee in the Giant Genie store, sat there in the car, killing time, for he was very early. He ran the heater to stay warm.

As far as he could tell, no one had followed him. But he really didn't care anymore.

He read the *Arizona Star*. Though the news of the nation and the world beyond were compressed to a few columns squeezed in above huge ads for underwear and lawn furniture, he saw no mention of any killings of FBI agents in Washington, no national manhunts.

That could mean something, or nothing.

He listened to the radio, killed more time.

When it was 10:30, he got his bag, locked the car. He walked to the border crossing. It was a light-travel day, only one other man going into Mexico on foot. Three of the six *immigración* booths were closed.

The Mexican *aduana* officer, wearing a jacket to stay warm, looked with some slight interest at all his charge card slips.

"You are in business?" he asked.

"Yes," Robinson.

"What kind?"

"Investments," said Robinson.

"What kind?"

"All kinds," Robinson said, adding, to ease the tension, real estate, tourism, etc.

The man shrugged, waved him in.

The northern world ended right there. He came across the line to find that the smells, the light, the way man touched the landscape, had changed, back to the folk, the tribal, the variegated.

Just as he turned from Avenida de la Gran Revolución onto Calle Segunda, Robinson thought he saw a familiar face or form in a small cluster of pedestrians who had gathered at the Ferrocarriles de México ticket window, a passing glance, a way of moving. He looked back discreetly but could identify no one.

The sun was quite warm, the day windless. On the eastern side of the street, with the sun approaching zenith, he actually felt overdressed.

The Cantina Fronteriza waited farther down, on the left.

He entered. He was alone, except for a woman who was in a back room, loading empty beer bottles into a crate.

It was 11:07 in the morning.

At 11:11, she noticed him sitting there and came out to assist him.

He ordered a Tecate beer, in a can.

At 11:13 the Tecate arrived. He opened it, and then went into the toilet at the back, carrying his bag with him. In order to do so he passed the woman, who was still loading the beer bottles. She waved him on to the toilet, farther back.

The toilet consisted of a foul-smelling gutter urinal, a sink with no water, and a mirror. Another closed door led presumably to the sit-down toilet. He stood there a moment.

He knocked on the toilet door. It opened, to reveal a Mexican man with a pistol pointed at him.

"*Buenos días*," Robinson said.

The gunman nodded and smiled. At that point, the outer door opened and "Señor García," the man with the widow's peak, the man who had tailed him on the Guatemalan trip and into Washington, came in, closing the door behind him. He also drew a gun.

Were they going to dispose of him here? They certainly could if they wanted to.

First they meticulously frisked him and searched the bag. They waved the wand of a bug detector over him and everything on his person.

But they did not kill him. They opened an outer door that led onto the back alley. A rusty panel truck with the name *Alfombras Abadi* and a painted panel of a man in a turban, sitting on a flying carpet, stood there, driven by a third man.

Robinson, widow's peak, and the Mexican got in back. The driver started south, immediately picking up a dirt road that ran parallel to Avenida de la Gran Revolución, marked by garbage cans and a running stream of sewage that must have emptied into the Santa Clara.

They bound his hands and his feet and blindfolded him. The jolts of the journey told him they were still on unpaved road. They drove this way for more than an hour, he guessed.

Then they came to a stop. Robinson thought perhaps they had

arrived at their destination, but then he heard an argument between the driver and someone outside. They discussed the road being blocked by a flock of sheep passing.

He could even hear their bleating.

They paused there for several minutes. Finally the sheep passed, and they were under way again.

They must have been gaining in altitude, for Robinson was getting cold. From the side-to-side roll he deduced switchbacks, climbing into the Sierra Madre. Up and up they went, the engine laboring as they did, temperature dropping almost by the minute, transmission grinding through its gears but finding no power beyond second and frequently having to drop back to first.

At last they drove on the level again, but just as they attained it, they slowed, then stopped. He heard another conversation between the driver and an outsider; slow acceleration followed, and then a definitive stop.

He surmised they had come into some kind of compound.

The back door of the panel truck opened up, and he was brought outside and untied. As his blindfold was taken away, the sweep of an ochreous panorama of canyonland and mesa hit him, redoubled by the power of the afternoon sun hitting his long-darkened eyes. Gradually things came into focus.

They stood on a flat mesa of moderate dimensions; immediately east and west, the land fell away into abyssal gorges. The landscape looked untouched, save for the miles-distant cut of roads crossing escarpments, gorge faces. At greater distances in both directions, larger sierras of roseate and wine basaltic flow cut them off from the far horizon. It was a position both of redoubt and of some exposure.

A beige hacienda stood at the center of the mesa, and a helicopter waited in an open area to the side. Saguaro cactus, piñon, and sagebrush dotted the aureate soil.

A striking setting, rendered melancholic by the aridity of the hills, the profundity of the shadows that fell into the gorges, the desolate character of the hacienda, which had been seemingly abandoned for decades, but more than anything by his own heightened emotional state.

A half-dozen men came down toward him from the house, most carrying weapons. Scanning the faces, Robinson saw an Arab in safari jacket, who seemed to dominate the delegation, and an American in blue jeans and suede jacket, aviator's cap and glasses, face rugged, a paramilitary look. The others included two Latins, the goateed Arab who had tailed him in Prague and Raver in Washington, and a man he guessed to be Laotian.

The Arab in safari jacket stuck out his hand in greeting.

"I am Tariq," he said, in flawless British-accented English. Robinson didn't shake his hand, but Tariq ignored the insult, continuing with gusto. "You have already met Mr. Ordóñez, who accompanied you." With this he pointed to widow's peak, who was a bit uncomfortable with the introduction.

"You must be tired," Tariq said. "Will you have lemonade or something stronger?"

Robinson declined. Tariq was in his late forties, having put on the weight that in his culture would indicate prosperity and middle age; the safari suit was perfectly tailored. His hair was oiled and combed sleekly back. His cologne was too strong but of high quality.

"Very well," Tariq said. "I see you have brought the documents. We shall have to take some time going over them, to make sure all is in order."

The bag with all the papers was handed over to the American in the aviator's glasses, who was more intent on looking at Robinson than at the papers. Robinson, in turn, thought the man looked familiar. He ran through in his head the roster of former company men who had fallen into the cracks over the years.

"My daughter," said Robinson hoarsely.

"Of course," said Tariq. "Sweet little girl. Misses Mommy and Daddy very much."

From the front door of the house Shannon emerged, still wearing her pajamas from three nights before, with new shoes and coat. She was on the verge of crying as she walked toward him, maintaining for whatever reason a slow, steady pace.

Was she on some kind of sedative?

Abyssal shadows, Shannon on the verge of tears, a hacienda on an ocher-colored mesa . . .

"Baby," he said, sweeping her up into his arms. She had circles under her eyes as if she had not slept well, and she coughed, having come down with a cold.

A triangle had been cut or scraped into her wrist.

Robinson himself was crying silently, seeing all the world

through the shifting prismatics of his tears, sun helianthin and exploding, great diagonals of light and dark cutting across the world. They stood for a time hugging, the situation being beyond the power of his words to console or resolve.

Through the film of tears Robinson became aware of a final figure coming down toward them from the house. Out of the shadow of the veranda into the backlight of the westerly falling sun, he saw mostly silhouette, distorted by the rainbow prismatics of his moist eyes. The figure was walking heavily, more heavily than the gaunt form would suggest. This man wore some kind of dark tweed overcoat and black-rimmed glasses. But as he came closer and the features solidified, Robinson was aware of the spectral lupine face, a face that he had at times thought might not even exist except in the imagination of Lhota and a long-dead Slovak psychiatrist, a projection of obsession and guilt.

Still holding Shannon in his arms, Robinson locked eyes with Dr. Emil Užhok.

The canyons of this man's face were almost as deep as the canyons of Mexico itself. The shock of white hair was slightly electrified, as if charged with some kind of energy. And Robinson could hear the man's breathing, the tubercular in and out, yet worse than tubercular, cadaverous, a guttural fibrillation of fluid and air, a constant saccular tremor, a thoracic tremolo that resounded deep and diseased.

This was the voice, yet reposing, that Dr. Michalský and Alena Moskowitz had described, the voice that would identify this man when nothing else could, the face having been changed at least once and possibly more by surgery to disguise its owner.

Robinson stood staring at the man for what in any other situation would have been an impolite interval. But in this case, it seemed warranted.

"*You are stupid,*" the awful voice said in Czech, coming up out of the spectral depths. Robinson tried to find a rejoinder, but none occurred. He stood about four feet from Emil Užhok.

Shannon was crying soundlessly now. The very proximity of Užhok disturbed her, and Robinson didn't want to know what this man had done to her in these two days.

"Mr. Robinson has kept up his end," said Tariq with slightly diminished bravado and verve. "All the papers are here."

Emil Užhok could not have cared less about the documents. He was looking deep into the soul of Daniel Robinson, plumbing the cellars of this person who had searched him out, not long on the heels of another who had done so, and was now dead.

It was much like staring down a big cat, a puma, caught in a mountain canyon. Outdoorsmen say eye contact can be fatal, because the animal takes it as a direct challenge. Similarly, averting the eyes can defuse an attack.

Dr. Emil Užhok, or whatever he called himself now, was about seventy years old.

He walked away from Robinson to the bag with the documents. He roughly took the bag from the American in the aviator glasses and rifled the papers. He found a copy of Michalský's journal, let the rest of the bag fall fluttering to the ground with an unceremonious whump.

Scowling, trembling with either rage or palsy, he skimmed over the pages.

"We should do this in systematic fashion," said Tariq, signaling to one of the minions to pick up the bundle. The goateed Arab began gathering up the documents and stuffing them in the bag. He was forced to chase across the mesa after several credit card tissues caught in the wind.

"Let's go in and sit down," said Tariq again, triggering a furious glance from Užhok, who was hunched over the journal. Tariq motioned to the foot soldiers to begin moving inside.

Shannon was now clinging more tightly than ever to Robinson, as if she sensed something he did not.

A basaltic mesa, abyssal canyons, lutescent sun declining in the west . . .

As if on cue, Užhok looked over at Ordóñez and waved his arm.

"Take the child from him," Užhok said.

With this the Cuban man who had assassinated someone in Chile long ago and probably killed Lhota and followed Robinson through Guatemala and right up to the gates of the White House itself, who had frisked him and bound him in the toilet of the Cantina Fronteriza in Heroica Nogales, now came to him a final time.

"Shouldn't we see what he knows?" asked Tariq, now hesitant. As Robinson and Shannon both resisted, Ordóñez restrained them, while the Mexican who had assisted in the bathroom frisking pulled Shannon away from her father. Shannon shrieked in fear, and Robinson felt the Cuban's forearm closing across his throat, the cuffs being put on by someone else.

Robinson was now making sounds of desperate petition, begging that his daughter be returned to him.

"We have won his eternal silence," Užhok intoned, losing interest in the conversation altogether.

The impossible harshness of sun on basalt, hard-edge aridity, earth stripped clean of life . . .

Now his daughter was once again receding from him, being dragged along sobbing by the Mexican toward the helicopter.

It became clear the American was the helicopter pilot, because he too had begun moving—in some confusion, apparently ahead of schedule, looking back at Tariq and Užhok for guidance—toward the helicopter.

Ordóñez cocked his pistol.

Shannon shrieked as she had on the tape, the shriek of helpless extermination.

Dr. Užhok was just passing between them, now also headed for the helicopter.

And it was then that they all heard another voice, amplified, coming up out of the earth behind Robinson, up out of the ravine, startling and yet ludicrous in its timbre, inflection.

Robinson knew this voice.

"Let go of the little girl," the amplified voice called, "or I blow your rotor off with a Hot-Chigger."

In the pandemonium that followed, as Wilson Raver and a crew of bedraggled but well-armed Mexican *campesinos* appeared at the ravine's edge, at least three of them waggling the barrels of shoulder-held missile launchers, one thing came through clear and unavoidably to Robinson: he himself would be shot. He knew García/Ordóñez held him in a bead and would not be deterred, even by this. It was a stupid feeling, a feeling almost akin to embarrassment, continuing as he dove to the ground to try and take some semblance of cover.

And he was right. The bullet came, it entered his upper chest, it was almost a relief.

As he lay there, gratified to see that Shannon had indeed been let go and was making her way back to him without injury, gunfire between the two groups began to increase, with one of Raver's team already down, the cockpit of the helicopter showing bullet holes.

From the cover of a boulder and a retaining wall, Ordóñez and the Laotian were trying to take out Raver's group, one by one, a beautifully run little delaying action that must have been perfected in the streets of Beirut and the villages of Afghanistan, while Tariq and his American chauffeur withdrew to the helicopter itself.

Užhok was in distress, having fallen hard after a shot in the leg, the old sorcerer choking and roaring with the bile and vengeance of one whose choices had long ago been made, now regaining the breath the pain had knocked out of him. And he was enraged to see his compatriots taking such a long time to dispose of the enemy. He managed to wrestle himself up, one or two teeth smashed, blood pouring out of his mouth, perhaps even a brittle bone broken, but those infernal eyes fully alert, intent on fulfillment of the plan.

"Give me a gun," gasped Užhok, still dazed and fully exposed, addressing Ordóñez.

The rotors of the helicopter were already turning. Waving a Mauser, Užhok came right toward Robinson and Shannon, somehow immune from the hail of gunfire, and it was clear he intended to finish the job. Robinson managed to raise himself up and shout over in desperation to Raver, who after a look of sheepish apology fired a Hot-Chigger at Užhok, since that was all he had at his disposal.

The Hot-Chigger is quite fast, moving at near-bullet speed from its launch tube, intending to seek the heat of an enemy aircraft or tank engine at some distance and then detonate. This was the case today, as it covered the space from Raver to Užhok in about a second, the warhead hitting Užhok mid-body and with a sound like a brick being thrown into wet mud, dividing him in two, legs remaining standing for an instant, head and abdomen whirling over to slam up against the porch of the hacienda. But the missile itself did not detonate, its first target being too soft and cool to trigger the firing cap, and so it roared across the porch, splintering an old rocking chair before it shrieked off the mesa and out into the expanse of northern Sonora, still howling and laying its contrail, guidance system locked onto the setting sun.

"Bull's-eye!" shouted Raver, breaking free of his cover to run over and join Robinson and Shannon. "I couldn't let you go down without a fight."

"Who are these people?" Robinson managed to ask. His voice sounded as though it were coming out of the hole in his chest.

"Some wonderful Mexicans. The minute I heard the recording two days ago I guessed Mexico; why else would they be taking you to Tucson? But I have some good contacts in Arizona too; we got a clear trace on that call to your motel. Of course you picked up my little coin transmitter. Did you mean to use it to pay for that beer in Nogales?"

Ordóñez and the Laotian had begun to run toward the departing helicopter, which rather than pausing to help them aboard repaid them with a blast of dust and a premature lift-off.

"A total rout!" Raver shouted again, watching the helicopter slowly rise into the air and begin a swing to the south. But the helicopter wasn't retreating, it was circling the site, the pilot taking bizarre evasive maneuvers in preparation for something else.

"Shit," said Raver. "He's gonna let fly. . . ."

Raver was shouting to one of his colleagues, one Yrigoyen, to shoot another Hot-Chigger, when the helicopter indeed launched its own attack.

This projectile arching out into the atmosphere above them had a lazy grace, an arc of white contrail almost festive and ceremonial.

Yrigoyen's Hot-Chigger made the five hundred feet to the copter's engine in an instant, and the engine and rotor blew out with a neat flash while the fuselage remained intact, hanging and then falling, falling, into the ravine.

"Beautiful," said Raver, ignoring the copter as it, complete with the openmouthed Tariq and the American pilot, fighting over a worthless stick, dove earthward. "I know that contrail."

The falling of the copter, the explosion as it crashed down into the ravine just behind Raver's battlement, was secondary now, peripheral to the sky show above. As was the capture and swift execution of Ordóñez and the Laotian by Raver's commandos.

No, all eyes were on the sky. It was filled with a magnificent nimbus of white light, a growing luminous fog that looked like a star falling to earth, a tiny sun, magnificent and ethereal, swelling and reaching down toward them.

"Hold your hats," cried Raver, both daubing at Robinson's massive chest wound and watching the star come closer. "They've done a beauty, Danny. Tactical neuropharmaceuticals, mounted on a solid-fueled Avian. But this luminosity . . . could be ionized, gas cloud modeling, or enhanced radiation . . . Yes, that's it, ERW! They've got gas behaving like a ray, Danny . . . a pulse. What devilment!"

From his backpack he was pulling out a jumble of clear polymer CBW suits, bubble-head enclosures, and breath-paks.

"I hate them and I salute them!" screamed Raver.

Raver saw to it that Shannon was well covered with the CBW suit and breath-pak before the first blast wave hit them, but both he and Robinson took it full force, unprotected.

At first it was as if they were inside a small star, Robinson and Raver and Shannon all shrouded in a ghostly glowing fog. But then Robinson thought—or did he dream—they'd all fallen inside a black-and-white television picture tube. For images of gray things, slight shadows, shot by him, like words, memories headed at high speed for someplace else. Only a snatch of color showed through, a few particles, as a reminder of a richer world.

There was an interval when not much happened. It might have lasted a second, or half a day. All Robinson could hear was a hissing that might have been gas, or blowflies cleaning their wings, or the sounds of his own collapsing chest. It was a most restful time, waiting in a quiet parlor of space.

And then a rude noise brought him back, a clattering series of impacts, an irritating sequence of detonations that baffled and deafened him with its force, so overwhelming that not for some time did he realize the noise was Raver firing his weapons with both hands, not at any visible foe but into the desert sky, all the while singing about Azrael, O Azrael, refrain of an Abbasid lyric poem remembered from his intensive Arabic studies at Monterey—yes, for Raver the final vision was of the Koranic angel of death fluttering down to make warfare, and he would answer him blow for blow, he would go down fighting.

But Robinson's own mind was quite tranquil, watching with detachment this final sterile battle even as a wind blew ochreous clouds of dust into his eyes, all seen through a rippling veil of blood and borealic solar glare. What he saw approaching from on high was not the angel of death but a glorious theophanic arrival, like one of those chariots coming straight down from heaven. And so he quite calmly accepted the crackling farewell hugs and plastic caresses of his daughter, wrapped in angel's placenta and umbilicus, sensing that though she was to remain here on earth she was under heaven's protection now.

He looked up at her as she knelt beside him, her head in the clear corona, this little girl smiling a look of such beatific peace and calm when it should have been one of horror. It was as though she had always understood what he now had to accept—that his end had come and the going up was nothing to be feared, but welcomed . . . that it was time to leave her behind and go up alone, up above that mesa in Sonora state, Mexico, where a zone of peace awaited him after the end of his twilight war.

ABOUT THE AUTHOR

Michael Hamilton Morgan has lived and traveled in 23 different countries. He has worked as a Washington journalist, a foreign service officer, and an official of a bipartisan presidential commission overseeing the Fulbright scholarships and Voice of America. In 1987, he joined Mobil Corporation as a public relations writer, and is currently the director of the Pegasus Prize for Literature. He lives in Virginia.